PENGUIN CLASSICS

NOTES FROM UNDERGROUND and THE DOUBLE

FYODOR MIKHAYLOVICH DOSTOYEVSKY was born in Moscow in 1821, the second of a physician's seven children. When he left his private boarding school in Moscow he studied from 1838 to 1843 at the School of Military Engineering in St Petersburg, graduating with officer's rank. His first novel to be published, *Poor Folk* (1846), was a great success. In 1849 he was arrested and sentenced to death for participating in the Petrashevsky Circle; he was reprieved at the last moment but sentenced to penal servitude, and until 1854 he lived in a convict prison at Omsk, Siberia. Out of this experience he wrote *The House of the Dead* (1860). In 1860 he began the journal *Vremya* (*Time*) with his brother; in 1862 and 1863 he went abroad, where he strengthened his anti-European outlook, met Apollinaria Suslova, who was the model for many of his heroines, and gave way to his passion for gambling. In the following years he fell deeply in debt, but in 1867 he married Anna Grigoryevna Snitkina (his second wife), who helped to rescue him from his financial morass. They lived abroad for four years, then in 1873 he was invited to edit *Grazhdanin* (*Citizen*), to which he contributed his *Diary of a Writer*. From 1876 the latter was issued separately and had a large circulation. In 1880 he delivered his famous address at the unveiling of Pushkin's memorial in Moscow; he died six months later in 1881. Most of his important works were written after 1864: *Notes from Underground* (1864), *Crime and Punishment* (1865-6), *The Gambler* (1866), *The Idiot* (1868), *The Devils* (1871-2) and *The Brothers Karamazov* (1880).

RONALD WILKS studied Russian language and literature at Trinity College, Cambridge, after training as a Naval interpreter, and later Russian literature at London University, where he received his Ph.D. in 1972. Among his translations for Penguin Classics are *My Childhood*, *My Apprenticeship* and *My Universities* by Gorky, *Diary of a Madman* by Gogol, filmed for Irish Television, *The Golovlyov Family* by Saltykov-Shchedrin, *How Much Land Does a Man Need?* by Tolstoy, *Tales of Belkin and Other Prose Writings* by Pushkin, and seven volumes of stories by Chekhov:

The Party and Other Stories, The Kiss and Other Stories, The Fiancée and Other Stories, The Duel and Other Stories, The Steppe and Other Stories and *Ward No. 6 and Other Stories*. In addition, he has also translated *The Shooting Party*, Chekhov's only full-length novel, as well as *The Little Demon* by Sologub, both for Penguin.

ROBERT LOUIS JACKSON, B. E. Bensinger Professor (Emeritus) of Slavic Languages and Literatures at Yale University, has written widely on Dostoyevsky, Tolstoy, Chekhov and other writers of nineteenth- and twentieth-century Russian literature. He is the author of *Dostoevsky's Underground Man in Russian Literature*, *Dostoevsky's Quest for Form: A Study of His Philosophy of Art*, *The Art of Dostoevsky. Deliriums and Nocturnes* and *Dialogues with Dostoevsky. The Overwhelming Questions*.

FYODOR DOSTOYEVSKY

Notes from Underground
and
The Double

Translated by RONALD WILKS
With an Introduction by ROBERT LOUIS JACKSON

PENGUIN BOOKS

In memory of Margaret – R. W.

PENGUIN CLASSICS

Published by the Penguin Group
Penguin Books Ltd, 80 Strand, London WC2R 0RL, England
Penguin Group (USA) Inc., 375 Hudson Street, New York, New York 10014, USA
Penguin Group (Canada), 90 Eglinton Avenue East, Suite 700, Toronto, Ontario, Canada M4P 2Y3
(a division of Pearson Penguin Canada Inc.)
Penguin Ireland, 25 St Stephen's Green, Dublin 2, Ireland (a division of Penguin Books Ltd)
Penguin Group (Australia), 250 Camberwell Road, Camberwell, Victoria 3124, Australia
(a division of Pearson Australia Group Pty Ltd)
Penguin Books India Pvt Ltd, 11 Community Centre, Panchsheel Park, New Delhi – 110 017, India
Penguin Group (NZ), 67 Apollo Drive, Rosedale, North Shore 0632, New Zealand
(a division of Pearson New Zealand Ltd)
Penguin Books (South Africa) (Pty) Ltd, 24 Sturdee Avenue, Rosebank, Johannesburg 2196, South Africa

Penguin Books Ltd, Registered Offices: 80 Strand, London WC2R 0RL, England

www.penguin.com

Notes from Underground first published 1864
The Double first published 1846
This translation first published in Penguin Classics 2009

013

Translation and Notes copyright © Ronald Wilks, 2009
Introduction copyright © Robert Louis Jackson, 2009
Further Reading © Robert Louis Jackson and Ronald Wilks, 2009
All rights reserved

The moral right of the translator and editor has been asserted

Set in 10.25/12.25 pt PostScript Adobe Sabon
Typeset by Rowland Phototypesetting Ltd, Bury St Edmunds, Suffolk
Printed in England by Clays Ltd, St Ives plc

ISBN: 978-0-140-45512-0

www.greenpenguin.co.uk

MIX
Paper from
responsible sources
FSC
FSC™ C018179

Penguin Books is committed to a sustainable
future for our business, our readers and our planet.
This book is made from Forest Stewardship
Council™ certified paper

Contents

Chronology

1821 (30 October)* Born Fyodor Mikhaylovich Dostoyevsky, in Moscow, the son of Mikhail Andreyevich, head physician at Mariinsky Hospital for the Poor, and Marya Fyodorovna, daughter of a merchant family.

1823 Pushkin begins *Eugene Onegin*.

1825 Decembrist uprising.

1830 Revolt in the Polish provinces.

1831–6 Attends boarding schools in Moscow together with his brother Mikhail (b. 1820).

1836 Publication of the 'First Philosophical Letter' by Pyotr Chaadayev.

1837 Pushkin is killed in a duel.
  Their mother dies and the brothers are sent to a boarding school in St Petersburg.

1838 Enters the St Petersburg School of Military Engineering as an army cadet (Mikhail is not admitted to the Academy).

1839 Father dies, apparently murdered by serfs on his estate.

1840 Lermontov's *A Hero of Our Time*.

1841 Obtains a commission. Tries his hand at historical drama without success. Early works, now lost, include two historical plays, 'Mary Stuart' and 'Boris Godunov'.

1842 Gogol's *Dead Souls*.
  Promoted to second lieutenant.

1843 Graduates from the Academy. Attached to St Petersburg Army Engineering Corps. Translates Balzac's *Eugénie Grandet*.

---

* Dates are old style, according to the Julian Calendar, in force in Russia until 1918.

1844 Resigns his commission. Translates George Sand's *La dernière Aldini*. Works on *Poor Folk*, his first novel.

1845 Establishes a friendship with Russia's most prominent and influential literary critic, the liberal Vissarion Belinsky, who praises *Poor Folk* and acclaims its author as Gogol's successor.

1846 *Poor Folk* and *The Double* published. While *Poor Folk* is widely praised, *The Double* is much less successful. 'Mr Prokharchin' also published. Utopian socialist M. V. Butashevich-Petrashevsky becomes an acquaintance.

1847 Nervous ailments and the onset of epilepsy. 'A Novel in Nine Letters' and 'The Landlady' are published.

1848 Several short stories published, including 'White Nights', 'A Weak Heart', 'A Christmas Party and a Wedding' and 'An Honest Thief'.

1849 *Netochka Nezvanova* published. Arrested along with other members of the Petrashevsky Circle, and convicted of political offences against the Russian state. Sentenced to death, and taken out to Semyonovsky Square to be shot by firing squad, but reprieved moments before execution. Instead, sentenced to an indefinite period of exile in Siberia, to begin with eight years of penal servitude, later reduced to four years by Tsar Nicholas I.

1850 Prison and hard labour in Omsk, western Siberia.

1853 Outbreak of Crimean War.
    Beginning of periodic epileptic seizures.

1854 Released from prison, but immediately sent to do compulsory military service as a private in the infantry battalion at Semipalatinsk, south-western Siberia. Friendship with Baron Wrangel, as a result of which he meets his future wife, Marya Dmitriyevna Isayeva.

1855 Alexander II succeeds Nicholas I as Tsar: some relaxation of state censorship.
    Promoted to non-commissioned officer.

1856 Promoted to lieutenant. Still forbidden to leave Siberia.

1857 Marries the widowed Marya Dmitriyevna Isayeva. Publication of 'The Little Hero', written in prison during the summer of 1849.

1858 Works on *The Village of Stepanchikovo and its Inhabitants* and *Uncle's Dream*.

1859 Allowed to return to live in European Russia; in December, the Dostoyevskys return to St Petersburg. First chapters of *The Village of Stepanchikovo and its Inhabitants* (the serialized novella is released between 1859 and 1861) and *Uncle's Dream* published.

1860 Mikhail starts a new literary journal, *Vremya (Time)*. Dostoyevsky is not officially an editor, because of his convict status. First two chapters of *Notes from the House of the Dead* published.

1861 (19 February) Emancipation of serfs. Turgenev's *Fathers and Sons*.

Vremya begins publication. *The Insulted and the Injured* published in *Vremya*. First part of *Notes from the House of the Dead* published.

1862 Second part of *Notes from the House of the Dead* and *A Nasty Tale* published in *Vremya*. Makes first trip abroad, to Europe, including England, France and Switzerland. Meets Alexander Herzen in London.

1863 *Winter Notes on Summer Impressions* published in *Vremya*. After Marya Dmitriyevna is taken seriously ill, travels abroad again. Begins liaison with Apollinaria Suslova. Nikolay Chernyshevsky's *What Is to Be Done?* is published.

1864 First part of Tolstoy's *War and Peace.*

In March with Mikhail founds the journal *Epokha (Epoch)* as successor to *Vremya*, now banned by the Russian authorities. *Notes from Underground* published in *Epokha*. In April death of Marya Dmitriyevna. In July death of Mikhail. The International Workingmen's Association (the First International) founded in London.

1865 *Epokha* ceases publication because of lack of funds. Suslova rejects his proposal of marriage. Gambles in Wiesbaden. Works on *Crime and Punishment*.

1866 Dmitry Karakozov attempts to assassinate Tsar Alexander II.

Crime and Punishment and *The Gambler* published. The

latter written in 26 days with the help of his future wife, the stenographer Anna Grigoryevna Snitkina (b. 1846).

1867 Marries and, hounded by creditors, the couple leave for Western Europe and settle in Dresden.

1868 Birth of daughter, Sofia, who dies only three months old. *The Idiot* published in serial form.

1869 Birth of daughter, Lyubov.

1870 V. I. Lenin is born in the town of Simbirsk, on the banks of the Volga. Defeat of France in Franco-Prussian War.
The Eternal Husband published.

1871 Moves back to St Petersburg with his wife and family. Birth of son, Fyodor.

1871–2 Serial publication of *Demons*.

1873 First *Khozdenie v narod* ('To the people' movement). Becomes contributing editor of conservative weekly journal *Grazhdanin* (*Citizen*), where his *A Writer's Diary* is published as a regular column. 'Bobok' published.

1874 Arrested and imprisoned again, for offences against the political censorship regulations.

1875 *The Adolescent* published. Birth of son, Aleksey.

1876 'The Meek One' published in *A Writer's Diary*.

1877 'The Dream of a Ridiculous Man' published in *Grazhdanin*.

1878 Death of Aleksey. Works on *The Brothers Karamazov*.

1879 Struggling with ill health, Dostoyevsky visits the health spa in Bad Ems, Germany, in the summer for treatment.
First part of *The Brothers Karamazov* published.

1880 *The Brothers Karamazov* published (in complete form). Anna starts a book service, where her husband's works may be ordered by mail. Speech in Moscow at the unveiling of a monument to Pushkin is greeted with wild enthusiasm.

1881 Assassination of Tsar Alexander II (1 March).
Dostoyevsky dies in St Petersburg (28 January). Buried in the cemetery of the Alexander Nevsky Monastery. The funeral procession numbers over 30,000.

Introduction: Vision in Darkness

> The underground, the underground, the *poet of the underground*
> – the feuilletonists keep repeating this as though there were some-
> thing demeaning in it for me. The little fools. This is my glory,
> because truth is here.
>
> F. M. Dostoyevsky, notebook for *The Raw Youth*, 22 March
> 1875[1]

'Tragedy and satire,' Dostoyevsky wrote in an entry for
December 1876 in his notebook for *Diary of a Writer*, 'are two
sisters who go hand in hand, and the name of both of them,
taken together, is *truth*.'[2] Dostoyevsky's tragic-comic novel *The
Double, A Petersburg Poem* (1846; 1866), originally subtitled
'The Adventures of Mr Golyadkin', and his novel *Notes from
Underground* (1864), initially titled *A Confession*, are both
amalgams of tragedy and satire, and both embody what Dostoyevsky called the truth of the underground. He took pride in
having foregrounded in these two works a new and tragic
underground social and literary type. In the most basic sense
the underground behaviour and outlook of the new social type,
as it pertains to Dostoyevsky's early works in particular, is
the consequence of a radical denial of man's organic need for
self-expression, of his natural drive to be himself and to occupy
his own space and place in the world. The suppression of the
basic drives of human nature, however, signifies not their death,
but their disfiguration.

The whimsical but keen chronicler of Dostoyevsky's 'Petersburg Chronicle'[3] (1847) touches on the roots of the underground when he writes that 'happiness lies ... in eternal

indefatigable activity and in the practical employment of all
our proclivities and capacities', but that 'if man is dissatisfied,
if he has no means to express himself and bring out what is
best in him (not out of vanity, but as a result of the most natural
human need to know, express, embody his "I" in real life)', he
undergoes some kind of extraordinary breakdown – drink,
card-playing, gambling, brawling,

> or, lastly, goes mad with concerns about status [*ambitsiia*], while
> at the same time privately disdaining preoccupation with status,
> and even suffering over the fact that one must suffer because of
> such trivialities as status. And so, involuntarily you arrive at the
> almost unjust, even insulting, but *likely very probable* conclusion
> – that we have very little sense of our own dignity, that we have
> very little necessary egoism. [4]

Dostoyevsky reported on the socially charged theme of 'Individualism and Egoism' in the radically oriented Petrashevsky
Circle[4] to which he belonged in the late 1840s – one of his
readings that contributed to his arrest in 1849 and sentence to
prison for four years in a labour camp in Siberia and an
additional six years in exile there.

After his return from Siberia in 1859, Dostoyevsky echoed
his thoughts on man's need for creative self-expression in 'A
Series of Articles on Russian Literature' (1861), where he wrote
that the 'need to affirm oneself, to distinguish oneself, to stand
out, is a law of nature for every individual; it is his right, his
essence, the law of his being'. He went on to note that this need
'in the crude unstructured state of society manifests itself in the
individual quite crudely and even savagely'.

In the most immediate sense, the problems of the 'dissatisfied'
man – personality breakdown, the absence of a sense of true
human dignity, of 'necessary egoism' – point backwards to
The Double and its underground protagonist, benighted Yakov
Petrovich Golyadkin, and forward to the unnamed man from
the underground, or the Underground Man, in *Notes from
Underground*, a work in which the theme of the basic needs and
rights of individuals to self-expression, and the consequences

of their suppression, hold a central place. In *The Double*, as in *Poor Folk* (1846), Dostoyevsky's first published work, the author dramatizes this theme in the social framework of St Petersburg's vast state bureaucracy and its minor clerks and functionaries. In *Notes from Underground*, the moral and psychological underground serves Dostoyevsky as a platform both for an attack on the radical theorists of the so-called 'Russian Enlightenment' of the 1860s and their doctrines of necessity, and as an illustration of rampant individualism. The underground emerges, finally, as a consequence of a profound moral and spiritual crisis of Russia's educated classes. 'The reason for the underground', Dostoyevsky wrote in his notebook for *The Raw Youth* in an entry dated 22 March 1875, is the 'destruction of faith and general norms. "*Nothing is sacred*".'

The Double and *Notes from Underground* are threshold works in the œuvre of Dostoyevsky: the first inaugurates his important motif of the 'double' and projects his concept of the underground and an underground social type; the second work, *Notes from Underground*, lays out the basic social, moral-philosophical and religious positions that Dostoyevsky will develop in the five great novels – *Crime and Punishment*, *The Idiot*, *The Devils*, *The Raw Youth* and *The Brothers Karamazov*. *Notes from Underground*, however, is not only an arresting and profound introduction to these works, but to the twentieth century, which recognized as its own the problems of reason and irrationality, freedom and self-will, human dignity and degradation.

I

Fyodor M. Dostoyevsky (1821–81), born in Moscow, educated in Moscow schools and a graduate of the Military Engineering Academy in St Petersburg, gave himself over fully to literature in 1844. In St Petersburg he came under the influence of Vissarion G. Belinsky (1811–48), reigning radical critic of the day, and leader of the so-called 'natural school' of Russian writing.[5]

It was Belinsky who ushered in Dostoyevsky's first published works, the social sentimental novel in letters, *Poor Folk* (1846), and, two weeks later, the social and psychological novel *The Double*.

Dostoyevsky matured as artist and thinker in the late 1830s and early 1840s, a period marked by the huge impact of German Romantic idealism and culture philosophy (Hegel, Schelling, Herder and Friedrich Schiller) and French utopian socialist thought (Charles Fourier, Saint-Simon and others) on Russian intellectual life and culture. He himself passed through a romantic infatuation with Schiller. Though he retained a deep, lifelong respect for Schiller and his aesthetic humanism, later in his works, especially in *Notes from Underground*, he mocked the Romantic infatuation over Schilleresque idealism.

Yet the lofty philosophical and social idealism prevalent among the Russian educated classes in that period was offset early on by a painful consciousness of the backwardness and barbarism of Russian society, one dominated for centuries by autocracy and serfdom.

Dostoyevsky responded acutely to the wounds inflicted on the Russian people by social and institutional violence. 'My older brother and I,' he wrote many years later of the journey he made with his brother Mikhail from Moscow to St Petersburg in 1838, 'were plunging at that time into the new life, we were dreaming intensely about something, about the "beautiful and the sublime" (this phrase was still fresh then and was spoken without irony).'[6] Dostoyevsky juxtaposes his Romantic state of mind at that time with an incident during the same trip at an inn near a posting station: he witnessed a tall, burly, strong and crimson-faced courier leap into his troika 'and silently, without so much as a word, raise his powerful right fist and bring it straight down painfully on the back of the coachman's neck . . . Here there was method and not anger . . . Again and again' blows would fall, while the coachman in turn, 'like one gone mad', kept lashing his horses. 'This repulsive little scene has remained in my memory all my life,' Dostoyevsky records. 'Not only dogs and horses are precious to the Russian Society for the Protection of Animals,' he wrote, 'but man, Russian man, whom it is necessary to re*form* [*obrazit*] and to humanize' (*Diary of a Writer*, January 1876 [3: 1]).

In his depiction of the Underground Man as 'dreamer' in Part II of *Notes from Underground*, Dostoyevsky will emphasize the tragic disjunction between the Romantic exaltation over the 'beautiful and sublime' and the reality of a ravaged soul that revenges itself for its humiliation by trampling on his own idealism in the person of Liza. Dostoyevsky's trajectory as man and writer passed from Romanticism to realism, though he himself remained permanently marked by the aesthetic and philosophical humanism of the period.

It was in St Petersburg,[7] as Dostoyevsky wrote later in an imaginative recreation of his artistic beginnings,[8] that he had his mystical 'vision on the Neva', an evocation of St Petersburg as a tragic and fantastic city of 'golden palaces and hovels' with inhabitants 'strong and weak', and a landscape resembling a 'magical dream', a world in which 'new buildings rose over old ones, a new city formed in the air'. Petersburg is the 'most abstract and fabricated city on earth', remarks the Underground Man. Impersonal, rational in conception and design, the city of Peter the Great, its palaces and chancelleries, was built on swamps and the bones of thousands of its serf builders.

The lower depths of Petersburg are the habitation of Dostoyevsky's first literary characters, his 'poor folk', timid civil servants, reclusive students, educated and brooding 'dreamers', and other survivors of Petersburg's attics and damp cellars. In his 'Petersburg Chronicle' he describes the city's fantastic netherworld as 'a Petersburg nightmare, embodied sin ... tragedy, silent, mysterious, gloomy, wild'.

In Pushkin's narrative poem *The Bronze Horseman* (1833), Petersburg is the stage for symbolic conflict between the all-powerful ruler of the autocratic state, Peter the Great, and the helpless 'little man' Eugene who, mad with misfortune, challenges the autocrat and perishes, but not before forcing Peter and his mount to pursue him through Petersburg.[9] The poem became a potent paradigm in Russian literary and social consciousness for Petersburg as a place of triumphant imperialism and catastrophe for the individual. This is the same tragic city that overwhelms Gogol's pathetic clerk, Akaky Akakievich, in 'The Overcoat' and Dostoyevsky's mad government clerk, Yakov Petrovich Golyadkin, in *The Double*, a story inspired, in part, by Gogol's 'Diary of a Madman' (1835).

The satirist and fantasist Nikolay Gogol (1809–52) was the giant who dominated the literary scene that Dostoyevsky entered as a writer in 1844. His collected *Petersburg Tales* (1842), with their uproarious mix of the absurd, the grotesque and the banal, contributed powerfully to the general image of Russia's imperial capital as a fantastic but also demonized and doomed metropolis. Gogol's vision of life and character in Petersburg and in Russia (for example, in his classic stories 'The Overcoat', 'Diary of a Madman', 'The Nose' and in his epic novel *Dead Souls*), constituted for many among the radical and liberal intelligentsia a fearful historical judgement on Russia. Alexander Herzen (1812–70), the founder of revolutionary populism in Russia and one of nineteenth-century Russia's greatest writers and thinkers, bluntly wrote of 'the universal and inexorable character of these [Gogolian] types because there can be no others in Russia'. Belinsky gloomily insisted in a letter of 22 November 1847 to the cultural historian and philosopher K. D. Kavelin: 'The concept of personality among us is only just taking shape and therefore the Gogolian types *for the time being* are the most authentic Russian types.'

Gogol's strange characters and types, what the critic and cultural historian Isaiah Berlin has referred to as the 'inhabitants of the teeming world of Gogol's terrible comic imagination',[10] deeply engaged the literary and social consciousness of the young Dostoyevsky. Russian writers, he wrote many years later, convey their 'real view' of life in literary types. 'The whole depth, the whole content of an artistic work consists . . . only in types and characters. And this is almost always the case.' Gogol's 'artistic types oppress the mind with the most profound and unbearable questions, evoke in the Russian mind the most disturbing thoughts, with which, one feels, we will cope only a long time from now; indeed, will we ever cope with them?' (*Diary of a Writer*, April 1876 [1: 2]).

The Russian critic and philosopher Vasily V. Rozanov

(1856–1919) once protested that any attempt to 'connect Gogol's writing with our [Russian] life . . . would mean to lift a hand against ourselves'. Yet that is precisely what Dostoyevsky did in his novels *Poor Folk* and *The Double*. His characters, however, were not 'dolls', as he once satirically dubbed Gogol's literary types, but psychologically and socially real people. Nonetheless, in their wounded and disfigured souls he disclosed the hidden underground of Gogol's grotesques. In *Poor Folk* and, in particular, in *The Double*, both works that richly borrow from and parody Gogol's writing, Dostoyevsky showed that Gogol had connected with Russian reality in a critical way. At the same time, Dostoyevsky's first two works gave, in their new psychological realism, clear evidence that his literary method was his own. Belinsky and others, he wrote boastfully to his brother on 1 February 1846, find 'a new and original element in me in the fact that I proceed by Analysis and not by Synthesis, that is, that I go into the depths and, picking things out atom by atom, I disclose the whole, whereas Gogol goes for the whole directly, and therefore is not as profound as I am'.

'The basic idea of all art in the nineteenth century', a 'Christian idea', Dostoyevsky wrote in his journal *Vremya* (*Time*) in 1862 in a preface to a translation of *Notre Dame de Paris* by the great French poet and novelist Victor Hugo (1802–85) is the 'restoration of the fallen man', the 'justification of the pariahs of society, humiliated and rejected by all'. In the figure of the humble and virtuous clerk Makar Devushkin, the desperately impoverished hero of *Poor Folk*, Dostoyevsky restores the image of the so-called 'little man', a frequent butt of humour in popular anecdote and story. At one point, Makar Devushkin reads Gogol's sentimental-satirical yet deeply humane story 'The Overcoat', but indignantly rejects it. The story, he insists, is 'simply lacking in truthfulness because it couldn't happen that there could be such a clerk'. Devushkin refuses to recognize himself in Gogol's crooked mirror. Gogol's image of his hero Akaky Akakievich violates Devushkin's self-image. His rejection of 'The Overcoat', of course, involves a naive misunderstanding of Gogol's art, yet it is one that signals his own

xviii   INTRODUCTION: VISION IN DARKNESS

inalienable sense of dignity as a human being. 'My self-respect,'
he declares, 'is more precious to me than anything else.'

Devushkin's good nature and benignity thinly veil a wounded
psyche, anxieties, resentments and worries about his 'enemies'.
He takes to drink, too. 'I saw everything double – goodness
only knows,' Devushkin says at one point of a drunken encounter with some officers. 'Neither can I remember what I said,
except that in my wild resentment I said many things.'

'Seeing double' points in the direction of the protagonist of
The Double, Yakov Petrovich Golyadkin, a civil servant whose
crazed and bizarre concerns over his status, dignity and 'place'
in the world have reached a breaking point. This banal and
pathetic creature, neither rich nor poor, neither high nor low
in rank, at once pretentiously humble and painfully posturing,
comic in his almost wooden physical movements and muddled
thoughts and yet tragic in the essence of his terrified being,
is seen slipping rapidly into delusional paranoia and schizo-
phrenia – this at the very beginning of his picaresque journey
through the sterile and barren landscape of Petersburg's bureaucratic world.

Dostoyevsky was never to forget the ecstatic reception given
by Belinsky and his circle to his novel *Poor Folk* and its engaging and affectionate hero. Belinsky hailed him for writing a
'humane and moving' work, for disclosing the 'dreadful truth'
of the lower depths of Petersburg. 'Honour and glory to the
young poet whose muse loves the people who live in attics and
cellars and says about them to the inhabitants of the golden
palaces: "These, too, are people, your brothers!"'

It is impossible, however, to love Yakov Petrovich Golyadkin
as one's brother, even at a distance. Critics at the time of the
appearance of *The Double* recoiled from it and from its hero:
the work, they declared, was an 'imitation' of Gogol, 'an
unpleasant and boring nightmare', 'pathological', 'madness for
madness' sake'. This is a 'monstrous creation', wrote the young
poet and critic Apollon A. Grigoriev (1822–64), with an
'immeasurably insignificant hero' who makes one feel 'sad to be
a human being'. Yet the same critic stumbles upon an important
truth. Dostoyevsky, he writes, has 'gone so deeply into the

analysis of bureaucratic life that boring, naked reality has already begun to take on the form for him of delirium bordering on madness'. Indeed, madness in *The Double* emerges both as a radical form of alienation and as a desperate underground response to what the German political philosopher and socialist Karl Marx (1818–83) in his early writings referred to as the '*devaluation* of the human world'.[11]

Makar Devushkin in his purity sustains a basic sense of humanity in spite of a system that psychologically, as well as economically, is breaking him down. In contrast, one finds in Golyadkin, as a social type, the construction of a faceless bureaucratic system that does not recognize individuality, but only service and production. He is a piece of bureaucratic machinery that can be used and replaced. His fate in his delusions is to be 'supplanted' by his ruthless, audacious and agile 'double', his extraordinary likeness in looks and name: Yakov Petrovich Golyadkin Junior. Dostoyevsky's point, of course, is that in the bureaucratic state such a likeness is *not* extraordinary. Indeed, the appearance of Golyadkin's double in the office evokes neither notice nor surprise among Golyadkin's associates. Though Golyadkin's fellow clerk Anton Antonovich after much prodding from Golyadkin casually concedes the striking likeness of the two Golyadkins, he dismisses the matter with the revealing comment that Golyadkin's double, after all, is 'a clerk like any other and . . . the efficient sort' – precisely the indifferent, functional point of view of the bureaucratic system to which Anton Antonovich himself belongs.

Golyadkin is anything but complacent. Yet, though terrified by his perfect likeness, he also senses in his double a man 'completely different'. The point is a crucial one in Dostoyevsky's design of Golyadkin's character: it is the first sign of a distinctive, irreducible and irreplaceable self in Golyadkin. His double gives expression to Golyadkin's own suppressed and base opportunism and ambitions, but he does not embody Golyadkin Senior's initially dormant moral sense.

'He's all right', he goes his 'own independent way', 'he was his own master, like anyone else', he has his own 'place' ('*mesto*' – 'place', but also 'job') – these anxious thoughts keep running through his mind. Golyadkin not only has a job (*mesto*), but a 'place' or 'space' (*mesto*) in the world; that is, he has a separate, independent nature, and a right to exist. Almost immediately on the appearance of his double, Golyadkin formulates his predicament in terms of justice and morality, a higher authority. A poor man's Job, he asks: 'What is this, a dream or not? . . . How can it be? By what right is all this happening? Who engaged such a clerk [his double]?' 'If it's fate, if it's fate alone,' he says of his double's appointment, 'should he then be treated like a dishcloth, shouldn't he be allowed to work. What justice would there be in that?' 'Someone' might have wanted to turn Mr Golyadkin into a 'rag, and not a Golyadkin' – the narrator's mocking voice invades and dominates Golyadkin's stream of consciousness throughout the narrative – but the 'result would have been a rag and not a Golyadkin – yes, a rag, a disgusting filthy rag . . . [but] this rag would have had its pride, this rag would have been endowed with animation and feelings, and even though those feelings would have been mute and hidden deep within the filthy folds of that rag, they would nonetheless have been feelings' (VIII). The presence of these feelings in the polluted rubble of Golyadkin's consciousness marks the 'difference' between himself and his soulless double.

Dostoyevsky is primarily an artist who 'thinks in imagery', Nikolay N. Strakhov (1828–96), the nineteenth-century literary critic, philosopher and close friend of Dostoyevsky, once remarked. In *The Double*, where the narratorial voice with ironic detachment enters the flow of Golyadkin's stream of consciousness, Dostoyevsky *thinks* the critical questions of the nature of human dignity and identity entirely in imagery.

Golyadkin's self-division and disintegration sets into motion a desperate urge to affirm his oneness. His feverish, despairing and mad efforts to affirm his own identity are a muddle of the social, legal and metaphysical absurd, but a muddle at the centre of which we find a person's broken personality. 'Save me from that scoundrel, that depraved man', he imagines himself saying to a high official. 'He's a different person, Your Excellency, and I'm another, too. He's someone apart and I'm also someone in my own right . . . Please be kind, please authorize the change and put an end to that godless, wilful substitution [his double]' (XII). He rails against those who 'desire to oust others from the positions occupied by those other people by reason of their very existence in this world and to supplant them'. Such relations, he declares, are 'strictly prohibited by the law and this, in my opinion, is perfectly just, since everyone should be content with his own place'. Golyadkin, of course, is a humble, law-abiding citizen, yet in his madness he is aware of the social implications of his deluded petitioning, for he hastily assures the official, a figment of his imagination, that the 'ideas outlined above regarding *knowing one's place* are purely moral' (IX).

There is no theophany or restoration of fortunes, however, for Dostoyevsky's mentally ill, painfully posturing and increasingly disoriented petty Job. He will end up in a lunatic asylum – a place of piercing terror for him. More symbolic of his fate, however, more relevant to his tragedy, is the image of the crazed Golyadkin rushing about the streets of Petersburg in 'anguish, terror and rage', pursued by 'perfect replicas [of himself] ... stretching out in a long chain like a gaggle of geese; ... a terrifying multitude of exact replicas was spawned that the whole city was finally jammed with these perfect replicas' (X). Petersburg itself is Golyadkin's sentence and hell. Golyadkin reaches the conclusion: 'I'm done for, I've disappeared, gone from this world completely and all this is in the natural order of things and just couldn't be otherwise.'

The 'tragedy of the underground' is the tragedy of disfigured souls adrift in what appears to them a meaningless, godless, fate-ruled world. Here there is no salvation, only the conviction that things 'cannot be otherwise'. The formulation of underground despair as a spiritual phenomenon belongs to the post-exile period of *Notes from Underground*. Yet it is already latent in Dostoyevsky's conception of Golyadkin's internal drama.

Golyadkin's madness, to be sure, is a real psychic illness, and Dostoyevsky has a keen psychiatric understanding of Golyadkin's breakdown. At the same time, he conceives of his hero's illness as an integral part of social disorder. Here there is not so much causality as mutuality. As a social type, Golyadkin is a casualty of a system whose values he shares. Man is his own environment. 'Perhaps there are not at all any bad people among us, but only trashy ones,' Dostoyevsky remarked in February 1876 in his *Diary of a Writer* [1: 2]. 'We have not grown up to the level of bad people.'

The mocking voice of the narrator throughout *The Double* is central to the dark comedy of the work. As is the case with Gogol's humour, Dostoyevsky traps the reader in his very own misplaced laughter, in the popular comedy of bedlam; he implicates him in the drama or melodrama of his hero's trivial and trashy life, and in the tragedy of Russian life where, as the narrator in Dostoyevsky's *The Brothers Karamazov* once observes, 'a Russian often laughs when he ought to weep'.

While writing *The Double*, in a letter to his brother Mikhail of 1 February 1846 (the same letter in which he had relayed Belinsky's appreciation of his work) the young Dostoyevsky enthusiastically called the work his 'chef d'œuvre', pronouncing it 'ten times better than *Poor Folk*'. He was sorely distressed, however, to learn that Belinsky and others of his circle were disappointed with his second published work. In his public criticism, however, Belinsky defended *The Double* against its critics, though not without reservations. He found 'more creative talent and depth of thought' in *The Double* than in *Poor Folk*, and remarked upon the work's 'deeply moving and deeply tragic coloration and tone'. Yet he complained that the 'deeply humanitarian and pathetic element' that he had found in *Poor Folk* was hidden behind the 'humour' of *The Double* and he bluntly, and blindly, asserted that the 'fantastic has no place in literature, only in lunatic asylums'.

In a subsequent review Belinsky faulted *The Double* for 'monstrous shortcomings' of a formal kind: long-windedness and an absence of 'measure' in the artistic development of the novel. The idea that he had 'spoiled something that could have been a major achievement', Dostoyevsky wrote in a letter of 1 April 1846 to his brother, was very distressing. Yet as his remarks on *The Double* in subsequent years attest, he entirely shared Belinsky's criticism of the formal flaws of his novel, and made serious plans to revise his work.

Arrest, trial and sentence to prison and Siberian exile in 1849 put an end to Dostoyevsky's literary endeavours. Revision of *The Double*, however, remained on his agenda. 'Believe me,' he wrote to Mikhail on 1 October 1859, on his return to Russia, 'this revision . . . will constitute a *new novel*. People will see at last what *The Double* is! . . . Why should I lose a splendid idea, an extraordinary type in its social importance that I was the first to discover and of which I am the herald?' In 1866, he published a revised version of *The Double*, but without introducing into the plot and design of the novel the new topical political and ideological elements he had sketched. He limited his revisions to bringing forward and clarifying the narrative and thematic lines of the original work.

In later years Dostoyevsky continued to emphasize his high estimation of *The Double*. The 'form' of the original work, he acknowledges in the November 1877 issue of *Diary of a Writer* [1: 2], had been a 'positive failure', but its 'idea was a most luminous one, and I have never put forward in literature a more serious idea than that one'. The serious idea as it pertains to *The Double* is not the idea of the double per se (the double motif, a familiar one in literature, had been variously worked by Jean Paul Richter, Adelbert von Chamisso, Heinrich von Kleist, E. T. A. Hoffmann, Gogol, Poe and others), but rather the idea of an underground type rooted in Russian social reality, one in whom self-division gives disfigured expression to man's natural but repressed need for self-expression and self-affirmation.

In his notebook for August 1875, well after publication of *Notes from Underground*, Dostoyevsky alludes to Golyadkin as his 'chief underground type' and refers to the generic underground type as 'the main person in the Russian world'. In another notebook entry, for 22 March 1875, one in which he expresses his pride in being the 'first to bring out the real man of the *Russian majority* and . . . the first to expose his disfigured and tragic side', Dostoyevsky (echoing phrases from the Underground Man himself in *Notes from Underground*) broadly defines the tragic world of the underground:

I alone brought out the tragedy of the underground, consisting in suffering, self-punishment, the consciousness of something better and of the impossibility of achieving it and, mainly, consisting in the clear conviction of these unfortunate ones that everyone is alike, and therefore it's not worth trying to improve oneself! What can support those who try to improve themselves? Reward, faith? There are rewards from nobody, faith in nobody! Take a step from here and you're at extreme depravity, crime (murder). Mystery.

The moral-psychological underground of *The Double* has broadened here into a spiritual underground involving all of Russian society. In a judgement that embraces both contemporary Russia and its historical past, Dostoyevsky writes in the same entry:

There are no *foundations* to our society, no norms that have been worked out in life, because there really has not been any life, either. A colossal shock, and everything is breaking down, collapsing, being negated as though it had not even existed, and not only externally as in the West, but internally, morally.

The Underground Man is a product of this collapsing world. He is a symbolic-character image of nineteenth-century man divorced from his national roots and faith, yet seeking, in the depths of his confession, for moral and spiritual foundations, for an 'ideal'. As a literary type he is a syncretic creation with deep roots in Dostoyevsky's own works and characters leading up to *Notes from Underground* (the 'little man', the 'civil servant', the 'dreamer' and others). Dostoyevsky acknowledges in his notebook in 1875 that 'others have written about [the underground type], because they could not but take note of him'. He maintains, however, that he has 'written more about him than all other writers'. Indeed, the Underground Man has broad affinities with the so-called 'superfluous man' who inhabits the works of Pushkin, Lermontov, Herzen and Turgenev (the latter's *The Diary of a Superfluous Man*, 1850, 'The Hamlet of Shchigrovy County', 1849, and 'Hamlet and Quixote', 1860), among other writers.[12]

One finds, too, in the conceptual foundations of *Notes from Underground* and its hero or anti-hero echoes from a broad range of European writers and thinkers: Schiller, Byron, Chateaubriand, Rousseau, Kant, Diderot, Hegel, Schelling, Schopenhauer, Heine and Max Stirner, to mention only a few.

Notes from Underground and its protagonist, finally, though shaped in the radical political climate and debates of the early 1860s, draw philosophical power and passion from Dostoyevsky's own tragic experience in prison in the years 1850 to 1854. These were years of intense suffering and thought. As he wrote to the poet Apollon N. Maikov from Siberia on 18 January 1856: 'I too thought and went through experiences, and in the kind of circumstances and conditions that obliged me to experience, rethink, and ponder far too much, beyond endurance.'

2

Years later in his 1873 *Diary of a Writer* [16] Dostoyevsky refers to his imprisonment as a time of 'rebirth of convictions'. That expression encompassed a resurgence of religious faith, a populist elevation of the Russian people, and a renewed interest in the relations of art and Christianity. Dostoyevsky's concern for the social and historical problems of Russian life grew more intense than ever, his outlook became more spiritualized and was marked by a tragic Christian idealism. Finally, incarceration in prison – an environment which he once called a kind of 'compulsory communism' – placed the questions of freedom in the foreground of his consciousness, a fact of special significance in the context of Dostoyevsky's polemics with the radical socialists of the 1860s.

Freedom as a basic psychological and spiritual need, and the tragic consequences of its suppression, is at the centre of his great artistic memoir, *Notes from House of the Dead* (1860–62). 'What is more important than money for the convict?' asks the narrator of this work. 'Freedom or at least some dream of freedom.' Through gambling, spending money on vodka, carousing, risk, seeking forbidden pleasures, smuggling, attempts at escape, or just speaking, acting, dressing in flamboyant or bizarre ways the convict seeks to act 'according to *his own free will*' (*po svoei voli*), to experience at least the 'illusion' of freedom (*svoboda*).[13] His longing for freedom, his hopes, however, are 'so utterly without foundation as almost to border on delirium'. Thus, the narrator remarks that sometimes even the ordinarily peaceable and model convict will suddenly and unaccountably burst out in a frenzy. Yet this is

> the anguished, hysterical manifestation of personality, an instinctive yearning to be oneself, the desire to express one's humiliated personality; a desire which suddenly takes shape and reaches the pitch of malice, of madness, of the eclipse of reason, of fits and convulsions. Thus, perhaps, a person buried alive in a coffin and awakening in it, would thrust at the cover and try to throw it off, although, of course, reason might convince him that all his efforts were in vain. But the whole point here is that it is not a question of reason [*rassudok*]: it's a question of convulsions [*sudoroga*] ... [1: 5]

Where the life impulse is suppressed, reason becomes irrational or, as Dostoyevsky suggests in a bit of verbal play with the key Russian words '*rassudok*' (reason, common sense) scrambles into '*sudoroga*' (convulsion). Such a phenomenon, in one form or another, is paradigmatic for the 'dead house' where, as the narrator remarks, 'almost every independent manifestation of personality in the convict is considered a crime'.

The convict's almost insane defence of his personality echoes Dostoyevsky's use of madness as a social metaphor in *The Double*, while at the same time it prefigures the Underground Man's psychology of underground protest, one in which man in extreme cases will go mad in order to insist on his own free will. Dostoyevsky's sympathies, to be sure, are with the convicts in their plight. At the same time, he views their rebellion, their excesses, as a tragic inversion of man's legitimate quest for self-expression, self-mastery and self-determination. His ambivalent attitude towards the convict's wild outbursts will mark his approach to underground rebellion in *Notes from Underground*.

In *Winter Notes on Summer Impressions* (1863), an account of Dostoyevsky's first trip to Europe in 1862 – a place he ironically refers to in the first pages of his work as the 'land of holy wonders' – the author broadly condemns Western individualism and social relations in general, and at the same time sets forth his own ideal concept of the relations between the individual and society.[14] He insists that the 'sign of the highest development of personality, of its supreme power, its absolute self-mastery, and its most complete freedom of its own will' is to be found in 'sacrifice of one's whole self for the benefit of all'. Society must recognize the rights of the individual, but the 'demanding rebellious individual ought first of all to sacrifice to society his whole "I", his whole self'. Authentic brotherhood must be grounded in 'feeling, in nature, not in reason', Dostoyevsky maintains. 'Love one another, and all these things will be added unto you.' [6] These thoughts, deeply rooted in Dostoyevsky's social thinking,[15] are central to the ethical-spiritual design of *Notes from Underground*.

Dostoyevsky regards both capitalist and socialist ideology and practice as providing deeply flawed and counterproductive models for social development. In Paris, Dostoyevsky had noted a 'struggle to the death between the general Western individualistic basis of the West and the necessity of at least somehow living together, at least somehow forming a community and settling down in a single anthill'. [5] The anthill will make another appearance in *Notes from Underground* when its narrator will sarcastically compare the utopian socialist's dream of completing the ideal social structure to the 'amazing' eternally indestructible 'anthill'.

Dostoyevsky's eight-day visit to London provided him with abundant material for his critique of bourgeois materialism. He noted, on the one hand, the immense wealth and spectacular technological advances in London that were a product of its great mid-century industrial revolution, but on the other saw the staggering poverty and destitution of the masses that accompanied that revolution. He knew well, of course, and admired,

the writings of 'the great Christian, [Charles] Dickens', as he
later in his June 1876 issue of *Diary of a Writer* [1: 2] referred
to the English novelist, a writer who in his novels and journalism had brought the epic world of London to life and at the
same time championed the poor and dispossessed. In an article
in 1851 in his journal *Household Words*, where in passing
he compares London to Babylon, the author of *Oliver Twist*
reminded the well-to-do classes who 'sleep in peace' and have
children in their houses to

> wake to think of, and to act for, the doomed childhood that
> encircles you out of doors, from the rising up of the sun unto the
> going down of the stars,[16] and sleep in greater peace. There is
> matter enough for real dread there. It is a higher cause than the
> cause of any rotten government on the Continent of Europe that,
> trembling, hears the Marseillaise in every whisper, and dreads a
> barricade in every gathering of men.[17]

In his chapter 'Baal' in *Winter Notes* Dostoyevsky gives
special attention to the much-hailed Crystal Palace that was the
centrepiece of London's Great Exposition in Hyde Park in
1851, and which both symbolized and embodied for many the
victory of Progress and the mastery of technology: here was a
palatial structure, a wrought-iron and glass 'wonder' with vast
exhibition spaces foregrounding the marvels of production from
lathes to perfume in the developing industrial and consumer-
oriented world.[18] Dostoyevsky's response to this wonder was
profoundly negative. This 'colossal palace', 'this Baal',[19] with its
aura of proud triumph and finality – a place to which millions
humbly stream from all corners of the earth – alarms him:

> Somehow or other you begin to fear something. However inde-
> pendent you may be, yet something begins to frighten you. 'Now
> really isn't all this in very fact the attainment of the ideal?' – you
> think. 'Isn't this really the ultimate? Is this not in fact the "one
> fold"?'[20] And won't one have to accept this as truth in its entirety,
> and then fall mute ... [Y]ou feel that here something final has
> been accomplished, accomplished and finished. This is some kind

of Biblical scene, something resembling Babylon, some kind of prophecy from the Apocalypse taking place before your very eyes. You feel that it would take a great deal of spiritual resistance and negation not to succumb, not to surrender to the impression, not to bow to the fact and not to deify this Baal, that is, not to accept the existing for one's ideal* * *

The Crystal Palace, idealized by the radical revolutionary Nikolay G. Chernyshevsky (1828–89) in his novel *What is to be Done?* (1863) as a model for his socialist society of the future, resurfaces in *Notes from Underground* where the Underground Man, precisely in a spirit of unremitting resistance and negation, will dismiss it as a sorry ideal, and one flawed not only by its wholly utilitarian and materialist essence, but by its deadly embodiment of stasis and finality.

As though in anticipation of the Underground Man, Dostoyevsky introduces in *Winter Notes* the image of an 'odd' fellow, a recognizable forerunner of the Underground Man in another respect – a person who will refuse to exchange even a 'drop of his personal freedom' for all the guaranteed benefits of this reason-based brotherhood. In his 'foolishness', Dostoyevsky writes ironically, it seems to this odd person that these arrangements are like 'a prison, and it's better to be on one's own, because that way one has absolute freedom of will [*polnaia volia*]'. [6] Dostoyevsky adds that in this state of liberty (*volia*) the odd fellow 'will be without work, beaten, and dying from hunger and really without any will [*volia*], yet all the same it seems to this odd fellow that his own will [*svoia volia*] is better'. Dostoyevsky, in essence, posits man's stubborn, seemingly irrational, will to be himself at all costs, as essential to his nature.

Finally, in lines and imagery both uncanny and prophetic, Dostoyevsky counterposes to the triumphalism of London with its worldwide trade, its Crystal Palace, and world fair, a dark and foreboding, indeed frightening image of mass underground resistance or rebellion, passive and for a moment undirected, but as Dickens in another context put it, 'a matter enough for real dread'. The wild, grotesque, dissolute behaviour at night of London's poor and dispossessed, these 'pariahs of society', represent to him

> a separation from our social formula, a stubborn, unconscious separation, an instinctive separation at any cost for the sake of salvation, a separation from us with disgust and horror. These millions of people, abandoned, banished from the human feast, shoving and crushing each other in the underground darkness into which they have been thrown by their elder brothers, grope about and knock at any gate, and seek a way out so as not to suffocate in the dark cellar. Here is a final, despairing effort to form their own group, their own mass, and to break with everything, even with the human image, just so as to be themselves, just so as not to be together with us. [5]

Dostoyevsky was never again to create another such fantastic, and yet at the same time realistic, scene of mass underground rebellion.[21]

3

When Dostoyevsky returned to St Petersburg in 1859 after nearly ten years in Siberian exile he found a changed and charged political and cultural landscape. The radical intelligentsia, the utopian socialists and dreamers of the 1840s had mutated into a new generation of strident activists and intellectuals with a press and a veiled but recognizable revolutionary agenda. The new representatives of the so-called Russian Enlightenment preached faith in reason, science and technology; they patterned much of their thinking after the utilitarian, deterministic and utopian ideas of English utilitarians and French utopian socialists Jeremy Bentham, John Stuart Mill, Charles Fourier, Saint-Simon and others, and their minds focused upon radical changes in society.

The leading representative of this new movement was the radical political thinker, literary critic and revolutionary socialist Nikolay Chernyshevsky. His frankly didactic, utopian novel

What is to be Done?, subtitled *From the Stories of the New Man*, aimed at promoting a new puritanical morality in the cause of social revolution. It held out the dream of eternal happiness for man on earth. Chernyshevsky's strangely cerebral heroes preach a philosophy of rational self-interest, or 'advantage', according to which 'lofty feelings, ideal strivings . . . are completely insignificant before the strivings of each person for his own advantage'. In the new man actions follow from the 'nature of things', he 'does not answer for them, and to blame them is foolish'. *Notes from Underground* constitutes a direct polemical and satirical assault on Chernyshevsky's denial of moral responsibility, freedom of will and his notion of the perfectibility of human nature.

Parts I and II of *Notes from Underground*, 'The Underground' and 'Apropos of Wet Snow', each appeared separately in two issues of Dostoyevsky's journal *Epokha* (*Epoch*) in the first half of 1864. The period of writing was a difficult one for him. His wife was dying of consumption. He himself was in ill health, suffering from epileptic attacks and other painful ailments. He worried over the reception of his work. In letters to his brother Mikhail in the spring of 1864 Dostoyevsky complains that an 'external fatalism' had laid too heavy a hand on *Notes from Underground*; he feels that the tone of this work is 'too strange', 'harsh, wild', though he trusts that its 'poetry' will have a mitigating effect. Yet he is confident that the work will be 'strong and frank; it will be the truth'.

The truth here is that of his critique of radical socialist doctrine, but it is also the truth of the underground – the underground as a consequence of the collapse of moral and spiritual foundations and of the alienation of the educated and cultured strata of Russian society from the mass of people and its faith. 'Scepticism and the sceptical view,' Dostoyevsky had written in a subscription prospectus to his journal *Time* for the year 1862, 'are killing everything, even the very view itself.' 'In our time everything is in confusion,' he writes in another prospectus for 1863, 'everywhere there are quarrels about foundations and principles.' 'Who among us in all honesty knows what is *good* and what is *evil*?' he asks again in an announcement of the publication of *Epokha* for 1865. The Underground Man is the epitome of this moral and intellectual confusion.

In his brief prefatory footnote to *Notes from Underground* (p. 3), Dostoyevsky goes out of his way to project the 'author of these notes', that is, the Underground Man, as a social type that 'not only can but even must exist in our society – taking into consideration those circumstances under which our society was formed'. He is a 'representative of a generation that has survived to this day'. It is this person who 'introduces himself and his views, and apparently wishes to explain those reasons as a result of which that generation appeared and was bound to appear in our midst'.

Dostoyevsky's unusually conspicuous statement of purpose suggests an anxious effort to distance himself from his protagonist. The Underground Man, a self-proclaimed 'anti-hero', is *not* his hero. A disillusioned idealist of the Hegel-dominated Romantic philosophical generation of the 1840s, the Underground Man gives expression in his polemic with the rationalists in the middle of the 1860s to Dostoyevsky's critique of radical ideology. Yet in his extremism, in his ravaged mental processes and in his moral and spiritual debacle, the Underground Man is at the same time Dostoyevsky's crowning illustration of what happens to a person whose mind and character have been shaped by a generation of Romantic and Hegelian-minded dreamers. The Underground Man emerges, finally, as a man without faith and foundations who has been caught up in a treadmill of consciousness. 'Where are my primary causes on which I can take a stand, where are my foundations? Where shall I take them from? I practise thinking and consequently every primary cause immediately draws another in its wake, one that is even more primary, and so on *ad infinitum*'[22] (Part I: v). Here is what the Underground Man calls the 'disease' of consciousness.

The first words of the Underground Man – 'I am a sick man . . .' (*Ya chelovek bol'noi . . .*) project the paradoxical and problematic nature of the anti-hero: the Underground Man is physically sick, but he is also spiritually ill. Yet he is a *man* (*chelovek*), a human being, first of all, conscious at the time of

writing of his condition and its roots. His basic humanity, albeit
a tormented one, finds resonance in his polemic in defence of
human dignity and free will. In the final analysis, the Underground Man, as the Russian scholar and critic Aleksandr
P. Skaftymov noted, is 'not only the accuser, but also the
accused'.[23] He is a brilliant polemicist who routs the rationalists, but he is also a causally determined 'anti-hero' who is
himself routed in the process.

A retired and educated civil servant of forty, an irritable,
jaundiced man, a 'mouse' in his underground and a man with
a pathological sense of humiliation, the Underground Man in
Part I introduces himself and polemicizes with the rationalists
of the 1860s. In Part II, his memoirs proper, he describes his life
and psychology, sixteen years earlier, as a sentimental-romantic
dreamer. Both polemics and memoirs move in parallel lines and
in tandem with each other towards a point of recognition of
intellectual, moral and spiritual bankruptcy.

In Part I the Underground Man's psychology of 'spite', one in
which reason and will are constantly at odds with one another,
becomes the foundation for an irrational will philosophy that
is directed against the rationalists' theory of enlightened self-
interest, or 'advantage'. According to this theory man does
bad things only because he doesn't know his true interests; if
'enlightened', however, he will do good because no man would
'act knowingly against his self-interest'. The rationalists further
project a 'Golden Age' at which time reason and science, the
discovery of the 'laws of our so-called free will', will have
thoroughly re-educated man and normalized human nature, so
that man will 'desire in accordance with the table' and will 'no
longer be responsible for his actions, and life will be extremely
easy for him'.

In his sharp and often sarcastic rebuttal, the Underground
Man insists on man's fundamental irrationality, his preference
for 'twice two is five' as opposed to 'twice two is four', which
is 'death'. Throughout history, the Underground Man argues,
man in his wilfulness and moral obliquity has 'knowingly' and
'stubbornly' acted against reason and what might appear to be
his 'advantage'. Moreover, sometimes 'human advantage not

only might but even must lie precisely in man desiring . . . what is bad for himself and not to his advantage'. Out of sheer boredom and caprice, the Underground Man argues, man will kick over all the rational benefit and prosperity of utopia. Central to his argument is that man wants to live according to his 'own free will'. Even if it were proven to him by mathematics and science that he was a 'piano key', he still 'wouldn't see reason', and would deliberately do something to have his own way. If necessary he would 'create chaos and destruction', curse the world and, if all that could be calculated, he would 'go insane in order to be rid of reason'. He would do all this for the sake of something dearer than his own very best interests, that is, the '*right to desire*', the right to act according to his own free will, a right that can be most 'advantageous', just because 'it preserves what is most precious and most important to us, and that is our personality and our individuality' (Part I: VIII).

The tragic paradox of the Underground Man's defence of personality is that in the defence of it he loses it, and sometimes, as in his final encounter with Liza, 'breaks with the human image', to borrow Dostoyevsky's words in *Winter Notes*. In his life, as in his polemic, the defence of free will passes into self-assertion, egoistic self-will. 'One's own whims however unbridled, one's fantasy, sometimes inflamed to the point of madness – here is the most advantageous of advantages,' declares the Underground Man. 'All man needs is *independent* volition, whatever that independence might cost and wherever it might lead' (Part I: VII). Ultimately he stands not 'for suffering, nor for prosperity', but for 'my own caprice and that it should be guaranteed me when the need arises' (Part I: IX).

Finally, the Underground Man equates his own personal drama, his own tragedy – an endless series of psychological actions and experiments to affirm his lost sense of dignity and integrity – with the fate of mankind. The whole human business would seem in fact to consist only in this, that 'he [man] might achieve his object and convince himself that he's a man and not a piano key' (Part I: VIII).

The Underground Man sees man as 'a predominantly creative animal condemned consciously to strive towards a goal', yet 'fond of destruction and chaos'. 'Perhaps the whole goal towards which mankind is striving in this world consists solely in the uninterrupted process of achievement – in other words, in life itself', and not in the goal which can only be twice two is four, i.e. the beginning of death. Mankind instinctively fears 'achieving his goal' and 'completing the building', and, indeed, leaves it for domestic animals, in particular to the ants who 'have one amazing building of this type, which is eternally indestructible – the anthill' (Part I: IX).

Dostoyevsky certainly is one with the Underground Man in his emphasis on the centrality in man's existence of the living process, of 'life itself', as opposed to any final earthly goal such as the Crystal Palace. Yet he in no way endorses the Underground Man's existentialist view that man is forever journeying without goal in a meaningless universe. Missing from the Underground Man's conception of man's destiny is what is missing from the utopian socialist's idea and ideal of the Crystal Palace: a spiritual dimension.

'Workers, when they finish ... go to the pub,' the Underground Man declares, and immediately asks: 'But where can man go?' Dostoyevsky had very definite views on this question. In a notebook entry of 16 April 1864, on the occasion of his wife's death, Dostoyevsky wrote that man's 'I' stands in the way of Christ's commandment to love a person *as one's own self*. 'Christ alone was able, but Christ was the eternal ideal towards which man strives and must by the laws of nature strive ... All history, be it of humanity or in part of every person separately, is only development, struggle, striving, and attainment of that goal.' In contrast to his Underground Man, Dostoyevsky posits a universe in which man's journey is made meaningful through endless striving for a moral and spiritual goal, but one that is *not* attainable on earth. Nowhere is Dostoyevsky's tragic religious idealism more evident than in his assertion at the end of the above-quoted entry that 'man on earth strives for an ideal that is *contrary* to his nature'. It is only through love and self-sacrifice, Dostoyevsky insists, that man fulfils the 'law of striving for the ideal ... Otherwise life on earth would be senseless.'

Dostoyevsky's ethical-religious ideal found expression in the original uncensored manuscript of *Notes from Underground*. In a letter to his brother Mikhail of 26 March 1864, Dostoyevsky complains of 'horrible misprints', and adds:

> It really would have been better not to have printed the penultimate chapter (the most important one where the main idea is expressed) [Part I: x] than to have printed it as it is, that is, with sentences thrown together and contradicting each other. But what is to be done! The swinish censors let pass those places where I mocked everything and sometimes blasphemed *for show*, but where I deduce from all this the need for faith and Christ – this is forbidden. Now who are these censors? Are they in a conspiracy against the government or something?

Yet even in his revision of Chapter x the Underground Man hints again and again at the presence in him of fervent 'ideals' and 'desires'. It is this fact that gives such immense force to his rejection of the rationalists' Crystal Palace. He can only compare it to a 'hen house' into which one might creep to get out of the rain. 'But what can I do if I've taken it into my head that this is not the sole purpose of living.' 'Give me another ideal ... Do away with my desires, eradicate my ideals, show me something better and I will follow you.' He would let his tongue be cut out 'if only that building could be so constructed that I would never again have the urge to stick it out again'. But there is no such edifice among 'your buildings', he emphasizes.

At the end of Chapter x, the Underground Man, in the symbolic form of three rhetorical questions, touches on issues, essentially religious in their inner content, relating to man's nature and origins: 'So why was I created with such desires? Could I possibly have been created solely and simply to reach the conclusion that my whole make-up is nothing but a swindle? Can that be the whole purpose? I don't believe it [*ya ne veriu*],' the Underground Man answers. He does not believe that his 'whole make-up', that is, his yearning for an ideal is a swindle, yet he cannot get beyond the stage of merely *not* believing it's a swindle. Dostoyevsky obliquely explains why in a play on the words '*Ya ne veriu*' (I don't believe it) – words that may *also* be translated as 'I do not believe', that is, 'I have no faith'. Such are the final words of the Underground Man at the end of Chapter x, the remnants, we may suppose, of Dostoyevsky's indication in the original uncensored version of Chapter x, of the 'need for faith and Christ'.

What the chapter does unmistakeably indicate to the reader is that the Underground Man is prime evidence of Dostoyevsky's spiritual 'law of striving for the ideal'. The Underground Man's striving for an ideal hints at his urgent need for faith. 'It's not the underground that's better,' he declares at the beginning of Chapter xi, 'but something else, something completely different, which I long for but which I just cannot find!'

It is impossible to know in what form the Underground Man gave expression to what Dostoyevsky calls the 'need for faith and Christ'. It is most unlikely that he used any of these terms or words.[24] Yet the uncensored text would have foregrounded the novelist's spiritual-religious idea. Further, it would have highlighted the importance of the episode in the penultimate chapter of Part II where love and sacrifice for a fleeting moment find expression in the embrace-in-tears of Liza and the Underground Man. It is the memory of the catastrophe of his encounter with Liza, his play with Romantic idealism, that 'weighs heavily' on the Underground Man's conscience and motivates him now, sixteen years later, to put down his recollections. 'For some reason,' the Underground Man writes at the end of Part I, 'I believe that by writing it down I shall rid myself of it' (Part I: xi).

'You know what a transition is in music? That's exactly what we have here,' Dostoyevsky wrote to Mikhail on 13 April 1864 regarding Part II of *Notes from Underground* in its original tripartite division. 'In the first chapter we have what appears to be chatter, but suddenly in the final two sections this chatter resolves itself in unexpected catastrophe.'

In one of his studies on Dostoyevsky, the Russian poet, thinker and scholar Vyacheslav I. Ivanov (1866–1949) wrote of the 'law of epic rhythm ... the law of the progressively gathering momentum of events' in the Dostoyevsky novel.

Action not only moves towards catastrophe, but in each synapse we are confronted with 'tragedy raised . . . to a higher power'.[25] The same may be said of the rhythm of underground polemic in Part I *of Notes from Underground*, and of the dramatic action in Part II of the novel.

The movement towards catastrophe is precipitous. Every wilful and proud attempt of the Underground Man to affirm his independence and self-mastery, every act of spite, every effort of his to introduce the irrational into the status quo of his existence only deepens his sense of dependence and humiliation, only locks him ever more firmly into the movement towards catastrophe. 'It's predestined, it's fate!' he cries at one point in words that define his interior paralysis. His every desperate and irrational act to affirm his personality and individuality parodies his notion that irrational behaviour preserves 'what is most precious and important, namely, our personality and our individuality'.

The tragic chain of actions, or confrontations, finds its last link in the episode with Liza. Here the catastrophe of the sentimental-romantic dreamer with its abstract and lofty humanism, and its disastrous psychological power game, is played out to its bitter end. The Underground Man takes out his humiliations on Liza, and finally, and cruelly, confesses to her his craving for power, his inability to conceive of love as anything but despotism. This raging yet self-denigrating moment of confession is suddenly interrupted: Liza, deeply feeling his sense of humiliation and pain, bursts into tears and reaches out to him. 'I couldn't hold myself back either and sobbed as I had never sobbed before.' Love, compassion and sacrifice are embodied in Liza's gesture of reaching out, in this embrace-in-tears. Yet the Underground Man's inability to conceive of love as anything but physical and moral despotism results in a fresh humiliation of Liza, that is, 'domination and possession'.

The Underground Man's sobbing confession to Liza – 'They won't let me . . . I can't be . . . good!' – signals his spiritual paralysis and failure to take responsibility. Yet his suffering, his guilt, his dialogue with himself and his interlocutors, and

finally his recollections, bring him to the threshold of Dostoyevsky's higher truth.

The motif of the 'double', of duality, finds various and rich
expression in almost all of Dostoyevsky's works. In Golyadkin,
self-division is an illness, both psychological and social; it
destroys him, even as his drama of disintegration testifies to his
core humanity. In his characterization and development of the
Underground Man, however, Dostoyevsky hints for the first
time in his fiction that the dynamics of duality, of divided
self-consciousness, can become a positive instrumentality in
moral and spiritual development. He set forth his ideas on the
subject of duality near the end of his life in a letter of 11 April
1880 to the artist Yekaterina F. Junge (1843–98) who had
written to him about her 'duality'. In his reply, Dostoyevsky
wrote that the phenomenon of duality was 'common to human
nature in general', though not in the intense form it took in
Junge. 'And it's for that reason that you are dear to me,' he
writes, 'because this *split* in you exactly resembles my own
life-long experience.' Dostoyevsky goes on to describe the
phenomenon of duality as a 'great torment, but at the same
time a great pleasure. It represents a strong sense of duty, a
need for self-appraisal, and the presence in one's nature of the
need for moral duty to oneself and to mankind. That is what
this duality means ... If you believe [in Christ] (or want very
much to believe),' Dostoyevsky adds significantly, 'then the
torments of this duality will greatly be mitigated, and you will
find a spiritual way out, and that is the main thing.'

The closing lines in Part II of the Underground Man's 'notes'
take on a choral character. One is conscious of the overvoice
of the author, Dostoyevsky. The drumbeat of egoistic 'I's' that
marks the opening of the Underground Man's notes yields in
places, symbolically, to the plural pronoun 'we'. The Underground Man has reached a partial understanding of his generation and of himself, and addresses the matter directly: '... we
are all cripples, each one of us to a greater or lesser degree ...
[we] are forever striving to become some kind of imaginary
generalized human beings. We are stillborn and we have long
ceased to be begotten of living fathers.' The Underground Man,

however, remains in limbo. He does not 'want to write any more from "The Underground",' but as the author tells us in a separate note at the end of *Notes from Underground*, he does go on writing. The Underground Man will not escape the underground, yet his confession, his desire at the end of Part II *not* to write any more from the underground, like his thirst for an ideal, marks a new stage of moral and spiritual awareness – some kind of vision in darkness.

Almost a decade after the publication of *Notes from Underground* Varvara V. Timofeeva (1850–1931), a young writer, remarked to Dostoyevsky after reading his novel: 'What a horror is this soul of man! But at the same time, what a terrible truth!' Dostoyevsky, Timofeeva recalls in her memoirs, 'smiled broadly and brightly', and remarked that a prominent journalist who regarded *Notes from Underground* as Dostoyevsky's chef d'œuvre had once advised him to keep on writing in that way. 'But I don't agree with him,' Dostoyevsky went on about his novel. 'It's really too sombre. *Es ist schon ein überwundener Standpunkt* ['that's past and over with', literally, 'that's already an outdated position, or "stand-point"']. I am *able* now to write in a more serene, more reconciliatory way. Now at the moment I'm writing something [*The Raw Youth*] [...].'[26] Dostoyevsky's words bring to mind his comments about *Notes from Underground* on the eve of its publication: the work is 'strong and frank', the 'truth', yet it is 'too strange', 'harsh, wild'.

Dostoyevsky never changed the moral-philosophical and religious views that constitute the conceptual foundation of *Notes from Underground*.[27] Had he in later years, however, come to feel that the tragic truth of the underground that he had so effectively mobilized in his attack on rationalist ideology had perhaps overshadowed his higher truth? 'What I especially like,' Dostoyevsky commented to Alexander Herzen in London about the latter's book *From the Other Shore* – a historical-philosophical dialogue between Herzen and his antagonist – 'is that your opponent is also very clever. You must agree that in many cases he has you with your back to the wall ... "Why that's the essence of the whole piece," replied Herzen, laughing' (*Diary of a Writer*, 1873 [1]).

That is perhaps the essence of *Notes from Underground*, but in a deeper, more visceral sense than in Herzen's book. Dostoyevsky's artistic-ideological design is in place. Those areas where he stands with the Underground Man and those where he stands against him can be marked out, though not in simple oppositions. His higher truth is manifest, but through a glass, darkly. The Underground Man is more than clever. Underground truth strains at the limits of authorial design and perspective. The work is a sombre one. Yet art has its own life and purposes. The brutal veracity of underground confession, the shock of recognition and the recoil, together with the power of ancient tragedy, the pity and the fear, lead to an opening of the spirit. As the Austrian-Czech writer Franz Kafka (1883–1924) once wrote, 'We must have those books that act upon us like ill-fortune, that pain us greatly, like the death of one who is dearer to us than ourselves . . ., like suicide – a book must be an axe to break the sea frozen within us.'[28]

Robert Louis Jackson

NOTES

1. Except for Ronald Wilks's translations in this Penguin edition of Dostoyevsky's *The Double* and *Notes from Underground*, all other translations from Dostoyevsky and works of other writers are mine. Russian references to works by Dostoyevsky – fiction, notebooks, *Diary of a Writer*, journalism and letters – are to *F. M. Dostoevskii, Polnoe sobranie sochinenii v tridtsati tomakh* (*F. M. Dostoyevsky, Collected Works in Thirty Volumes*, Nauka, Leningrad: 1972–90). When a Dostoyevsky work (fiction, *Diary of a Writer*, journalism, notebook entries or letters) is mentioned or cited in this introduction, the date of the work is given; where major quotations are concerned the number of the chapter and of the section (if there are subdivisions) are provided in square brackets at the end of the quotation. Where quotations from Ronald Wilks's translations are cited, references are provided in round brackets.

2. Throughout his life Dostoyevsky wrote journalistic and critical essays. 'Petersburg Chronicle' in 1847 (four articles on various aspects of Petersburg life) was an early example of his creative journalistic style. In 1861, he and his brother Mikhail inaugurated a journal of criticism and opinion called *Vremya (Time)* (1861–3), and later, in 1865, after the closing of *Vremya*, the short-lived *Epokha (Epoch)*. Both journals, edited by Dostoyevsky and his brother, published literary and social criticism, translations from foreign writers, as well as work of Russian writers, including Dostoyevsky's *Notes from Underground* (1864) and *Winter Notes on Summer Impressions* (1863). In 1873, Dostoyevsky became editor of the journal *Grazhdanin (Citizen)* and, under the title of *Dnevnik literatora (Diary of a Man of Letters)*, began contributing a wide range of formal and informal journalistic, fiction and critical writing, and social commentary. He ceased publishing his *Diary* in 1874 in order to write his novel *Podrostok (The Raw Youth)*, but renewed publication of his *Diary* (this time under the title of *Dnevnik pisatelia – Diary of a Writer*) in 1876–7; after an interval in which he wrote *The Brothers Karamazov*, he renewed his *Diary* in 1880, scarcely a year before his death. The *Diary* was published in a monthly format and divided into chapters and sections. Dostoyevsky fills his *Diary* with his own short stories, criticism, journalistic sketches and commentary that treated matters autobiographical, contemporary, historical, social, political, psychological, philosophical and religious. The *Diary* is unique in the way it conflates various genres of writing, blends fiction and criticism, memoirs with imaginative writing, authorial judgement with opinions of fictive narrators, and so forth. Thus, for example, there are short stories that grow out of journalistic material in the *Diary*, and journalistic pieces that suddenly turn into fiction. Here, too, are to be found the bare, often limited politics and prejudices of Dostoyevsky and, side by side with them, analyses, meditations and thoughts of a profound thinker and moralist. However one defines the *Diary of a Writer* as a literary genre, both its form and content add up to an enormously rewarding journey into the mind and art of a literary-philosophical genius.

3. 'Petersburg Chronicle' – an occasional popular column in the Sunday edition of the *St Petersburg Gazette*, to which Dostoyevsky contributed four journalistic articles, or, as they were known at the time, 'feuilletons'. The narrator in each of Dostoyevsky's

four feuilletons talks about Petersburg, its events, inhabitants, cultural, literary and social life.

4.   The 'Petrashevsky Circle' was an informal discussion group of intellectuals, writers, civil servants, teachers and students who met in the apartment of M. B. Butashevich-Petrashevsky (1821–66), a civil servant and translator for the Russian Ministry of Foreign Affairs. His personal library contained many prohibited books that were read by members of the Circle. This informal group was one of a number of literary and philosophical groups engaged in studying the writings of the utopian socialists – social thinkers and reformers, such as Saint-Simon, Pierre Leroux, Etienne Cabet, Louis Blanc and, in particular, Charles Fourier (1772–1837). Some of the members of the Petrashevsky Circle, including Dostoyevsky, constituted a smaller group that planned to print anti-government proclamations using a secret printing press. The general thinking of the participants in these circles was sharply critical of the repressive Russian autocracy and of serfdom, a feudal system of agriculture officially abolished only in 1861. Tsar Nicholas I (b. 1796, Emperor of Russia, 1825–55) played a direct role in the trial and sentencing of members of the Petrashevsky Circle. Nicholas instituted a harsh system of rule under the slogan of 'Autocracy, Orthodoxy, and Nationality'. He suppressed the Decembrist revolt of 1825 in Russia, crushed the November 1831 uprising in Poland, and helped suppress rebellions in Europe in 1848, earning himself the nickname of the 'gendarme of Europe'.

5.   The 'natural school' – a literary movement of mid-century Russia of diverse trends that marked the shift of Russian narrative prose from the influence of German Romantic literature and idealist philosophy to a social and realistic orientation; it had strong links to contemporary French literature (Balzac, Hugo, George Sand and others). Belinsky, who focused primarily on a writer's content and social perspective, was the most influential voice of the new realism. Although privately he acknowledged the strange character of Gogol's writing, he nevertheless insisted that Gogol perceived the sickness of Russian society. Hence his close association of the 'natural school' with Gogol. Dostoyevsky was a member of Belinsky's circle in the mid-1840s, though his relationship with the critic gradually cooled.

6.   The 'beautiful and the sublime'. The term is used by, among others, the British statesman, writer and orator Edmund Burke, in his treatise *A Philosophical Enquiry into the Origin of Our*

Ideas of the Sublime and the Beautiful (1757) and the German philosopher Immanuel Kant's *Observations on the Feeling of the Beautiful and the Sublime* (1764). As Dostoyevsky notes, the term was used without irony in the Romantic 1830s and early 1840s. The Underground Man, a disillusioned idealist and one-time Romantic dreamer, employs that term with great irony in *Notes from Underground*.

7. St Petersburg was founded by Peter the Great (1682–1725) in 1703. The city was erected on swampy ground and built by peasants under brutal conditions and with great loss of life. In 1712 Peter moved the capital of Russia from Moscow to St Petersburg, where it remained, except for a short interval, until 1918, when Moscow again became the capital of Russia. The imperial city, designed by architects from Europe, and surrounded by myth in poetry and prose in subsequent Russian literature, became and has remained one of the most extraordinary monuments to Russian and European culture.

8. *Peterburgskie snovideniia v stikhakh i proze* (*Petersburg Dreams in Verse and Prose*), 1861.

9. At the centre of Pushkin's poem is the equestrian statue of Peter the Great on Senate Square in St Petersburg. It was created by the French rococo sculptor Etienne-Maurice Falconet (1716–91). The monument was commissioned by Catherine the Great as a tribute to Peter the Great. Set upon a huge piece of granite, the figure of Peter the Great, the great reformer, is seen seated on a huge rearing horse, one arm raised and pointing towards the Neva River, while the horse tramples on a snake, generally perceived as symbolizing the enemies of Peter's reforms. It is this equestrian statue that pursues poor Eugene in Pushkin's poem.

10. Isaiah Berlin, *Russian Thinkers*, edited by Henry Hardy and Aileen Kelly, with an introduction by Aileen Kelly (Penguin Books, Harmondsworth: 1981), p. 180.

11. Karl Marx, *Early Writings*, translated and edited by T. B. Bottomore, and with a new foreword by Erich Fromm (McGraw Hill Book Company, New York, Toronto, London: 1963) p. 121.

12. The term 'superfluous man' (*lishnii chelovek*) entered into general usage after the appearance of Turgenev's *The Diary of a Superfluous Man* (1850) and came to designate, both negatively and positively, a whole range of characters in Russian nineteenth-century literature. As a rule, the 'superfluous man' was a member of the upper class, intelligent, capable and desirous of engaging in useful social activity, but condemned to inactivity because of

his heightened moral or social consciousness, or his inability to adapt to the oppressive tsarist bureaucratic world or provincial society; or because of his comfortably secure, and therefore undemanding, economic status; or because of some personal idiosyncrasy, or for all of these reasons. Such individuals, typically outsiders, would lapse into states of indolence and boredom, become alienated from their social peers and society. Others out of boredom, cynicism, spiritual emptiness became fatalists, gamblers and duellists. Dostoyevsky's concept of the 'dissatisfied' man – one who is denied the possibility of actively employing his abilities and talents in life – certainly overlaps with the social and cultural type of 'superfluous man'. At the same time, his dissatisfied man is inclusive of other social types, mostly urban, such as his underground type, Golyadkin, hero of *The Double*.

13. '*Svoboda*', like its English counterpart 'freedom', is used in the sense of freedom of speech, or freedom, as opposed to slavery. It implies rights and obligations. The Russian '*volia*', essentially outside of law (though not necessarily opposed to it), is psychological or psychic in character; it embraces both the concept of will (volition, desire or wanting), as well as that of freedom. This kind of freedom is the felt and organic right to act as one pleases, to do what one wills with one's own life, according only to one's own sense of right or wrong. The will to be free, to be one's own master, to occupy one's own space, or to revel in the freedom of space, can also take on a romantic or capricious character. Finally, if frustrated or suppressed, '*volia*' can turn into self-will (*svoevolie*), arbitrary action (*proizvol*), or a feeling that 'all is permissible' (*vsedozvolennost*'). Here, of course, is an important element of Dostoyevsky's 'tragedy of the underground'.

14. The expression 'land of holy wonders' (*strana sviatykh chudes*) was used by the poet, philosopher of history and theologian Aleksey S. Khomyakov (1804–60) in his poem 'Dream' (*Mechta*), where he presents the West as a world that has lost its former glory and is now covered by a 'deathly shroud'. One of his central ideas – also to be found in Dostoyevsky's own thought – is the Orthodox religious idea of '*sobornost*' (from '*sobor*', 'council' and 'church'), a Russian word variously translated as 'conciliarity', 'ecumenicity', 'harmony' or 'unanimity'. 'It is the liberty in love that unites believers,' writes the Russian theologian Sergius Bulgakov in his book *The Orthodox Church*, translated by Elizabeth C. Cram, edited by Donald A. Lowrie (Morehouse Publishing Co., New York and Milwaukee, and Centenary Press,

London: 1935), p. 75. This religious idea finds expression in Dostoyevsky's social views on 'authentic brotherhood' in *Winter Notes on Summer Impressions* and in Father Zosima's concept in *The Brothers Karamazov* of the connectedness of all phenomena, and of universal responsibility 'for all and everyone'. He speaks of the 'magnificent communion' of the future when man will not seek servants but will strive to be the servant of everybody [V 1:3].

15. Commenting on a self-oriented social type inhabiting Petersburg's isolated corners and social circles, the narrator of Dostoyevsky's early 'Petersburg Chronicle' in 1847 remarks that 'life is a whole art, that to live means to make an artistic work out of oneself, [but] that only in accord with the communal interests, in sympathy with the mass of society, with its direct, immediate requirements, and not in drowsiness, not in indifference from which follows the disintegration of the mass, and not in solitude' can the individual find genuine fulfilment. [1]

16. A paraphrase of Psalm 113: 3.

17. See 'The Metropolitan Protectives', in the 26 April 1851 issue of Dickens' journal, *Household Words*, in Charles Dickens' *Uncollected Writings from Household Words, 1850–1859*, edited with an introduction and notes by Harry Stone (Indiana University Press, Bloomington and London: 1968), p. 273. The article was co-authored by W. H. Wills, but the lines quoted have been attributed to Dickens.

18. The Exhibition building was 1,850 feet (564m) long, with an interior height of 408 feet (124m), and 990,000 sq feet of floor space. Fourteen thousand exhibitors from various countries occupied the floor space of the Crystal Palace, displaying an extraordinary range of machinery and products of what has been called the second Industrial Revolution in Europe. The building, originally erected in Hyde Park, was rebuilt on Sydenham Hill, in south London, where it remained a major attraction until it burned down in 1936.

19. 'Baal' – literally 'lord' – a pagan god of ancient Semitic peoples to whom human sacrifices were offered in times of calamity. Dostoyevsky's 'Baal' emerges as a god of modern bourgeois materialist society – a 'proud and sombre spirit' who reigns like an emperor over a 'giant city'. Full of contempt for the people he rules, 'he does not even demand submission, because he is convinced of it'. He is not at all troubled by the 'poverty, suffering, grumbling, and stupefaction of the masses', and 'contemptu-

ously and calmly, distributes organized charity, just in order to dispose of it'. [5] Dostoyevsky's Baal in certain features, such as his contempt for the masses, anticipates the Grand Inquisitor in *The Brothers Karamazov* (1880).

20. 'And there shall be one fold, and one shepherd' (John 10: 16).

21. The reality of London's nineteenth-century slums, it must be said, fully testifies to the truth of Dostoyevsky's fantastic realism. In his account of London's slums in the early 1880s, Andrew Mearns described its tenements as places 'where tens of thousands are crowded together amidst horrors which call to mind what we have heard of the middle passage of the slave ship. To get into them you have to penetrate courts reeking with poisonous and malodorous gases arising from accumulations of sewage and refuse scattered in all directions and often flowing beneath your feet; courts, many of them which the sun never penetrates, which are never visited by a breath of fresh air, and which rarely know the virtues of a drop of cleansing water. You have to ascend rotten staircases, which threaten to give way beneath every step ... You have to grope your way along dark and filthy passages swarming with vermin.' See Mearns, *The Bitter Cry of Outcast London: An Inquiry into the Condition of the Abject Poor*, edited with an introduction by Anthony S. Wohl (Leicester University Press; Humanities Press, New York: 1970), p. 58.

22. The Underground Man's words come across almost as a parody of Kant's handwritten comment in his own printed copy of his *Observations on the Feeling of the Beautiful and Sublime*: 'Everything goes past like a river and the changing taste and various shapes of men make the whole game uncertain and delusive. Where do I find fixed points in nature, which cannot be moved by man, and where can I indicate the markers by the shore to which he ought to adhere?' See Immanuel Kant, *Observations on the Feeling of the Beautiful and Sublime*, translated by John T. Boldthwait (University of California Press, Berkeley and Los Angeles, California: 1960), pp. 8–9. If we take into account Dostoyevsky's remarks in a letter to his brother Mikhail about censored passages in *Notes from Underground* (see p. xxxvi of this introduction), as well as other indications in the text, the Underground Man would appear to be searching half-unconsciously for fixed points grounded in Christianity.

23. Aleksandr P. Skaftymov, *Nravstvennye iskaniia russkikh pisatelei* (*The Moral Quest of Russian Writers*) (Khudozhestvennaia Literatura, Moscow: 1972), p. 90. Skaftymov's discussion of

Notes from Underground originally appeared in the Czech publication *Slavia* in 1929–30, and was the first major analytical essay to place *Notes from Underground* in the context of the polemics of the 1860s.

24. It seems most unlikely, considering the muted character of the Underground Man's religious consciousness, that Dostoyevsky had him directly use the words 'Christ' or 'faith'. More likely, the Underground Man's allusion was indirect, as in Dostoyevsky's later brilliant tale, 'A Gentle Creature' ('Krotkaia', 1876), where the pawnbroker, one of Dostoyevsky's last great underground figures, exclaims in his despair over his wife who had committed suicide as a result of his cruelty and confession: 'People, love one another? Who said that, whose testament is that?'

25. Vyacheslav Ivanov, *Freedom and the Tragic Life. A Study in Dostoevsky*, translated [from the German] by Norman Cameron, edited by Professor S. Konovalov (Oxford), foreword by Sir Maurice Bowra (Noonday Press, New York, NY: 1952), p. 11. Ivanov's book was originally written and published in Germany in 1932. Ivanov reworked and incorporated in the book some of his earlier pre-First World War Russian writings on Dostoyevsky.

26. V. V. Timofeeva (O. Pochinkovskaya), 'God raboty s znamenitym pisatelem' ('One Year at Work with a Renowned Writer') in *F. M. Dostoevskii v vospominaniiakh sovremennikov v dvukh tomakh* (*F. M. Dostoyevsky in the Recollections of his Contemporaries in Two Volumes*), Vol. II (Khudozhestvennaia Literatura, Moscow: 1990), p. 186.

27. It should be emphasized that Dostoyevsky did *not* use the idiomatic or colloquial German phrase '*Es ist schon ein überwundener Standpunkt*' in a sense that implies that his intentional point of view in *Notes from Underground* had changed or become outdated, but rather in the sense that the work represented a kind of writing that is past. He no longer writes 'in that way'. Dostoyevsky's particular use of the German idiom finds numerous parallels in German writing, e.g., '*Der Typhus ist für uns ein überwundener Standpunkt*' (Typhus for us is a thing of the past); '*Briefe sind ein überwundener Standpunkt*' ([Writing] letters is a thing of the past, i.e. it's been replaced by a new technology). What was unique about *Notes from Underground* was its use as a polemical device of an all-dominating narratorial first-person focus on the world 'from the underground', with all the various

consequences that derive from focusing on the world from that position or, literally, 'stand-point'.

28. Letter to Oskar Pollak, 27 January 1904, in *Franz Kafka, Briefe*, Vol. 1, edited by Hans-Gerd Koch (F. Fischer, Frankfurt am Main: 1999), p. 36.

Further Reading

CRITICAL WORKS

Bakhtin, M., *Problems of Dostoevsky's Poetics*, edited and translated by Caryl Emerson, introduction by Wayne C. Booth (Minneapolis, Minn., 1984).

Berdyaev, Nicholas, *Dostoevsky*, translated by Donald Attwater (Cleveland and New York, 1973).

Berlin, Isaiah, *Russian Thinkers*, edited by Henry Hardy and Aileen Kelly, with an introduction by Aileen Kelly (Harmondsworth, 1978; 1981).

Carr, E. H., *Dostoevsky (1821–1881)* (London, 1930).

Catteau, Jacques, *Dostoevsky and the Process of Literary Creation*, translated by Audrey Littlewood (Cambridge, 1989).

Chizhevsky, Dmitry, 'The Theme of the Double in Dostoevsky', in *Dostoevsky: A Collection of Critical Essays*, edited by René Wellek (Englewood Cliffs, NJ, 1962).

De Jonge, Alex, *Dostoevsky and the Age of Intensity* (London, 1975).

Fanger, Donald, *Dostoevsky and Romantic Realism. A Study of Dostoevsky in Relation to Balzac, Dickens, and Gogol* (Cambridge, Mass., 1967).

Frank, Joseph, *Dostoevsky: The Seeds of Revolt, 1821–1849* (Princeton, NJ, 1976).

— *Dostoevsky: The Years of Ordeal, 1850–1859* (Princeton, NJ, and London, 1983).

— *Dostoevsky, The Stir of Liberation, 1860–1865* (Princeton, NJ, 1986).

Gide André, *Dostoevsky* (London, 1952).

Hingley, Ronald, *The Undiscovered Dostoevsky* (London, 1962).

Holquist, Michael, *Dostoevsky and the Novel* (Princeton, 1977).

Ivanov, Vyacheslav, *Freedom and the Tragic Life. A Study in Dostoevsky* (New York, 1952).

Jackson, Robert Louis, *Dostoevsky's Underground Man in Russian Literature* (The Hague, 1958).

— *Dostoevsky's Quest for Form. A Study of his Philosophy of Art* (New Haven, Conn.; London, 1966).

— *The Art of Dostoevsky. Deliriums and Nocturnes* (Princeton, NJ, 1981).

— *Dialogues with Dostoevsky. The Overwhelming Questions* (Stanford, Calif.).

Jones, John, *Dostoevsky* (Oxford, 1985).

Jones, Malcolm V., *Dostoyevsky: The Novel of Discord* (London, 1976).

— *Dostoyevsky After Bakhtin: Readings in Dostoyevsky's Fantastic Realism* (Cambridge, 1990).

Knapp, Liza, *The Annihilation of Inertia. Dostoevsky and Metaphysics* (Evanston, Illinois, 1996).

Leatherbarrow, W. J., *Fedor Dostoevsky: A Reference Guide* (Boston, Mass., 1990).

Lednicki, Waclaw, 'Dostoevsky – The Man from the Underground', in *Russia, Poland, and the West; Essays in Literary and Cultural History* (London, 1954).

Magarshack, David, *Dostoevsky* (London, 1960).

Matlaw, Ralph, 'Structure and Integration in *Notes from Underground*', PMLA [Publications of the Modern Language Association of America] 73 (1958).

Meyer, Priscilla and Rudy, Stephen, *Dostoevsky & Gogol, Texts and Criticism* (Ann Arbor, Mich., 1979).

Miller, Robin, 'Dostoevsky and Rousseau: The Morality of Confession Reconsidered', in *Dostoevsky. New Perspectives*, edited by Robert Louis Jackson (Englewood Cliffs, NJ, 1984).

Mochulsky, Konstantin, *Dostoevsky: His Life and Works*,

translated with an introduction by Michael A. Minihan (Princeton, NJ, 1967).

Neuhäuser, Rudolph, 'Romanticism in the Post-Romantic Age: A Typological Study of Antecedents of Dostoevsky's Man from the Underground, *Canadian-American Slavic Studies* 8 (1974).

Offord, D. C., 'Dostoevsky and Chernyshevsky', *Slavonic and East European Review* LVII, No. 4 (1979).

Peace, Richard, *Dostoevsky: An Examination of the Major Novels* (Cambridge, 1971; republished Bristol, 1992).

— *Dostoevsky's Notes from the Underground* (London, 1993).

Rice, Martin P., 'Current Research in the English Language on *Notes from the Underground*', *Bulletin of the International Dostoevsky Society*, No. 5 (November, 1975).

Rozanov, V. V., *Dostoevsky and The Legend of the Grand Inquisitor*, translated and with an afterword by Spencer E. Roberts (Ithaca, NY, 1972).

Seduro, Vladimir, *Dostoyevski in Russian Literary Criticism: 1846–1956* (New York, 1957).

Shestov, Lev, *Dostoevsky, Tolstoy and Nietzsche*, translated by Bernard Martin and Spencer E. Roberts (Athens, Ohio, 1969).

Steinberg, A., *Dostoievsky* (London, 1966).

Steiner, George, *Tolstoy or Dostoevsky: An Essay in the Old Criticism* (New York, 1971; first published 1959).

Terras, Victor, *The Young Dostoevsky, 1846–49: A Critical Study* (The Hague, 1969).

Wasiolek, E., *Dostoevsky: The Major Fiction* (Cambridge, Mass., 1964).

Note on the Text

The text used in these translations is the thirty-volume complete collection, chief editor G. M. Fridlender, and published by Nauka, Leningrad, 1972–90.

Table of Ranks

Since the different civil service ranks are mentioned frequently throughout this volume they are listed here for ease of reference. The Table of Ranks was introduced by Peter the Great in 1722 for the civil service. Each civil rank had its equivalent in the army and navy, the clergy and the imperial court. The system survived in slightly modified form until the 1917 Revolution.

The fourteen ranks are (beginning with the highest):

Class	Rank
1	Chancellor
2	Actual privy counsellor
3	Privy counsellor
4	Actual state counsellor
5	State counsellor
6	Collegiate counsellor
7	Court counsellor
8	Collegiate assessor
9	Titular counsellor
10	Collegiate secretary
11	Ship secretary
12	Government secretary
13	Provincial secretary
	Senate registrar
	Synod registrar
	Cabinet registrar
14	Collegiate registrar

Hereditary nobility was conferred on those holding minimum rank eight (collegiate assessor). Although civil ranks had their parallels in the army and navy, the armed services took precedence over the civil.

NOTES FROM
UNDERGROUND

I

*The Underground**

I'm a sick man . . . I'm a spiteful man. I'm an unattractive man.
I think there's something wrong with my liver. But I understand
damn all about my illness and I can't say for certain which part
of me is affected. I'm not receiving treatment for it and never
have, although I do respect medicine and doctors. What's more,
I'm still extremely superstitious – well, sufficiently to respect
medicine. (I'm educated enough not to be superstitious, but I
am superstitious.) Oh no, I'm refusing treatment out of spite.
That's something you probably can't bring yourselves to understand. Well, I understand it. Of course, in this case I can't
explain exactly to you whom I'm trying to harm by my spite. I
realize perfectly well that I cannot 'besmirch' the doctors by
not consulting them. I know better than anyone that by all this
I'm harming no one but myself. All the same, if I refuse to have
treatment it's out of spite. So, if my liver hurts, let it hurt even
more!

I've been living like this for a long time – about twenty years.
I'm forty now. I used to work in a government department, but

* The author of these notes and the *Notes* themselves are, of course, fictitious.
Nevertheless, such people as the writer of these notes not only can but even
must exist in our society – taking into consideration those circumstances in
which our society was formed. I wanted to bring before the public more
distinctly than usual one of the characters of the recent past. He is a representative of a generation that has survived to this day. In this fragment entitled *The
Underground*, this person introduces himself and his views, and apparently
wishes to explain those reasons as a result of which that generation appeared
and was bound to appear in our midst. In the second fragment there appear
the actual notes of this person about certain events in his life.

Fyodor Dostoyevsky

I don't work there any more. I was a spiteful civil servant. I was rude and enjoyed being rude. You see, I never took bribes, so I had to compensate myself in some way. (That's a rotten joke, but I don't intend striking it out. I wrote it down thinking it could come across very witty, but now that I've seen that I only wanted to do a spot of vulgar bragging I shall let it stand on purpose!) Whenever people came with their petitions to the desk where I sat I would snarl at them and I felt inexhaustible pleasure whenever I succeeded in upsetting someone. And I was nearly always successful. For the most part they were a timid bunch – we all know what people asking for favours are like. But among those fops there was one particular officer whom I just couldn't stand. He simply wouldn't be brought to heel and had a nasty way of rattling his sabre. For eighteen months he and I waged war over that sabre. In the end I triumphed. He stopped the rattling. However, this happened when I was still young. And do you know, gentlemen, what was the main point of my malice? Well, the main point, indeed the crowning nasti-ness, was that even during my most splenetic moments I was constantly, shamefully, aware that not only was I not seething with spite but that I wasn't even embittered, and was merely scaring sparrows in vain, for my own amusement. I might foam at the mouth, but just bring me some kind of toy, give me a cup of tea with sugar and most likely I'd calm down or even be deeply touched, although I'd be so ashamed. I would most cer-tainly grumble at myself afterwards and suffer from insomnia for several months. I've always been like that.

Well, I lied about myself just now when I said I was a spiteful civil servant. I lied out of spite. I was simply having a little fun with these petitioners and the officer, as in fact I could never really be spiteful. I was always conscious of the abundance of elements within me that were diametrically opposed to that. I felt that they were literally swarming inside me, those warring elements. I knew that they had been swarming there all my life, begging to be set free, but I wouldn't set them free, oh no, I wouldn't, I deliberately wouldn't set them free. They tormented me until I felt ashamed; they brought on convulsions and – in the end – they bored me, oh how they bored me! So don't you think, gentlemen, that I'm repenting of something to you, asking you to forgive me for something? I'm certain that's what you think. But I assure you that it's all the same to me if that's what you're thinking . . .

Not only did I not become spiteful, I never even managed to become anything: neither spiteful, nor good, neither a scoundrel nor an honest man, neither a hero nor an insect. And now I'm living out my life in my corner, teasing myself with the spiteful and utterly worthless consolation that an intelligent man cannot make himself anything and that it's only fools who manage to do that. Oh yes, your intelligent, nineteenth-century man ought to be and is in fact morally obliged to be essentially without character; a man of character, a man of action, is primarily a very limited creature. That's my conviction as a forty-year-old. Yes, I'm forty now – mind you, forty is an entire lifetime, it's extreme old age. To go on living after forty is unseemly, vulgar and immoral! Who lives longer than forty? Give me a straight, honest answer. I'll tell you who does: fools and rogues. I shall tell all those venerable old men, all those hoary-haired, sweet-smelling worthies that to their faces! I shall tell the whole world to its face! I have the right to talk like this, since I myself shall live to be sixty. I'll live to be seventy! To be eighty! Now wait a moment! Let me get my breath back . . .

You're probably thinking, gentlemen, that I want to make you laugh. Well, there you're mistaken too. I'm not in the least the jolly type you think I am, or perhaps may think I am. If, however, you find all this chatter irritating (and I can sense that you *are* irritated) and are thinking of asking me who I am exactly, I'd give you this answer: I'm just an ordinary collegiate assessor.[1] I worked in the civil service in order to earn my bread (but solely for that reason) and when a distant relative left me six thousand roubles in his will last year I resigned immediately and settled down in my little corner. I did live for a while in this corner before, but now I've taken up permanent residence in it. My room is cheap and filthy, on the outskirts of town. My maidservant is an old peasant woman, ill-tempered from stupidity, and what's more she always smells terribly. I'm told the St Petersburg climate is bad for me now and that with my paltry means it must be very expensive living in St Petersburg. I know all that, better than all those experienced and extremely wise counsellors and head-shakers. But I shall stay in St Petersburg – I shall not leave St Petersburg! I shan't leave it because ... Ah well! – it doesn't make a damned bit of difference whether I leave it or not.

However, what can a decent chap talk about with the greatest pleasure?

Answer: about himself.

Very well, I'll talk about myself.

II

Now I'd like to tell you, gentlemen, whether you want to hear it or not, why I didn't even manage to become an insect. I solemnly declare that many times have I wanted to become an insect. But even that hasn't been granted me. I assure you, gentlemen, that to be excessively conscious is a disease, a real, full-blown disease. For the needs of everyday life ordinary human consciousness should be more than sufficient – that is, half or even a quarter less than the portion which falls to the lot of an educated man in our unhappy nineteenth century and, on top of that, of one who has the twofold misfortune of living in St Petersburg, the most abstract and premeditated city on earth. (Cities tend to be either premeditated or unpremeditated.) For example, the consciousness possessed by all our so-called spontaneous people and men of action should be quite sufficient. I'd wager that you think I'm writing all this simply to show off, to score off those men of action and, what's more, that I'm rattling my sabre like my officer, also to show off – and in very bad taste. But gentlemen, who could possibly pride himself on his infirmities, let alone brag about them?

But what am I saying? – everyone does it – everyone vaunts his illnesses – and perhaps myself more than anyone. But don't let us argue about it. I put it rather clumsily. All the same, I'm firmly convinced that not only a great deal of consciousness but even any amount of consciousness is a disease. I firmly maintain that. But let's put that to one side for a moment. Tell me this: why did it invariably happen, as if deliberately, that at those very moments when I was most capable of appreciating all the subtleties of the 'sublime and beautiful'[2] as we once used to say, I not only would fail to comprehend but would perform the most contemptible actions . . . well . . . the kind of which everyone is guilty, but which I happened to perform precisely when I was most conscious that I should not be performing them at all? The more I recognized goodness and the whole question of the 'sublime and beautiful', the deeper I sank into the mire and the more capable I became of completely immersing myself in it. But the main feature of all this was that it wasn't within me by accident, but as if it were bound to be there. It was as if this were my normal condition and far from being an illness or the fruits of corruption, so that finally I lost the desire to combat that corruption. It all ended by my almost coming to believe (or perhaps I really did believe) that this was probably my normal condition. But at the very outset how much agony I was forced to endure in that struggle! I didn't believe the same could happen to others and so all my life I have kept it to myself, like a secret. I was ashamed (and perhaps I'm ashamed now). It reached the point where I felt an abnormal, secret, base thrill of pleasure when returning to my corner on some positively foul St Petersburg night and I would feel intensely aware that once again I had done something vile that day, that what's done cannot be undone, and inwardly, secretly, I would keep gnawing, gnawing, nibbling and eating away at myself until the bitterness finally turned into some shameful, damnable sweetness and finally into serious, definite pleasure. Yes, pleasure, pleasure! I stand by that. I broached the subject because I'd like to find out for certain: do others experience the same kind of pleasure? Let me explain: the pleasure I experienced came directly from being too vividly aware of my own degradation, from the feeling of having gone too far; that it was foul but that it couldn't be otherwise; that there's no way out for you, that you'd never make yourself a different person; that even if there remained enough time and faith to change yourself into something different you most probably wouldn't want to change yourself. And that even if you did want to, you'd end up by doing nothing because there might in fact be nothing to change yourself into. But finally, and most importantly, all this proceeds from the normal, fundamental laws of heightened consciousness and from the inertia which is the direct result of those laws and therefore not only could you *not* change yourself, you'd simply do nothing at all. For instance, as a result of this intensified awareness you are justified in being a scoundrel, as if it's of any comfort to a scoundrel that he himself feels that he's in fact a scoundrel. But that's enough . . . Good Lord, I've been waffling away, and what have I explained? How can one explain this feeling of pleasure? But I shall explain it! I shall pursue it to the bitter end! That's why I picked up my pen . . .

I, for example, am extremely touchy. I'm as suspicious and as quick to take offence as a hunchback or a dwarf, but in fact there have been moments when, if someone had slapped my face, I might have been glad even of that. I mean this in all seriousness: very likely I would have managed to derive pleasure of a kind even from that – I mean of course the pleasure of despair; but it's in despair that you discover the most intense pleasure, especially when you are acutely conscious of the hopelessness of your predicament. And here too, after that slap in the face, you are crushed by the realization of what filth you're being smeared with. The main thing is that, whichever way I look at it, it invariably turns out that I'm the first to be blamed for everything and, what hurts most of all, that I'm blamed when innocent, according to the laws of nature, so to speak. First of all I'm to blame, as I'm cleverer than anyone else around me. (I've always considered myself cleverer than everyone else around me and sometimes, would you believe, even felt ashamed of it. At all events, all my life I've somehow always looked away and could never look people straight in the face.) And finally, I'm guilty, since even if I'd had the magnanimity within me, my awareness of its utter futility would have caused me greater torments. I should probably have been unable to do anything because of my magnanimity: neither forgive, since the offender might have slapped me according to the laws of nature and you can't forgive the laws of nature; nor forget, since even if these are laws of nature it still hurts. Finally, even had I not wanted to be magnanimous at all but, on the contrary, if I'd wanted to take revenge on the offender, most probably I wouldn't even have been able to avenge myself on anyone for anything, since I probably would never have had the determination to do anything even if I could. Why shouldn't I have had the determination? I'd like to say a few words about that in particular.

III

Now, with those people who, for example, know how to take revenge and generally stand up for themselves – how do they do it? They are so obsessed, let's suppose, by this feeling of revenge that during that time all that remains in their entire being is this feeling. This kind of gentleman simply heads straight for his goal like a maddened bull with lowered horns and is stopped only by a wall. (Incidentally, such gentlemen, that's to say, these spontaneous men of action, genuinely give up when faced with a wall. For them a wall is not simply a diversion, as it is, for example, for men like us who think and who consequently do nothing. Nor is it a pretext for turning back, a pretext in which people like us don't normally believe but of which we are always very glad. No, they capitulate in all sincerity. For them a wall provides something reassuring, something morally decisive, definitive, perhaps even something mystical . . . But more about the wall later.) So, it's precisely this kind of spontaneous man whom I consider the real, normal person, such as tender Mother Nature herself wished to see him as she lovingly brought him into being on this earth. This kind of man makes me green with envy. He is stupid – that I don't dispute with you, but perhaps your normal man ought to be stupid – how do you know? Perhaps it's even a very fine thing. And I'm all the more convinced of this suspicion, so to speak, because if one takes for example the antithesis of the normal man, that is, the man of heightened consciousness, who of course has not sprung from the bosom of nature but from a test tube (this is already verging on mysticism, gentlemen, but I'm suspicious of that, too), then this test-tube man will sometimes capitulate when confronted with his antithesis, to such a degree that for all his heightened awareness he will in all good conscience consider himself a mouse and not a man. Granted, an intensely aware mouse, but a mouse all the same, whereas the other is a man, so consequently . . . etc, etc. The important thing is that he, of his own accord, considers himself a mouse: no one asked him to do so – and that's an important point.

But now let's take a look at this mouse in action. Let's suppose, for example, that he too has been offended (and his feelings are almost invariably hurt) and is also thirsting for revenge. Perhaps there is even more anger accumulated in him than in *l'homme de la nature et de la vérité*.[3] That nasty, mean, petty desire to repay the offender in his own coin might possibly gnaw away inside him more viciously than in *l'homme de la nature et de la vérité*, because *l'homme de la nature et de la vérité*, given his inborn stupidity, considers his revenge nothing more than simple, straightforward justice, whereas the mouse, with his heightened awareness, denies there is any justice here. Finally, we come to the deed itself, the act of revenge. In addition to that original nastiness, the hapless mouse has this time managed to accumulate so much additional nastiness in the form of questions and doubts; it has piled up so many other unresolved questions in addition to the original problem that it has involuntarily surrounded itself with a lethal brew, a stinking bog consisting of its doubts and emotions, and finally of the spittle showered on it by all the spontaneous men of action solemnly gathered around in the guise of judges and dictators who are laughing their heads off at him. Of course, it's obvious that all that remains for him to do is wave his little paw dismissively and creep ignominiously back into his little hole with a smile of simulated contempt in which he doesn't even believe himself. There, in his foul, stinking cellar, our offended, downtrodden and ridiculed mouse immerses himself in cold, venomous and, chiefly, everlasting spite. For forty years on end he will remember the offence, down to the smallest and most shameful detail, constantly adding even more shameful details of his own, maliciously teasing and irritating himself with his own fantasies. He himself will be ashamed of his fantasies, but nevertheless he will remember all of them, weighing them up and inventing all sorts of things that never happened to him, on the pretext that they too could have happened and he'll forgive nothing. Probably he'll start taking his revenge, but somehow in fits and starts, pettily, anonymously, from behind the stove, believing neither in his right to take revenge, nor in the success of his revenge and knowing beforehand that he will suffer one hundred times more from every single one of his attempts at revenge than the object of his revenge, who, most likely, won't give a damn. On his deathbed he will recall the whole thing with compound interest for all that time and . . . But it is in this cold, loathsome half-despair, this half-belief, this conscious self-interment in the underground for forty years from sorrow, in that powerfully created but nonetheless partially dubious hopelessness of his situation, in all the poison of inwardly turned, unfulfilled desires, in all those feverish vacillations, in all those decisions taken once and for all only to be regretted a few minutes later, that lies the very essence of that strange pleasure of which I was speaking. It is so subtle and sometimes so little subject to consciousness that even marginally limited people or even strong-nerved people cannot make head or tail of it. Perhaps you will interrupt with a grin – those who have never had their faces slapped won't understand it either – and thus you politely point out to me that at some time in my life I too have perhaps been slapped and that's why I'm speaking as an expert. I'm ready to bet that's what you think. But don't worry, gentlemen, I've never received any slaps, although I'm completely indifferent to what you may think about it. Perhaps I even still regret having distributed so few slaps in my lifetime. But that's enough, not another word on this subject which is so extraordinarily interesting for you.

I shall calmly continue about those people with strong nerves who don't understand certain refinements of pleasure. Although, on different occasions, these gentlemen may roar full-throatedly like bulls and although this supposedly does them the greatest credit, as I've already said, when confronted with an impossibility they immediately capitulate. Impossibility is a stone wall. Now what do I mean by stone wall? Well, the laws of nature, the conclusions of natural science and mathematics of course. Once it is proven to you, for example, that you're descended from the apes,[4] it's no good pulling a long face – you must accept things as they are. Or when they demonstrate that one ounce of your own fat should essentially be dearer to you than a hundred thousand of your fellow men and that this demonstration finally settles the whole question of so-called virtues and duties and other such ravings and prejudices, you must simply accept it, there's nothing you can do about it, since twice two is mathematics. Just you try and refute it.

'If you don't mind!' they'll shout at you, 'you can't fight it: this is twice two is four! Nature doesn't ask for your permission; she's not concerned about your wishes or whether or not you care for her laws. You are obliged to accept her as she is and consequently all her end results. That is, a wall is a wall . . . etc, etc.' Good heavens! What do the laws of nature and arithmetic have to do with me if, for some reason, I don't happen to like those laws and that twice two is four? Naturally, I shan't break through that wall with my forehead, if in fact I don't have the strength, but I won't capitulate simply because I'm confronted with a stone wall and don't have the strength to break through.

As if a stone wall really did bring reassurance and really did have some message for the world, solely because it is twice two is four. Oh, absurdity of absurdities! How much better to understand everything, to be conscious of everything, of every impossibility, every stone wall; not to capitulate before a single one of those impossibilities or stone walls – if capitulating sickens you. To arrive by way of the most inexorable syllogisms at appalling conclusions on the eternal theme that somehow you are to blame even for that stone wall although once again it's abundantly clear that you're in no way to blame and consequently silently and impotently to grit your teeth and sink voluptuously into inertia, dreaming that there isn't even anyone for you to be angry with; that no object can be found and perhaps never will be; that it's all deception, juggling with facts, sharp practice, and that here there's nothing but a vile brew – we know neither what nor who – but despite all the uncertainties and juggling with facts you are still in pain and the less you know the more you ache!

IV

'Ha, ha, ha! Next you'll be finding pleasure even in a toothache!' you'll laugh out loud.

'What of it? There's pleasure even in toothache,' I'll reply. 'I once had toothache for a whole month; I know what it's like. People don't rage in silence, of course – they groan. But these aren't sincere groans – they are malicious groans and the whole point is in this malice. Through his groans the sufferer is expressing his pleasure. If he didn't find pleasure in them he wouldn't have started groaning. This is an excellent example, gentlemen, and I shall develop it. Firstly, in these groans the whole pointlessness of your pain – so humiliating for our consciousness – is expressed; the whole legitimacy of nature, for which you don't give a damn, of course, but from which you suffer all the same, while she doesn't. They express your awareness that even though your enemy is nowhere to be found you are in pain; your awareness that despite all the Wagenheims in the world[5] you are at the complete mercy of your teeth; that if someone should so wish, they could stop your teeth aching, but should they not so wish, they'll go on aching for another three months; and finally, that if you still disagree and carry on protesting, the only consolation that remains is to practise self-flagellation or hit the wall harder with your fists, but definitely no more than that. Well then, it's from these bloody insults, from these practical jokes carried out by persons unknown, that pleasure finally arrives, pleasure that sometimes reaches the peak of voluptuousness. I ask you, gentlemen, to listen sometimes to the groans of an educated man of the

nineteenth century who is suffering from toothache, on the
second or third day of his indisposition, when he's groaning
quite differently from the way he did on the first day – that is,
not simply because he has toothache; not like some coarse
peasant, but rather like a man touched by enlightenment and
European civilization groans, like a person "divorced from the
soil and his native roots"[6] as they put it these days. His groans
become something vile, viciously bad-tempered and continue
all day and all night ... And yet he himself knows perfectly
well that his groans won't bring him any relief; better than
anyone he knows that he is only irritating and overtaxing himself and everyone else for nothing. He knows that even the
audience before whom he is performing with such fervour, and
his whole family, are sick and tired of listening to him, that
they don't believe him one bit and know in their heart of hearts
that he could very well groan differently, in a more natural
fashion, without the flourishes and affectation, and that he is
merely indulging himself out of malice and bad humour. Well,
the voluptuousness lies precisely in all this consciousness and
disgrace. "I'm disturbing you," he says, "I'm lacerating your
feelings, not letting anyone in the house sleep. Well, don't sleep,
you ought to be experiencing every minute of my toothache.
I'm no longer the hero I wanted to appear before, but merely a
nasty fellow, a good-for-nothing. Very well, so be it! I'm
delighted you've seen through me. Does it disgust you, listening
to my ignoble groans? Well, let it disgust you; now I'm going
to regale you with an even more disgusting roulade of
groans ..." Do you understand now, gentlemen? Well, one has
to be highly developed and intensely aware to understand all
the twists and turns of this voluptuous pleasure! Are you laughing? I'm absolutely delighted. Of course, my jokes, gentlemen,
are in bad taste, uneven, muddled, lacking in confidence. But
don't you see – that's because I have no self-respect. Can any
thinking person have any kind of respect for himself?'

V

And can a man who has sought pleasure even in the actual consciousness of his degradation really have one atom of self-respect? I'm not speaking out of any feeling of unctuous remorse. And in general I never could bring myself to say: 'Forgive me, Papa, I won't do it again' – not because I was incapable of saying it – on the contrary. Perhaps it was precisely because I was all too capable of saying it – and do you know when? As if deliberately.

I used to get into awkward situations, just on those occasions when I wasn't to blame in any way. That was the most degrading part of it. On such occasions I would once again be deeply moved, I would repent, shed tears and of course I was fooling myself, although I was far from pretending. It was my heart that was somehow defiled . . . Here I couldn't even blame the laws of nature, although the laws of nature have constantly offended me all the same, more than anything else, my whole life.

I find it degrading to recall all this now and it was degrading at the time. You see, after a minute or so I would be bitterly reflecting that the whole thing was a lie, a lie, a loathsome, hypocritical lie, that is all these regrets, all this emotion, all these promises of regeneration. And if you ask why I tormented and mangled myself like that the answer is: because I was already terribly bored idly sitting around and so I indulged in all manner of capers. Really, that's how it was. If you observe yourselves a little more closely, gentlemen, you'll understand that it's so. I used to imagine adventures for myself, I invented a life, so that I could at least exist somehow. How many times, for example, have I taken offence, just like that, for no reason. And I myself knew very well that I had no reason to take offence and that I was putting it on, but I would work myself up to such a degree that in the end I really did feel offended. All my life I've been attracted to playing games like that, so that finally I lost all self-control. Once or even twice I wanted to force myself to fall in love. I really did suffer for it, gentlemen, I can assure you. Deep down within me I just cannot believe in my own suffering; there's a hint of self-mockery here, but I suffer all the same – and in an authentic, genuine fashion. I'm jealous, I lose all control over myself . . . And it all stems from boredom, gentlemen, from sheer boredom; I am crushed by inertia. After all, the immediate, legitimate, direct fruit of consciousness is inertia – that is, consciously sitting twiddling your thumbs. I've mentioned this before. I repeat, I repeat most emphatically: all spontaneous people and men of action are active because they are dull-witted and limited. What is the explanation for this? Well, it's like this: as a result of their limitations they take immediate and secondary causes for primary ones and are thus persuaded more quickly and easily than others that they have found an indisputable basis for whatever they do and so they are reassured. And that's the main thing. You see, in order to begin to act you must be completely sure in advance that there are no residual doubts whatsoever. But how can I, for example, reassure myself? Where are my primary causes on which I can take a stand, where are my foundations? Where shall I take them from? I practise thinking and consequently every primary cause immediately draws another in its wake, one that is even more primary, and so on *ad infinitum*. And that is precisely the essence of all thought processes or self-awareness. Again, this must therefore be the laws of nature. And what is the final result? Well, exactly the same. Remember that I was talking of revenge not so long ago. (You probably didn't get my meaning very well.) I said that a man avenges himself because he finds justice in it. That means he has found his primary cause, has found a basis for his actions, namely, justice. Therefore he is completely reassured on all counts and consequently takes his revenge calmly and successfully, convinced that what he is doing is just and honourable. But for the life of me I can see neither justice here nor virtue and consequently, if I start taking my revenge, it's really out of spite. Spite, of course, can over-come everything – all my doubts – and therefore it could quite successfully serve instead of a primary cause for the simple reason that it's not a cause. But what can I do if I don't even feel spite (after all, that's what I began with a short time ago)? Again, as a result of those damned laws of consciousness, my spite is subject to chemical decomposition. Just look – and the object vanishes into thin air, reasons evaporate, the culprit is nowhere to be found and the offence is no longer an offence but becomes destiny, something in the nature of a toothache for which no one is to blame and consequently there again remains the same way out – that is, banging your head against the wall so that it hurts even more. And so you give it up as a bad job because you've failed to find a primary cause. But just you try letting yourself be carried along blindly by your emotions, without reasoning, without primary cause, banishing your consciousness at least for the time being: hate or love – do anything but sit there not doing a stroke. The day after tomorrow, at the very latest, you will begin to despise yourself for having knowingly deceived yourself. The result is a soap bubble and inertia. You see, gentlemen, perhaps I only consider myself an intelligent person because all my life I've never been capable of starting or finishing anything. All right, so I'm a windbag, a harmless, tiresome windbag, as all of us are. But what can one do about it if the direct and sole purpose of any intelligent man is idle chatter, that is, deliberately milling the wind?

VI

Oh, if only it were simply out of laziness that I did nothing! Heavens, how I should have respected myself then! I should have respected myself precisely because I was at least capable of being lazy. At least I should have possessed one positive quality of which I myself could have been certain. Question: what is he? Answer: a lazy devil. Of course, it would be really most pleasant to have heard that said of oneself.

It implies something positively defined, that there's something to be said about me. 'Lazy devil!' Why, that's a rank and a calling, that's a career. Don't joke about it – it's true. Then I should by rights be a member of the most exclusive club and my sole occupation would be nursing my self-esteem. I once

knew a gentleman who all his life prided himself on being a
great connoisseur of Château Lafite. He considered this his own
positive merit and never doubted himself. He died, not so much
with an easy conscience but with a triumphant one and he was
absolutely right. And I should have chosen a career for myself
at the time: I would have been a loafer and a glutton – but not
a simple one, rather one who for example empathizes with all
that is sublime and beautiful. How do you like that? I was
haunted by visions of it long ago. This 'sublime and beautiful'
is a real pain in the neck now that I'm forty. But that's because
I'm forty – but then, oh then it would have been different! I
should at once have sought out a suitable sphere of activity for
myself, namely, toasting the health of all that is sublime and
beautiful. I would have seized every opportunity of first shedding a tear into my glass and then draining it in honour of
the sublime and beautiful. Then I would have transformed
everything in the world into the sublime and beautiful; I should
have sought out the sublime and beautiful in the most revolting,
indisputable filth. I should have become as lachrymose as a wet
sponge. For example, the artist Ge[7] has painted a picture and
I immediately drink the health of that artist Ge, the painter
of that picture, because I am a lover of all that is sublime
and beautiful. An author has written 'For your satisfaction';
immediately I toast the health of 'your satisfaction' since I love
all that is sublime and beautiful. I insist on being respected for
that and I shall hunt down anyone who fails to show me respect.
Thus I live peacefully and die in triumph. Why, that's delightful,
simply delightful! And then I should have developed such a
paunch, cultivated such a triple chin, produced such a purple
nose for myself that any passer-by would exclaim on looking
at me: 'Well, there's a fine fellow! He's really got something
about him!' Say what you like, gentlemen, it's extremely pleasant to hear such tributes in this negative age of ours.

VII

But all these are golden dreams. Oh, do tell me who first
announced, who first proclaimed, that man only does vile things
because he doesn't know his own true interests; that if he were
enlightened, if his eyes were to be opened to his real, normal
interests he would immediately cease doing vile things and
at once become virtuous and honourable; since, once he is
enlightened and understands what will truly benefit him, he
will see that his own best interests lie in doing good; that since
it's common knowledge that no man can act knowingly against
his own best interests he would necessarily do good. Oh, the
child! Oh, the pure, innocent babe! In the first place when did
man, in all these thousands of years, ever act solely in his
own best interests? What about the millions of cases that bear
witness to the fact that people *knowingly*, that is, while fully
comprehending their own best interests, relegating them to the
background and following a different, uncertain and risky path,
not because they are being forced to do that by anyone or
anything, but simply as if reluctant to follow the appointed
path, stubbornly and wilfully choose to forge ahead along
another difficult and absurd path, seeking it in almost total
darkness? This can only mean that for men this obstinacy and
wilfulness was in actual fact more agreeable to them than any
kind of personal advantage . . . Advantage! What is advantage?
Would you care to volunteer an absolutely exact definition of
what human advantage consists of? And what if it should
sometimes happen that human advantage not only might, but
even must lie precisely in man desiring, in different cases, what
is bad for himself and not to his advantage? And if this is so, if
such things are at all possible, then the whole rule goes to
blazes. What do you think – can such cases occur? You laugh?
Well, laugh, gentlemen, but just answer me this: are human
advantages calculated with perfect accuracy? Are there not
some that not only have not been classified but cannot even be
classified at all? After all, gentlemen, as far as I know, you have
deduced your whole register of human advantages by taking

averages from statistics and scientifico-economic formulae. And
since your advantages are prosperity, wealth, freedom, peace
and so on, and so on, so that anyone who, for example, were
to act openly and knowingly against the whole register would,
in your opinion and in mine too of course, be an obscurantist
or a complete madman – isn't that so? But the really amazing
thing is surely this: how does it always happen that all these
statisticians, sages and lovers of the human race, when enumer-
ating human advantages, invariably omit a particular one? They
don't even take it into account as it should be taken and on this
the entire calculation depends. In effect, there would be no
great harm in taking this advantage and adding it to their list.
But the snag is that this abstruse advantage doesn't fit into
any classification, or cannot be accommodated in any list. For
instance, I have a friend ... Oh, gentlemen! He's a friend of
yours too and in fact to whom is he not a friend? When he
undertakes to do something this gentleman will immediately
expound to you, lucidly and grandiloquently, exactly how he
should proceed, according to the laws of truth and logic. And
that's not all: he'll talk to you with enthusiasm and passion
about true, normal human interests; he'll scornfully sneer at
those short-sighted fools who understand neither their own
interests nor the true meaning of virtue; and then, exactly
a quarter of an hour later, without any sudden, outside
mediation, but rather prompted by some inner impulse which
is stronger that all his interests, he'll take a completely different
tack, that is to say, he'll blatantly go against what he was just
saying: against the laws of reason and against his own best
interests – in short, against everything ... I'm warning you that
my friend is a collective person, so it's rather difficult to pin the
blame on him individually. Now that's just the point, gentlemen: doesn't there exist, in fact, something that is dearer to
almost everyone than his own very best interests or (not to
violate logic) there exists one most advantageous advantage (to
be precise, the omitted one of which we were talking just now)
which is more important and advantageous than any other
advantage and for the sake of which man, should the need arise,
is ready to oppose all the laws, that is, reason, honour, peace,

prosperity – in short, all these fine and useful things, provided he attains this primary, most advantageous advantage which is dearest of all to him?

'Well,' you'll interrupt, 'they're advantages all the same.' If you don't mind, we'll clarify matters – yes, we're not talking about plays upon words, but the fact that this advantage is remarkable precisely because it destroys all our classifications and is constantly demolishing all systems devised by lovers of humanity for the happiness of the human race. In short, it interferes with everything. But before I give a name to this advantage I want to compromise myself personally and therefore I boldly declare that all these fine systems, all these theories that explain to humanity its best, normal interests, and assert that by striving out of necessity to attain them, it will immediately become virtuous and noble, are in my opinion pure sophistry! Oh yes, sophistry! You see, even to affirm this theory of the regeneration of the entire human race by means of this systematic classification of its own personal advantages is, in my opinion, almost the same as affirming with Buckle,[8] for example, that civilization softens man and therefore he becomes less bloodthirsty and less inclined to wage war. He appears to argue it very logically. But man is so partial to systems and abstract conclusions that he is ready deliberately to distort the truth, ready neither to hear nor see anything, only as long as he can justify his logic. That's why I take this as an example, because it is an all too striking one. Just take a look around you: blood is flowing in rivers and in such a jolly way you'd think it was champagne. There's your entire nineteenth century, in which Buckle lived too. There's your Napoleon – both the great Napoleon and the present-day one.[9] There's your North America[10] the everlasting Union. Finally, there's your grotesque Schleswig-Holstein . . .[11] And what does civilization soften in us? Civilization develops in man only the many-sidedness of his sensations and decidedly nothing more. And through the development of this many-sidedness man may advance still further to the stage where he will find pleasure in bloodshed. Well, that's already happened to him. Have you noticed that the most refined bloodshedders have almost invariably been highly civilized gentlemen, to whom all those different Attilas and Stenka Razins could not have held a candle. And if they don't arrest your attention as powerfully as Attila[12] and Stenka Razin,[13] that's precisely because you meet with them so often, they are too commonplace and too familiar. At all events, if as a result of civilization man hasn't grown more bloodthirsty, he has certainly become viler in his quest for blood than before. Formerly he saw justice in bloodshed and exterminated those he needed to with an easy conscience. But nowadays, although we consider bloodshed something abhorrent, we still participate in it – and more than ever. Which is worse? – that you must decide for yourselves. They say that Cleopatra[14] (apologies for taking an example from Roman history) was fond of sticking gold pins into the bosoms of her slave girls, taking keen delight in their screams and contortions. You will say that this happened in relatively barbarous times; that today too times are still barbarous because (also relatively speaking) we still stick pins into people; and that even now, although man has learned to see more clearly than in barbarous times, he's a long way from *accustoming* himself to act as science and reason dictate. For all that you are absolutely convinced that man is bound to grow accustomed once certain bad old habits have been discarded and when science and common sense have fully re-educated and directed human nature along normal lines. You are convinced that man will then, *of his own accord*, cease making mistakes and – so to speak – willy-nilly refuse to divorce his volition from his normal interests. And that's not all: you say that then science itself will teach man (although in my opinion this is already a luxury) that in actual fact he possesses neither will nor whims and never did have them and that he is nothing more than a sort of piano key or organ stop; and, what is more, that there do exist in this world the laws of nature, so that whatever he does is not of his own volition at all, but exists according to the laws of nature. Consequently these laws of nature need only to be revealed and man will no longer be responsible for his actions and life will be extremely easy for him. All human actions, it goes without saying, will then be calculated according to these laws, mathematically, like a

logarithm table, reaching 108,000 and entered in a directory.
Better still, certain orthodox publications will appear, rather
like our modern encyclopaedic dictionaries, in which everything
will be so accurately calculated and specified that there will
no longer be either independent actions or adventures in this
world.

And then – it's still you who maintain this – a new political
economy will appear on the scene, ready-made and also calculated with mathematical precision, so that in a flash all conceivable questions will vanish, simply because all conceivable
replies to them will have been provided. Then the Crystal
Palace[15] will be erected. Then . . . well, the Golden Age will
dawn. Of course, it's quite impossible to guarantee (it's me
speaking now) that things won't be incredibly boring, for
example (because what will there be left to do once everything
is calculated according to tables?); but, on the other hand,
everything will be extraordinarily rational. Of course, when
you're bored you can think up all sorts of things! After all, it's
from boredom that gold pins are stuck into people, but none
of that would matter. The bad thing is (and again it's me
speaking) that then – who knows? – people might be glad even
of gold pins. Man is so stupid, phenomenally stupid. I mean to
say, he may not be so completely stupid, but then he's so
ungrateful that you couldn't find another like him, even if you
were to look hard. For example, I wouldn't be in the least
surprised if some gentleman of dishonourable – better, of reactionary and mocking – appearance were suddenly to spring up
from nowhere amidst this universal good sense, stand hands on
hips and tell every one of us: well, gentlemen, why don't we get
rid of this good sense once and for all by giving it a good kick,
just so that we can send all these logarithms to hell and once
again be able to live according to our own foolish will? That
wouldn't be so bad, but the really galling thing is that he would
undoubtedly find followers: that's the way men are fashioned.
And all this for the most trivial reason which, one would think,
is hardly worth mentioning: to be precise, because man, whoever he may be, has always and everywhere preferred to act as
he chooses and not at all as his reason or personal advantage

dictate; indeed, one can act contrary to one's own best interests and sometimes it's *absolutely imperative* to do so (that's my idea). One's own free, independent desire, one's own whims, however unbridled, one's fantasy, sometimes inflamed to the point of madness – all this is precisely that same, invariably omitted, most advantageous of advantages which cannot be accommodated within any classification and because of which all systems and theories are constantly consigned to the devil. And where on earth did all those sages get the idea that man needs some kind of virtuous, some kind of normal desire? How did they come to imagine that man categorically needs rational, advantageous desire? All man needs is *independent* volition, whatever that independence might cost and wherever it might lead. Anyway, the devil only knows what volition is.

VIII

'Ha, ha, ha! Well, if you like, essentially there's no such thing as volition!' you interrupt with your guffaws. 'By now science has made such advances in anatomizing man that we know that volition and so-called free will are nothing other than . . .'

'Hold on, gentlemen, that's how I myself wanted to begin. I do confess that I even took fright. I was just about to shout out loud that the devil knows what volition depends on – and we may perhaps thank God for that – and then I remembered about science and I . . . quietened down. At that point you joined in. As it happens, if they do in fact discover one day a formula for all our desires and caprices – that is, what they depend on, exactly from what laws they originate, exactly how they are disseminated, to what they are aspiring in one case or the other, and so on and so on, that's to say a real mathematical formula, then man will very likely at once stop desiring anything and most probably cease to exist altogether. What is the point of desiring by numbers? What's more, he would immediately change from a man into an organ stop or something like that. Because what is man without his volition but a stop on a

barrel-organ cylinder? What do you think? Consider the prob-
abilities – could it happen or couldn't it?'

'Hm,' you opine, 'for the main part our desires are erroneous
because of an erroneous view of what is in our own best interest.
The reason why we sometimes desire pure nonsense is that in
our stupidity we see in that nonsense the easiest route to achieving some kind of previously assumed advantage ... Well, when
all this is explained and calculated on paper (which is highly
possible since it is base and senseless to believe in advance that
there are certain laws of nature that man will never discover)
then of course there will no longer be any of these so-called
desires. You see, if volition should ever come to be completely
identified with reason, then we shall of course reason and not
desire, precisely because it's obviously impossible to *desire* nonsense while preserving our reason and thus knowingly go
against reason and desire what is harmful ... And since all
volition, all reasoning, can actually be tabulated, because one
fine day they will discover the laws of our so-called free will,
then, in all seriousness, they will be able to draw up some kind
of table, ensuring that we really shall desire in accordance with
that table. You see, if at some time it could be calculated and
proven to me, for example, that if I cocked a snook at someone,
it was because I could not help it and that I was bound to stick
my finger up that way, then how could there be anything left
in me that could be called *free*, especially if I'm a scholar and
have attended a science course somewhere? In that case I'd be
able to calculate the next thirty years of my life in advance; in
brief, if that's how things were to be arranged, there would of
course be nothing left for us to do. We'd have to accept it all
the same. And in general we should have to keep repeating to
ourselves, without flagging for one moment, that without fail,
at certain moments and in certain circumstances, nature does
not stop to ask our permission; that we must accept her as she
is and not as we imagine her to be; and that if we really
are speeding towards tables and directories and ... well, even
towards test tubes, then what can we do but accept the test tube
too! Otherwise the test tube will be accepted without us ...

'Oh yes, sir – that's just where the snag is as far as I'm

concerned! Forgive me, gentlemen, for philosophizing away like
this – that comes from forty years underground! Allow me to
indulge in a little fantasizing. You see, gentlemen: reason is a
good thing, there's no denying it, but reason is only reason
and satisfies only man's rational faculty, whereas volition is a
manifestation of the whole of life – and by that I mean the
whole of life, together with reason and all the headscratching
that goes with it. And even if, in this manifestation, our life
frequently turns out to be rubbish, it is still life and not simply
the extraction of a square root. As for me, I quite naturally
want to live in order to satisfy my whole capacity for living and
not solely to satisfy my capacity for reasoning, which is only
one-twentieth of my entire capacity for living. What does reason
know? Reason only knows what it has managed to discover
(the rest, perhaps, it will never discover; that's little comfort,
but why not say it outright?), whereas human nature acts as a
whole, with everything it comprises, conscious or unconscious;
it may talk nonsense, yet it lives. I suspect, gentlemen, that
you're looking at me with pity; you keep repeating that an
enlightened and intellectually mature person – in short, man as
he will be in the future – cannot knowingly desire something
that is not to his advantage and that this is mathematics. I
entirely agree, it really is mathematics. But I repeat to you for
the hundredth time that there is one case and only one, when
man may deliberately and consciously desire something that is
downright harmful even stupid, even extremely stupid, and that
is: to *have the right* to desire what is even extremely stupid and
not to be duty bound to desire only what is intelligent. You see,
this height of stupidity is your caprice, gentlemen, and in fact
might be more advantageous to us than anything else on earth,
especially in certain circumstances. But in particular it can be
more advantageous than any other advantage even when it
obviously does us harm and contradicts the soundest conclusions of our reasoning about advantage, because at any rate
it preserves what is most precious and most important to us,
and that is our personality and our individuality. In fact some
would claim that this is in fact more precious than anything
else to man. Of course, volition may coincide with reason if it

so wishes, especially if it is not abused but used in moderation; this is useful and occasionally even laudable. But very often and for the main part volition is directly and obstinately at loggerheads with reason and . . . and . . . do you know that this too is useful and sometimes even highly laudable? Let's suppose, gentlemen, that man is not stupid. (Actually, it's absolutely impossible to say this about him, for the sole reason that if he's stupid then who is clever?) But if he's not stupid, he's monstrously ungrateful all the same. Phenomenally ungrateful. I even think that the best definition of man is this: he's a two-legged creature and an ingrate. But that's not all – that isn't even his principal shortcoming; his principal shortcoming is his constant improper behaviour, constant from the time of the Flood to the Schleswig-Holstein period of human history. Improper behaviour and therefore lack of reason, since it has long been known that irrationality originates from nothing else than improper behaviour. Just cast your eye over the history of mankind – and what do you see? Is it grand? All right, then let's say it's grand. Just think how much the Colossus of Rhodes[16] alone is worth! It's not for nothing that Mr Anayevsky[17] testifies that whereas some people claim it is the work of human hands, others maintain that it was created by nature herself. Variety? Well, perhaps even variety. Consider only the ceremonial uniforms, military and civilian of all nations, at all times and think what they must be worth! And if you include civil service uniforms – well, the mind boggles! Not a single historian would cope with them. Monotony? Well, I suppose monotony too. Fighting and fighting – they're fighting now, they fought before and will fight again.

'You must agree it's already excessively monotonous. In brief, you can say anything you like about world history, anything that could be conceived only by the most disordered imagination. Only one thing cannot be said, however – that it's in any way rational. You'd choke on the first word. And there's another thing that keeps cropping up: such moral and sensible people are always appearing in life, such sages and lovers of mankind who have made it their lifetime's ambition to conduct themselves as decently and sensibly as possible, to enlighten

their neighbours, strictly speaking, to prove to them in effect
that it really is possible to live both morally and rationally in
this world. What then? We know very well that sooner or later
many of these philanthropists have, in their twilight years,
betrayed themselves by committing some foolish act, sometimes
of the most scandalous variety. Now I ask you: what can one
expect of man, as a creature endowed with such strange qualities? Yes, shower him with all earthly blessings, immerse him
so completely in happiness that the bubbles dance on the surface
of his happiness, as though on water; grant him such economic
prosperity that he will have absolutely nothing else to do but
sleep, eat gingerbread and concern himself with the continuance
of world history – and that man, out of sheer ingratitude, out
of sheer devilment, will even then do the dirty on you. He will
even put his gingerbread at risk and deliberately set his heart
on the most pernicious trash, the most uneconomical nonsense
solely in order to alloy all this positive good sense with his
pernicious, fantastic element. It's precisely his fantastic dreams,
his gross stupidity, that he wants to cling to, solely to convince
himself (as if this were absolutely essential) that people are still
people and not piano keys upon which the laws of nature
themselves are not only playing with their own hands, but
threatening to persist in playing until nothing can be desired
that is not tabulated in the directory. And that's not all: even if
it were really the case that man turned out to be a piano key
and if this were to be proven to him even by the natural sciences
and mathematics – even then he wouldn't see reason but would
deliberately do something to contradict this, out of sheer
ingratitude, just to have things his own way. And in any situation where he didn't have the means to carry this out he
would create chaos and destruction and devise various modes
of suffering and still insist on having things his own way! He'll
unleash his curse on the world and since only man is able to
curse (that's his privilege, which principally distinguishes him
from the other animals) then, through cursing alone he might
achieve his object and convince himself that he's a man and not
a piano key! If you say that even all this – the chaos, gloom and
imprecations – can be calculated according to tables, so that

the mere possibility of advance calculations will put a stop to everything and reason would prevail – in that case man would deliberately go insane in order to be rid of reason and still have things his own way. I believe in this, I'm prepared to vouch for it, because this whole human business would seem in fact to consist only in this, that man should always be proving to himself that he's a man and not an organ stop! He's always proved it, however much it takes – he's proved it even by becoming a troglodyte. And after that how can one fail to transgress, to applaud that this has not yet come about and that meanwhile volition depends on the devil knows what . . .

You will shout out to me (if you still deign to favour me with your shouts) that here in fact no one is trying to deprive me of my free will; that all they're doing is fuss: about how to arrange things so that my will should of its own accord coincide with my normal interests, with the laws of nature and with arithmetic.

'Ah, gentlemen! What will become of your will once the whole business ends up with tables and arithmetic, when only twice two is four is in demand? Twice two will make four without my willing it. So much for your will!'

IX

Of course I'm joking, gentlemen, and I myself know that I'm not joking very successfully, but really, you mustn't take everything as a joke. Perhaps I'm joking with clenched teeth. Gentlemen, I'm tormented by various questions; answer them for me. For example, here you are, wanting to wean man from his old habits and correct his will in conformity with the demands of science and common sense. But how do you know that man not only can, but *must* be modified this way? On what grounds do you conclude that man's volition *must*, of necessity, be corrected that way? In short, how do you know that such a correction will really benefit man? All said and done, why are you so *utterly* convinced that not opposing man's real, normal advantages, which are guaranteed by the deductions of reason and arithmetic, is really always to his advantage and is a law for all mankind? Surely this is as yet only your supposition. Let's assume it's a law of logic, but perhaps not a law at all for mankind. You might be thinking I'm insane, gentlemen. Allow me to make one proviso. I agree that man is, above all, a predominantly creative animal, condemned consciously to strive towards a goal and to engage in the art of engineering, that is, eternally, unceasingly constructing a road for himself *wherever it may lead.* And the reason why he perhaps sometimes wants to swerve to the side is precisely that he is *condemned* to follow that path and also, perhaps, because however stupid your plain man of action may be in general, he will sometimes get the idea into his head that this path, as it turns out, almost always leads *wherever it's going to lead,* and that the important thing is not where it's leading, but that it should lead somewhere and that our well-behaved child, scorning the art of engineering, should not surrender to that ruinous idleness which, as we all know, is the mother of all vices. Man loves to construct and lay down roads, no question about it. But why is he so passionately fond of destruction and chaos? Tell me that!

But here I myself would like to say a few words about that in particular. Isn't man perhaps so passionately fond of destruction and chaos (and there's no disputing that he's sometimes very fond of them, that really is the case) that he himself instinctively fears achieving his goal and completing the building in course of erection? How do you know – perhaps he only likes the building from a distance and not at all at close quarters; perhaps he only likes building it and not living in it, leaving it afterwards *aux animaux domestiques,*[18] such as ants, sheep, etc. Now these ants' tastes are completely different. They have one amazing building of this type, which is eternally indestructible – the anthill.

The worthy ants began with an anthill and they'll most probably finish with an anthill, which does much credit to their persistence and positive outlook. But man is a superficial and unseemly creature and perhaps, like a chess player, is fond only of the actual process of achieving his goal rather than the goal itself. And who knows (no one can say for sure), perhaps the whole goal towards which mankind is striving in this world consists solely in the uninterrupted process of achievement – in other words, in life itself and specifically in the goal which, needless to say, can be nothing other than twice two is four – in other words, a formula; but twice two is four is no longer life, gentlemen, but the beginning of death ... At least, man has always somehow been afraid of this twice two is four and I'm still afraid of it. Let's suppose that man does nothing but seek out this twice two is four formula, sails across oceans, devoting his life to the quest but never really finding it – God, he's afraid of it somehow! You see, he feels that once he's found it there'll be nothing left to look for. When they finish work, labourers at least take their money and off they go to the pub and end up at the police station. Well, that's a good week's work. But where can man go? At all events one can observe something uncomfortable about him every time he achieves his goal. He loves progressing towards his goal but not quite reaching it, and this of course is terribly funny. In short, man is a comically fashioned creature and evidently there's a joke behind all this. Twice two is four is nevertheless an intolerable thing. Twice two is four is, in my opinion, nothing more than a damned cheek. Twice two is four looks on smugly, hands on hips, stands in your path and defies you. I agree that twice two is four is an excellent thing, but if we're going to praise everything then twice two is five can sometimes be a most charming little thing as well!

And why are you so soundly, so solemnly convinced that only the normal and the positive – in brief, convinced that prosperity alone is advantageous to man? Can't reason make mistakes about advantages? Perhaps prosperity isn't the only thing that man loves? Perhaps he likes suffering just as much? Perhaps suffering is just as advantageous to him as prosperity? Sometimes man loves suffering intensely, passionately – and that's a fact. In this instance it's no good consulting world history. Just ask yourself, if you're a man with any experience of life. As for my personal opinion, to love only prosperity is even somehow unseemly. Whether it's a good thing or a bad thing, smashing something is occasionally very pleasant too.

I'm not campaigning for suffering, or for prosperity. I'm advocating . . . my own caprice and that it should be guaranteed me when the need arises. In vaudevilles, for example, suffering is taboo, I know that. In the Crystal Palace it's unthinkable: suffering is doubt, negation, and what kind of Crystal Palace could it be where there's room for doubt? And yet I'm convinced that man will never renounce true suffering, that is, destruction and chaos. Suffering – yes, that's surely the sole cause of consciousness. Although I did maintain at the beginning that, in my opinion, suffering is man's greatest misfortune, I know that man loves it and would not exchange it for any gratification whatsoever. Consciousness, for example, is infinitely superior to twice two is four. After twice two is four, of course there'll be nothing left, not only to do but even to discover. All that would then be possible would be to shut off your five senses and bury yourself in meditation. Well, even if you arrive at the same result with consciousness, that is, there won't be anything for you to do either, but at least you could sometimes give yourself a good flogging, which is stimulating all the same. This may be retrograde, but it's still better than nothing.

X

You believe in the Crystal Palace, eternally indestructible – that is, in something at which you can neither stick out your tongue nor cock a snook on the sly. Well, perhaps the reason I fear this edifice is that it is made of crystal and eternally indestructible and because you cannot even furtively stick your tongue out at it.

So, you see: if instead of a palace there were a hen house and if it started raining I might perhaps creep into the hen house to avoid getting soaked, but I would never take the hen house for a palace, out of gratitude for protecting me from the rain. You're laughing, you're even telling me that in this case it doesn't matter whether it's a hen house or a mansion. Yes, I reply, if one's only aim in life is not getting wet.

But what can I do if I've taken it into my head that this is not the sole purpose of living and that if one has to live it might as well be in a mansion. That is my volition, that is my desire. You'll only rid me of it by changing my desire. Well, change it, tempt me with something else, give me another ideal. But in the meantime I shan't take a hen house for a palace. It might even be that the Crystal Palace is a sham, that it's not provided for by the laws of nature and that I only invented it as a result of my stupidity and certain outmoded, irrational habits of our generation. But what's it to do with me if it's not provided for? Isn't it all the same, so long as it exists in my desires – better, if it exists as long as my desires exist? Perhaps you're laughing again? Well, by all means laugh. I'll put up with your derision but I still won't say I'm full when I'm hungry. For all that, I know that I'll never settle for compromise, for a constantly recurring zero simply because it exists according to the laws of nature and *in actual fact* exists. I shall not accept as the crown of my desires a big tenement block with flats for impoverished tenants on thousand-year leases, with the dentist Wagenheim's name on the sign board for emergencies. Do away with my desires, eradicate my ideals, show me something better and I will follow you. You'll probably say that it's not worth getting involved; but in that case I could give you the same reply. This is a serious discussion; if you don't want to honour me with your attention I shan't come begging for it. I have my underground.

Meanwhile I carry on living and desiring – may my hand fall off if I carry one brick to that tenement block! Ignore the fact that just now I rejected the Crystal Palace for the sole reason that it would be impossible to stick one's tongue out at it. By no means was I saying this because I'm so fond of sticking out my tongue. Perhaps I was only angry because, out of all your buildings, not one edifice at which you couldn't stick out your tongue has been found up to now. On the contrary, I would let my tongue be cut off, from sheer gratitude, if only that building could be so constructed that I would never again have the urge to stick it out again. What does it concern me if it were impossible to construct and that we had to content ourselves with tenement blocks? So why was I created with such desires? Could I possibly have been created solely and simply to reach the conclusion that my whole make-up is nothing but a swindle? Can that be the whole purpose? I don't believe it.

However, do you know what? I'm convinced that under-ground people like me must be kept under strict control. They might well be capable of sitting in their underground for forty years without uttering one word, but the moment they emerge into the light of day and break their silence they just talk and talk and talk . . .

XI

To sum up, gentlemen: the best thing is to do nothing! Better conscious inertia! So, long live the underground! Although I may have said that I envy the normal man with all the rancour of which I'm capable, I wouldn't care to be him, in the situation in which I see him (although I shan't stop envying him all the same. No, no, in any event the underground is more advantage-ous!). There one can at least . . . Ah! You see, here again I'm lying! I'm lying because I myself know, as sure as twice two is four, that it's not the underground that's better in any way, but something else, something completely different, which I long for but which I just cannot find! To hell with the underground! Even this would be better: if I myself could believe just a little of all that I've written now! I solemnly assure you, gentlemen, that I don't believe one word, not a single word of what I've just scribbled here. I mean to say, perhaps I really do believe it but at the same time, I don't know why, I feel and suspect I'm lying like a bootmaker.

'So why have you written all this?' you ask me.

'Well, I'd like to shut you away for forty years with nothing at all to do and then come and visit you after forty years to see what had become of you. Surely a man can't be left alone for forty years with nothing to do?'

'But isn't that disgraceful, isn't that humiliating!' you may possibly ask me, scornfully wagging your heads. 'You thirst for life and yet you try to solve life's problems with muddled logic. And how tiresome, how impudent your outbursts are – and at the same time how frightened you are! You talk nonsense and are happy with it. You come out with insolent remarks, yet you constantly fear for the consequences and apologize. You assure us that you are afraid of nothing yet you come crawling for our approval. You assure us that your teeth are clenched and at the same time you crack jokes in order to amuse us. You know that your jokes are not very witty, but you're evidently satisfied with their literary merit. Perhaps you really have had to suffer at times, but you have no respect whatsoever for your suffering. There is even truth in you, but no integrity; out of the pettiest vanity you carry your truth to the marketplace to be paraded in public and put to shame ... You really do want to say something, but from fear you conceal your last word, since you haven't the resolve to say it, only craven impudence. You boast of your consciousness, but all you do is vacillate, since although your brain is functioning your heart is darkened by depravity and without a pure heart there can never be full, authentic consciousness. And how importunate you are, how pushy, how pretentious! Lies, lies and more lies!'

Of course, I've just now invented all these words of yours myself. This too comes from the underground. I've been listening to these words of yours through a chink for forty years on end. I thought them up myself – you see, there was nothing else for me to think up. So it's not surprising they were learnt by heart and acquired literary form ...

But surely, surely you're not so gullible as to imagine that I'm going to publish all this and, what's more, give it to you to read? And I have another problem on my hands: why do I in fact address you as 'gentlemen', why do I treat you as if you really were my readers? Such confessions as I intend committing to paper don't get printed or given to others to read. At least, I don't have sufficient firmness of purpose for that, nor do I consider it necessary. Don't you see? A certain fantasy has entered my head and at all events I wish to realize it. Now this is what it's all about.

In every man's memories there are certain things that he will
not reveal to everyone but only to his friends. And there are
things that he will not even disclose to his friends, only to
himself and even then under a veil of secrecy. But, finally, there
are things that he's afraid of divulging even to himself and every
decent man has quite an accumulation of these. It might even
be the case that the more respectable a person is the more he
will have of them. At least, only recently I decided to recall
some of my earlier adventures which up to now I had always
passed over with a certain degree of uneasiness. But now, when
not only am I recalling them but have even decided to write
them down, what I really wish to put to the test is: can one be
perfectly honest with oneself and not be afraid of the whole
truth? Apropos of this I would point out that Heine claims that
true autobiographies are almost impossible and that a man will
most certainly lie about himself.[19] In his opinion, Rousseau, for
example, undoubtedly lied about himself in his *Confessions* –
even lied deliberately, out of vanity. I'm convinced that Heine
is right; I can understand perfectly well how one can sometimes
accuse onself of all sorts of crimes solely out of vanity and I
even understand very well the nature of that vanity. But Heine
was passing judgement on a man who was making a *public*
confession. But I'm writing for myself alone and declare once
and for all that if I'm writing as if I'm addressing readers, then
it's purely for show, since it's easier writing like that. It's only
a form, an empty form. I shall never have any readers. I've
already said as much . . .

I don't want to be restricted in any way in editing my notes.
I shan't introduce any order or system. Whatever I happen to
remember I shall write down.

But here you might start quibbling and ask: if you're not
counting on having any readers then why do you make such
compacts with yourself – on paper, what's more; that is to say,
that you won't be introducing any order or system, that you'll
just write down what you happen to remember, and so on and
so on? Why are you explaining all this, why all these excuses?

'Well, you just think,' I reply.

There's a whole psychology here, however. Perhaps it's that

I'm simply a coward. But perhaps it's because I'm deliberately imagining I have an audience before me so that I conduct myself more fittingly when I come to write things down. There could be a thousand reasons.

But there's something else: why, why exactly do I want to write? If it's not for the public then couldn't I very well commit everything to memory without putting pen to paper?

Quite so; but it will turn out somehow grander on paper. There's something inspirational about it, one can be more self-critical, and it makes for better style. Besides, perhaps by writing things down I really shall find relief. Only today, for example, I'm particularly oppressed by some very ancient memory. It came vividly to mind only recently and since then has plagued me like some tiresome musical motif that one can't get rid of. But meanwhile I must get rid of it. I have hundreds of similar memories, but at times one of them stands out from the hundreds and weighs heavily on me. For some reason I believe that by writing it down I shall rid myself of it. So why not try?

Lastly, I'm bored, I do nothing the whole time. Writing things down is really work of a kind. They say that work makes a man good and honest. Well, at least there's a chance.

Just now it's snowing – almost wet, yellowish, dirty snow. Yesterday it snowed too and the day before that. I think that the wet snow reminded me of that incident which refuses to stop pestering me. So, let this be a tale apropos of the wet snow.[20]

II

Apropos of the Wet Snow

When from error's murky ways,
I freed your fallen soul,
With burning words of exhortation.
When, filled with profound torment
You wrung your hands and cursed
All-ensnaring vice.
When with memory punishing
Your conscience so unmindful,
You told me the tale
Of all that was before me.
Then suddenly, hiding your face,
Overcome with shame and horror,
Indignant and shaken,
You tearfully resolved . . .
Etc, etc, etc . . .[21]
From the poetry of N. A. Nekrasov

At that time I was no more than twenty-four years old. Even then my life was gloomy, chaotic and wildly lonely. I didn't socialize with anyone, I even avoided conversations and withdrew further and further into my corner. At work, in the office, I even tried not to look at anyone and I realized perfectly well that my colleagues not only regarded me as a crank – and this is how it always struck me – but seemed to look on me with a kind of loathing. I used to wonder: why does no one else but me get the impression he's looked upon with loathing? One of our office clerks had a repulsive, extremely pock-marked face, rather like a criminal's, even. With such a repulsive face like that, I thought, I would never have dared look at anyone. Another clerk had a uniform that was so tatty there was a nasty smell if you went near him. And yet neither of these two gentlemen was embarrassed, neither on account of his clothes nor his face, nor on moral grounds, so to speak. Neither one of them imagined for one moment that he was being looked upon with loathing; and if they did imagine that, they didn't care one rap, as long as their superiors didn't deign to look at them. Now it's abundantly clear to me that because of my unbounded vanity, and the demands I made upon myself, I very often looked upon myself with furious dissatisfaction that amounted to disgust and consequently I mentally attributed my own attitude to everyone else. For example, I hated my face, I found it vile, I even suspected that it had a kind of base expression and so whenever I appeared at the office I suffered agonies in attempting to behave as independently as possible, to ensure that they didn't suspect me of baseness and to give my face the most dignified expression possible. 'Well, what if my face *is* unsightly,' I thought, 'it doesn't matter as long as it has a noble, expressive and above all *extremely* intelligent look.' But I knew without any doubt, I was painfully aware, that my face could never express all these perfections. But what was worse than anything, I found it positively stupid. I would have been quite happy to settle for intelligence. I would even have been content with a base expression, as long as my face struck people as awfully intelligent at the same time.

Needless to say, I hated all the office clerks from first to last and despised them all, yet at the same time I was also somehow afraid of them. Sometimes, it happened that I would even rate them as superior to myself. It was all very sudden: one moment I would despise them and the next I'd rate them superior to myself. A cultured, self-respecting person cannot be vain without making unlimited demands on himself and without at other times despising himself to the point of hatred. But whether I despised them, or classed them as my superiors, practically at every encounter I would lower my eyes. I even used to make experiments to discover whether I could bear someone – whoever it might be – staring at me, and I was invariably the first to look down. This tormented me to distraction. Also, the fear of appearing ridiculous made me ill and so I slavishly followed routine in everything that had to do with outward appearances.

Enthusiastically, I fell into the common rut and with my heart and soul feared the least sign of eccentricity in myself. But how was I to keep it up? I was painfully cultivated, as any cultivated man of our times should be. But they were a dim-witted lot, each like the other as a flock of sheep. Perhaps I was the only clerk in the whole office who always looked upon himself as a coward and slave and that's precisely why I felt I was cultivated. But not only did I appear to be, in actual fact I *was* a coward and a slave. I say that without the least embarrassment. Every self-respecting man of our time is, and is bound to be, a coward and a slave. That's his normal condition. Of that I'm deeply convinced. That's how he's fashioned, that's what he's created for. And it is not simply in our time, as a consequence of certain random events, but it's generally true at all times that any self-respecting man is bound to be a coward and a slave. This is a law of nature that applies to every decent person in this world. Even if one of them happens to put on a show of bravery over something, he shouldn't take any comfort from it or get carried away, he'll still make a fool of himself in front of others. This is the only and eternal outcome. Only asses and cross-breeds try to appear brave and even then to a certain extent. But it's not worth paying attention to them, since they don't matter one little bit.

At that time one other thing tormented me – to be precise, no one was like me, nor was I like anyone else. 'I am one person and they are *everybody*,' I thought, becoming very pensive.

From all this it is obvious that I was still a complete child.

At times completely contradictory things happened. Occasionally, going to the office utterly repelled me: things reached the point where many times I went home feeling quite ill. Then suddenly, out of the blue, a bout of scepticism and indifference would set in (everything with me was in bouts) and then I would laugh at my own intolerance and squeamishness, and reproach myself with romanticism. I did not want to talk to anyone, but now I would go so far as to start a conversation with people and even consider striking up friendships with them. Suddenly, for no obvious reason, my fastidiousness would vanish at one stroke. Who knows, perhaps it had never even existed in me and was only assumed, borrowed from books? To this day I haven't solved this question. Once I even became great friends with them, started visiting their homes, playing preference, drinking vodka and discussing promotion . . . But please allow me to digress a little here.

Generally speaking, we Russians have never had in our ranks those stupid, starry-eyed romantics of the German variety, especially the French type who don't turn a hair at anything – even if the ground were to open up beneath them, even if the whole of France were perishing at the barricades they would still stay the same, they would not change, not even out of common decency, but would carry on singing their transcendental songs to their dying day, so to speak, because they are fools. But here, on Russian soil, we have no fools, that's a well-known fact; that's why we differ from other, Germanic, countries. Consequently, transcendental natures are not to be found among us in their pure form. It was our 'positive' publicists and critics of those days who, in pursuit of Kostanzhoglos and Uncle Pyotr Ivanoviches,[22] stupidly taking them as our ideal, invented all that stuff about our romantics, considering them just as other-worldly as in France or Germany. On the contrary – the characteristics of our romantics are the complete and diametrical opposite of the transcendental European variety and not one European criterion applies here. (Permit me to use this word 'romantic' – it is an ancient, venerable, time-honoured word and familiar to all.) The characteristics of our romantic type are: *to see everything and often to see it incomparably more clearly than our finest intellects*; not to be reconciled with anyone or anything, but at the same time not to baulk at anything; always evading difficulties; deferring to everyone and behaving tactfully to everyone; never losing sight of useful, practical goals (such as rent-free apartments, nice little pensions, or medals) and never forgetting those aims for all these enthusiasms and dainty volumes of lyrical verse, while at the same time preserving inviolate in himself to his dying day the 'sublime and beautiful' and appropriately preserving himself completely cocooned in cotton wool, like some piece of jewellery, ostensibly for the benefit of that very same 'sublime

and beautiful'. Our romantic is a man of broad vision and the
most accomplished of all our swindlers – I can assure you of
that . . . even from personal experience. Of course, all this only
applies if the romantic is clever. But what am I saying? The
romantic is always clever and I merely wished to point out that
even if we may have had our romantic fools they don't count,
solely because when they were in their prime they were finally
reborn as Germans, and to preserve their jewel more con-
veniently they settled somewhere over there, chiefly in Weimar
or the Black Forest. I, for instance, genuinely despised my office
job and it was only sheer necessity that prevented me from
saying to hell with it, since all I did was sit there and get paid
for it. Therefore – please note – I didn't say to hell with it. Our
romantic would sooner go insane (which is very rare, however)
but he doesn't give a damn if he has no other job in mind and
he'll never be thrown out on his neck, although he might be
hauled off to the madhouse because he thinks he's the 'King of
Spain'[23] – and that's only if he really has gone stark raving mad.
You see, only the anaemic and fair-haired go out of their minds
in Russia. But we have an incalculable number of romantics
and they subsequently attain exalted rank. Such astonishing
versatility! And what capacity for the most contradictory sensations! Even at that time these thoughts comforted me and
even now I hold the same views. That's why we have so many
'broad natures' who, even in their ultimate decline, never lose
sight of their ideal. And though they may not lift a finger
for that ideal, although they may be out-and-out thieves and
gangsters, they still respect their original ideal to the point of
tears and are uncommonly pure of heart. Oh yes, sir, it's only
with us that the most inveterate scoundrel can be utterly and
even sublimely pure of heart without at the same time ceasing
to be a scoundrel in any way. I repeat, from among our romantics such businesslike rogues (I use the word 'rogue' with affection) emerge pretty often and they suddenly display such a
feeling for reality, such practical awareness, that their astonished superiors and the public can only click their tongues at
them in utter amazement.

This versatility is truly staggering and God only knows what

it might turn into, how it will subsequently develop and what
it holds in store for us in future. And the material isn't at all
bad! I don't say this out of some sort of ridiculous or jingoistic
patriotism. However, I'm convinced that again you're thinking
that I'm trying to be funny. And who knows, perhaps the
opposite's true, that is you're convinced that's what I really do
think. At any rate, gentlemen, I shall consider either of your
views as an honour and a particular pleasure. But please forgive
this digression.

Of course, I didn't keep up my friendship with my colleagues;
very soon I fell out with them and owing to my still youthful
inexperience at the time even stopped greeting them, giving
them the cold shoulder, as it were. However, this happened to
me only once. In general I was always alone.

To begin with, at home I spent most of my time reading. I
wanted to stifle all that was continuously boiling up inside me
through external impressions. Out of all external impressions,
reading was the only one possible for me. Of course, reading
helped a lot – it excited, delighted and tormented me. But at
times it bored me to death. For all that I still wanted to be doing
things and I would suddenly plunge into dark, subterranean,
vile, not so much depravity as petty dissipation. My mean,
trivial, lusts were keen and fiery as a result of my constant,
morbid irritability. The surges were hysterical, always accompanied by tears and convulsions. Apart from reading I had
nowhere to turn – I mean, there was nothing in my surroundings
that I could respect then or to which I might have been attracted.
Moreover, dreadful ennui was seething within me, a hysterical
craving for contradictions and contrasts would make its presence felt, and so I launched into debauchery. I haven't just told
you all this simply to excuse myself – not at all . . . But no! I've
lied! To justify myself is exactly what I wanted, that's why
I'm just making this trifling observation for my own benefit,
gentlemen. I don't want to lie. I've given you my word.

My debauchery was solitary, nocturnal, furtive, timorous
and sordid, and it was accompanied by a feeling of shame that
did not desert me at the most depraved moments, at such times
even culminating in curses. Even in those days I carried my

underground deep within me. I was terrified that I might somehow be seen, or meet someone, be recognized. I frequented
various extremely shady places.

One night as I was passing some wretched tavern, through a
brightly lit window I saw some gentlemen standing around a
billiard table doing battle with their cues and then one of their
company was thrown out of the window. Any other time this
would have positively sickened me, but I envied the ejected
gentleman so much that I even walked straight into the billiard
room. 'Perhaps,' I told myself, 'I'll get into a fight and I'll be
thrown out of the window too.'

I wasn't drunk, but what should I do? To what state of
hysteria depression can sometimes reduce one! But nothing
came of it.

As things turned out I was even incapable of jumping out of
the window and I finally made my exit without having had a
fight. From the start I was confronted by an officer.

I was standing by the billiard table, inadvertently blocking
the way of this officer who wanted to get past. He took me by
the shoulders in complete silence and without a word of warning or explanation shifted me from where I was standing to
another place and then walked on, as if he hadn't even seen
me. I would have forgiven him for beating me, but in no way
could I forgive him for moving me from one place to another
and completely failing to notice me.

The devil knows what I would have given then for a real, for
a more correct quarrel – a more proper, a more *literary* one, so
to say! They'd treated me like a fly. The officer was about six
feet tall, and I was short and emaciated. However, it was within
my power to start a quarrel. All I needed to do was protest and
of course I would have been thrown out of the window. But I
reconsidered and preferred to . . . withdraw from the scene with
bitter feelings.

I left the tavern confused and distressed, went straight home,
and the very next day I continued my petty debauchery even
more timidly, feeling more downtrodden and despondent than
ever before and with tears in my eyes, so it seemed, but for all
that, I persevered. Don't imagine, however, that I shied away

from that officer through cowardice. I've never been a coward at heart, although in fact I constantly behaved like one – but wait a little before you laugh, there's an explanation for this. I have an explanation for everything that concerns me, rest assured.

Oh, if only that officer had been the type to agree to a duel! But no, he was one of those gentlemen (alas, long vanished!) who preferred to take action with billiard cues or, like Gogol's Lieutenant Pirogov,[24] complain through the authorities. These gentlemen never fought duels and in any case would have considered a duel with the likes of me, a wretched civilian clerk, not the done thing at all; and, generally speaking, for them a duel was something unthinkable, free-thinking and very French, but they themselves were ready to dish out insults, especially if they happened to be six feet tall.

So now it was not cowardice that made me withdraw, but unbounded vanity. I was not scared of the height of six feet, nor that I might be painfully beaten and thrown out of the window; true, I had sufficient physical courage, but I lacked moral courage. I was afraid that everyone there, from that smart aleck of a marker to the last diseased, pimply, miserable greasy-collared clerk, would fail to understand and would ridicule me when I made my protest and addressed them in literary language. Because to this day it's impossible for us to discuss a point of honour – I don't actually mean honour, but point of honour (*point d'honneur*) in anything but literary language. In ordinary language 'points of honour' are never mentioned. I was perfectly convinced (this instinct for reality, despite all my romanticism!) that all of them would simply die laughing and that the officer wouldn't simply (that is, inoffensively) have laid into me, but would certainly have shoved me with his knee all around the billiard table and only then would he have taken pity and thrown me out of the window. Of course, I couldn't allow this wretched episode to end just like that. Afterwards I often met the officer in the street and I observed him very closely. Only, I can't say whether *he* recognized *me*. Most probably not – certain indications led me to this conclusion. But as for me, I ... looked at him with anger and loathing, and so it went on – for several years! My anger grew and

strengthened as the years passed. At first I started making dis-
creet inquiries about this officer. This I found most difficult, as
I didn't know a soul. But once someone hailed him in the street
when I was following at a short distance, as if I were on a lead,
and so I discovered his surname. Another time I followed him
right up to his flat and for ten copecks learnt from the caretaker
where he lived, on which floor, whether on his own or with
someone, etc – in short, everything that could be learnt from a
caretaker. One morning, although I had never engaged in literary activities, I suddenly hit on the idea of denouncing that
officer by caricaturing him in a short story. I took great delight
in writing that story. I exposed him, I even libelled him. At
first I disguised his name in such a way that it was instantly
recognizable, but later, on mature reflection, I changed it and
sent it off to *Fatherland Notes*.[25] But in those days there was
still no denunciatory literature and my story wasn't published.
This I found deeply annoying. At times I simply choked with
anger. Finally I decided to challenge my enemy to a duel. I
composed a beautiful, charming letter, begging him to apologize; in the event of a refusal I hinted at a duel in fairly strong
terms. The letter was written in such a way that if the officer
had had the least inkling of the 'sublime and beautiful' then no
doubt he would have come running to me to throw his arms
around my neck and offer me his friendship. Oh, how wonderful that would have been! What a life we would have spent
together, what a life! He would have protected me with his
exalted rank; I would have ennobled him with my culture and
. . . well, with my ideas all kinds of things – so many – would
have been possible! But just imagine, two years had passed
since he first insulted me and my challenge was nothing but a
glaring anachronism, despite all the skilfulness of my letter in
explaining and concealing the anachronism. But thank God (to
this day I tearfully thank the Almighty) I didn't send the letter.
It makes my blood run cold when I recall what might have
happened had I sent it. And then suddenly . . . suddenly I took
my revenge in the simplest, most incredibly ingenious way! All
of a sudden the most brilliant idea dawned on me. Sometimes,
on holidays, I used to knock around the Nevsky Prospekt,[26]

strolling down the sunny side between three and four o'clock.
I mean to say, I didn't stroll at all there – rather, I suffered
innumerable torments, humiliations and attacks of spleen; but
most probably that was necessary. I darted along between
passers-by in the ugliest manner, like a minnow, constantly
making way for generals, Horse Guards officers or hussars, or
genteel ladies. At those moments I had sharp shooting pains in
my heart and a burning sensation down my back at the very
thought of the sorry state of my outfit and of the wretchedness
and vulgarity of my small darting figure. This was the most
excruciating agony, an uninterrupted, intolerable humiliation
brought about by the thought which turned into the most
palpable and unvarying feeling that I was a fly in the eyes of all
those society people, a revolting, obscene fly – more intelligent
and nobler than anyone else – that goes without saying – but a
fly nonetheless, always giving in to others, humiliated by everyone and insulted by everyone. Why I had brought this torment
on myself, why I had to go to Nevsky Prospekt I really don't
know, but I was simply *drawn* there at every opportunity.

At that time I was already beginning to experience surges of
those pleasures of which I've already spoken in my first chapter.
After that incident with the officer I was drawn to Nevsky
Prospekt more strongly than ever. It was there that I met him
most often, there that I feasted my eyes on him. He too used to
go there, mostly on holidays. Although he would step aside
for generals and other high-ranking personages and also dart
between them like a minnow, nobodies like me – and even those
just a cut above me – were trampled on; he would bear right
down on them as if there were simply empty space before him
and under no circumstances would he give way. Looking at
him I revelled in my own anger and . . . bitterly made way for
him every time. It tormented me to think that not even in the
street could I be on anything like an equal footing with him.
'Why is it invariably *you* who are first to make way?' I kept
questioning myself in a mad fit of rage, sometimes waking up
at two o'clock in the morning. 'Why is it always *you* and not
him? There can't be a law about it, surely it's not written down
anywhere? Why shouldn't there be a little give and take, as is

normally the case when refined gentlemen meet in the street? So, he steps back halfway and you do the same and in that way you pass each other in mutual respect.' But that never happened and *I* was the one who always stepped aside and he didn't even notice that I was giving way. And then the most amazing idea suddenly dawned on me: what if we should meet and I ... didn't step to one side? Deliberately not step aside, even if it meant colliding with him? What about that? This daring idea gradually so possessed me that it gave me no peace. I dreamt of it incessantly and horribly and I deliberately went to Nevsky Prospekt more often in order to get a clearer picture of how I would do it when the time came. I was ecstatic. More and more my plan came to strike me as both practicable and possible. 'Of course, I won't exactly give him a shove,' I thought, already mellowing in advance at the idea from sheer joy, 'I'll simply not make way, bump right into him, not too painfully, but shoulder to shoulder, strictly according to the rules of etiquette; I'll bump into him only as hard as he bumps into me.' At last my mind was completely made up. But the preparations took ages. The first thing I did when I put my plan into action was to make myself more presentable and take a little trouble over my clothes. 'Just in case there should be a public scandal (and there the public is highly refined: a countess promenades there, Prince D— promenades there – the whole of literature promenades there), I have to be dressed decently – that creates a good impression and in certain ways puts one at once on an equal footing in the eyes of high society.' With this in mind I asked for my salary in advance and bought myself black gloves and a respectable hat from Churkin's. Black gloves struck me as more impressive and *bon ton* than the lemon ones that first tempted me. 'The colour's too bright, it makes it look as if I want to show off', so I didn't take the lemon ones. Long before this I had a good shirt ready, with white bone studs, but the overcoat seriously delayed matters. In itself my overcoat wasn't all that bad and it did keep me warm. But it was wadded, with a racoon collar that was the height of servility. Whatever the cost, it had to be changed for a beaver one, the kind worn by army officers. To acquire one I started frequenting the Gostiny Dvor[27] and after several attempts settled on cheap German beaver. Although German beavers show signs of wear in no time and begin to look terribly shabby, when newly bought they are really quite decent. And, after all, I only needed it for the one occasion. I asked the price, but it was still too expensive. After profound deliberation I decided to sell my racoon collar. As for the rest of the money, which was a tidy sum for someone like me, I decided to try and borrow it from Anton Antonych Setochkin, my head of department, a rather withdrawn, but solid and worthy gentleman who never lent money to anyone but to whom I had been specially recommended when I first started work by the important personage who had appointed me to the post. I suffered agonies. To ask Anton Antonych for a loan struck me as monstrous and shameful, I even didn't sleep for two or three nights – in general I slept very little at the time and felt delirious; my heartbeats would become very faint or suddenly my heart would start racing, racing, racing! ... At first Anton Antonych was taken aback, then he frowned, pondered the matter and in the end lent me the money, in return for a signed receipt which gave him the right to have the loan repaid out of my salary within a fortnight. So at last everything was ready. A fine beaver collar reigned in place of the filthy racoon and gradually I prepared for action. I couldn't come to an immediate decision without first thinking the thing had to be managed skilfully, step by step. But I confess that after repeated attempts I had even begun to despair: we'd never collide with each other – and that was that! Either I wasn't quite ready or determined enough – once we seemed on the point of colliding, but then I again gave way and he walked on without noticing me. I even prayed every time I approached him that God might strengthen my resolve. Once, after I had finally made my mind up, it only ended by my getting in his way, since at the very last moment, when I was only a few inches away, my courage failed me. He calmly walked right through me and I rolled to one side like a ball. That night I was again feverish and delirious. And then suddenly everything came to the happiest possible conclusion. The previous night I had finally decided not to persevere with an enterprise doomed

to failure and to abandon it all as a lost cause; with this in mind
I went for a stroll along Nevsky Prospekt for the last time, just
to see how I would abandon it all as hopeless. Suddenly, about
three paces from my enemy, I unexpectedly made up my mind,
screwed up my eyes – and we collided squarely, shoulder to
shoulder! I didn't yield one inch and I passed him – on an
absolutely equal footing! He didn't even look round and pretended not to have noticed. But he was only pretending, of that
I am certain. To this day I'm quite sure of that! Of course, I
came off the worse, as he was the stronger; but that wasn't the
point. The point was, I had achieved my purpose, upheld my
dignity, hadn't yielded an inch, and had put myself on the same
social footing as him in public. I went home feeling completely
avenged. I was jubilant. I celebrated my triumph and sang
Italian arias. Of course, I shan't describe what happened to me
three days later. If you've read the first chapter of the *Notes
from Underground* you can guess for yourselves. The officer
was later posted somewhere else; I haven't set eyes on him for
fourteen years. What's he doing now, my dear old chum? Who's
he trampling on now?

II

But my spell of petty dissipation was coming to an end and
I became heartily sick of it all. I had pangs of remorse, but I
drove them away: I felt nauseated enough already. Gradually,
however, I grew accustomed to this too. I grew accustomed
to everything, that is, I didn't actually grow accustomed but
somehow agreed of my own free will to grin and bear it. But I
had a certain outlet which reconciled me to everything and this
was to escape into all that was 'sublime and beautiful' – in my
dreams, of course. I indulged in an orgy of dreaming. I dreamt
for three months on end, huddled up in my little corner and,
believe me, at those moments I bore no resemblance to that
gentleman who, in his chicken-hearted confusion, had sewn a
German beaver collar onto his overcoat. Suddenly I became a

hero. I wouldn't even have allowed that six-foot officer to visit
me then. I couldn't even visualize what he looked like then.
What my dreams were about and how I could be satisfied with
them is difficult to say now, but at the time they did satisfy me.
Yes, even now I gain a certain degree of satisfaction from them.
My dreams were especially sweet and powerful after a bout of
dissipation, when they were accompanied by remorse and tears,
by curses and rapture. There were moments of such positive
ecstasy, of such happiness, that I swear I didn't feel even the
slightest stirring of derision within me. Yes, there was faith,
hope, love. But that's precisely the point – at that time I blindly
believed that by some miracle, through some external circumstance, all this would suddenly open up, offering a wide prospect of appropriate activity – philanthropic, beautiful and, most
important, ready-made (what kind of activity I never knew but,
most important, it should be ready-made) and then I would
suddenly step out into the wide world, to all intents and purposes mounted on a white steed and crowned with laurel. I
couldn't imagine myself playing a secondary role and this was
exactly why in reality I quite happily adopted the last. Either a
hero or muck – there was nothing in between. And this was my
undoing, since in the muck I consoled myself with the thought
that at other times I was a hero, but a hero who was disguising
himself in the muck. It's shameful, I thought, for an ordinary
person to wallow in muck, but a hero is too exalted to dirty
himself completely, so therefore I could wallow in it a little.
Remarkably, these surges of the 'sublime and beautiful' came
upon me during bouts of dissipation and precisely when I was
plumbing the depths. They arrived just like that, in distinct
pulses, as if to make their presence felt, but their appearance
didn't put paid to my debauchery, however. On the contrary,
they seemed to enliven it by way of contrast and came in just
the right quantity needed to make a good sauce. In this case
the sauce consisted of contradiction and suffering, of agonized
introspection, and all these torments and pinpricks lent a certain
piquancy, even a meaning, to my debauchery – in brief, they
performed the function of a good sauce perfectly. None of this
was even lacking in a certain profundity. Indeed, how could I

have agreed to a simple, vulgar, immediate, clerkish debauchery and yet borne all that filth! What could there have been in it to attract me and lure me out into the streets at night? Oh no, sir, I had a decent loophole for everything . . .

But how much love, oh Lord, how much love I used to experience in those dreams of mine, in those escapes into all that was 'sublime and beautiful'! Although that love was pure fantasy, although in reality it could never be applied to anything human, there was such an abundance of that love that later on I never felt the need to project it on to anything: that really would have been a superfluous luxury! Everything, however, always ended extremely happily, in a lazy and intoxicating transition into art, that is, into beautiful, ready-made forms of existence, forcibly stolen from poets and novelists and adapted to every possible kind of use and requirement. For example, I triumph over everyone; of course, all have crumbled to nothing and are compelled willy-nilly to recognize all my perfections and I forgive them all; a famous poet and courtier, I fall in love; I inherit untold millions and immediately donate them to the human race and at once confess my vices to the whole nation, which of course are not simple vices, but incorporate an extraordinary amount of the 'sublime and beautiful', something in the Manfredian[28] style. Everybody weeps and kisses me (otherwise what insensitive brutes they would be!) and I set off barefoot and hungry to preach new ideas and to rout the reactionaries at Austerlitz.[29] Then they strike up a march, an amnesty is called and the Pope agrees to leave Rome for Brazil.[30] Next there's a ball for the whole of Italy at the Villa Borghese,[31] which is on Lake Como, since Lake Como has been transported to Rome specifically for the occasion. And then a scene in the bushes, etc – as if you didn't know! You'll say that it's vulgar and ignoble to parade all this in public now after personally confessing to so many raptures and tears. But why should it be ignoble? Surely you don't think that I'm ashamed of all this or that it's sillier than anything in your own lives, gentlemen? What's more, let me assure you that some of it wasn't at all badly staged by me . . . Not everything took place on Lake Como. But you're quite right; it really is vulgar and contemptible. But most contemptible of all is that I've started justifying myself to all of you. But even more contemptible than that is the fact that I'm making this observation now . . . Well, enough of this, or I'll never finish: one thing will be more contemptible than what came before it . . .

I was never capable of spending more than three months on end dreaming and I began to feel an irresistible need to plunge into society. For me, plunging into society meant going to visit my head of department, Anton Antonych Setochkin. He was the only regular acquaintance I had in my whole life, a circumstance that surprises me even now. But I only visited him during one of those bouts and my dreams reached such a peak of bliss that it was an absolute necessity to embrace people and all mankind immediately. To do that I needed to have at least one person at hand, someone who really existed. However, I could only visit Anton Antonych on Tuesdays (that was the day he received visitors), so therefore I had to postpone this need to embrace the whole of humanity until a Tuesday came along. This Anton Antonych lived at Five Corners,[32] in a third-floor flat with four low-ceilinged rooms, each smaller than the last, all very spartan and jaundiced-looking. He had two daughters – and there was an aunt, who used to pour out the tea. The daughters – one was thirteen, the other fourteen – had little snub noses and they always made me feel terribly embarrassed by their constant giggling and whispering. The host would usually sit in his study on a leather sofa in front of the table, together with some grey-haired guest, an official from our department or even from some other. I never saw more than two or three guests there, always the same. They would talk about excise duty, haggling in the Senate, salaries, promotion, His Excellency and how to get into his good books, etc, etc. I had the patience to sit next to these people like a complete idiot for four hours at a stretch, listening to them, neither daring to nor capable of discussing anything with them. I would sit there in a dull stupor and on several occasions I broke into a sweat, with a feeling of paralysis hanging over me. But all this was useful and good for me. When I returned home I would temporarily set aside my desire to embrace all mankind.

However, I apparently had another acquaintance, Simonov, an old school friend of mine. Very likely there were many of my former school-fellows in St Petersburg, but I didn't mix with them and even stopped greeting them in the street. Perhaps the reason for my moving to another government department was to distance myself from them and to cut myself off at one stroke from my loathsome boyhood. Curse that school and those terrible years of penal servitude! In short, I broke with my school-fellows the moment I regained my freedom. There remained just two or three whom I still greeted when I met them. One of them was Simonov, a very quiet and even-tempered person who hadn't distinguished himself in any way at school but in whom I discerned a certain independence of character and even integrity. I don't even think he was as limited as all that. Once we used to spend some fairly cheerful moments together, but they were short-lived and suddenly seemed to become shrouded in mist. Obviously he found these reminiscences oppressive and always appeared afraid that I might lapse into my former tone with him. I suspected that he found me extremely repulsive, but as I wasn't really certain of this I still visited him.

And then, one Thursday, unable to bear my solitude any longer and knowing that Anton Antonych's door would be closed on Thursdays, I remembered Simonov. As I climbed the stairs to his third-floor flat I was in fact thinking that this gentleman found my company disagreeable and that I was wasting my time going there. However, as it always came about that reflections of this kind only egged me on all the more, as if deliberately, to put myself in an ambiguous situation, I went in. It was almost a year since I had last seen Simonov.

III

I found two more of my school-fellows with him. They were evidently discussing something very important. Not one of them paid much attention to my arrival, which was rather odd, since

I hadn't seen them for years. Apparently they considered me some kind of common house-fly. Even at school I hadn't been treated like this, although all of them had hated me there. I realized, of course, that they were bound to despise me now because of my unsuccessful civil service career and because I had let myself go so badly and went around in scruffy clothes and so on – things that in their eyes proclaimed my ineptitude and mediocrity. All the same, I never expected such contempt. Simonov was even surprised when I arrived. Even before he had always seemed surprised whenever I turned up. All this puzzled me. Somewhat dejected, I sat down and started listening to their conversation.

A serious and even heated conversation was in progress about a farewell dinner that these gentlemen wanted to organize jointly the very next day for their friend Zverkov,[33] an army officer who had been posted to some remote part of the provinces. Monsieur Zverkov had been at school with me the whole time I was there. I grew to hate him, particularly in the upper forms. In the lower forms he was just a pretty, lively little chap whom everyone liked. I, however, loathed him even in the lower forms – just because he was such a pretty, lively little chap. He was consistently bad at lessons and the longer he was at the school the worse he got. But he passed his final exams because he was well connected. In his last year there he was left an estate of two hundred serfs and since most of us were poor he started bragging about it to us. He was vulgar in the highest degree, but for all that a decent fellow, even when he was bragging. Despite our superficial, far-fetched and stereotyped formulae of honour, all of us, with very few exceptions, toadied to Zverkov the more he boasted. And we didn't ingratiate ourselves in the hope of gaining something by it, but because he was a person blessed with the gifts of nature. Besides, it had somehow become accepted among us to consider Zverkov an expert in the department of social skills and good manners. The latter particularly infuriated me. I hated the piercing, cocksure sound of his voice, the way he adored his own witticisms which invariably came across as extremely silly, although he did have a very sharp tongue. I hated his handsome but stupid face (for which, however, I would willingly have exchanged my *intelligent* one) and those casual forties-style officer's manners. I hated the fact that he talked of his *future* successes with women (he had decided not to start womanizing until he received his officer's epaulettes, which he was impatiently awaiting) and said that he would be fighting duels non-stop. I remember how once, although I was always the silent type, I suddenly came to grips with Zverkov when he was chatting with his friends in a free period about his forthcoming amours and finally growing as playful as a puppy in the sunshine, he suddenly announced that not one of the peasant girls on his estate would escape his attentions, that this was his *droit de seigneur*,[34] and that if the peasants so much as protested he'd have the lot of them flogged and would double that bearded rabble's rent. Our louts applauded him, while I argued with him – not because I felt at all sorry for the girls and their fathers, but simply because they were applauding an insect like him. On that occasion I won the day, but although Zverkov was a fool, he was cheerful and cheeky and laughed the whole thing off so well, that in fact I didn't really win at all: the laugh was on his side. After that he got the better of me several times, but without any malice, jokingly as it were, casually, laughing. I was too angry and contemptuous to offer a rejoinder. After we left school he made overtures to me; I offered little resistance, I was so flattered, but we quickly and naturally went our own ways. Later I heard of his success as a barrack-room lieutenant and of his *boozing*. Then other rumours circulated about how he was *succeeding* in the army. No longer did he greet me in the street and I suspected he was afraid of compromising himself by exchanging greetings with a nobody like me. Once I spotted him in the theatre, in the third row of the circle, already sporting aiguillettes. He was bowing and scraping, and making up to the daughters of some very ancient general. In three years he had gone terribly to seed, although he was still quite handsome and sprightly. He had a somewhat bloated look and had put on weight. Obviously, by the time he was thirty, he'd be really flabby. It was in honour of this same finally departing Zverkov that our friends wanted to give a dinner. They had hung around with him for the entire three years, although in their heart of hearts they didn't consider themselves his equal – of that I am convinced.

Of Simonov's two guests one was a Russo-German, Ferfichkin, a short fellow with an ape-like face, a perfect idiot who poked fun at everyone and who had been my bitterest enemy ever since the lowest forms – an odious, insolent show-off, posing as someone of the most refined arrogance, although he was of course a rotten coward at heart. He was among those admirers of Zverkov who played up to him from ulterior motives and often borrowed money from him. Simonov's other guest, Trudolyubov, was an unremarkable character – the military type, tall, with a chilly air, fairly honest but one who worshipped success of any kind and who was incapable of discussing anything except promotion. Apparently he happened to be a distant relative of Zverkov's and this, stupidly enough, gave him a certain status among us. He always considered me a nonentity; but he treated me if not altogether politely at least tolerably.

'All right,' said Trudolyubov, 'if it's seven roubles each and there's three of us – that makes twenty-one roubles and for that we can dine jolly well. Of course, Zverkov won't be paying.'

'Of course not, if we're inviting him!' Simonov said decisively.

'Do you really think,' Ferfichkin cut in haughtily, with the fervour of an insolent lackey boasting of his master the general's decorations, 'do you really suppose that Zverkov will allow us to foot the whole bill? He'll accept out of tactfulness, but then he'll stand us a half-dozen bottles.'

'But what are the four of us going to do with a half-dozen bottles?' observed Trudolyubov, concerned only with the half-dozen.

'Well then, three of us – four with Zverkov – that's twenty-one roubles – at the Hôtel de Paris, tomorrow at five o'clock,' concluded Simonov, who had been chosen to organize proceedings.

'But how do you arrive at twenty-one?' I said with some agitation, making myself out to be rather offended. 'If you include me it makes twenty-eight, not twenty-one.'

I felt that my sudden and totally unexpected offer would

strike them as a handsome gesture and that they would all be
won over and look upon me with respect.

'Surely *you* don't want to come too, do you?' Simonov replied
in annoyance, somehow avoiding eye contact with me. He knew
me through and through.

I was furious that he knew me through and through.

'Why not? After all, I was at school with him as well. I must
confess I'm rather hurt at being left out,' I spluttered again.

'And where were we supposed to look for you?' Ferfichkin
rudely put in.

'You never hit it off with Zverkov,' added Trudolyubov,
frowning. But now I had seized on the idea I wouldn't let go . . .

'It strikes me that no one has the right to judge that,' I
retorted with trembling voice, as if God knows what had happened. 'Perhaps it's precisely because we didn't hit it off that
I want to come now.'

'Who the hell can make you out? . . . All these lofty
sentiments . . .' Trudolyubov sniggered.

'We'll put your name down,' decided Simonov, turning to
me. 'Tomorrow at five o'clock, at the Hôtel de Paris. Don't get
it wrong.'

'What about the money?' Ferfichkin said in a low voice to
Simonov, nodding towards me, but he stopped short, since even
Simonov was embarrassed.

'All right,' said Trudolyubov, 'if he wants to come so badly
then let him.'

'But really, we're just an intimate little circle of friends,'
fumed Ferfichkin as he picked up his hat. 'It's not an official
gathering. Perhaps we don't want you to come at all . . .'

They left. Ferfichkin did not even bow to me as he went and
Trudolyubov nodded slightly, without looking at me. Simonov,
with whom I was now left face to face, appeared to be in a state
of vexed bewilderment and gave me an odd look. He did not
sit down, nor did he invite me to.

'Hmm . . . yes . . . so, it's tomorrow. Are you going to hand
over the money now? I'm asking, as I'd like to know for
certain . . .' he muttered, with an embarrassed look.

I flared up but as I did so I remembered that from time

immemorial I'd owed Simonov fifteen roubles and although I'd never forgotten them, I'd never paid them back either.

'You yourself must agree, Simonov, I couldn't have known when I came here . . . and I'm very upset that I forgot . . .'

'All right, all right, it doesn't matter. Pay me tomorrow at the dinner. I only wanted to know . . . Now please don't . . .'

He stopped short and started pacing the room with even greater annoyance. As he did this he came down on his heels, stamping all the harder.

'I'm not keeping you, am I?' I asked after a two-minute silence.

'Oh no,' he replied with a start. 'Well, to be honest . . . yes . . . You see, I've got to drop in somewhere . . . not very far from here . . .' he added rather apologetically and somewhat ashamed.

'Good Lord! Why on earth didn't you say so?' I cried, grabbing my peaked cap in a surprised but nonchalant manner, which came from God knows where.

'It's not far at all . . . just a couple of steps . . .' Simonov repeated, seeing me to the front door with a busy look, which did not suit him at all.

'So, tomorrow at five o'clock sharp!' he shouted down the stairs. He was truly delighted that I was leaving. But I was absolutely fuming.

'Whatever possessed me, whatever made me put myself forward?' I said to myself, gnashing my teeth as I strode along the street. And as for that rotten swine Zverkov! Of course, I shouldn't really go; of course, I should say to hell with it. I don't have to go, do I? I'll send them a note in the post tomorrow . . .'

But what so infuriated me was that I knew very well that I would go; that I would go on purpose; and that the more tactless, the more inappropriate it was to go, the more certain it was that I would go.

And there was even one positive obstacle to my going: I didn't have the money. All I had in the world was nine roubles. But out of that I had to pay seven to my servant Apollon, who lived with me, as his month's wages, without keep.

Given Apollon's character, not to pay him was out of the question. But more about that swine, that thorn in my flesh, later.

However, I knew that I wouldn't pay him all the same and that I would definitely go.

That night I had the most terrible nightmares. And no wonder: the whole evening I was oppressed by memories of those miserable years of penal servitude at school and I couldn't shake them off. I had been dumped at that school by some distant relatives on whom I depended and of whom I've since heard nothing. I was sent there as an orphan, already crushed by their reproaches, already introspective, silent and looking at everything around me like a savage. My school-fellows greeted me with spiteful and merciless sneers because I wasn't like any of them. But I couldn't bear those sneers, I couldn't get on with them as easily as they got on with each other. I conceived an immediate loathing for them and sought refuge in my timorous, wounded but excessive pride. Their uncouthness deeply disturbed me. They laughed cynically at my face, at my clumsy figure – yet how stupid their own faces were! In our school facial expressions tended to become particularly stupid and degenerate. So many handsome boys entered the school but within a few years it simply revolted you to look at them. By the time I was sixteen I looked upon them in sullen amazement; even then I was startled by the triviality of their ideas, the stupidity of their pursuits, their games, their conversations. They had little understanding of what really mattered, took so little interest in the most stimulating, inspiring subjects that I couldn't help considering them my inferiors. It wasn't wounded vanity that drove me to that and for God's sake don't try and get at me with such sickeningly banal retorts as: 'I was only dreaming, whereas they understood real life.'

They understood nothing, nothing of real life, and I swear it was this that exasperated me most about them. On the contrary, their conception of the most strikingly obvious reality was fantastically stupid and even then they were used to worshipping nothing but success. Everything that was just, but downtrodden and oppressed, they mocked callously and disgracefully. They

took rank for intelligence; at sixteen they were already discussing cushy little jobs. Of course, much of this could be
blamed on the stupidity and bad examples that were the constant companions of their childhood and adolescence. They
were monstrously depraved. Of course, this was more of a
façade, more affected cynicism; of course, youth, and a certain
freshness could be glimpsed in them despite their depravity. But
in them even the freshness was unappealing and manifested
itself in a kind of rakishness. I hated them intensely, although I
was perhaps even worse than they were. They repaid me in
kind and made no attempt to conceal their loathing for me. But
I no longer wanted them to like me; on the contrary, I constantly
longed for their humiliation. To escape their sneers I deliberately began to study as hard as I could and soon advanced to
the top of the class. That did impress them. Moreover, they
were all gradually coming to realize that I was already reading
books that were well beyond them and understood things (not
part of our special curriculum) of which they had never even
heard. They looked on all this with wild mockery, but they
were morally subservient, all the more so since in this respect
even the teachers paid attention to me. The sneers ceased, but
the hostility remained and from now on cold, strained relations
were established. In the end I myself couldn't hold out any
longer: with the passing years I developed the need for people,
for friends. I tried to get close to a few of them, but this
attempted rapprochement always turned out unnatural and so
it simply fizzled out of its own accord. I did once have a friend.
But I was already a despot at heart, I wanted to have unlimited
authority over his soul; I wanted to instil in him a contempt for
his surroundings; I demanded that he should make an arrogant
and definitive break with those surroundings. I frightened him
with my passionate friendship, I reduced him to tears, to nervous convulsions. He was a naive, submissive soul, but when
he surrendered himself completely to me I immediately hated
him and brushed him aside – it was just as if I'd needed him
only to win victory over him, simply to bring about his total
submission. But I couldn't get the better of everyone. My friend
was also quite unlike any of the others and in this he was an

extremely rare exception. The first thing I did on leaving school was to abandon the special career for which I was earmarked in order to sever all ties, cursing the past and scattering it to the winds . . . The devil only knows what made me drag myself off to Simonov's after that! . . .

Early next morning I leapt out of bed feeling terribly excited, as if everything would come to fruition right away. I believed that some radical turning-point in my life was approaching and was bound to come that very day. Whether it was through lack of experience, perhaps, but all my life it had struck me that whenever any external event occurred, even the most trivial, some radical change in my life would immediately take place. However, I went to the office as usual, but slipped away two hours early to get ready. The important thing, so I thought, was not to arrive first or they might think I was only too delighted to be going to the dinner. But there were thousands of important things like this and all of them worried me into a state of impotence. I polished my boots again myself: nothing in the world would have induced Apollon to polish them twice a day – that would have been quite out of order. So I cleaned them myself, sneaking the brushes from the hall so that he couldn't see me and despise me for it later. Then I gave my clothes a close inspection and found that everything was old, worn out, threadbare: I'd really become terribly slovenly. However, my office uniform was fairly presentable, but I simply couldn't go out to dinner in my uniform! The main problem was the huge yellow spot right on the trouser knee. I anticipated that this spot alone would deprive me of nine-tenths of my personal dignity. I knew that it was very low of me to think like that. 'But now's not the time for thinking, now reality is approaching!' I thought – and at that my spirits drooped. I also knew very well even then that I was monstrously exaggerating all these facts, but what could I do? I was no longer in control of myself and I was shaking feverishly. In my despair I visualized how patronizingly and icily that 'scoundrel' Zverkov would greet me; with what stupid, positively invincible contempt that block-head Trudolyubov would look at me; how nastily and insolently that louse Ferfichkin would sneer at my expense, just to worm his way into Zverkov's favour; how perfectly Simonov would understand all this and despise me for the meanness of my vanity and my faint-heartedness; and, most of all, how sordid, how *unliterary*, how pedestrian it would all be. Of course, the best thing was not to go at all. But this was more impossible than anything: once I had got the idea in my head I was totally committed. For the rest of my life I would have taunted myself: 'You got cold feet, you were frightened of *reality* – yes, you got cold feet!' But no, I dearly wanted to show that 'riff-raff' that I wasn't such a coward as I myself imagined. What's more, in my most violent paroxysm of feverish cowardice I still dreamed of gaining the upper hand, making mincemeat of them, winning them over, forcing them to like me – well, if only for the 'loftiness of my thoughts and undeniable wit'. They would desert Zverkov and he would take a back seat, silent and ashamed, and I would crush him. Later, perhaps, I might make it up with him and drink with him as an intimate friend; but the most galling and most hurtful thing for me was that even then – I knew this without any shadow of doubt – in actual fact, I needed none of this and that, in actual fact, I didn't have the slightest inclination to crush, subjugate or attract them and that even if I were to achieve all that I myself would be the first not to give a damn for the outcome. Oh, how I prayed for that day to be over quickly! In inexpressible anguish I went over to the window, opened the hinged pane and peered out into the murky dimness of the thickly falling wet snow . . .

Finally my shoddy wall clock wheezed five o'clock. I grabbed my hat and, trying not to look at Apollon who had been waiting for me to hand over his wages since morning but was too proud to broach the matter first, slipped past him through the door and in a smart cab that I had specially hired with my last fifty copecks, I bowled along like a lord to the Hôtel de Paris.

IV

I already knew since the previous evening that I'd be first to arrive. But it wasn't a matter of who arrived first.

Not only was no one there, but I even had difficulty finding our room. The table wasn't fully laid yet. What could that mean? After much questioning I finally ascertained from the waiters that dinner had been ordered for six o'clock, not for five. This was confirmed in the bar. I even felt ashamed that I had to ask. It was still only twenty-five past five. If they had changed the time then they should at least have informed me – that was what the post was for – and not subjected me to this 'indignity', both in my own eyes and in front of the waiters. I sat down; a waiter started laying the table. Somehow I felt even more humiliated in his presence. Towards six o'clock candles were brought in, in addition to the lamps that were already lit – the waiter hadn't thought of bringing them immediately I arrived. In the next room two gloomy, angry-looking hotel guests were dining in silence at separate tables. From one of the rooms furthest away came a dreadful racket. There was even shouting and I could hear the loud guffaws of a whole gang of people and some foul, French-sounding shrieks: there were ladies dining there too. In short, it was all truly sickening. Rarely have I lived through worse moments, so that when they all arrived at exactly six o'clock I was initially so delighted to see them, as if they were my liberators, that I almost forgot that I was supposed to look offended.

Zverkov entered at the head of them – obviously he was the leader. He and all the others were laughing, but on seeing me Zverkov assumed a dignified air, came over to me without hurrying himself, bending slightly forward from the waist as if to show off and offering his hand – amiably but not too familiarly – with the somewhat guarded courtesy of a general, as if by doing so he was protecting himself from something. I had imagined that, on the contrary, the moment he entered he would have laughed that shrill, high-pitched laugh of his right from the start and immediately produced those weak jokes and witticisms of his. I had been preparing myself for them from the day before, but I hadn't in the least expected such condescending, such overbearing affability. So, now he considered himself immeasurably superior to me in every respect. If he had only wanted to insult me by behaving like a general that wouldn't have mattered, I thought. One way or the other I would have shrugged it off. But what if, in actual fact, without any wish to cause offence, he had seriously got the idea in his stupid mutton-head that he was immeasurably superior to me and that the only way he could possibly treat me was patronizingly? This assumption alone made me choke with anger.

'It came to me as a surprise when I learnt of your desire to join us,' he began, lisping affectedly, drawling and mouthing his words in a way he never used to. 'Somehow we never seem to meet. You fight shy of us. There's no need to. We're not so frightening as you think. In any event I'm pleased to re-ne-ew . . .'

And he turned away nonchalantly to put his hat on the window sill.

'Have you been waiting long?' asked Trudolyubov.

'I arrived at five sharp, as I was told to yesterday,' I replied in a loud voice, with irritation that threatened an imminent explosion.

'Surely you must have told him we changed the time?' asked Trudolyubov, turning to Simonov.

'I didn't – I forgot,' he replied and, without a trace of remorse, and without even a word of apology, he went off to see about the hors d'œuvre.

'So, you've been here an hour already – oh, you poor chap!' Zverkov exclaimed sarcastically, since in his opinion the whole thing was really terribly funny. And after him that rotter Ferfichkin broke into his nasty high-pitched laughter that sounded like a wretched little dog squealing. He too found my situation amusing and embarrassing.

'It's not in the least funny!' I shouted at Ferfichkin, growing increasingly incensed. 'It's the others' fault, not mine. No one bothered to tell me. It's . . . it's . . . it's simply absurd!'

'Not only absurd, but more than that,' Trudolyubov muttered, naively standing up for me. 'That's putting it too mildly! It's downright rude! Of course, it wasn't intentional. But how could Simonov have . . . hm!'

'If someone had treated me like that,' observed Ferfichkin, 'I'd have . . .'

'But you could have ordered a little something in the meantime,' interrupted Zverkov, 'or simply dined without waiting for us . . .'

'You'll agree that I didn't need anyone's permission for that,' I snapped. 'If I waited it was because . . .'

'Come on, let's sit down, gentlemen,' cried Simonov as he came back. 'Everything's ready and I can vouch that the champagne's beautifully chilled . . . You see, I didn't have your address, so where was I supposed to find you?' he said, suddenly turning to me but again avoiding eye contact. Clearly he had something against me. He must have had second thoughts after yesterday.

Everyone sat down and I followed suit. The table was a round one. On my left I had Trudolyubov, with Simonov on my right. Zverkov was sitting opposite, with Ferfichkin next to him, between him and Trudolyubov.

'Now, ple-ea-se te-tell me . . . do you work in a government department?' Zverkov continued, still giving me his attention. When he saw that I was upset he seriously imagined that I should be shown some kindness, that I needed to be cheered up, so to speak. 'What does he want? Does he want me to chuck a bottle at him?' I thought, in a terrible rage. Not being used to this sort of thing I grew excited unnaturally quickly.

'In a certain office,' I replied brusquely, peering at my plate.

'And do y-you f-find it r-r-remuner-rative? Tell me, what ind-d-duced you to leave your previous job?'

'What ind-d-duced me was that I just w-w-anted to l-leave my previous j-j-job,' I drawled three times as much as him, barely able to control myself. Ferfichkin snorted. Simonov glanced at me ironically; Trudolyubov stopped eating and began looking me over quizzically. Zverkov winced, but pretended not to notice.

'We-well now, what's your p-pay?'

'My pay?'

'I mean – your s-salary?'

'Why this cross-examination?'

However, I immediately told him what my salary was and flushed crimson.

'That's nothing much,' Zverkov observed pompously.

'Oh no, you can't dine in smart restaurants on that!' Ferfichkin added insolently.

'In my opinion it's a mere pittance,' Trudolyubov remarked gravely.

'And how thin you've grown, how you've changed . . . since those days,' added Zverkov, not without venom, eyeing me and my clothes with brazen pity.

'Now stop embarrassing him,' tittered Ferfichkin.

'My dear sir, I'll have you know that I'm not in the least embarrassed,' I finally blurted out. 'Do you hear? I'm dining here, in this "smart restaurant", at my own, at my *own* expense and not at other people's. Please take note, Monsieur Ferfichkin.'

'Wha-at!? Which one of us here isn't dining at his own expense? It seems you . . .' Ferfichkin latched on, turning red as a lobster and looking me frenziedly in the eye.

'Well now,' I replied, feeling I'd gone a bit too far. 'I suggest we have a rather more intelligent conversation.'

'It seems you're determined to demonstrate your intelligence!'

'Don't worry, it would be really wasted here.'

'What on earth are you ca-ca-cackling about, my dear sir, eh? You haven't gone off your r-rocker in your *l*epartment, have you?'

'Enough, gentlemen, enough!' Zverkov cried imperiously.

'This is all so silly! Here we are, gathered together as good friends to wish a dear comrade bon voyage,' observed Trudolyubov, rudely addressing me alone, 'and you're counting the cost. It was you who thrust yourself on us yesterday, so don't go upsetting the general harmony . . .'

'That's enough, enough,' exclaimed Zverkov. 'Stop it, gentlemen, this won't do at all. You'd better let me tell you how I nearly got married the day before yesterday . . .'

And he embarked on some scandalous story about how he had nearly got married two days before. However, there wasn't a word about a marriage and the narrative was peopled with generals and colonels and even gentlemen of the bedchamber, with Zverkov almost the leading light. There followed bursts of approving laughter; Ferfichkin positively yelped.

They all abandoned me and I sat there, crushed and humiliated.

'Heavens! Is this my kind of company?' I thought. 'And what a laughing-stock I've made of myself in front of them! All the same, I let Ferfichkin get away with murder. Those boobies honestly think they've done me an honour by giving me a place at their table, but they don't seem to understand that it's me, it's *me*, who's doing *them* the honour and not the other way round. "You've got thinner! That suit!" Oh, damn those trousers! Zverkov must have noticed the yellow spot on the knee just now ... Well, what of it ... ? I should really get up now, this instant, take my hat and simply leave, without a word ... Out of contempt! Even if it means a duel tomorrow. The bastards! As if I grudged a measly seven roubles. But perhaps they'll think ... Oh, what the hell! I don't grudge seven roubles! I'm going this instant ... !'

Needless to say, I stayed.

I drowned my misery in Château Lafite and sherry by the glassful. Being unused to drink, I very soon got tipsy and the more I drank the more incensed I became. Suddenly I felt the urge to insult the lot of them in the most audacious manner and then make my departure. Just seize the right moment and show them who they're dealing with – then they could at least say: he may be ridiculous but he's very intelligent ... and ... and ... in short, to hell with them!

Insolently, I looked them all over with glazed eyes. But it seemed they had completely forgotten about me. *They* were noisy, boisterous, cheerful. Zverkov did all the talking. I listened hard. He was telling them about some ravishing lady whom he had finally brought to the point of declaring her love for him (naturally, he was lying like a trooper) and how he had been greatly assisted in this affair by a bosom pal, a certain princeling called Kolya, an officer of the Hussars, who owned three thousand serfs.

'And yet this Kolya with the three thousand serfs is obviously not here to see you off,' I said, suddenly breaking into the conversation. For a moment no one said a word.

'You're drunk already,' Trudolyubov said, at last deigning to acknowledge my presence and casting a contemptuous glance in my direction. Zverkov was silently eyeing me as if I were some nasty insect. I looked down. Simonov hurriedly started pouring the champagne.

Trudolyubov raised his glass and everyone except me followed suit.

'Your very good health and a prosperous journey!' he shouted to Zverkov. 'To old times, gentlemen, and to the future. Hurrah!'

Everyone drained his glass and went over to embrace Zverkov. I didn't budge. My full glass was standing in front of me, untouched.

'Surely you're going to drink his health?' bellowed Trudolyubov, losing patience and turning towards me menacingly.

'I wish to make a speech of my own, separately . . . and then I'll drink, Mr Trudolyubov.'

'Bad-tempered brute!' growled Simonov.

I drew myself up in my chair and feverishly clutched my glass, preparing myself to say something out of the ordinary, although I didn't have any idea what it would be.

'Silence!' shouted Ferfichkin. 'I'm sure we're going to hear something intelligent!'

Realizing what was going on, Zverkov waited very gravely.

'My dear Lieutenant Zverkov,' I began, 'I'd have you know that I detest big talk, phrase-mongers and tight waists . . . That's point number one and the second follows on from that . . .'

Everyone stirred uneasily.

'Point number two: I hate smutty stories and those who tell them. Especially those who tell them!'

'Point number three: I love truth, sincerity and honesty,' I continued almost mechanically as I was starting to freeze with

terror and I didn't understand how I could be saying all this
... 'I love ideas, Monsieur Zverkov. I love true comradeship,
on an equal footing and not ... hm ... I love ... But what's
the point? I'll drink your health, too, Monsieur Zverkov. Now
go and seduce all those Circassian maidens, shoot the enemies
of the fatherland ... and ... and ... your health, Monsieur
Zverkov!'

Zverkov got up from the table, bowed and said: 'I'm really
most obliged to you.'

He was terribly insulted and even turned pale.

'To hell with you!' roared Trudolyubov, banging his fist on
the table.

'Oh yes, sir, people get punched in the mug for that!' shrieked
Ferfichkin.

'He should be thrown out,' muttered Simonov.

'Not another word, gentlemen, don't do anything!' Zverkov
solemnly shouted, putting a stop to the general indignation. 'I
thank you all, but I myself am quite capable of showing him
how much I value his words.'

'Mr Ferfichkin,' I said in a loud voice, imperiously turning to
Ferfichkin. 'Tomorrow you will give me satisfaction for what
you've just said.'

'You mean a duel, sir? With pleasure,' he replied. However,
I really must have cut such a comical figure challenging him, it
was so at odds with my diminutive stature, that everyone simply
collapsed with laughter, Ferfichkin last of all.

'Yes, of course, chuck him out! He's obviously dead drunk!'
Trudolyubov said with loathing.

'I'll never forgive myself for including him,' Simonov growled
once more.

'Right now I'd like to throw a bottle at the lot of them,' I
thought and I picked one up ... and filled my glass to the brim.
'No ... I'd better sit it out to the bitter end!' I thought.

'You'd be only too delighted if I left, gentlemen. Fat chance
of that. I'll deliberately sit here and drink right to the end to
show that I don't consider you of the slightest importance. I
shall sit and drink because this is a low-class dive and I paid
good money to come in. I shall sit here and drink, because I

think you're a lot of nobodies – non-existent nobodies. I shall sit here and drink . . . and sing if I want to . . . yes . . . I'll sing, because I have the right to . . . sing . . . hmm.'

But I didn't sing. I merely tried to avoid looking at any of them; I adopted the most detached air and waited impatiently for them to speak first. But alas, they did not speak. And how I longed, how I longed to make it up with them at that moment! It struck eight and finally nine. They moved from the table to the divan. Zverkov stretched out on the sofa, resting one leg on a small round table. They took their wine with them. Zverkov did in fact contribute three bottles of his own. Of course, he didn't invite me. They all gathered around him on the divan, listening to him almost reverentially. Obviously they were very fond of him. 'Why? Why?' I wondered. Now and then they went into drunken raptures and embraced each other. They spoke of the Caucasus, the nature of true passion, the most advantageous postings in the army, how much a certain Hussar officer, Podkharzhevsky (whom none of them knew personally) earned and were delighted that he had such a large income; about the exceptional grace and beauty of Princess D—, whom none of them had ever set eyes on either; and finally they came to the conclusion that Shakespeare was immortal.

I smiled contemptuously and walked along the wall on the other side of the room, directly opposite the sofa, back and forth, from table to stove. I was trying my hardest to show them that I could do without them; at the same time I deliberately stamped on the floor, coming down hard on my heels. But it was all in vain. *They* took no notice whatsoever. I had the patience to keep walking up and down like that, right in front of them, from eight to eleven o'clock, always keeping to the same line from table to stove and back again. 'So, I'm walking because I want to and no one can forbid me.' A waiter stopped several times to look at me whenever he entered the room; the frequent turns made me feel giddy and at times I thought I was delirious. During those three hours I became soaked in sweat and three times I dried out again. At times the thought flashed through my mind and pierced my heart with the most excruciating pain that ten, twenty, forty years might pass and

I would still – even after forty years – recall with revulsion and humiliation these nastiest, most ridiculous and ghastliest moments of my whole life. To humiliate myself more shamefully and voluntarily was impossible – this I fully, all too fully, understood – yet still I continued my pacing from table to stove and back. 'Oh, if you only knew what feelings and thoughts I'm capable of and how cultured I am!' I thought at times, mentally addressing the divan on which my enemies were seated. But my enemies were behaving as if I wasn't even in the room. Once, only once, did they turn towards me – to be exact, just as Zverkov started holding forth about Shakespeare and I suddenly broke into contemptuous laughter. I gave vent to such artificial, revolting snorts that they all broke off their conversation at once and for about two minutes – gravely and without laughing – watched me as I walked along the wall, from table to stove, *without paying them the least attention*. But nothing happened: they said nothing and within two minutes had again deserted me. It struck eleven.

'Gentlemen!' cried Zverkov, rising from the divan. 'Let's all go *there* – now!'

'Of course, of course!' exclaimed the others.

I turned sharply towards Zverkov. I was so exhausted, so shattered that I felt like ending it all, even if it meant cutting my throat! I was feverish ... My sweat-soaked hair stuck to my forehead and temples.

'Zverkov! I ask you for forgiveness!' I said brusquely and determinedly. 'And yours too, Ferfichkin – everyone's, everyone's. I've insulted everyone!'

'Aha! So duels aren't your cup of tea, eh?' Ferfichkin hissed venomously.

I felt a sharp stab of pain in my heart. 'Oh no, duels don't scare me, Ferfichkin! I'm ready to fight you tomorrow, even after a reconciliation. I insist on it and you cannot refuse. I want to show you that I'm not afraid of duels. You'll fire first and I'll fire into the air.'

'Likes his little joke!' observed Simonov.

'A load of hogwash!' retorted Trudolyubov.

'Now please allow me to pass, you're in my way! ... Well,

what is it you want?' Zverkov replied contemptuously. All of them were red-faced and their eyes were shining: they'd had a great deal to drink.

'I'm asking for your friendship, Zverkov. I offended you, but . . .'

'Offended me? Y-you!? Offended *m-me*?! I'll have you know, my dear sir, that never, not under any circumstances, could you ever offend *me*!'

'We've just about had enough of you, so clear out!' said Trudolyubov, rounding things off. 'Let's go.'

'Olympia's all mine, gentlemen. Agreed?' shouted Zverkov.

'We won't argue!' they replied, laughing.

I stood there, totally rebuffed. The gang left the room noisily, Trudolyubov striking up some stupid song. Simonov stayed behind for a brief moment to tip the waiters. Suddenly I went up to him.

'Simonov! Lend me six roubles!' I said resolutely and desperately.

He looked at me in absolute amazement with his bleary eyes. He too was drunk. 'You don't mean to say you're coming *there* with us?'

'Oh yes!'

'I don't have any money!' he snapped, grinning disdainfully and sweeping out of the room.

I grabbed him by his overcoat: it was a nightmare. 'Simonov! I saw you had money, so why do you refuse? And am I really such a scoundrel? Now, mind you don't refuse me: if only you knew, if only you knew why I'm asking! Everything depends on it, my entire future, all my plans . . .'

Simonov took out some money and virtually hurled it at me.

'Take it, if you're so shameless!' he said mercilessly and ran off to catch up with the others.

For a minute I was left on my own. Disorder, leftovers, a broken glass on the floor, spilt wine, cigarette ends, intoxication and wild gibberish in my head, tormenting anguish in my heart – and finally that all-seeing, all-hearing waiter staring me curiously in the eye.

'*There!*' I yelled. 'Either they'll all go down on their knees,

clasp my legs and beg for my friendship . . . or I'll give Zverkov
a slap in the face!'

                                  V

'So, here it is, here it is at last, that collision with reality,' I
muttered, rushing headlong down the stairs. 'This, of course,
is no longer the Pope leaving Rome and travelling to Brazil, it's
obviously not a ball on Lake Como!'

'You're a scoundrel,' ran through my mind, 'if you can laugh
at this now.'

'Oh, what the hell!' I shouted, answering myself. 'It's all over
anyway!' There was no sign of them, but that didn't matter:
I knew where they'd gone.

By the steps stood a solitary night cabby, his coarse peasant
greatcoat completely powdered with snow that was still falling
in wet, seemingly warm flakes. It was steamy and close outside.
His shaggy little skewbald horse was also powdered with snow
and was coughing – that I remember very clearly. I rushed to
the sledge, but no sooner had I raised one foot to step in when
the recollection of the way Simonov had given me those six
roubles was the last straw and I slumped into it like a sack . . .

'No, I'll have to do a lot to redeem all this!' I shouted. 'But
I shall redeem it, or I'll perish on the spot, this very night.
Drive on!'

We moved off. A whole whirlwind was raging in my head.

'Going down on their knees to beg for my friendship – that
they won't do! That's a mirage, a vulgar mirage, disgusting,
romantic, fantastic, just like the ball on Lake Como. That's
why I *must* slap Zverkov's face! I'm obliged to do that. So,
that's settled. Now I'm tearing off to give him a slap.'

'Faster!'

The driver jerked the reins.

'I'll do it the moment I go in. But shouldn't I perhaps say a
few words before the slap, by way of introduction? No! I'll just
walk in and give him one. They'll all be sitting in the lounge

and he'll be on the sofa with Olympia. Damn that Olympia! Once she laughed at my face and refused me. I'll drag Olympia to one side by the hair and pull Zverkov along by the ears. No, better by one ear, I'll haul him right round the room by one ear. Very likely they'll all start beating me and throw me out. In fact, that's almost a certainty. Let them – I'll have delivered the first slap: that's my prerogative and according to the code of honour that's everything. He'll be branded for life and no amount of blows will ever wipe out that slap – only a duel. He'll *have* to fight. Well, let them thrash me now. Let them, the base swine! Trudolyubov will lay into me particularly hard – he's so strong. Ferfichkin will pounce on me from the side and almost certainly grab me by the hair. So, let them, let them! That's my whole reason for going. They'll finally have to get into their mutton-heads that there's a whole tragedy here. When they drag me to the door I'll call out loud that they aren't worth my little finger.'

'Faster, driver, faster!' I shouted at the cabby.

He gave a sudden start and flourished his whip. (My shout was a really wild one.)

'We'll fight at dawn, that's settled. I'm finished with the department. A moment ago Ferfichkin said *l*epartment instead of department. But where shall I get pistols? Nonsense! I'll take an advance on my salary and buy them. What about powder and bullets? That's the second's affair. And how can I arrange all this before dawn? And where am I to find a second? I don't have any friends . . .'

'Nonsense!' I shouted, growing increasingly ruffled. 'Nonsense!'

'The first person I ask in the street is obliged to be my second – it's just the same as pulling a drowning man out of the water. The most exceptional circumstances must be allowed for. And even if I were to ask the head of my department himself tomorrow, to be my second, he too would have to agree, simply out of chivalry – and to keep the secret! Anton Antonych . . .'

The fact was, at that very moment I could see more clearly and vividly than anyone in the whole wide world the vile absurdity of my assumptions and the reverse side of the coin, but . . .

'Faster, driver, faster, you rogue!'

'But sir!' groaned that son of the soil.

Suddenly I went cold all over. 'Wouldn't it be better ...
wouldn't it be better to go straight home? God – why did I have
to invite myself to that dinner yesterday? No, it's impossible!
And all that promenading for three hours, from table to stove?
No, they alone, no one else, should pay for all those promenades! They must wipe out the dishonour!'

'Faster!'

'But what if they should hand me over to the police? They
wouldn't dare! They'd be afraid of the scandal. And what if
Zverkov turns down the duel, out of contempt? That's even
highly likely. But then I'll show them ... I'll dash to the posting-
station when he's leaving, grab his leg and rip off his overcoat
as he's getting into the coach. Then I'll sink my teeth into his
arm. I'll bite him. "Just look, everyone, see to what lengths a
desperate man can be driven!" Let him punch me on the head
and the others from behind. I'll shout to all the people there:
"Just look at this young puppy who's off to captivate Circassian
girls with my spit on his face!"

'Of course, after that everything is finished! The department
vanishes from the face of the earth. I'm arrested, tried, given
the sack and sent to a Siberian penal settlement. But never
mind! When I'm released fifteen years later, a beggar, all in
rags, I'll drag myself after him. I'll seek him out in some provincial town. He'll be married and happy. He'll have a grown-up
daughter ... I'll tell him: "Look, you monster, just look at my
hollow cheeks, look at my rags! I've lost everything – my career,
my happiness, art, science, *the woman I loved* – and all because
of you. Here are the pistols. I've come to discharge mine – and
... and ... I forgive you." Then I'll fire into the air and that's
the last he'll hear of me ...'

I was even on the verge of tears, although at that very moment
I knew perfectly well that all this came out of *Silvio*[35] and
Lermontov's *Masquerade*.[36] And suddenly I felt terribly
ashamed, so ashamed that I stopped the horse, got out of the
sledge and stood in the snow in the middle of the street. The
cabby looked at me in amazement and took a deep breath.

What could I do? I couldn't possibly go *there* – the whole thing had turned into a farce. And I couldn't leave things as they were, since then there would be . . . Good God! How could I possibly leave things as they were! And after such insults!

'No!' I called out, flinging myself back into the sledge. 'It's predestined, it's fate! Drive on – *there*! Let's go!'

And in my impatience I thumped the driver on the neck with my fist.

'What's that for? What yer 'itting me for?' cried my poor old peasant, but he whipped on his miserable nag, which made it kick out with its hind legs.

The wet snow was falling in large flakes; I unbuttoned my coat – I wasn't concerned about the snow. I had forgotten everything else since I finally decided on the slap and I realized with horror that it was all *bound to happen* right now and that *no power on earth could prevent it*. The solitary street lamps were glimmering mournfully through the snowy haze like torches at a funeral. The snow was packed under my overcoat, under my frock-coat, under my tie and melting there. I didn't bother to cover myself again – after all, it was a lost cause! Finally we arrived. I leapt out, scarcely aware of what I was doing, raced up the steps and started hammering on the door with fists and feet. My legs were becoming terribly weak, especially at the knees. The door seemed to open quickly, as if they knew I was coming. (In actual fact, Simonov had forewarned them that another person might be coming, as it was a place where you had to give prior notice and generally take precautions. It was one of those 'fashion shops' of the time, long since closed down by the police. During the day it was in fact a shop, but in the evenings those with suitable recommendations could go there as guests.) With hurried steps I walked across the dark shop and went into the familiar salon where a single candle was burning and I stopped in bewilderment: no one was there.

'Where are they?' I asked someone.

But of course they'd already managed to disperse . . .

Standing before me was a person with a stupid smile, the madam herself, who knew me slightly. A moment later the door opened and another character appeared.

Without paying attention to anything I paced up and down the room, seemingly talking to myself. It was as if I had been saved from death and I was rejoicing in the fact with my whole being. Indeed, I would most certainly have delivered that slap – most certainly would I have delivered it! But now they weren't there and . . . everything had vanished, everything had changed . . . ! I looked around. Still I couldn't make head or tail of it. Mechanically I glanced at the girl who had come in: before me I saw a fresh, young, rather pale face with straight, dark eyebrows and a serious, as it were faintly surprised expression. This I liked immediately; I would have hated her had she been smiling. I began to stare at her more intently and with some effort, so to speak. I still hadn't collected my thoughts. There was something kind and simple-hearted in that face, but also something somehow strangely serious. I am certain that this was to her disadvantage in that place and that not one of those idiots had noticed her. Besides, she could not have been called a beauty, although she was tall, strong and well-built. She was dressed extremely simply. Suddenly something nasty cut me to the quick. I went straight over to her . . .

By chance I caught sight of myself in the mirror. My agitated face struck me as utterly repulsive: pale, vicious, mean, my hair dishevelled. 'That's fine, I'm glad of it,' I reflected. 'Yes, I'm really glad that I'll strike her as repulsive; that pleases me . . .'

VI

. . . Somewhere behind the partition, as if under immense pressure and as if someone were strangling it, the clock suddenly wheezed. After an unnaturally prolonged wheeze there followed a rather thin, nasty, somewhat unexpectedly rapid chime, as if someone had suddenly leapt forward. It struck two. I regained consciousness, although I hadn't been asleep, merely lying in a half-trance.

In the cramped, narrow, low-ceilinged room, crammed with a huge wardrobe, cluttered with cardboard boxes, rags and all kinds of scraps of clothing, it was almost completely dark. The candle-end on the table at the other end of the room had almost gone out, feebly flickering now and then. In a few minutes the whole room would be completely dark . . .

It did not take me long fully to come to my senses; all at once, without any effort, everything came back to me in a flash, as if it had been lying in wait in order to attack me again. And in that half-conscious state itself there constantly remained a kind of focal point in my memory that hadn't been forgotten at all and around which my sleepy reveries wearily revolved. But the strange thing was that all the events of that day seemed to me now I was awake to have taken place long, long ago, as if I had lived through everything in the remote past.

My head was feeling muzzy. Something seemed to be hovering over me, nagging at me, rousing and disturbing me, Once again, anguish and spleen seethed within me and sought an outlet. All at once I saw right next to me two wide-open eyes surveying me curiously and intently. Their look was cold, indifferent and sullen, like a stranger's. This I found oppressive.

A gloomy thought stirred in my brain and swept through my whole body like some foul sensation, similar to the kind you experience on going into a damp and mouldy cellar. It was somehow unnatural that only at that precise moment did those two eyes decide to start scrutinizing me. I also remembered that in the course of two hours I hadn't spoken one word to that creature and even considered it quite unnecessary; until a few moments before I was even pleased about it for some reason. But now there suddenly and vividly appeared to me, as absurd and repulsive as a spider, a vision of lust which, without love, crudely and shamelessly, begins exactly where true love is crowned. We looked at each other for a long time, but she didn't lower her eyes before mine, nor did she alter her expression, so that finally I was overcome by a kind of eerie feeling.

'What's your name?' I asked brusquely, to get it over with as soon as possible.

'Liza,' she replied, almost in a whisper but somehow quite ungraciously – and she looked away.

For a while I said nothing.

'The weather today . . . snow . . . it's foul!' I muttered almost to myself, wearily putting my hand behind my head and gazing up at the ceiling. She didn't reply. It was all very ugly.

'Are you from St Petersburg?' I asked a moment later, almost in a temper and turning my head slightly towards her.

'No.'

'Where are you from?'

'From Riga,' she replied reluctantly.

'Are you German?'

'Russian.'

'Been here long?'

'Where?'

'In this house?'

'Two weeks.'

She was speaking more and more abruptly. The candle had gone out altogether and I could no longer distinguish her face.

'Are your mother and father alive?'

'Yes . . . no . . . yes, they are.'

'Where are they?'

'There . . . in Riga.'

'Who are they?'

'Just . . .'

'What do you mean "just"? Who are they, what do they do?'

'They're tradespeople.'

'Have you always lived with them?'

'Yes.'

'How old are you?'

'Twenty.'

'Why did you leave them?'

'I just . . .'

This *just* meant: leave me alone, I'm sick of all this. We said nothing.

God knows why I didn't leave. I myself was feeling increasingly depressed and disgusted. Visions of all that had happened the previous day started drifting through my mind, disjointedly, as if of their own accord, against my will. Suddenly I remembered a scene I had witnessed that morning in the street when I was anxiously trotting along to the office.

'This morning they were carrying a coffin out and very nearly dropped it,' I suddenly said out loud, without the slightest wish to start a conversation – almost unintentionally as it were.

'A coffin?'

'Yes, in the Haymarket.[37] They were taking it out of a cellar.'

'Out of a cellar?'

'Well, not exactly a cellar – a basement ... you know ... down below ... from a house of ill fame. There was such filth everywhere ... eggshells, litter ... nasty smells ... it was disgusting.'

Silence.

'A dreadful day for a funeral!' I began again, simply for the sake of saying something.

'Why dreadful?'

'The snow ... the damp ...' (I yawned).

'Doesn't make any difference ...' she said suddenly, after a brief pause.

'No, it's horrible ...' (I yawned again). 'I'm sure the grave diggers must have been swearing because they were wet from the snow. Most probably there was water in the grave.'

'Why should there be water in the grave?' she asked with some curiosity, but speaking even more rudely and disjointedly than before. Suddenly something spurred me on.

'Well, yes, there's water at the bottom – six inches of it. In Volkovo Cemetery,[38] you can't dig a dry grave.'

'Why is that?'

'What do you mean "why"? Because the whole place is waterlogged. There's marsh everywhere. They just lower them into the water. I've seen it myself ... many times ...'

(I had never seen it, nor had I ever been to Volkovo – I'd only heard others talk about it.)

'So it's all the same to you – dying?'

'Why should I die?' she replied, somewhat defensively.

'Well, one day you'll die and I reckon you'll die just like that woman did. She too was a young girl like you ... died of consumption.'

'A whore would have died in hospital.' (She knows about it already, I reflected – she said 'whore' instead of 'young girl'.)

'She was in debt to the madam,' I continued, warming more and more to the argument, 'and she served her almost right to the end, despite having consumption. The cab drivers around here were telling some soldiers about it. Most likely they were former acquaintances of hers. They were laughing and planning on having a few drinks to her memory in the pub. (Much of this too was my own invention.)

Silence, profound silence. She didn't even stir.

'So, you think it's better to die in hospital?'

'Isn't it all the same ... And why should I die?' she added irritably.

'If not now, then later on.'

'All right, later on ...'

'But things don't work out like that! You're young now, pretty and fresh – that's why you're worth quite a lot to them. But another year of this kind of life and you won't be the same, you'll fade away.'

'After a year?'

'At any rate, after a year you'll be worth less,' I continued sadistically. 'You'll have to leave here for somewhere even lower, another house. A year after that – to a third house, sinking lower and lower and about seven years later you'll end up in a cellar in the Haymarket. That wouldn't be so bad, but the trouble is if on top of that you contracted some illness, let's say, a weak chest ... or caught a cold, or something. In that sort of life it's very hard to shake off an illness. It will take a grip on you and you won't be able to get rid of it. And then you'll die.'

'So, I'll die,' she replied, very bad-temperedly and with a quick change of position.

'But I feel sorry.'

'Sorry for whom?'

'Sorry for the life you're leading.'

Silence.

'Did you ever have a boyfriend? Eh?'

'What's it to do with you?'

'Well, I'm not interrogating you, I'd just like to know. Why are you so angry? Of course, you probably had your share of trouble. Why should I care? I just feel sorry.'

'For whom?'

'Sorry for you.'

'There's no point . . .' she whispered almost inaudibly and she restlessly shifted about again.

This immediately made me see red. So! I had been so gentle with her, but she . . .

'Well, what do you think? That you're on the right path, eh?'

'I don't think anything.'

'Well, that's bad, not thinking anything. Open your eyes while there's still time. And there *is* time. You're still young, pretty, you could fall in love, get married and be happy . . .'

'Not all married women are happy . . .' she cut me short with her rude patter of before.

'Of course not all, but it's still a good sight better than being here. Incomparably better. And where there's love you can even live without happiness. Life is sweet, even in sorrow. It's good to be alive in this world, however you live. But what's here except . . . a foul stench? Ugh!'

I turned away, disgusted. I was no longer coolly rational: I myself was beginning to be affected by what I was saying and I was becoming heated. I was longing to expound those cherished *little ideas* that I had nurtured in my corner. Suddenly something caught fire within me, some kind of purpose 'revealed' itself.

'Don't take any notice of my being here, I'm no example for you. Perhaps I'm even worse than you. However, I was drunk when I came here,' I added, hurrying to excuse myself all the same. 'Besides, a man is no example for a woman at all. They're totally different. Although I may degrade and dirty myself, I'm no one's slave. I came here – and then I'll be gone. I can shake it all off and again be a different man. But consider the fact that you're a slave right from the start. Yes, a slave! You give everything up, your entire freedom. And later, if you want to break these chains, it will be too late: the fetters will bind you tighter and tighter. And it's such a damnable chain! I know it. And I'm not talking about anything else, as you probably wouldn't even understand. Now tell me this: you must already be in debt to your mistress, eh? There, you see!' I added,

although she didn't answer but simply listened in silence with
her whole being ... There's a chain, for you! You'll never pay
her off. That's what happens. Same as selling your soul to the
devil ...

'And besides, for all you know, I might be a miserable wretch
like you and I'm deliberately wallowing in muck because I'm
sick at heart too. Sorrow drives people to drink, so I'm here –
out of sorrow. Now tell me – what's good about all this? You
and I ... we made love just a few moments ago ... and the
whole time we didn't say one word to each other and afterwards
you began staring at me like a wild woman. And I stared back.
Is that the way to love? It's really shocking, that's what!'

'Yes,' she agreed, sharply and hastily. The hastiness of that
'yes' even surprised me. Was the same thought perhaps running
through her mind just then, when she was watching me? Did it
mean that she too was capable of some thought ... ?

'Damn it, this is very curious, this *kinship*,' I thought, almost
rubbing my hands. And how could she fail to cope, with such
a young spirit as hers ... ?'

It was the game more than anything that appealed to me.

She had turned her head closer to me and in the darkness
seemed to be leaning on her elbow. Perhaps she was scrutinizing
me? How sorry I was that I couldn't distinguish her eyes ...
I could hear her heavy breathing.

'Why did you come here?' I began, now with a certain
authority.

'Because ...'

'I suppose it was nice, living in a family home, so warm and
free – your own little nest!'

'And supposing it was worse than here?'

The thought: 'I must strike the right note' flashed through my
mind, 'sentimentality probably won't get me very far with her.'

However, it was just a passing thought. I swear that she really
did interest me. Besides, I was feeling rather relaxed and in the
mood. After all, knavery gets on so easily with sentiment.

'Who can tell?' I hastened to reply. 'Anything is possible.
You see, I'm convinced that someone wronged you and *they*
were more to blame than you were. You see, I know nothing

of your background, but a girl like you doesn't end up in a place like this because she wants to, does she?'

'So, what kind of girl am I?' she whispered barely audibly – but I could make out what she said.

"To hell with it, I'm flattering her! That's low of me. Or perhaps it's all right . . ." She remained silent.

'Look here, Liza, I'll tell you about myself. If I'd grown up in a family when I was a child, I wouldn't be as I am now. I often think about it. You see, however bad it may be in a family, they're still your own father and mother and not your enemies, not strangers, even though they may show their love for you just once a year. At any rate, you can be sure that you're at home. I grew up without any family – that's certainly why I turned out the way I am – without feelings.'

Again I waited for her to speak.

'Perhaps she doesn't understand,' I thought. 'What's more, she must find all this moralizing rather comical.'

'If I were a father and had a daughter I think I'd love the daughter more than a son really, I would,' I began obliquely, as if on another subject, to divert her attention. I was blushing, I do confess.

'Why's that?' she asked.

Ah! So she was listening!

'Well, I don't really know, Liza. You see, once I knew a father who was a very strict, grim kind of man, but he used to kneel before his daughter and kiss her hands and feet. Really, he couldn't stop feasting his eyes on her. She'd be dancing at a party and he'd stand in the same spot for hours without taking his eyes off her. He was besotted with her – that I can understand. At night, when she was tired and fell asleep, he'd wake up and go and kiss her in her sleep and make the sign of the cross over her. He went around in a greasy old frock-coat, was tight-fisted towards everyone else, but he would spend his last copeck on her, buy her expensive presents – and the joy it brought him if the gift was to her liking! Fathers always love their daughters more than a mother does. For some girls home is a very happy place. But I don't think I would let a daughter of mine get married.'

'But why not?' she asked with the faintest of laughs.

'I'd be jealous, really! How could she kiss someone else, love a stranger more than her father? The thought of it pains me. Of course, all this is nonsense, in the end everyone comes to see reason. But I think that before letting her marry I'd have exhausted myself with worry; I'd have found fault with every suitor. However, in the end I'd let her marry the one she loved. You see, the man the daughter falls in love with always strikes the father as worst of all. It's always been like that. It causes a lot of trouble in families.'

'Others are glad to sell their daughters rather than give them in marriage honestly,' she suddenly said.

Ah! So that was it!

'That only happens in those cursed families where there's neither God nor love, Liza,' I threw in heatedly. 'For where there's no love there's no reason. There are such families, that's true, but it's not them I'm talking about. From what you say you can't have known any kindness in your family. You are a genuinely unfortunate person. Hm ... all that mainly comes about through poverty.'

'And is it any better among gentlefolk? Honest folk can live decently even if they're poor.'

'Hm ... yes, perhaps so. But there's something else, Liza: people only like to count their sorrows and not their good fortune. But if they were to take account of things as they should then they'd see that everyone has his fair share laid in store for him. So, supposing all goes well with your family, if God gives his blessing, if your husband turns out to be a good man, who loves you, cherishes you and doesn't leave you! Life is so good in that family! And sometimes it's good even if one half of it is beset with sorrow. And is there anywhere without sorrow? Should you marry perhaps you'll *find out for yourself*. But then consider the early days of married life to the man you love: what happiness sometimes comes along! And that happens time and again. In the early days even quarrels with the husband end happily. Sometimes, the more a woman loves her husband the more quarrels she picks with him. It's true; I once knew someone like that. "You know I love you very much", she would say, "and it's because I love you that I torment you, so that you can feel it." Do you know that someone can deliberately torment another, out of love? Mainly women do that. The woman thinks to herself: but then I'll be so tender and loving to him afterwards that it's no sin if I make him suffer a little now! And everyone in the house is happy for you, everything is so good, so happy, so peaceful and honest ... And there's others who are jealous as well – I knew one like that – if the husband went out somewhere she couldn't bear it and in the middle of the night she'd leap out of bed and go snooping about to discover whether he was there, in that house, with that woman. That's very bad. And she knows it's bad and her heart sinks and she blames herself; but she loves him – it's all for love. And how good it is to make peace after a quarrel, to admit that it was her fault and to forgive him! And how good it is for both of them, how good everything suddenly becomes – just as if they were newly met, newly wed and their love was born anew. And nobody, positively nobody, need know what goes on between husband and wife if they love each other. Whatever quarrels they get into they should never summon their own mother as judge, when they each tell tales about the other. They are their own judges. Love is a divine mystery and must be kept hidden from all other eyes, no matter what happens. That way it's holier, it's better. They respect each other more and much is founded on respect. And if once there was love, if they married for love, why should love ever pass? Is it really impossible to keep it alive? Those cases are rare when it's impossible to keep it alive. And if the husband succeeds in being a good and honest man, how could love ever fade? It's true, the first, conjugal love passes, but then even finer love comes along. Their souls will be as one and they will do all things together; they will hold no secrets from one another. And when children come along, every moment, even the hardest, will seem like happiness. As long as they love one another and are steadfast. And then work itself is a joy – even if you sometimes have to go hungry for your children that's a joy too. For they will love you for it later, as it means you're storing things up for yourself. As the children grow up you feel that you're setting them an example, that you're a support to them; that were you to die they will carry your thoughts and feelings with them, all their lives, since they have received from you your image and taken your likeness. That means it's an immense duty. So, in this case, how can the father and mother not grow closer together? Do they say that having children is a great burden? Who says this? It's heavenly bliss! Do you love little children, Liza? I love them, terribly. Just think – a tiny, rosy baby sucking at your breast – well, every husband's heart must turn to his wife when he sees her sitting there with his little child. A rosy, chubby little baby, stretching itself and snuggling up to you. Those plump little arms, those tiny clean nails – so tiny it makes you laugh to look at them; little eyes that seem already to understand everything. And it sucks away, the tiny hand plucking playfully at your breast. Father comes over and it tears itself from the breast, leans over backwards, looks up at the father and laughs – it's so screamingly funny – again, again, it goes on sucking. And then it might suddenly go and bite the mother's breast, if it's already teething, and artfully look at her with its little eyes as if to say: "Look, I've bitten you!" Surely that's the height of happiness when all three – husband, wife and baby – are together? Much can be forgiven for those moments. No, Liza, you must first learn to live yourself, and then you can blame others!'

'It's with little pictures, it's with these little pictures that you must show her!' I thought to myself, although I really was speaking with genuine feeling. And suddenly I blushed. 'What if she suddenly bursts out laughing; where shall I put myself then?' The very thought drove me into a frenzy. Towards the end of my speech I'd become positively heated and now my vanity was suffering somewhat. The silence dragged on. I felt like giving her a little shove.

'What are you on about?' she said and then stopped.

But now I understood everything: in her voice there sounded a different note, tremulous, not harsh or rude and defiant as before, but somehow soft and bashful – indeed, so bashful that I myself felt ashamed and guilty.

'What did you say?' I asked with tender curiosity.

'Well, you . . .'

'What?'

'Well, you ... sound just like a book,' she said and again I seemed to detect a hint of mockery in her voice.

This remark cut me to the quick. I hadn't been expecting that. And I didn't understand that she was deliberately using that mockery as a mask and that this was the last subterfuge of those who have been subjected to vulgar and persistent probing, of those who out of pride will not yield until the very last moment and who are afraid of unbosoming themselves in front of you. From the very timidity with which she made several attempts at mockery and only then finally brought herself to speak out I should have been able to guess this. But I didn't guess and I was gripped by feelings of spite.

'Just you wait,' I thought.

VII

'That's enough, Liza. What do books have to do with it when I'm feeling rotten on your behalf? Or perhaps it isn't on your behalf?

'I've only just woken up to all this myself ... Surely, surely, you yourself must find it loathsome here? But apparently not – habit counts for a lot! The devil only knows what habit can do to a person. You don't seriously think, do you, that you'll never grow old, that you'll always stay pretty and that they'll keep you on for ever and ever? And I'm not talking about the dirty tricks they play, here ... However, I'm going to tell you this, about your present life here. You're still young, comely, attractive, with spirit and feelings. Well, do you know, as I came to just now I immediately felt disgusted at being here with you? You need to be drunk to come to this sort of place. If you happened to be somewhere else, living as normal, decent people live, I'd not only run after you – I'd positively fall in love with you and be glad of one look from you, let alone one word. I'd be waiting for you by your gate, I'd go down on my knees to you; I'd look on you as my bride-to-be and consider myself honoured. I wouldn't dare harbour one unclean thought about you. But here I know very well that I only have to whistle and whether you like it or not you'll come to me, as it wouldn't be *me* who has to do your bidding, but you would have to do mine. Even the meanest peasant can hire himself out, but he won't be enslaving himself altogether, because he knows it's just for a limited time. But where's your limited time? Just think what it is you're giving up here, what you are enslaving! It's your soul, your soul, over which you have no command that you are enslaving, together with your body! You let your love be desecrated by any old drunkard. Love! – that's everything, that's a precious jewel, a virgin's treasure – love! Some men are ready to sacrifice their souls or go to their deaths to earn that love. And what is your love worth now? You are sold, every part of you, and why should anyone try to win your love when he can get all he wants without any love? There's no worse insult for a young girl than that, do you understand? I've heard people say that to keep you silly fools happy they let you have lovers here. But that's just to spoil you, it's downright deceit, they're only laughing at you – and you believe them. And does this lover in fact love you? I think not. How can he love you when he knows you might be called away from him at any moment? He'd be a filthy devil to do that! But how can he have one drop of respect for you? What do you have in common with him? He'll laugh at you and steal from you – that's what his love amounts to! And you'll be lucky if he doesn't beat you. Or maybe he will. And if you have one of those gentlemen with you, just go and ask if he'll marry you. Yes, he'll laugh right in your face – that is, if he doesn't spit at you or knock you down. And perhaps he's not worth more than a brass farthing himself. And for *what* have you ruined your life here? To be plied with coffee and given plenty to eat? And why do they feed you so well? Any decent woman wouldn't allow one crumb to pass her lips for she'd know very well *why* they're feeding her. In this place you're in debt and you'll always be in debt, right up to the very end, up to the time when customers give you a wide berth. And that time isn't far off – don't rely on your youth. You see, in this kind of place all that passes in a flash. They'll throw you out. And not simply throw you out, since long before that they'll have started finding fault with you, reproaching you, cursing you, as though it wasn't *you* who sacrificed your health and allowed your youth and soul to perish for madam's benefit, but as if you'd ruined *her*, robbed her, sent her out begging. And don't expect any support: the others, your friends, will also turn against you, so that they can get into her good books, because everyone here is a slave and has lost all conscience and sense of compassion long ago. They are defiled and there's nothing on earth more repulsive, obscene and offensive than their abuse. And you'll have given up everything, everything – your health, youth, beauty, your hopes, with no redemption and at twenty-two you'll look like thirty-five and you'll be lucky if you still have your health – pray to God for that! Perhaps you're thinking now that it's not really work you're doing, that it's all one long holiday! But in fact there is no work in the world harder or more back-breaking and there never has been. Anyone would think it's enough to make you cry your heart out. And you won't dare utter a word, not one syllable when they turn you out and you'll leave as if it were all your fault. And you'll move on to another place, then to a third, then somewhere else, until finally you end up in the Haymarket. And there they'll beat you as a matter of course; that's their way of welcoming you. The customers just can't fondle a woman without first giving her a good thrashing. You don't believe that it's so awful there? Well, just you go along some time and take a look for yourself – then you might see with your own eyes. One New Year's Day I saw one of those women standing by a door. She'd been turned out in ridicule by her own people to cool off a bit because of her dreadful howling and they'd locked the door behind her. By nine o'clock in the morning she was already dead drunk, dishevelled, half-naked and bruised all over. Her face was powdered, but she was black all around the eyes. She was bleeding from nose and mouth – some cabby had given her a bashing. She sat down on the stone doorsteps holding some kind of salted fish and howling, as if bemoaning her "lot", banging the fish against the steps. A crowd of cabbies and drunken soldiers stood in the doorway taunting her. You

don't believe that you'll end up like her? And I wouldn't like to
believe it either, but how do you know? Perhaps eight or ten
years before, that same woman with the salted fish arrived here
fresh from somewhere, pure and innocent as a cherub, knowing
no evil and blushing at every word . . . Perhaps she was just like
you – proud, sensitive, unlike the others, looking like a queen,
aware that perfect bliss was awaiting the man who fell in love
with her and whom she fell in love with. But you see how it all
ended? And what if at that very moment when, drunk and
dishevelled, she was banging that fish against the filthy steps –
what if at that very moment she recalled all those pure, earlier
years spent at her father's house, when she went to school and
a neighbour's son waited for her on the road and assured her
that he would love her all his life and place his destiny in her
hands? And when they pledged their love for each other for
ever and would marry as soon as they grew up? No, Liza, it
would be a blessing, a real blessing if you died of consumption
in some corner or cellar, like that girl I was telling you about.
In hospital, you say? All right, if they take you there, but what
if your mistress still needs you? Consumption is an odd sort of
illness: it's not like a fever. A person suffering from that might
go on hoping to the very last minute and say she's well. She
reassures herself – and that suits your mistress. Don't worry,
it's true. It means you've sold your soul and you owe money
into the bargain, so you daren't utter a word. And when you're
dying they'll all desert you, turn their backs on you, because
what use are you to them? What's more, they'll take you to
task for using up space for nothing and not getting on with
your job and dying. You'll have to beg for a drink and they'll
curse when they give it you. "When are you going to kick the
bucket, you slut! You keep us awake, you never stop moaning
and the customers won't go anywhere near you." It's true; I
myself have overheard things like that. And when you're actually dying they'll shove you in the most foul-smelling corner of
the cellar, in the dark and damp. And what will you be thinking,
as you lie there all alone? You'll die and you'll be carted off in
a hurry, by impatient, grumbling strangers. No one will say a
prayer for you, no one will sigh for you – all they'll want is to

get you off their backs as quickly as they can. They'll buy a cheap coffin and then they'll go and carry you out like that poor girl today and then they'll go and say prayers for you in the pub. There'll be slush, rubbish and slime in the grave – the gravediggers won't stand on ceremony for the likes of you. "Let 'er down, Vanyukha. Well, just 'er luck, even now she's got 'er legs up in the air, that's the sort she was. Now, shorten the ropes and stop mucking about." "She's all right as she is ain't she?" "All right, you say? Can't you see she's lying on 'er side? She were a 'uman being once, weren't she? Oh, go on then, fill it in." And they won't waste much time arguing because of you. They'll hurry up and shovel the wet blue clay over you and then it's off to the pub. And that'll be the last anyone will remember about you in this world. Children, fathers and husbands go to other women's graves, but for you there'll be no tears, no sighs, no memorial prayers and no one, no one in the whole world will ever come to visit you. Your name will vanish from the face of the earth, as if you'd never even existed, never been born! There'll only be mud and swamp and you can knock as much as you like on your coffin lid at night when the dead awaken: "Let me out, kind folk, so I can live in the world again! Once I lived but I didn't see life, I frittered it away, I drank it away in a pub in the Haymarket. Set me free, kind folk, I want to live in the world again . . . !"'

I had laid it on so thick I felt a lump rising in my throat . . . and suddenly I stopped, raised myself a little in fright, bowed my head apprehensively and my heart pounded as I started listening: I had good reason to feel confused.

For some time I'd had the feeling that I'd brought about a great spiritual upheaval in her and broken her heart, and the more certain I was of this the more eager I was to achieve my goal as quickly and comprehensively as possible. It was the game, the game that fascinated me. However, it wasn't only the game . . .

I knew I was speaking in a stiff, artificial, even bookish manner – in brief, I couldn't talk in any other way except 'just like a book'. But it wasn't that which troubled me: after all, I knew, I felt that I would be understood and that this very

bookishness might perhaps advance my cause. But now it had
made such an impact my nerve suddenly failed me. No, never,
never before had I witnessed such despair! She lay there prone,
her face buried in the pillow, clasping it with both hands.
Her bosom was heaving. Her whole young body was violently
shaking, as if she were having convulsions. Stifled sobs con-
stricted her chest, then they rent it – and suddenly they broke
free in wails and shrieks. And then she pressed her face even
more firmly against the pillow: she didn't want anyone there,
not a single living soul, to know of her sufferings and tears. She
bit the pillow, bit her hand until it bled (I noticed this later),
clutching at her tangled plaits and weakening from the effort,
holding her breath and clenching her teeth. I was about to speak
to her, to beg her to calm herself, but I felt that I simply didn't
dare and suddenly, in a fit of violent trembling, almost in terror,
I began groping around for my clothes so that I could somehow
get dressed and leave as soon as possible. It was dark, and hard
as I tried I couldn't get my clothes on quickly. Suddenly I found
a box of matches and a candlestick with a new candle.

The moment the light filled the room Liza suddenly leapt up
and sat looking at me almost vacantly, with a half-demented
smile on her distorted face. I sat down beside her and took her
hands. She came to her senses, threw herself towards me as if
wanting to clasp me in her arms, but she did not dare and
quietly bowed her head before me.

'Liza, my dear, I didn't mean to ... please forgive me,' I
began, but she squeezed my hand in hers so violently that
I guessed I was saying the wrong thing and I stopped.

'Here's my address, Liza, come and see me.'

'I will!' she whispered emphatically, but without raising her
head.

'And now I'm going ... goodbye ... until we meet again.'

I stood up and so did she, and then suddenly, blushing furiously, she shuddered, seized the shawl that was lying on the
chair and flung it over her shoulders, covering herself up to the
chin. Then she smiled again rather painfully, blushed and gave
me a strange look. I felt dreadful; I was in a hurry to leave, to
get right away from that place.

'Wait a moment,' she said suddenly when we were already at the entrance hall door; holding me back with one hand on my overcoat she hastily put down the candle and ran off – clearly she had remembered something or wanted to bring something to show me. As she did so her face was flushed, her eyes were sparkling and there was a smile on her lips – what could it be? Reluctantly I waited. After a minute she returned with a look that seemed to be begging forgiveness for something. Altogether this was no longer the same face or the same look as before – so sullen, distrustful, obstinate. Now her look was imploring, gentle and at the same time trusting, warm and timid. That was the way children look at those whom they love very much and from whom they are asking for something. Her eyes were hazel, so beautiful, alive, capable of expressing both love and sullen hatred.

Without offering me a word of explanation, as if I were some higher being who understood everything without the need for explanation, she handed me a piece of paper. At that moment her whole face was radiant with the most naive, almost childlike exultation. I unfolded the letter. It was from a medical student, or someone like that, a terribly high-flown and flowery, but extremely polite declaration of love. I can't recall the precise wording, but I do remember very well that through the elevated style one could distinguish the kind of genuine feeling that cannot be feigned. When I had read it through I met her ardent, inquisitive and childishly impatient gaze. Her eyes were glued to my face as she impatiently waited to hear what I had to say. In a few hurried words, but somehow joyfully, almost proud of the fact, she explained that she had gone to a party at the house of 'some very, very nice people – *family people* – where they *still knew* nothing, absolutely nothing', as she was still fairly new there and only . . . but that she was far from deciding whether to stay but would definitely leave once she had repaid her debt . . . "So, this student had been there and danced with her the whole evening. He talked to her and it turned out that he had known her when they were children in Riga, that they'd played together, but that was a long time ago. And he'd known her parents, but knew absolutely nothing *about this*

and suspected nothing. And the very next day after the party
(three days ago) he had sent her that letter through the friend
who had gone to the party with her . . . and . . . well . . . that
was all."

When she had finished her story she dropped her sparkling
eyes rather bashfully.

Poor girl, she was keeping that student's letter as a treasure
and had run off to fetch this, her only treasure, reluctant that I
should leave without knowing that she was loved, honourably
and sincerely, that even *she* was spoken to respectfully. That
letter was certainly destined to lie in a box, without any consequences. But that didn't matter. I am certain she would treasure
it all her life, as her pride and justification and now, at this
moment, she had remembered that letter and fetched it in all
naivety to show off in front of me, to resurrect herself in my
eyes, so that I would praise her after seeing it. I said nothing,
pressed her hand and left. I was dying to get away . . . I walked
the whole way home, although the snow was still falling in
large, wet flakes. I was exhausted, crushed, perplexed. But the
truth was already shining through the perplexity. The vile truth!

VIII

However, it took some time before I was prepared to acknowledge that truth. Waking next morning after a few hours of
deep, leaden sleep and immediately mulling over all the events
of the previous day, I was even astonished at my *sentimentality*
with Liza and then at all those 'horrors and miseries of yesterday'. 'Phew, a fine attack of womanish nerves!' I thought. 'And
what possessed me to foist my address on her? What if she
came? Well, let her come, it doesn't matter . . .' But *evidently*
that wasn't the most important, the most urgent matter now:
what I needed to do was to hurry up and – at any price and as
soon as possible – to salvage my reputation in the eyes of
Zverkov and Simonov. That was the most important thing.
And in my frantic activity that morning I forgot all about Liza.

First of all I had to repay yesterday's debt to Simonov without further delay. I decided on a desperate measure: to borrow the entire fifteen roubles from Anton Antonych. Luckily, he was in the best of moods that morning and gave me the money the moment I asked. I was so delighted with this that as I signed the IOU with a somewhat jaunty air I *casually* informed him that the previous day I had been 'living it up with some friends at the Hôtel de Paris where we were seeing off an old friend, one might even say a childhood friend and – you know – a hard drinker, a spoilt darling, but of course of good family, very well off, with a brilliant career, witty, a good chap in fact, always intriguing with certain ladies – you know what I mean; we drank the extra "half dozen" and . . .' Well, no harm done. All this was spoken with the greatest ease, familiarity and smugness.

The moment I arrived home I wrote to Simonov.

To this day I am lost in admiration when I recall the truly gentlemanly, genial and frank tone of my letter. Deftly, nobly and – most importantly – without one superfluous word I had blamed myself for everything. I excused myself – 'if I still may be permitted to excuse myself' – by the fact, that, being completely unused to drink, the very first glass I had (allegedly) drunk before they arrived, while I was waiting for them in the Hôtel de Paris from five to six o'clock, had gone to my head. I apologized chiefly to Simonov and asked him to convey my apologies to all the others, especially to Zverkov, whom I vaguely remembered having insulted. I added that I would have called on all of them personally, but that my head was splitting and, most of all, I was deeply ashamed. I was particularly pleased with a certain 'lightness of touch', even verging on the casual (perfectly polite, however), which suddenly found expression through my pen and which gave them at once to understand better than any possible argument that I took a rather detached view of 'that beastly affair of yesterday'. By no means, not by any reckoning, was I finished outright as you're no doubt thinking, gentlemen, but on the contrary, I look upon the affair as any coolly self-respecting gentlemen ought. Yes, let bygones be bygones!

'Isn't there even a touch of marquis-like playfulness here?' I said admiringly, reading the letter over again. And all because I'm such an intellectually mature and educated person! Other men in my position wouldn't have known how to get themselves out of this mess, but just look how I've managed to extricate myself and now I can start living it up again – and all because I'm a 'mature and educated man of our time'. Yes indeed, very likely it was all because of yesterday's alcohol. Hm . . . well, no . . . not because of alcohol. I didn't touch a drop of vodka between five and six while I was waiting for them. I'd told Simonov a lie – I'd lied shamelessly. And even now I don't feel ashamed . . .

Anyway, to hell with it! The important thing was that I'd got out of it.

I put six roubles in the letter, sealed it and asked Apollon to take it to Simonov. Learning that there was money in the letter, Apollon became more respectful and agreed to go. Towards evening I went out for a stroll. My head was still aching and going round from last night. But the more evening drew on and the thicker the twilight grew, the more my impressions changed and grew muddled – and after them my thoughts. Something deep inside me, in the very depths of my heart and conscience, refused to die and proclaimed itself in burning anguish. For the most part I knocked around the most crowded shopping streets – the Meshchanskaya, the Sadovaya, and near the Yusupov Gardens.[39] I have always been particularly fond of strolling along these streets at dusk, just when crowds of workers and tradespeople returning home from their daily labours are at their thickest, their faces careworn to the point of anger. It was precisely that common bustle, the blatantly prosaic nature of it all, that appealed to me On this occasion all that jostling in the streets only irritated me even more. I could no longer cope, I couldn't find a way out. Something was rising, constantly and painfully rising in my soul, and wouldn't calm down. Positively distraught, I went home. It was as if I had some crime weighing on my conscience.

The thought that Liza might come was a constant torment. I found it strange that of all the memories of yesterday it was hers that particularly tormented me, somehow quite separately. By evening I had managed to forget all the rest, to shrug it off, and I still remained satisfied with my letter to Simonov. But even here I didn't really feel so very satisfied. It was as if I were tormenting myself with Liza alone. 'What if she comes?' I couldn't stop thinking. 'Ah well, let her come. Hm. Only, the rotten thing is, she'll see how I live, for instance. Yesterday I made myself out to be such a . . . hero . . . but now, hm! It's really shocking, though, the way I've let myself go. The flat has such a poverty-stricken look. And how could I possibly have gone out to dinner yesterday in a suit like that! And my oilskin sofa with the stuffing sticking out! And my dressing-gown with which I can't even cover myself up! What rags . . . And she'll see everything – and she'll see Apollon. That swine's bound to insult her. Just to be rude to me he'll start picking on her. And as usual I'll play the coward of course, shuffling around in front of her and wrapping my dressing-gown skirts around me; I'll start smiling and I'll tell lies. Ugh! How vile! And that's not the vilest thing! There's something more important, even viler, even more despicable! Yes, more despicable! Again, once again, I'll don that dishonest, lying mask! . . .'

Having arrived at this thought I simply flared up. 'Why dishonest? What's dishonest about it? I was being quite sincere in what I said yesterday. I remember, my feelings were genuine too. I only wanted to arouse noble sentiments in her . . . if she cried a little that was a good thing, it was bound to have a salutary effect . . .'

All the same, in no way could I rest easy.

The whole of that evening, after I had returned home, even after nine o'clock, when I reckoned that there was no chance of her coming, the thought of her still haunted me and for the main part I remembered her in exactly the same situation. To be precise, one moment from all that had happened yesterday stood out particularly vividly in my memory: that was when I struck a match and saw her pale, distorted face, with that martyred look in her eyes. How pathetic, how unnatural, how twisted her smile had been at that moment! But I couldn't know then that fifteen years later I would still go on picturing Liza to myself with precisely the same twisted, superfluous smile she wore at that moment.

Next day I was again prepared to consider the whole thing nonsense, the result of frayed nerves and above all as an *exaggeration*. I had always acknowledged that as my weak spot and sometimes I feared it greatly. 'I keep exaggerating everything and that's my downfall,' I would repeat to myself hourly. But 'however, Liza will very likely come all the same' – that was the refrain with which all my reasoning invariably concluded at the time. I was so terribly anxious that occasionally I would fly into a mad rage. 'She'll come, she's bound to come!' I would exclaim, dashing round the room, 'if not today then tomorrow and she'll find me!' For that's the typical damned romanticism of all these *pure hearts*! Oh, the loathsomeness, the stupidity, the narrow-mindedness of these 'vile, sentimental souls'! Well, how can she not understand, how is it she doesn't even appear to understand! . . . ?' But at this point I would stop, feeling greatly confused.

'And how few words, how few words were really necessary,' I thought in passing, 'how little need there was of the idyllic (and such an artificial, bookish and contrived idyll at that) in order immediately to shape a human being's entire soul the way I wanted. That's chastity for you! That's virgin soil for you!'

At times I considered going to see her myself, to 'tell her everything' and beg her not to come and see me. But at the very thought of it such anger would seethe within me that I could have crushed that 'damned' Liza if she were suddenly to appear at my side. I would have insulted her, humiliated her, driven her away, struck her!

However, one day passed, then another, a third and still she didn't come and I began to relax. I became particularly cheerful and carefree after nine o'clock; sometimes I even began having dreams – and rather sweet ones at that! for example: 'I'm saving Liza precisely by virtue of the fact that she's coming to see me and I'm talking to her . . . I'm developing her, educating her. Finally I notice that she loves me, loves me passionately. I pretend not to understand (I don't know why I'm pretending, though – probably for a little embellishment). Finally, in complete confusion, beautiful, trembling and sobbing, she throws herself at my feet and tells me that I am her saviour and that she loves me more than anything else in the world. I am amazed, but . . . "Liza," I say, "surely you don't think I haven't noticed that you love me? I saw everything, I guessed, but I didn't dare to be the first to encroach upon your heart, because I influenced you and was afraid that you would deliberately force yourself to respond to my love out of gratitude, that you would try to force emotions that possibly don't exist. But I didn't want that since that is . . . despotism . . . That's indelicate" (well, in short, here I am blathering away with some variety of European, George Sandish, inexpressibly noble finesse . . .). "But now, now – you are mine, you are my creation, pure and beautiful . . . you are my lovely wife.

> And boldly and freely
> Enter my house, mistress of all!" [40]

And then we start living happily ever after, go abroad, etc, etc. In brief, the whole thing became so vile for me that I would end up by sticking out my tongue at myself.

'And they won't let her out, "the slut",' I thought. 'After all, I don't think they let them go out very much, least of all in the evenings (for some reason I invariably felt that she would come in the evening, at exactly seven o'clock). However, she did say that she wasn't entirely under their thumb and that she had special privileges; that means – hm! What the hell, she'll come, she's bound to come!'

Fortunately at that time Apollon was there to distract me with his boorishness. He tried my patience to the limit. He was the plague of my life, a scourge visited upon me by Providence. For years on end he and I had been constantly at loggerheads and I hated him. God, how I hated him! I don't think I've ever in my life hated anyone as much as him, especially at certain moments. He was a pompous, middle-aged man who did occasional tailoring. For some reason he despised me, even beyond all measure, and treated me with intolerable condescension. However, he looked down on everyone. You only had to

take one look at that sleek, flaxen head, at that quiff greased
with vegetable oil that stuck up over his forehead, at that solid
mouth always pursed into a 'V' shape, and you felt you were
in the presence of some creature perpetually bristling with self-
assurance. He was a pedant in the highest degree, the greatest
pedant I had ever met on this earth; and besides that, his vanity
was perhaps worthy only of an Alexander of Macedon. He was
enamoured of every single one of his buttons, every single
fingernail – oh yes, truly infatuated – that was him in a nutshell!
He treated me utterly despotically, spoke to me very seldom
and if he did sometimes bring himself to glance at me, it was
with a firm, majestically self-assured and invariably supercilious
look that sometimes drove me into a frenzy. He performed his
duties in a way that suggested he was doing me an enormous
favour. However, he hardly ever lifted a finger for me and
didn't even consider himself in the least obliged to do anything.
Without a shadow of doubt, he looked upon me as the greatest
fool on earth and if he 'retained me' it was solely because he
could receive his monthly salary from me. He had agreed 'to
do nothing' for me, for seven roubles a month. Many sins will
be forgiven me for his sake. Sometimes my hatred reached such
fever pitch that his walk alone almost sent me into convulsions.
But the thing I loathed most of all was the way he lisped. His
tongue was a little too long, or something like that, so that he
was always lisping and hissing, of which he seemed inordinately
proud, imagining that it lent him an extraordinary degree of
distinction. He spoke in soft, measured tones, his arms folded
behind his back and his eyes fixed on the ground. It particularly
infuriated me when he started reading from the psalter behind
the partition. I endured many a battle over those recitations.
He was passionately fond of reading in the evening in his quiet,
drawling voice, as if he were chanting over a corpse. Curiously
that's what he ended up doing: now he's employed to read
psalms over the dead and he also exterminates rats and makes
boot polish. But at that time I couldn't dismiss him, as his
existence seemed chemically fused to mine. Besides, on no
account would he have agreed to leave. I couldn't live in fur-
nished rooms: my flat was my private property, my shell, my

container, in which I hid myself from all humanity, and Apollon, the devil knows why, seemed to be part and parcel of that flat and for seven whole years I couldn't get rid of him.

To keep back his wages, for example, for two or even three days, was out of the question. He would have made such a fuss that I shouldn't have known what to do with myself. But in those days I was feeling so embittered towards everyone that I decided for some reason or other to *punish* Apollon by stopping his wages for a fortnight. I had been intending to do this for a long time, for two years, simply to show him that he should not presume to lord it over me and that I could always stop his wages if I wanted to. I proposed not to mention it to him and even deliberately remained silent in order to conquer his pride and compel him to be first to raise the subject of wages. Then I would take all seven roubles out of a drawer, show him that I had them and was putting them aside because 'I didn't want to, I didn't want to, I simply didn't want to pay him his wages because *that's what I wanted*', because those were 'the Master's wishes', because he was disrespectful, because he was an oaf; but if he were to ask me politely, then I might perhaps relent and pay him; if not, he'd have to wait another fortnight, three weeks – he'd have to wait a whole month . . .

But for all my anger he still got the better of me. I couldn't even hold out for four days. He would begin the way he always did in similar cases, as there *had* been similar cases before; it had all been tried and tested (let me point out that I knew all this in advance, I knew his underhand tactics by heart), that's to say: he would start by keeping his extremely severe glance riveted on me, without dropping it, for several minutes on end, especially when he let me in or out of the flat. If, for instance, I didn't flinch and pretended not to notice these stares, he would, still maintaining his silence, embark on further torments. Suddenly, for no earthly reason, he would glide quietly into my room while I was walking about or reading, stop by the door, put one hand behind his back, part his legs and fix his stare on me – a stare not so much severe as highly contemptuous. If I should suddenly ask what he wanted, he would say nothing, continue staring straight at me for a few more seconds and with those peculiarly pursed lips and a very significant look, slowly turn round and slowly retire to his room. Two hours later he would suddenly emerge and appear before me as before. It sometimes happened that I was too incensed to ask him what he wanted, but I would simply raise my head sharply and imperiously, and then I too would stare back at him. And so we would stare at each other, for about two minutes; finally, slowly and pompously, he would turn round and retire for another two hours.

If this still failed to make me see reason and I continued to be rebellious, he would suddenly start sighing as he looked at me, drawing long, deep sighs as if by them alone he were gauging the whole depth of my moral decline, and needless to say this always ended in his complete victory over me: I would rage and scream, but I would still be compelled to do whatever had to be done.

On this occasion the usual manoeuvre of 'withering looks' had barely begun when I immediately lost my temper and flew at him in a fit of fury: I was exasperated enough as it was.

'Stop!' I shouted in a wild frenzy when, slowly and silently, one hand behind his back, he turned round to retire to his room. 'Stop! Come back, come back, I'm talking to you!' And I must have bellowed so unnaturally that he turned back and started eyeing me with some amazement. However, he still wouldn't say a word and it was this that really made me see red.

'How dare you come in here without permission and look at me like that! Answer me!'

But after calmly surveying me for half a minute he again started turning away.

'Stop!' I roared, running over to him. 'Don't move! That's it! Now answer me: why have you come in here to gawk at me like that?'

'If you have any orders for me right now it's my duty to carry them out,' he replied after another silence, with his soft, measured lisp, raising his eyebrows and calmly shifting his head from one shoulder to the other – all this with the most maddening composure.

'No, it's not that, that's not what I'm asking you about, you torturer!' I cried, shaking with anger. 'I'll tell you myself, you torturer, why you came here. You see that I'm not paying you your wages and since you're too proud to come and ask for them that's why you come in here to punish me with those inane stares of yours, to torment me. You do not sus-pe-ect for one moment, you torturer, how stupid it is, how stupid, stupid, stupid, stupid!'

He was again about to turn away without speaking, but I grabbed him.

'Listen!' I shouted. 'Here's the money. Look – look! Here it is (I took it out of the table drawer), all seven roubles, but you won't receive them, you won't re-ce-ive them until you come to me cap in hand, admitting your guilt and begging forgiveness. Do you hear me?!'

'But that can never be!' he replied with a kind of unnatural self-assurance.

'Oh yes it can!' I shouted. 'I give you my word of honour it can!'

'But I've no reason to ask for forgiveness,' he continued as if he simply hadn't noticed my shouts, 'because you called me "torturer" and for that I could always go along to the police station and put in a complaint.'

'Go then! Go and complain!' I roared. 'Go right away, this minute, this second! But you're a torturer all the same. Torturer, torturer!' But he merely glanced at me, then wheeled round, turned a deaf ear to my adjurations and sailed off to his quarters without once looking back.

'If it weren't for Liza none of this would have happened,' I said to myself. And then, after standing still for a moment, I followed him to his room behind the screen, solemnly and with dignity, but with my heart beating slowly and violently.

'Apollon!' I said with calm deliberation, although I was choking with anger. 'Go now, without a moment's delay and fetch the local police inspector.'

Meanwhile he had seated himself at his table, donned his spectacles and applied himself to some sewing. But on hearing my command, he suddenly snorted with laughter.

'Now, go this minute – go, or you can't imagine what will happen!'

'You must be truly out of your mind,' he remarked without even looking up, with that same slow lisp and continuing to thread his needle. 'Whoever heard of someone going to report himself to the police? And as for scaring me, you're wasting your energy, because nothing will come of it.'

'Go!!' I screeched, grabbing him by the collar. I felt I was on the verge of hitting him.

But I hadn't heard the entrance hall door quietly and slowly open all of a sudden and a figure entered and stopped to stare at us in bewilderment. I took one look, was stricken with shame and rushed off to my room. There, clutching my hair with both hands, I leant my head against the wall and froze in that position.

Two minutes later I heard Apollon's slow footsteps.

'There's a certain *person* asking for you,' he said, giving me a particularly severe look and then he stood aside to make way for Liza. He didn't want to leave and kept staring at us sarcastically.

'Get out! Get out!' I ordered, losing all self-control.

At that moment my clock exerted itself, wheezed and struck seven.

IX

> And boldly and freely
> Enter my house, mistress of all . . .
> From the same poem

I stood before her, crushed, disgraced, sickeningly embarrassed – and, I think, smiling and making a concerted effort to wrap the skirts of my ragged old quilted dressing-gown around me – well, in every respect, exactly as I imagined shortly before, when my spirits were so low. After hovering over us for about two minutes Apollon went out, but I didn't feel any easier. And the worst of it was that she too suddenly became embarrassed, to a degree I had never even expected. Needless to say, it was from looking at me.

'Sit down,' I said mechanically, bringing a chair up to the table for her. She sat down immediately, obediently, all eyes, and she was evidently expecting something from me there and then. The naivety of this expectancy drove me into a frenzy but I controlled myself.

At this point I should have pretended not to notice anything, as if everything were normal, but she ... And I vaguely sensed that she would make me pay dearly *for all this*.

'You've caught me in a strange situation, Liza,' I began, stammering and fully aware that this was exactly the wrong way to begin. 'No, no, don't think badly of it!' I cried, seeing that she had suddenly blushed, 'I'm not ashamed of my poverty ... On the contrary, I look upon it with pride. I'm poor but honourable ... It's possible to be poor and honourable ...' I muttered. 'However ... would you like some tea?'

'No.' she began.

'Wait a moment!'

I leapt up and dashed off to get Apollon. I had to disappear somewhere.

'Apollon,' I whispered in a feverish patter, tossing him the seven roubles that had been in my fist the whole time. 'Here's your wages. You see, I'm paying you, but in return you must save me. Now run down to the pub right away and bring some tea and ten dry biscuits. If you refuse you'll make me the unhappiest of mortals. You don't know what kind of woman she is ... That's the whole point! Perhaps you're thinking things ... But you don't know what kind of woman she is ... !'

Apollon, who had already settled down to his work and had donned his spectacles again, without putting down his needle, at first squinted at the money in silence; then, ignoring me completely and still without a word, carried on fiddling with the thread, still trying to get it through the eye of the needle. I waited for about three minutes, standing before him with my arms folded à la Napoléon. My temples were damp with sweat and I sensed my face was pale. But, thank God, just looking at me must have made him feel sorry. Having finished with his thread, he slowly got up, slowly moved his chair back, slowly took off his spectacles, slowly counted the money and finally left the room after asking me over his shoulder whether he should fetch two full teas. As I went back to Liza the thought occurred to me of simply running away, just as I was, in my old dressing-gown, wherever my feet carried me – and come what may.

I sat down again. Liza looked at me anxiously. For a few minutes neither of us spoke.

'I'll kill him!' I suddenly shrieked, banging my fist so violently on the table that the ink splashed out of the inkwell.

'Ah, what are you saying?' she cried, shuddering.

'I'll kill him, I'll kill him!' I shouted, again banging on the table in a terrible rage, at the same time terribly aware how stupid it was to get into such a rage . . .

'You don't know how he tortures me, Liza. He's my executioner . . . Now he's gone out for some biscuits, he . . .'

And suddenly I burst into tears. It was a genuine attack of nerves. How ashamed I felt in between my fits of sobbing, but I was powerless to restrain them. She took fright.

'What's the matter with you? What's wrong?' she cried, fussing around me.

'Water, give me some water . . . it's over there,' I muttered feebly, aware, however, that I could very well manage without water and stop those feeble mutterings. But I was play-acting, as they say, to save face, although the nervous attack was real enough.

She gave me some water and looked at me with a lost expression. At that moment Apollon brought in the tea. This ordinary, prosaic tea suddenly struck me as so inappropriate and miserable after all that had happened that I blushed. Liza even glanced at Apollon in fright. He went out without so much as looking at us.

'Liza, do you despise me?' I asked, staring intently at her and trembling with impatience to discover what she was thinking.

She became flustered and was at a loss for a reply.

'Drink your tea!' I said angrily. I was furious with myself, but of course I had to make her suffer for it. Suddenly terrible anger towards her boiled up within me. I really think I could have killed her. To take revenge on her I vowed to myself not to say one word to her the whole time. 'She's to blame for everything,' I thought.

Our silence had already lasted about five minutes. The tea stood on the table but we didn't make any attempt to touch it. I had reached the point where I deliberately refused to begin first in order to make things even harder for her; for her to begin would have been awkward.

Several times she glanced at me in sad bewilderment. I remained stubbornly silent. Of course, the principal sufferer was myself, since I fully recognized the sickening meanness of my stupid anger and at the same time in no way could I restrain myself.

'I want ... to get away from that place ... altogether ...' she began in an attempt to break the silence somehow. But poor girl! That was precisely *not* the thing to bring up at a moment that was stupid enough already – and particularly to a stupid man like myself. My heart even ached with pity at her awkwardness and needless honesty. But something very nasty immediately stifled all pity within me. Indeed, it even spurred me on all the more. To hell with the whole world! Another five minutes went by.

'I'm not disturbing you, am I?' she began timidly and barely audibly, starting to get up.

But as soon as I saw this first flash of wounded dignity I simply shook with rage and immediately erupted.

'Why have you come here? Please tell me that,' I began, choking with anger and without considering even the logical sequence of my words. I wanted to get it all out at once, in one salvo, and I couldn't even be bothered about where to begin.

'Why did you come? Answer me! Answer me!' I shouted, beside myself. 'I'll tell you why you came, my dear woman. You came because I spoke *words of sympathy* to you the other night. Well, now you've gone soft and want to hear 'words of sympathy' again. Well, let me tell you that I was laughing at you then. And I'm laughing at you now. Why are you trembling? Yes, I was laughing! I'd been insulted before at a dinner by that same crowd who arrived before me. I came to your place intending to give one of them – an officer – a good

thrashing. I wasn't successful, as he'd already left. So, I needed
to vent my anger on someone because of that insult, to get my
own back, and then you turned up, so I vented my anger on
you and had a good laugh about it. I'd been humiliated, so I
too wanted to humiliate someone. I'd been treated like a door-
mat, so I wanted to show my power ... That's how it was, but
you were thinking that I'd come specially to rescue you, weren't
you? Isn't that what you were thinking? Isn't it?'

I knew that she was perhaps getting confused and wouldn't
grasp every detail; but I also knew that she understood the
essence of what I was saying perfectly. And so she did. She
turned white as a sheet, tried to speak, but her lips became
painfully distorted and she slumped back into her chair as if
felled by an axe. And all the time after this she listened to me
open-mouthed, wide-eyed, trembling with terrible fear. The
cynicism, the cynicism of my words had crushed her ...

'To save you!' I continued, leaping from my chair and running up and down the room in front of her, 'to save you from
what? Well, perhaps I'm worse than you. Why didn't you fling
it all back in my mug when I was preaching to you? You asked:
'Why did you come here? To teach us morality?' It was power,
power that I wanted then and I wanted some sport, I needed
your tears, your humiliation, your hysterics – that's what I
needed then! But I myself couldn't go through with it because
I'm trash, I panicked and the devil knows why I was stupid
enough to give you my address. Later, even before I got home,
I was cursing you to high heaven, because of that address. I
really did hate you because I'd lied to you then. Because I only
wanted to have a little game with words, to fill my head with
dreams – but do you know what I really wanted? For you to
vanish into thin air, that's what! I need peace and quiet. And
in order not to be disturbed I'd sell the whole world right now
for a copeck. Should the world vanish or should I go without
my tea? I'm telling you, the whole world can vanish as long as
I always have my tea to drink. Did you know that or not? What
I do know is that I'm a scoundrel, a cad, an egotist, a loafer.
Oh yes, for the past three days I've been shaking for fear that
you might come. And do you know what particularly worried

me during those three days? That I'd made myself out to be such a great hero before you then – and that suddenly you'd find me here in this shabby old dressing-gown, destitute and loathsome. I told you just now that I wasn't ashamed of my poverty. Well, please understand that I *am* ashamed, ashamed of it more than anything. I fear it more than anything, more than if I'd stolen something, because I'm so vain – it's as if I've been flayed alive and the very air causes me pain. Surely you must realize even now that I'll never forgive you for having caught me in this wretched old dressing-gown, just when I was hurling myself like a vicious little cur at Apollon. The saviour, the former hero, flying like a mangy, shaggy mongrel at his servant – and he just laughs at him! And as for those tears which I couldn't hold back just before, like some old crone who's been put to shame – I shall never forgive you those! Nor will I ever forgive *you* for what I'm confessing to you now! Oh yes, you – you alone must answer for everything, now that you've turned up, because I'm a cad, the vilest, most ridiculous, pettiest, stupidest, most jealous of all the worms on earth, not one jot better than me but who, the devil knows why, are never embarrassed. But all my life I'll be insulted by any little nit because that's what my character's like! And what's it to do with me if you don't understand a word of all this! And why should it concern me whether you perish in that place or not? And do you realize that now, having said all this, how I shall hate you for having been here and listened to me? After all, it's only once in a lifetime that a man speaks his mind like this and then only if he's hysterical! What more do you want? Why are you still hanging around after all this, tormenting me by not leaving?'

But then something very odd happened.

I was so used to thinking and imagining things as they happened in books and picturing everything in the world as I myself had previously created it in my dreams, that at first I couldn't understand that strange event. What happened was this: Liza, whom I had so humiliated and crushed, understood a lot more than I imagined. She understood from all this what a woman will always understand first and foremost if she loves sincerely, namely, that I myself was unhappy.

At first the terrified and wronged expression on her face turned into sorrowful amazement. But when I began to call myself a cad and a rotter and my tears started flowing (I had delivered all of my tirade in tears) her whole face was distorted by some kind of convulsion. She wanted to get up, to stop me; but when I had finished it wasn't to my cries of 'Why are you here, why don't you leave?' that she paid attention, but to the fact that it must have been extremely hard for me to say all I had said. And she was so dispirited, poor thing; she considered herself infinitely beneath me. But why should she feel animosity and take offence? Suddenly, on some kind of irresistible impulse, she leapt from her chair and then, her whole body straining towards me – timidly, though, and without daring to move from her seat – she held out her arms to me ... At this point my heart too turned over. Then she suddenly rushed towards me, threw her arms around my neck and burst into tears. I couldn't hold myself back either and sobbed as I had never sobbed before ...

'They won't let me ... I can't be ... kind!' I barely managed to say and then I reached the sofa, fell face downwards on it and sobbed really hysterically for a quarter of an hour. She pressed herself against me, embraced me and seemed to freeze in that embrace.

All the same, the point was that my hysterics could not last for ever. And now (I'm writing the whole sickening truth), as I lay face down, pressing hard against the sofa, my face buried in my cheap leather cushion, I began gradually, as if from a distance, involuntarily but irrepressibly, to feel that it would be awkward if I were to raise my head now and look Liza straight in the eye. What was I ashamed of? I don't know, but I was ashamed. And the thought also entered my overwrought brain that our roles had now been completely reversed, that she was the heroine and that I was just such a humiliated and crushed creature as she had appeared to me that night – four days before ... And all this occurred to me just when I was lying face down on the sofa!

Good God! Could I have envied her even then?

I don't know, to this day I still cannot decide, but then I was of course even less able to understand it than I am now. Without power and tyranny over someone I cannot survive. But ... but reasoning won't solve anything, so there's no point in reasoning.

However, I pulled myself together and raised my head slightly – I had to raise it some time or other ... And then, I am convinced of it to this day, it was precisely because I was ashamed of looking at her that another feeling was suddenly kindled in my heart and flared up ... a feeling of mastery and possession. My eyes gleamed with passion and I squeezed her hand hard. How I hated her and how powerfully I was drawn to her at that moment! One feeling reinforced the other. This was almost tantamount to revenge ... ! At first her face expressed what seemed to be perplexity, perhaps even fear, but only for a fleeting instant. Rapturously and fervently she embraced me.

X

A quarter of an hour later I was rushing up and down the room in frantic impatience, constantly going over to the screens and peeping at Liza through the narrow gap between them. She was sitting on the floor, leaning her head on the bed and she must have been crying. But she was not leaving and it was this that irritated me. This time she knew everything. I had insulted her definitively, but there's no point in telling that story. She had guessed that my fit of passion was indeed revenge, a fresh humiliation for her, and that to my former, almost aimless hatred there was now added a *personal, jealous* hatred of her ... However, I'm not claiming that she exactly understood all of this. On the other hand, she understood well enough that I was a loathsome person and, most important, incapable of loving her.

I know that people will tell me that it's incredible – incredible to be as spiteful and stupid as I am. And perhaps they will add that it was incredible not to fall in love with her, or at least appreciate her love. But why incredible? Firstly, I was incapable of falling in love because, I repeat, to me love meant tyrannizing and being morally superior. All my life I've been unable even to imagine any other kind of love and I've reached the point where I sometimes think that love consists in the right, voluntarily given by the loved one, to be tyrannized. Even in my underground dreams I couldn't conceive of love as other than a struggle that I invariably embarked upon with hatred and finished with moral subjugation, after which I couldn't imagine what to do with the vanquished victim. And in fact the incredible thing here is that I had already managed to become so morally corrupt and had grown so accustomed to 'real life' that only just now had I thought of reproaching her and putting her to shame for coming to hear my 'words of sympathy'. And I didn't guess that she hadn't come to hear words of sympathy at all, but to love me, since for women love comprises their total resurrection, their total salvation from any kind of ruin, their total regeneration and cannot manifest itself in any other kind of way. However, I no longer hated her so much as I scurried around the room, peeping through the gap between the screens. I only felt it intolerably oppressive with her being there. I wanted her to disappear. I longed for 'peace', I wanted to be left alone in my underground. I had become so unused to 'real life' that it crushed me until I even found it hard to breathe.

But a few more minutes passed and still she didn't get up, as if she were in a trance. I was shameless enough to knock gently on the screen to remind her . . . Suddenly she roused herself, leapt from her place and hurriedly started looking for her shawl, her hat, her fur coat, as if escaping from me somewhere. Two minutes later she slowly came out from behind the screens and gave me a pained look. I produced a spiteful smile, that was forced however, *for the sake of decency*, and turned away from her stare.

'Goodbye,' she said, heading towards the door.

I suddenly ran after her, grabbed her hand, unclasped it, put something into it and then clasped it again. Then I immediately turned away and rushed as fast as I could to the far corner so that at least I wouldn't see . . .

At that moment I wanted to tell a lie, to write that I had done it unintentionally, without thinking, while beside myself, out of stupidity. But I don't want to lie and therefore I say straight out that I unclasped her hand and put something into it . . . out of spite. The idea had occurred to me when I was running up and down the room while she was sitting behind the screens. But what I can say for certain is this: although I committed this act of cruelty deliberately, it came not from the heart but from my wicked head. This cruelty was so artificial, so cerebral, so deliberately contrived, so *bookish*, that I myself couldn't sustain it even for a minute – first I dashed into the corner in order not to see, then, ashamed and desperate, I rushed after Liza. I opened the hall door and listened hard.

'Liza! Liza!' I called down the stairs, timidly though, in an undertone . . .

There was no answer and I thought I could hear her footsteps on the lower stairs.

'Liza!' I shouted, louder this time.

No reply. But at that moment I could hear the heavy glazed street door creak open and slam shut. The noise carried up the staircase.

She had gone. Hesitantly, I returned to my room. I felt utterly miserable.

I stopped at the table near the chair where she had been sitting and gazed vacantly in front of me. About a minute passed, then suddenly I trembled all over: right before me on the table I saw . . . in brief, I saw a crumpled, blue five-rouble note, the very one that I had thrust into her hand a moment before. It was the *same one*: it couldn't have been any other, as there was no other in the house. She must have managed to fling it on the table just as I was dashing to the opposite corner.

What then? I might have expected her to do that. Might have expected? No. I was such a egotist and in actual fact had so little respect for others that I couldn't imagine that she would do such a thing. This was more than I could bear. A moment later I rushed like a madman to get dressed, throwing on whatever I could in my frantic hurry and then rushing headlong after

her. She hadn't gone more than a couple of hundred yards when
I ran out into the street.

It was quiet and the snow was coming down in large flakes,
falling almost perpendicularly and spreading a soft white
blanket over the pavement and the deserted street. There were
no passers-by, not a sound could be heard. The street lamps
glimmered mournfully and uselessly. I ran about two hundred
paces to the crossroads and stopped.

'Where had she gone? And why am I running after her? Why?
To go down on my knees, to break into repentant sobs, to kiss
her feet, to beg her forgiveness? That was just what I wanted.
My heart was being torn to shreds and never, never shall I recall
that moment with indifference. But why – why?' I thought.
'Surely I'd hate her, perhaps tomorrow, precisely because I
kissed her feet today? Could I really have made her happy?
Surely I'd recognized my own true worth again today, for the
hundredth time? Surely I'd torment the life out of her!'

I stood in the snow, peering into the dull haze and thought
about it.

'And isn't it better, wouldn't it be better,' I daydreamed later
at home, trying to deaden the sharp pain in my heart with my
fantasies, wouldn't it be better if she took that insult to her
pride away with her for ever? After all, an insult is purification;
it is the most caustic and painful form of consciousness!
Tomorrow I would have defiled her soul and wearied her heart
by my presence. But now that insult will never die within her
and however vile the filth that is in store for her, that insult will
elevate and purify her ... through hatred ... hm ... and perhaps through forgiveness. However, will all this make life any
the easier for her? And in fact I'll now pose one idle question:
which is better – cheap happiness or exalted suffering? Tell me,
which is better?

All this dimly appeared to me as I sat at home that evening,
half-dead with spiritual pain. I have never endured such suffering and repentance. But really, could there ever have been even
the slightest doubt, when I ran out of the flat, that I would turn
back halfway and go home? Never again did I meet Liza, nor
did I hear what became of her. I will add that for a long time I

remained pleased with my *windy rhetoric* about the usefulness of insults and hatred – despite the fact that I myself became almost ill with anguish at the time.

And even now, after so many years, all this comes back as a *nasty* memory. Many things are now nasty memories, but ... shouldn't I really end the 'Notes' here? It seems that writing them in the first place was a mistake. At least, I felt ashamed the whole time I was writing this *tale*. That means it is not literature, but corrective punishment. For example, telling a long story about how I missed out on life in my corner through moral decay, through lack of human contact, through losing the habit of living and through my narcissistic, underground spite – God, that's of no interest! A novel needs a hero but here I've *deliberately* gathered together all the features of an anti-hero and the main thing is, all this will produce a most unpleasant impression, since we have all lost touch with real life, we are all cripples, each one of us to a greater or lesser degree. We have even become so unaccustomed to living that we sometimes feel a kind of loathing for 'real life' and that's why we cannot bear to be reminded of it. You see, we have reached the point where we look upon real life almost as a burden, almost as servitude, and we are all agreed among ourselves that it's better to live according to books. And what are all of us sometimes rummaging around for, why are we so capricious, what is it we are begging for? We ourselves don't know. It would be even worse for us if our capricious requests were granted. Well, just try, give us more independence, for intance, loosen the bonds of any one of us, broaden our field of activity, relax surveillance and we ... yes, I assure you we should all immediately be begging for that surveillance to be reimposed. I know that you will perhaps be angry with me because of this, you'll stamp your feet and say: 'You are speaking of yourself alone and your underground misery, so don't you dare say *all of us*.' But excuse me, gentlemen, I'm not trying to justify myself by this *all of usness*. Strictly speaking, as far as I'm concerned, I've merely carried to extremes in my life things that you've never had the courage even to take halfway and what's more you've interpreted your cowardice as common sense and found comfort in deceiving yourselves. So perhaps I'll prove to be 'more alive' than you. And just take a closer look. After all, we don't even know where this 'living' life is lived these days, what it is or what its name is. Leave us to our own devices, without our books, and we'll immediately get into a muddle and lose our way – we shan't know what side to take, where to place our allegiance, what to love and what to hate, what to respect and what to despise. We even find it a burden being human beings – human beings with our *own* real flesh and blood; we are ashamed of it, consider it a disgrace and are forever striving to become some kind of imaginary generalized human beings. We are stillborn and we have long ceased to be begotten of living fathers – and this we find increasingly pleasing. We are acquiring a taste for it. Soon we'll devise a way of being somehow born from an idea. But that's enough: I don't want to write any more from 'The Underground . . .'

On the other hand, the 'Notes' of this purveyor of paradoxes do not end here. He couldn't help continuing with them. But we also feel that here we might call a halt.

THE DOUBLE

A Petersburg Poem

CHAPTER I

It was a little before eight o'clock in the morning when Titular Counsellor[1] Yakov Petrovich Golyadkin awoke after a long sleep, yawned, stretched and finally opened his eyes wide. However, for about two minutes he lay motionless on his bed like a man not yet entirely certain if he has woken up or is still asleep, if everything around him was now actually happening or was simply a continuation of his chaotic daydreaming. But soon Mr Golyadkin's senses began to take in more clearly and distinctly their normal, everyday impressions. The dirty-green, grimy, dusty walls of his little room, his mahogany chest of drawers, his imitation mahogany chairs, his red-painted table, his sofa upholstered with reddish oilskin patterned with tiny green flowers, and finally the clothing he had hastily discarded the night before and thrown in a heap on the sofa glanced familiarly at him. And finally that foul, murky, dreary autumn day, peeping into his room through the dim windows with such an angry, sour look that Mr Golyadkin no longer had any doubts whatsoever that he was lying in bed, in his own fourth-floor flat, in a huge tenement block in Shestilavochnaya Street,[2] in the capital city of St Petersburg and not in some distant fairy realm. After making such a momentous discovery, Mr Golyadkin convulsively closed his eyes as if feeling regret for his recent slumbers and wishing to recall them if only for one brief moment. But a minute later, he leapt out of bed in one bound, having in all probability finally hit upon the idea around which his scattered and thoroughly disorganized thoughts had so far been revolving. Once out of bed he immediately ran over to a small round mirror that stood on the chest of drawers.

Although the sleepy, weak-sighted countenance and somewhat balding head reflected there were so insignificant as to command no attention at first glance, its owner was obviously perfectly satisfied with all he saw in the mirror. 'A fine thing it would be,' said Mr Golyadkin under his breath, 'a fine thing it would be if there were something not quite right with me today – if, for example, some kind of unwanted pimple had popped out up, or something else just as unpleasant. However, it's not too bad. So far so good.' Positively delighted that all was well, Mr Golyadkin replaced the mirror and, although he was barefoot and still wearing the same apparel in which he usually retired for the night, ran to the window and started anxiously searching for something in the courtyard that was overlooked by the windows of his flat. Evidently what he discovered in the courtyard was also to his entire satisfaction; his face lit up with a complacent smile. After first taking a peep behind the partition into his servant Petrushka's cubby-hole and convincing himself that he wasn't there, he tiptoed over to the table, unlocked one of the drawers, rummaged around in a far corner and finally extracted from beneath some old, yellowing papers and various rubbish, a worn, green wallet, cautiously opened it and carefully and delightedly peered into its furthest, most secret compartment. Probably the bundle of nice green, grey, blue, red and other brightly coloured banknotes[3] looked at Mr Golyadkin approvingly and cordially as his face was radiant as he placed the open wallet before him on the table and vigorously rubbed his hands in a manner that indicated the greatest satisfaction. At length he drew out his comforting bundle of banknotes and, what's more, for the hundredth time since the previous day started counting them, carefully smoothing out each note between thumb and index finger. 'Seven hundred and fifty roubles in notes!' he finally murmured in a half-whisper, 'seven hundred and fifty roubles ... a tidy sum! A most agreeable sum!' he continued in a voice that was trembling and somewhat weakened by pleasure, squeezing the wad of notes and smiling significantly. 'A most agreeable sum! An agreeable sum for anyone! I'd like to see the man for whom that might be a trifling sum! A man could go far with a sum like that ...'

'But what's going on here?' wondered Mr Golyadkin. 'Where's that Petrushka got to?' Still in the same apparel, he took another look behind the partition: again there was no sign of Petrushka, only the samovar that had been set on the floor, and was quite beside itself, fuming, working itself into a frenzy, constantly threatening to boil over, lisping and burring in its own mysterious language something that sounded like: 'Come and take me, good people, I've boiled now and I'm quite ready!'

'To hell with him!' thought Mr Golyadkin. 'That lazy devil could drive a man to distraction! Where's he loafing around now?' In righteous indignation he went out into the hall that consisted of a small passage with the entrance door at the end, opened it a little and caught sight of his servant surrounded by a sizeable crowd of footmen, sundry menials and chance riff-raff. Petrushka was busily regaling them with some story and they were all ears. Evidently neither the topic of conversation nor the conversation itself were to Mr Golyadkin's liking, for he immediately summoned Petrushka and returned to his room looking thoroughly dissatisfied and even upset. 'That wretch would sell anyone for a song – and particularly his master!' he mused. 'And he's sold me, no doubt about that – and for a few lousy copecks, I'm prepared to bet. Well, what is it?'

'They've brought the livery, sir.'

'Put it on and come over here.'

After donning the livery, Petrushka went into his master's room, grinning stupidly. His costume was bizarre in the extreme: he was attired in the green, second-hand livery of a footman, trimmed with gold braid, very worn and clearly fashioned to fit someone a good two feet taller than Petrushka. He was holding a hat that was also trimmed with gold braid and adorned with feathers, and at his side he wore a footman's sword in a leather scabbard.

Finally, to complete the picture – and faithful to his favourite practice of always going around in a state of domestic undress – Petrushka had nothing on his feet. Mr Golyadkin inspected Petrushka from all angles and was apparently well satisfied. The livery had obviously been hired for some ceremonial occasion. What was more, throughout the inspection one could clearly see that Petrushka was eying his master with a strange air of expectancy and following his every movement with marked curiosity, which embarrassed Mr Golyadkin no end.

'Well, what about the carriage?'

'That's arrived too.'

'Do we have it for the whole day?'

'The whole day. For twenty-five roubles.'

'And have they brought the boots?'

'Yes, they've brought the boots.'

'Nitwit! Can't you say, . . . "Yes, they've brought them, *sir*"? Now, give them to me.'

Having expressed his satisfaction that the boots were a good fit, Mr Golyadkin ordered his tea and his things for washing and shaving. He both shaved and washed with extreme care, hurriedly sipping his tea in between and embarking on the principal and definitive enrobing. Then he donned an almost completely new pair of trousers, a shirt-front with little brass buttons, a waistcoat with a nice, extremely bright little floral pattern; around his neck he tied a multicoloured silk cravat and finally pulled on his uniform jacket, also quite new and carefully brushed. As he dressed he glanced lovingly at his boots several times, first raising one foot and then the other to admire their style, constantly whispering something under his breath and occasionally winking with an expressive grimace at every thought that came to him.

However, that morning Mr Golyadkin appeared to be extremely preoccupied, since he hardly noticed the little grins and grimaces directed at him by Petrushka as he helped him dress. At last, when he had checked that all was as it should be and was completely dressed, Mr Golyadkin slipped his wallet into his pocket and cast a final, admiring glance at Petrushka, who by now had put on his boots and was thus in complete readiness. Observing that everything was duly completed, he scurried busily down the stairs, his heart throbbing with trepidation. A light-blue, hired carriage, embellished with a coat of arms of sorts, came rolling up to the door with a loud clatter. After exchanging winks with the driver and some idle bystanders, Petrushka saw that his master was seated; in a peculiar voice and barely able to suppress his idiotic laughter, he shouted: 'Drive off!', leapt up on to the footboard and with much jingling and creaking the entire equipage thundered off towards Nevsky Prospekt.[4] No sooner had the light-blue carriage passed through the gates than Mr Golyadkin rubbed his hands feverishly and broke into a soft, barely audible chuckle, like some bright spark who has brought off a splendid joke and is tickled pink about it. Immediately after this fit of merriment, however, the laughter gave place to a strange, apprehensive expression on Mr Golyadkin's face. In spite of the damp weather he lowered both windows and started scrutinizing passers-by to left and right, immediately adopting a decorous and dignified air the moment he noticed someone looking at him. At the junction of Liteynaya Street and Nevsky Prospekt, a most disagreeable sensation made Mr Golyadkin shudder and, frowning like some poor devil whose corn has been accidentally trodden on, he shrank back hurriedly and even fearfully into the darkest corner of his carriage. The fact was, he had encountered two of his colleagues, two young clerks from the same department where he himself worked. For their part the clerks, so it seemed to Mr Golyadkin, were utterly bewildered at meeting their colleague in these circumstances; one of them even pointed his finger at him. The other, so it appeared to Mr Golyadkin, even shouted his name out loud, which was of course most improper in the street. Our hero hid himself and didn't respond. 'Those urchins!' he reflected. 'So, what's so strange about it? If a man needs a carriage he simply goes and hires one! But all they are is riff-raff! I know them – just little brats who could do with a good thrashing! All they can think of after they're paid their wages is playing pitch-and-toss, or roaming around the streets. That's all they're concerned with! I'd like to give them a piece of my mind, only . . .' Mr Golyadkin didn't finish and he froze. A pair of lively Kazan horses, very well known to Mr Golyadkin and hitched to a fancy droshky, were rapidly overhauling his carriage on the right. The gentleman seated in the droshky, happening to catch sight of the face of Mr Golyadkin, who had rather rashly poked his head out of the window, also appeared absolutely amazed at such an unexpected encounter. Leaning out as far as he could, he started peering with the greatest curiosity and interest into that corner of the carriage where our hero had made haste to conceal himself. The gentleman in the droshky was none other than Andrey Filippovich, head of the same department where Mr Golyadkin was employed as assistant to his chief clerk. When he realized that hiding was impossible, since Andrey Filippovich had fully recognized him and was staring at him wide-eyed, Mr Golyadkin blushed to his ears. 'Should I bow or not? Should I respond or not? Should I acknowledge it's me or not?' wondered our hero in indescribable anguish. 'Or should I pretend it's not me, but someone else remarkably like me, and look as if nothing were the matter? Really, it's not me, it's not me at all – and that's the end of it!' exclaimed Mr Golyadkin, doffing his hat to Andrey Filippovich and without taking his eyes off him. 'I'm . . . I'm all right,' he barely managed to whisper, 'I'm all right, quite all right, it's not me at all, not me at all, Andrey Filippovich – oh no! And that's all there is to it.' However, the droshky soon overtook the carriage and no longer was he subjected to the magnetic power of the head of department's gaze. But he was still blushing, smiling and muttering to himself: 'I was a fool not to respond!' he thought at length. 'I should simply have taken a bolder approach and, with an outspokenness not lacking in nobility, I should have told him: 'So that's how it is, Andrey Filippovich. I've been invited to dinner as well – so there you are!' And then, suddenly remembering that he had made a hash of things, our hero reddened like fire, scowled and cast a terrible and defiant look at the front corner of the carriage – a look positively calculated to reduce all his enemies to ashes in one instant. Finally, in a sudden fit of inspiration, he tugged the cord attached to the driver's elbow, stopped the carriage and gave instructions to turn back to Liteynaya Street. The truth was, Mr Golyadkin had an urgent need – probably for his own peace of mind – to tell his doctor, Krestyan Ivanovich Rutenspitz, something of the greatest interest. And although he hadn't known the doctor for very long at all – he'd called on him only once for something he needed the previous week – but, as they say, a doctor is like a confessor and it would have been stupid to hide himself away since, after all, it is a doctor's responsibility to know his patients. 'Will it be all right?' our hero continued, alighting from his carriage at the entrance to a five-storey building in Liteynaya Street where he had ordered the driver to stop. 'Will it be all right? Will it be proper to call on him? Will it be convenient? Ah well, what of it!' he added, pausing to catch his breath as he mounted the stairs to stop his heart pounding, as it was wont to do on the staircases of others. 'Well, what of it? After all, I've come about what concerns me personally and there's nothing reprehensible about that. It would have been stupid to hide myself away. So, I'll just pretend I'm all right, that I came for no special reason but simply happened to be passing. He'll see that I'm in fact doing the right thing.'

Reasoning thus, Mr Golyadkin went up to the second floor and stopped outside flat number five, whose door bore a handsome brass plate with the inscription:

KRESTYAN IVANOVICH RUTENSPITZ
DOCTOR OF MEDICINE AND SURGERY

As he stood there our hero lost no time in giving his countenance a relaxed, seemly expression that was not lacking in a certain degree of affability and prepared to pull the bell. But just as he was about to ring he immediately and quite appropriately concluded that might it not be better to return to tomorrow as for the time being there was nothing he really needed. However, when Mr Golyadkin suddenly heard footsteps on the stairs he hastily reversed his decision and at the same time rang Dr Rutenspitz's bell with the most determined air.

CHAPTER II

Krestyan Ivanovich Rutenspitz, Doctor of Medicine and Surgery, an extremely healthy, although rather elderly gentleman, endowed with thick, greying eyebrows and side-whiskers, with

an expressive twinkle in his eyes, which alone appeared sufficient to banish all ailments and wearing an important decoration on his chest, was sitting that morning in his consulting
room, in his comfortable armchair, smoking a cigar, drinking
coffee that his wife herself had brought him and writing out
prescriptions for his patients from time to time. After prescrib-
ing a draught for his last patient, an old gentlemen with piles,
and seeing him out through a side door, Krestyan Ivanovich was
sitting down awaiting the next caller. In came Mr Golyadkin.

Evidently Krestyan Ivanovich wasn't in the least expecting
Mr Golyadkin, nor did he want to see him, since all of a sudden
he was taken aback and involuntarily assumed a strange –
some might say even disgruntled – expression. For his part, Mr
Golyadkin would almost invariably, and at precisely the wrong
moment, falter and become flustered just when he was about
to approach someone about his personal affairs – and so it was
now: having failed to prepare the opening sentence, which was
always a real stumbling block for him on such occasions, he
became dreadfully embarrassed, muttered something – apparently an apology – and, at a loss what to do next, took a
chair and sat down. However, realizing that he had sat down
uninvited, he immediately acknowledged the impropriety of his
action and made haste to rectify his mistake and ignorance of
etiquette and good form by immediately rising from the seat he
had occupied so discourteously. Then, collecting himself and
dimly perceiving that he had committed two blunders simultaneously, he decided, without a moment's delay, to commit a
third, that is, he tried to make excuses, muttered something
with a smile, became flushed and embarrassed, lapsed into
eloquent silence, finally sat down for good and, to safeguard
himself against all eventualities, protected himself with that
defiant look which had the extraordinary power of allowing
him to crush all his enemies and reduce them to ashes, without
saying one word. Besides, it was a look that fully expressed Mr
Golyadkin's independence, that is, it showed quite clearly that
'all was well' with Mr Golyadkin, that he was his own master,
like anyone else, and that in any case what other people did
was no concern of his. Krestyan Ivanovich coughed to clear

his throat, apparently as a sign that he approved and agreed to all this, and directed an inquisitorial, searching look at Mr Golyadkin.

'Krestyan Ivanovich,' Mr Golyadkin began, smiling. 'I've come to trouble you a second time and for a second time I venture to crave your indulgence.' Mr Golyadkin clearly had difficulty in choosing the right words.

'Hm ... yes!' said Krestyan Ivanovich, emitting a stream of smoke and placing his cigar on the table. 'But you *must* take what I prescribed. I did explain that your treatment should consist of a change of routine. Yes, I mean diversions. And ... we ... you should visit friends and acquaintances – and at the same time don't be an enemy of the bottle! And regularly keep only cheerful company.'

Still smiling, Mr Golyadkin hastened to observe that he considered himself to be just like anyone else, that he was his own master, that he had his diversions like anyone else ... and that of course he could go to the theatre since, like anyone else, he too had the means; that he was busy at the office during the day, but was at home in the evening; that he was quite 'all right'; he even mentioned in passing that, as far as he knew, he too was as well off as the next man, that he was living in his own flat and that, finally, he had his servant Petrushka. At this point Mr Golyadkin hesitated.

'Hm ... no, that kind of routine is not what I meant ... that wasn't what I wanted to ask you about. What I'm really interested in is whether you are a great lover of cheerful company, whether you spend your time cheerfully. Now, do you lead a melancholy kind of life or a cheerful one?'

'Krestyan Ivanovich ... I ...'

'Hm,' interrupted the doctor, 'what I'm telling you is that you need to radically change your whole lifestyle and in a sense you must completely transform your character.' (Krestyan Ivanovich particularly emphasized the word 'transform' and paused for a moment with an extremely significant look.)

'Don't shun the gay life, go to theatres and clubs, and in any case don't be an enemy of the bottle. Staying at home is out of the question for someone like you.'

'I love peace and quiet, Krestyan Ivanovich,' Mr Golyadkin said, casting a meaningful glance at the doctor and obviously seeking the words that would most successfully convey his thoughts. 'In the flat there's no one but myself and Petrushka . . . I mean, my manservant, Krestyan Ivanovich. What I want to say is that I go my own way, my own independent way, Krestyan Ivanovich. I keep to myself and as far as I can see I don't depend on anyone. I also go for walks, Krestyan Ivanovich.'

'What? . . . Oh yes! But it can't be much fun going for walks at the moment, the weather's simply awful.'

'Yes, Krestyan Ivanovich, as I've already had the honour of explaining to you, I'm a peace-loving man, but my path lies in a different direction from other people's. The road of life is broad . . . what . . . what I mean to say is, Krestyan Ivanovich . . . Oh do forgive me, I'm no expert at fine phrases . . .'

'Hm . . . you were saying?'

'I was saying that you must excuse me, Krestyan Ivanovich, for not having, as far as I can judge, a gift for fine phrases,' Mr Golyadkin said in a half-offended tone, growing a little muddled and confused, 'in this respect, Krestyan Ivanovich, I'm not like other people,' he added with a peculiar kind of smile. 'I'm not a good talker and I never learned to embellish my style with fancy expressions. On the other hand I – act, Krestyan Ivanovich. I *act*, Krestyan Ivanovich.'

'Hm . . . what's that . . . you . . . *act*?' replied Krestyan Ivanovich. There was a minute's silence. The doctor glanced somewhat strangely and incredulously at Mr Golyadkin, who in turn squinted rather incredulously at the doctor.

'I, Krestyan Ivanovich,' continued Mr Golyadkin in the same tone as before, rather irritated and puzzled by Krestyan Ivanovich's extreme stubbornness, 'I love peace and quiet and not the hurly-burly of society. With that class of people – I mean, people in high society – you must know how to polish parquet floors with your boots . . .' (Here Mr Golyadkin gently scraped one foot on the floor.) 'That's what they expect of you – they also ask you to make clever puns and you must know how to pay scented compliments – yes, that's what they expect of you. But I've never learned to do that kind of thing, Krestyan

Ivanovich, I've never learned all those cunning tricks – never
had time for them. I'm a simple, straightforward sort of person,
there's no surface brilliance about me. On this point, Krestyan
Ivanovich, I lay down my arms – in that sense of the words
I lay them down!'

Of course, Mr Golyadkin said all this in a way that made it
quite clear that our hero had no regrets whatsoever about laying
down his arms *in that sense*, that he had never learned cunning
tricks – the exact reverse, in fact. As Krestyan Ivanovich listened
he gazed at the floor with a very unpleasant grimace, as if he had
somehow been expecting something like this. Mr Golyadkin's
tirade was followed by a long and significant silence.

'I think you've rather strayed from the subject,' Krestyan
Ivanovich said at length, in a low voice. 'I do confess, I couldn't
quite get your drift.'

'I'm not skilled in eloquence, Krestyan Ivanovich, I . . . I've
already had the honour of informing you of this,' said Mr
Golyadkin, this time in a sharp, determined voice.

'Hm . . .'

'Krestyan Ivanovich!' Mr Golyadkin began again in a low
but significant and to a certain extent solemn voice, dwelling
on every point. 'Krestyan Ivanovich, when I arrived I began by
apologizing. Now I repeat what I said before and again I crave
your indulgence for a while. I, Krestyan Ivanovich, have nothing
to hide from you. I'm a little man, you know that yourself. But
fortunately I don't regret being a little man. Even the contrary,
Krestyan Ivanovich. And to be perfectly frank, I'm even proud
of being a little man and not a big one. And I'm proud that I'm
not an intriguer either. I don't act furtively, but openly, without
deception, and although I in turn could harm people – and do
it very well – although I even know whom to harm and how to
do it, I don't want to sully myself and in this sense I wash my
hands. Yes, in this sense I wash my hands of it, Krestyan
Ivanovich!' For a moment Mr Golyadkin lapsed into an
expressive silence again. He had been speaking with mild
enthusiasm.

'I go about my business openly and honestly,' our hero continued, 'I don't act deviously because that's what I despise and

leave to others . . . I don't like double-talk, I abhor slander and gossip, I've no time for wretched duplicity. Only when I go to masquerades do I wear a mask, but I don't parade one in front of people every day. All I'm asking is this: how would *you* go about taking revenge on your enemy, your deadliest enemy, or on whom you considered such?' concluded Mr Golyadkin with a defiant glance at Krestyan Ivanovich.

Although Mr Golyadkin had expounded all this with the utmost clarity, distinctness and self-assurance, weighing his words and counting on their maximum impact, he was now looking at Krestyan Ivanovich with ever-increasing alarm. Now he was all eyes, timidly awaiting Krestyan Ivanovich's reply with morbid, vexed feelings of impatience. But to Mr Golyadkin's amazement and utter dismay, all the doctor did was mutter something under his breath; then he pulled his chair up to the table and announced – rather coolly but nonetheless politely – something to the effect that his time was precious, that somehow he didn't quite follow and that he was prepared, as far as he could, to be of service, but beyond that he would not delve into matters that did not concern him. Here he picked up his pen, drew a sheet of paper towards him, cut off a piece the size of a prescription and announced that he would prescribe what was appropriate right away.

'No, Krestyan Ivanovich, that's not appropriate, not appropriate at all,' said Mr Golyadkin, half-rising from his seat and grabbing the doctor's right arm. 'There's no need for that at all in my case.'

While Mr Golyadkin was saying this, a weird transformation came over him. His grey eyes shone with a strange fire, his lips quivered and every muscle, every feature of his face twitched and shifted. He was shaking all over. Following his first movement, holding Krestyan Ivanovich by the arm, Mr Golyadkin now stood motionless, as if he had lost all confidence and was awaiting inspiration for further action. And then a rather bizarre scene followed.

Somewhat puzzled, Krestyan Ivanovich momentarily stayed glued to his chair, quite taken aback and gazing wide-eyed at Mr Golyadkin, who gazed back in similar fashion. Finally the doctor stood up, supporting himself to some degree by one of Mr Golyadkin's coat lapels. For a few seconds they both stood there like that, without budging or taking their eyes off each other. Then followed Mr Golyadkin's second impulsive movement, moreover in a most peculiar manner. His lips trembled, his chin twitched and quite unexpectedly our hero burst into tears. Sobbing and nodding, beating his breast with his right hand whilst grasping the lapel of Krestyan Ivanovich's domestic attire with the other, he tried to speak, to offer some immediate explanation, but he was unable to utter one word. At last Krestyan Ivanovich recovered from his amazement.

'Come, come! Please calm yourself! Sit down,' he said, trying to seat Mr Golyadkin in the armchair.

'I have enemies, Krestyan Ivanovich, I have vicious enemies who have vowed to ruin me . . .' Mr Golyadkin replied in a frightened whisper.

'Now, that's enough of enemies! No need to bring enemies into it – absolutely no need to. Now sit down, please do sit down,' continued Krestyan Ivanovich, finally getting Mr Golyadkin into the armchair.

Mr Golyadkin settled down, without taking his eyes off the doctor, who began pacing his consulting room from one end to the other with an extremely disgruntled look. A long silence ensued.

'I'm grateful to you, Krestyan Ivanovich, extremely grateful and I deeply appreciate all you've done for me. I shall not forget your kindness until my dying day, Krestyan Ivanovich' Mr Golyadkin finally said, rising from the chair with a hurt look.

'Now that's enough, enough! I'm telling you that's enough!' exclaimed Krestyan Ivanovich, reacting rather severely to Mr Golyadkin's outburst as he once again made him sit down. 'What's the matter with you? Tell me what's bothering you now?' Krestyan Ivanovich continued, 'and who are these enemies you keep mentioning? What's it all about?'

'No, Krestyan Ivanovich, we'd better leave that for now,' replied Mr Golyadkin, looking down at the floor. 'We'd better put that aside for the time being . . . for another time, when it's more convenient, when all will be revealed, when masks will fall from certain faces and various facts will come to light. But in the meantime, after what's happened between us, of course . . . you yourself will agree, Krestyan Ivanovich . . . Please allow me to wish you good day,' said Mr Golyadkin, this time solemnly and determinedly rising from his chair and reaching for his hat.

'Ah well, as you like . . . hmmm . . .'

(A minute's silence followed.)

'If, for my part . . . well, you know, if there's anything I can do . . . and I sincerely wish you well . . .'

'I understand you, Krestyan Ivanovich, I understand you perfectly now. At all events please forgive me for disturbing you.'

'Hm . . . no, that's not what I meant. However, as you wish. Carry on with the same medication as before.'

'I shall carry on with the same medication as you say, Krestyan Ivanovich, I shall carry on with it and get it at the same chemist's. It's quite a big thing, Krestyan Ivanovich, being a chemist these days.'

'How so? In what sense?'

'In a very ordinary sense, Krestyan Ivanovich. I mean, that's what the world has come to these days . . .'

'Hm . . .'

'And any little urchin – and not only in chemists' shops– sticks his nose up at respectable citizens nowadays.'

'Hm . . . what do you mean by that?'

'I'm talking about someone we both know, a mutual acquaintance, Krestyan Ivanovich – Vladimir Semyonovich, for example.'

'Ah!'

'Yes, Krestyan Ivanovich. And I know several people who aren't so enslaved by public opinion that they can't occasionally speak the truth.'

'Ah! And how is that?'

'Well, that's how things are. But this is a totally different matter. Sometimes people know how to serve an egg with sauce.'

'Serve *what*?'

'Serve an egg with sauce, Krestyan Ivanovich. It's a Russian proverb.[5] Sometimes they know how to congratulate someone at the appropriate time, for example. There are people like that, Krestyan Ivanovich.'

'Congratulate?'

'Yes, congratulate, Krestyan Ivanovich, as a close acquaintance of mine did the other day.'

'A close acquaintance ... ah! And how was that?' said Krestyan Ivanovich, looking intently at Mr Golyadkin.

'One of my close acquaintances congratulated another close acquaintance – what's more, a comrade, a bosom pal as they say, on his promotion to assessor's rank.[6] He put it like this: "I'm genuinely delighted, Vladimir Semyonich," he said, "at this opportunity of offering you my congratulations, my *sincere* congratulations on your promotion. All the more so, as nowadays, as the whole world knows, those in high places who give others a leg up have become virtually extinct!"' Here Mr Golyadkin gave a roguish nod and screwed up his eyes as he looked at Krestyan Ivanovich.

'Hm ... he said that, did he?'

'Yes he did, Krestyan Ivanovich, that's what he said – and then he looked at Andrey Filippovich, our little treasure Vladimir Semyonovich's uncle. But what do I care, Krestyan Ivanovich, if he's been promoted to assessor? Is it any concern of mine? What's more, he's wanting to get married, when he's still wet behind the ears, if you'll pardon the expression. That's just what he said. Now, I've told you everything, so please allow me to be on my way.'

'Hm ...'

'Yes, Krestyan Ivanovich, please allow me to take my leave. But to kill two birds with one stone, after I'd cut that young whippersnapper down to size with that talk of friends in high places I turned to Klara Olsufyevna (it happened the day before yesterday at her father Olsufy Ivanovich's) and she'd just sung a sentimental ballad, so I told her: "The way you sang that ballad was full of feeling, but those who are listening to you are not pure of heart." And with this I dropped a clear hint, you understand, Krestyan Ivanovich, I dropped a clear hint that it was not her they were interested in but had set their sights a little higher.'

'And what did *he* say?'

'He looked as if he'd just bitten into a lemon, as the saying goes.'

'Hm . . .'

'Oh yes, Krestyan Ivanovich, I spoke to the old man too. "Olsufy Ivanovich," I said, "I know how I'm indebted to you, I fully appreciate the favours you've showered me with almost since I was a little child. But open your eyes, Olsufy Ivanovich," I said. "Take a good look around you. I myself do things fairly and squarely, Olsufy Ivanovich."'

'Well – you don't say! So, that's how things are . . .'

'Yes, Krestyan Ivanovich, that's how things are.'

'But what did he say?'

'Oh yes, what indeed, Krestyan Ivanovich! He mumbled this and that, that I know you and that His Excellency's a benevolent person – laid it on pretty thick, he did. Well, what can you expect? He's gone doddery from old age, as they say.'

'Ah! So that's how things are now!'

'Yes, Krestyan Ivanovich, that's how we all are! Poor old chap. He's got one foot in the grave – at death's door, as they say. And when they start spinning old wives' tales he's there listening. They can't do a thing without him.'

'Old wives' tales, you say?'

'Yes, Krestyan Ivanovich, they've spun some sort of tale. And our friend the Bear and his nephew – the little treasure – had a hand in it. They're in league with the old crones of course and they've cooked something up. And what do you think? They've conceived a plan to murder someone . . .'

'*Murder* someone!?'

'Yes, Krestyan Ivanovich, to murder someone, murder someone morally. They've put out a rumour . . . I'm still talking about this close acquaintance of mine . . .'

Krestyan Ivanovich nodded.

'They've spread a rumour about him. I do confess, Krestyan Ivanovich, I'm even too ashamed to talk about it.'

'Hm . . .'

'They've spread the rumour that he'd given a written undertaking to marry someone when he was already engaged to someone else. And who do you think it was, Krestyan Ivanovich?'

'I really don't know.'

'Some brazen German slut who owns an eating-house and
cooks his dinner. Instead of paying her what he owes her in
cash he's offering her his hand.'

'Is that what they say?'

'Can you believe it, Krestyan Ivanovich? A nasty, vile, shameless German slut – Karolina Ivanovna ... if you've heard of
her ...'

'I must confess, for my part ...'

'I understand you, Krestyan Ivanovich, I do understand you
and for my part I feel ...'

'Now, please tell me where you're living now?'

'Where I'm living now, Krestyan Ivanovich?'

'Yes ... I'd like to ... I seem to remember you used to live
before ...'

'Oh yes, I used to live, Krestyan Ivanovich! Yes, I did live
before – I must have done, mustn't I?' Mr Golyadkin replied,
accompanying his words with a little laugh and somewhat
taking Krestyan Ivanovich aback with his answer.

'No, you've misunderstood me. What I wanted to say was,
for my part ...'

'For my part, Krestyan Ivanovich, I wanted to as well,' Mr
Golyadkin continued, laughing. 'I too wanted to ... However,
I've really outstayed my welcome, Krestyan Ivanovich. I hope
you will now permit me to wish you good morning ...'

'Hm ...'

'Yes, Krestyan Ivanovich. I understand you, I understand you
perfectly now,' our hero said, showing off a little before the
doctor. 'So if you'll permit me to wish you good morning ...'

At this our hero clicked his heels and walked out of the room,
leaving Krestyan Ivanovich utterly stunned. As he went down
the doctor's staircase he smiled and gleefully rubbed his hands.
Once he reached the front steps and breathed in the fresh air
and felt he was free he was even quite prepared to admit that
he was the happiest of mortals and ready to go later straight to

the office, when suddenly his carriage rumbled in through the gate. He took one look and remembered everything. Petrushka was already opening the carriage door. A peculiar, extremely unpleasant sensation held Mr Golyadkin totally in its grip. For a moment he appeared to flush; then something seemed to prick him. As he was about to plant his foot on the carriage step he suddenly turned round and looked up at Krestyan Ivanovich's windows. Just as he thought! Krestyan Ivanovich was standing at one of them, smoothing his side-whiskers with his right hand and looking at our hero rather inquisitively. 'That doctor's stupid,' thought Mr Golyadkin, hiding in the carriage. 'Terribly stupid. He may be a good doctor – all the same he's as thick as two planks!' Mr Golyadkin sat back, Petrushka shouted 'Drive on!' and the carriage once more rolled out on to Nevsky Prospekt.

CHAPTER III

That entire morning was spent by Mr Golyadkin in frenzied activity. When he reached Nevsky Prospekt our hero ordered the driver to stop at the Gostiny Dvor.[7] Leaping down from his carriage he ran down the arcade, accompanied by Petrushka, and made a beeline for a shop that sold gold and silver articles. From Mr Golyadkin's appearance alone one could tell that here was a man with a lot on his plate and a whole pile of things to do. After haggling over a complete dinner and tea service for 1,500 roubles, striking a bargain over an elaborately fashioned cigar case and a full silver shaving set for a similar amount, and after asking the price of some little trifles that were useful and pleasant in their own way, Mr Golyadkin finished by promising to return the very next day, without fail – or even to send for his purchases that same day, noting the shop number, listening attentively as the shopkeeper made a fuss about a small deposit and promising to put down a small deposit in due course. After that, he hurriedly bade the astonished shopkeeper good day and walked between the rows of shops, pursued by a whole swarm of assistants, constantly looking back at Petrushka and carefully seeking out some new shop. On his way he darted into a money changer's and changed his large notes into smaller denominations, and although he lost on the transaction his wallet fattened considerably as a result, which evidently afforded him the greatest satisfaction. Finally he stopped at a shop that sold various materials for ladies. After bargaining over goods worth a significant sum, here too Mr Golyadkin promised the shopkeeper to call back without fail, noted the shop number and when he was asked for a small deposit he again confirmed that it would follow, all in good time. Then he visited a few more shops, bargained in all of them, inquired about the prices of various articles, occasionally engaged in lengthy arguments with the shopkeepers, leaving the shops only to return three times to each one of them – in brief, he was extraordinarily busy. From the Gostiny Dvor our hero headed for a well-known furniture store, where he struck a deal over enough furniture to fill six rooms, admired a highly elaborate and fashionable lady's dressing-table, in the very latest style, and after assuring the shopkeeper that he would send for everything without fail, he left the shop with his usual promise of a small deposit and then drove off somewhere to order something else. In short, there was evidently no end to his furious activity. Finally all this became tiresome in the extreme for Mr Golyadkin himself and God knows why, right out of the blue, he even began to be troubled by twinges of conscience. Not for anything would he now have agreed to meet Andrey Filippovich or Krestyan Ivanovich, for example. At last the city clocks struck three in the afternoon. When Mr Golyadkin finally took his seat in his carriage, all that his actual acquisitions of that morning amounted to was a pair of gloves and a bottle of perfume, to the value of one and a half roubles. Since it was still rather early for him, Mr Golyadkin ordered the driver to stop at a well-known restaurant on Nevsky Prospekt, which he had known of only by hearsay until then, alighted from the carriage and hurried in for a snack and a rest and to wait until the time was right.

After eating like a man who has a sumptuous banquet in prospect, that is, having a little snack to stave off the pangs as they say, after downing a glass of vodka, Mr Golyadkin seated himself in an armchair and after modestly taking a look around, quietly settled down with a certain flimsy national newspaper.[8] When he had read a line or two, he stood up, looked at himself in the mirror, spruced himself up and smoothed his clothes. Then he went over to the window to see if his carriage was there ... then he sat down again and picked up the paper. Clearly our hero was extremely agitated. Glancing at the clock and seeing that since it was only a quarter past three and that consequently he still had quite a while to wait, and at the same time reasoning that it was indecorous to sit there just like that, Mr Golyadkin ordered some chocolate, for which he really didn't feel much inclination just then. After drinking the chocolate and noting that time had moved on a little, he went up to the counter to pay. Suddenly somebody clapped him on the shoulder.

He turned round and saw before him two of his colleagues from the office, the same ones he had met that morning in Liteynaya Street, both young lads, very junior in age and rank. Our hero's relations with them were neither one thing nor the other, neither friendly nor openly hostile. Of course, propriety was observed on both sides but there was no close intimacy, nor could there have been. An encounter at this particular time was extremely unpleasant for Mr Golyadkin. He frowned slightly and for a moment became somewhat flustered.

'Yakov Petrovich, Yakov Petrovich!' twittered the two clerks. 'You here? For what ... ?'

'Oh, it's you, gentlemen!' Mr Golyadkin hurriedly interrupted, somewhat put out and scandalized by the clerks' surprise and at the same time by the familiarity of their approach, but playing, however, the easy-going fellow, despite himself.

'So, you've deserted, gentlemen! He he he!' And then, in order not to lower himself by behaving condescendingly towards his office juniors, with whom he always stayed within proper bounds, he tried to pat one of the young men on the shoulder. But on this occasion his attempt at camaraderie didn't succeed and instead of a seemly and friendly gesture something quite different resulted.

'Well, is that Bear of ours still in the office?' he asked.

'Who's that, Yakov Petrovich?'

'Why, the Bear. As if you didn't know who's called the Bear!' Mr Golyadkin laughed and turned to the waiter to take his change. 'I'm talking about Andrey Filippovich, gentlemen,' he continued, having finished with the waiter and this time addressing the clerks with an extremely grave air. The clerks exchanged knowing winks.

'He's still there and he was asking for you, Yakov Petrovich,' one of them replied.

'Still there, eh? In that case let him stay there, gentlemen. And he was asking for me, eh?'

'That's right, Yakov Petrovich. But what's all this – pomading and perfuming yourself like a regular fop!'

'Well, that's how things are, gentlemen! But that's enough . . .' replied Mr Golyadkin, looking away with a strained smile. Seeing Mr Golyadkin smiling, the clerks burst into loud guffaws. Mr Golyadkin started sulking a little.

'Let me tell you, gentlemen, as a friend,' our hero said after a brief pause, as if he had decided to reveal something to the clerks. 'You all know me, gentlemen, but up to now you've only known one side. For this no one can be criticized and I must confess that I myself was partly to blame.'

Mr Golyadkin pursed his lips and glanced meaningfully at the clerks. The clerks again exchanged winks.

'Up to now, gentlemen, you haven't really known me. To explain here and now wouldn't be entirely appropriate, so I'll tell you something casually, in passing. There are people, gentlemen, who don't like devious behaviour and who don masks only for masquerades. There are people who don't see as man's true purpose in life the ability to polish the parquet with their boots. There are even people, gentlemen, who don't admit they're happy and who live life to the full when, for example, their trousers are a good fit. Finally, there are people who don't like prancing and whirling around to no purpose, flirting, toadying to others – and, most important of all, poking their noses in where they're positively not asked to . . . I've told you almost everything, gentlemen. Now, please allow me to leave.'

Mr Golyadkin stopped. As the registrar clerks[9] were by now thoroughly satisfied they both suddenly started splitting their sides with laughter in the rudest manner. Mr Golyadkin flared up.

'You may laugh, gentlemen, you may laugh for the present! But just you wait and see when you're older!' he said with a feeling of wounded dignity, taking his hat and retreating to the door.

'But I shall say more, gentlemen,' he added, addressing the clerks for the last time. 'I shall tell you more, now that you're face to face with me. These are my rules, gentlemen: if things are bad I stand firm – if they go well I hold my ground. And in any event I undermine no one. I'm not an intriguer and of that I'm proud. I'd never have been any good as a diplomat. As they say, gentlemen, the bird flies to the huntsman of its own accord. That's true and I'm ready to agree. But who's the huntsman here and who's the bird? Answer that one, gentlemen!'

Mr Golyadkin lapsed into eloquent silence and with the most significant expression – that is, with his eyebrows raised and lips pursed as tightly as possible – he bowed to the gentlemen clerks and walked out, leaving them utterly stunned.

'Where to?' asked Petrushka, quite gruffly, as he was probably sick and tired of hanging around in the cold. 'Where do you want to go?' he again asked Mr Golyadkin and met with that terrifying, all-destroying look with which our hero had already twice protected himself that morning and to which he now resorted for a third time as he went down the steps.

'Izmaylovsky Bridge.'[10]

'Izmaylovsky Bridge! Let's be off!'

'They don't usually have dinner before four, perhaps not even until five,' thought Mr Golyadkin. 'Isn't it still too early? But surely I could arrive a little early? After all, it's just a family dinner. I could simply go there *sans façon*,[11] as respectable people put it. Why shouldn't I go *sans façon*? The Bear also said it would all be *sans façon*, so therefore I too . . .' – such were Mr Golyadkin's thoughts; but meanwhile his agitation was growing by the minute. One could see that he was preparing himself for something extremely troublesome, to say the least, whispering to himself, gesticulating with his right hand, constantly gazing out of the carriage windows so that nobody looking at Mr Golyadkin now would have said that he was preparing for a fine meal, informally, within his own family circle as well, *sans façon*, as respectable people say. At length, right by Izmaylovsky Bridge, Mr Golyadkin pointed out a particular house; the carriage clattered through the gates and stopped at an entrance on the right. Noticing a woman's figure at a first-floor window, Mr Golyadkin blew her a kiss. However, he himself barely knew what he was doing, for at that moment he positively felt neither dead nor alive. Pale and distraught, he emerged from the carriage, went up into the porch, removed his hat, mechanically straightened his clothes and went upstairs, feeling a slight trembling in his knees.

'Olsufy Ivanovich?' he asked the servant who opened the door to him.

'He's at home, sir – I mean, he's not. The Master's not home, sir.'

'What? What do you mean, my dear man? I've come to dinner, old chap. Surely you know me?'

'How could I not know you, sir? But my orders are not to receive you, sir.'

'You ... you ... old chap, are most likely mistaken. It's *me*. I, old chap, have been invited. I've come to dinner,' Mr Golyadkin said, throwing off his overcoat and showing every intention of entering the main reception rooms.

'Sorry, sir, but you can't. Orders are not to receive you, that's how it is.'

Mr Golyadkin turned pale. At that moment the door from one of the inner rooms opened and Gerasimych, Olsufy Ivanovich's old butler, came out.

'This gentlemen wants to come in, Emelyan Gerasimovich, but I ...'

'You're a fool, Alekseich. Now go into the rooms and send that scoundrel Semyonich here. You can't, sir,' he said politely but firmly, turning to Mr Golyadkin, 'it's out of the question, sir. The Master asks to be excused, sir, but he can't receive you.'

'So that's what he said – that he can't receive me?' Mr

Golyadkin asked uncertainly. 'Forgive me, Gerasimych, but why is it out of the question?'

'It's quite impossible, sir. I did announce you, sir, but the Master said: "Ask him to excuse me." He said he can't receive you.'

'But why not? How can this be? How . . .'

'Please, sir, please!'

'But how can this be? I'm not standing for this! Now go and announce me. How can this be? I've come to dinner.'

'Please, sir, please!'

'Well, if he's asking to be excused that's a different matter. But how can this be, Gerasimych, if you'll allow me to inquire?'

'If you don't mind, sir!' retorted Gerasimych, very determinedly shoving Mr Golyadkin to one side to allow a broad passage for two gentlemen who were entering the hall just at that moment. They were Andrey Filippovich and his nephew Vladimir Semyonovich. Both looked at Mr Golyadkin in bewilderment. Andrey Filippovich appeared about to say something, but Mr Golyadkin had already made up his mind; his eyes downcast, blushing, smiling and with a thoroughly lost expression, he was already leaving Olsufy Ivanovich's entrance hall.

'I'll call back later, Gerasimych . . . I'll have it out with him. I hope all this won't delay a proper and timely explanation,' he said, partly from the threshold and partly from the stairs.

'Yakov Petrovich! Yakov Petrovich!' resounded the voice of Andrey Filippovich, who had followed Mr Golyadkin out.

Mr Golyadkin had already reached the first landing. He turned quickly to confront Andrey Filippovich.

'What can I do for you, Andrey Filippovich?' he asked in quite a determined tone of voice.

'What's the matter with you, Yakov Petrovich? How is it that you're . . . ?'

'I'm all right, Andrey Filippovich. I'm here on my own account. This is my personal life, Andrey Filippovich.'

'What did you say, sir?'

'I said that this is my *personal* life and as far as I can see there's nothing reprehensible to be found with regard to my *official* relations.'

'What!? With regard to your official . . . What's the matter with you, sir?'

'Nothing, Andrey Filippovich, absolutely nothing. An insolent slut – that's all . . .'

'What? *What!?*' Andrey Filippovich exclaimed, lost in amazement. Mr Golyadkin, who, until then, while talking to Andrey Filippovich from the bottom of the stairs, had looked as if he were ready to jump right down his throat, seeing that the head of his department was somewhat disconcerted, took a step forward almost without realizing it. Andrey Filippovich drew back. Mr Golyadkin climbed one stair after the other. Andrey Filippovich looked around anxiously. Suddenly Mr Golyadkin rapidly bounded up the stairs. Even more rapidly Andrey Filippovich leapt into the room and slammed the door behind him. Mr Golyadkin was left alone now. Everything went dark before his eyes. He was utterly flummoxed and stood there in some kind of muddled meditative state, as if recalling some event that was also extremely stupid and that had taken place very recently. 'Oh dear! Oh dear!' he whispered, smiling from the strain. Meanwhile he could hear the sound of voices and footsteps from the stairs below – probably those of some of Olsufy Ivanovich's newly arrived guests. Mr Golyadkin partly came to his senses, hastily turned up the racoon collar of his coat to conceal himself as much as possible, and started hobbling, stumbling, scurrying down the stairs. He felt a kind of weakness and numbness. So extreme was his confusion that when he came out on to the porch he didn't wait for his carriage, but hurried straight to it across the muddy courtyard. As he approached it and prepared to get in, Mr Golyadkin mentally evinced the desire for the earth to swallow him up, or to hide away, in a mousehole, carriage and all. It struck him that every single person in Olsufy Ivanovich's house was now staring at him from every window. He knew that he was bound to drop dead on the spot if he turned round.

'What are you laughing at, you blockhead!' he rattled away at Petrushka who was preparing to help him into the carriage.

'What have *I* got to laugh about? Wasn't doing anything! Where are we going now?'

'Home . . . Let's go . . .'

'Home!' shouted Petrushka to the driver, perching himself on the footboard.

'Caws like a crow!' thought Mr Golyadkin. Meanwhile the carriage had already travelled some distance beyond Izmaylovsky Bridge. Suddenly our hero pulled the cord with all his might and shouted to the coachman to turn back immediately. The coachman turned the horses and within two minutes drove once again into Olsufy Ivanovich's courtyard. 'No, there's no need, you fool, no need! Back again!' shouted Mr Golyadkin – and it was as though the coachman were expecting these instructions, for without a word of protest or stopping at the entrance, he drove right round the courtyard and then out again into the street.

Mr Golyadkin did not go home, however, but after they passed Semyonovsky Bridge he ordered the coachman to turn down a side street and stop outside a tavern of rather modest appearance. After getting out of the carriage our hero settled up with the coachman and then, thus finally rid of his carriage, ordered Petrushka to go home and await his return, while he entered the tavern, took a private room and ordered dinner. He felt very unwell and his head was in utter turmoil and chaos. For a long time he paced the room in great agitation. Finally he sat down, propped his forehead on his hands and made a concerted effort to weigh the whole situation up and to try and come to some conclusion regarding his present situation.

CHAPTER IV

That day, the day of great festivity, the birthday of Klara Olsufyevna, only daughter of State Counsellor[12] Berendeyev, benefactor of Mr Golyadkin in bygone days – that day was celebrated with a splendid, sumptuous banquet – such a banquet as had not been seen for many a day within the walls of civil servants' apartments in the neighbourhood of Izmaylovsky Bridge and thereabouts, a banquet more like Belshazzar's

Feast,[13] redolent of something Babylonian in its brilliance, luxury and good taste, a banquet with Veuve Clicquot, oysters and the fruits of Yeliseyev and Milyutin,[14] with every kind of fatted calf, with an official list showing the rank of every civil servant present – that festive day, commemorated with so festive a dinner, was concluded with a brilliant ball – a small, intimate, family ball, yet brilliant nonetheless in its taste, elegance and decorum. Of course, I entirely agree that such balls do take place, only rarely. Such balls, more like joyful family occasions than balls, can only be given in houses such as State Counsellor Berendeyev's, for example. I shall go further: I even doubt whether every state counsellor could give such a ball. Oh, if I were a poet – of course, at least like a Homer or a Pushkin . . . (with lesser talent I would not dare poke my nose in) – then I would unfailingly portray for you, oh reader, with vivid colours and broad brush, that day of pomp and ceremony in its entirety. Oh yes, I would begin my poem with the banquet and pay particular attention to that striking and at the same time solemn moment when the first goblet was raised in honour of the Queen of Festivities. First I would depict for you the guests, plunged in reverential silence and expectation – more reminiscent of Demosthenic eloquence[15] than silence. Then I would portray Andrey Filippovich – who, as the oldest guest, even had certain claims to precedence, adorned with silvery hair and civil orders befitting that silvery hair, who rose from his seat and held aloft a celebratory goblet of sparkling wine, a wine more like nectar than wine, a wine expressly brought from some distant realm to celebrate such moments. Then I would portray for you the guests and the happy parents of the Birthday Queen following the example of Andrey Filippovich in raising their glasses and gazing at him with eyes full of expectation. Then I would portray for you how this so frequently mentioned Andrey Filippovich, after first shedding a tear in his glass and offering his congratulations and good wishes, proposed a toast and drank the health . . . But I must confess, I fully confess, that it would be beyond my powers to depict all the solemnity of that moment when the Birthday Queen herself, blushing like a vernal rose with the flush of blissful modesty, sank from fullness of

emotion into her tender mother's embrace; how the tender
mother dissolved in tears and how, at this, her father himself
began to sob, that venerable elder and State Counsellor Olsufy
Ivanovich, who had lost the use of his legs in long years of
service to the State and who had been rewarded by fate for his
zeal with a nice little capital, a house, some small estates and a
beautiful daughter, began to sob like a child and proclaimed
through his tears that His Excellency was the most benevolent
of men. I could not, no, I really could not portray for you the
general stirring of heartfelt emotion that immediately followed,
a stirring of emotion clearly expressed even by the behaviour
of a young registrar clerk (at that moment he looked more
like a State Counsellor than a humble registrar) who was also
shedding tears himself as he listened to Andrey Filippovich.
Andrey Filippovich in turn, at that solemn moment, did not
in the least resemble a collegiate counsellor[16] and head of a
department – no, he appeared to be someone else . . . I do not
know exactly what, but definitely not a collegiate counsellor.
He was more elevated! And finally . . . oh, why don't I possess
the secret of the lofty, powerful style, the solemn style, to
portray all these beautiful and edifying moments of human life,
which seem to be expressly devised, as it were, to demonstrate
how virtue can sometimes triumph over disloyalty, free-
thinking, vice and envy! I shall say nothing, but will silently
point out to you – this will be better than eloquence alone –
that happy youth entering his twenty-sixth spring, Vladimir
Semyonovich, Andrey Filippovich's nephew, who in turn has
risen to his feet and who in turn is proposing a toast and on
whom are turned the tearful eyes of the parents of the Birthday
Queen, the proud eyes of Andrey Filippovich, the bashful eyes
of the Birthday Queen herself, the enraptured eyes of the guests
and even the decorously jealous eyes of some of that brilliant
young man's colleagues. I shall say nothing, although I cannot
help observing that everything about that young man who
(speaking in a favourable respect) was more like an old man
than a young one – everything, his blooming cheeks to the very
rank of Assessor invested in him – all this spoke at that solemn
moment of the dizzy heights to which good conduct can raise

a man. I shall not describe how, finally, Anton Antonovich Setochkin, head of a section in a certain department, a colleague of Andrey Filippovich's and formerly of Olsufy Ivanovich, and at the same time an old friend of the family and godfather to Klara Olsufyevna, how that little old man with hair as white as snow who, when proposing a toast, crowed like a cock and recited some jolly verses; how, by this decorous neglect of decorum, if I may thus express it, he reduced the whole gathering to tears of laughter and how Klara Olsufyevna herself, at her parents' bidding, rewarded him with a kiss for such gaiety and amiability. I shall merely say that the guests, who after such a banquet naturally felt like brothers and kinsfolk, at last rose from the table; how the old men and solid citizens, after a short interval spent in friendly conversation and even in the exchange of the most proper and needless to say polite confidences, repaired, with much decorum, to another room and, without wasting precious time, broke up into small groups and, conscious of their own dignity, settled themselves at tables covered with green baize; how all the ladies, having seated themselves in the drawing-room suddenly became unusually amiable and started chatting about various dress materials; how finally the highly esteemed paterfamilias himself, who had lost the use of his legs in true and loyal service and been rewarded for this by all that has been mentioned above, started hobbling among his guests on his crutches, supported by Vladimir Semyonovich and Klara Olsufyevna; and how, suddenly waxing extraordinarily amicable too, he decided to improvise a modest little ball, regardless of expense; how, to this end, a certain smart youth (the very one who at dinner looked more like a state counsellor than a youth) was dispatched to fetch musicians; how they subsequently arrived, no fewer than eleven of them; and how, finally, at exactly half past eight, were heard the inviting strains of a French quadrille and various other dances ... I need hardly say that my pen is too feeble, too sluggish and dull to do full justice to the ball improvised with such uncommon kindness by the hoary-haired host. And, I ask, how can I, humble chronicler of Mr Golyadkin's adventures, extremely interesting though they are in their own way – how

can I depict that rare and decorous blending of beauty, brilliance, gentility, gaiety, amiable sobriety and sober amiability,
playfulness, all those games and jests of the high-ranking
officials' wives, more like fairies than ladies – I say this in their
favour – with their lilac-pink shoulders and faces, their ethereal
figures and their nimble (to speak in the high style), their homeo-
pathic feet? And finally, how can I portray for you these brilliant
civil service cavaliers, so cheerful and sedate, young and elderly,
gay and decorously melancholy, smoking a pipe in the intervals,
between dances, in a remote small green room, or not smoking
pipes; cavaliers from first to last, all of becoming rank and name,
cavaliers deeply imbued with a sense of the elegant and their
personal dignity, cavaliers for the most part speaking to their
ladies in French, or if in Russian, with the most refined expressions, with compliments and profound phrases; cavaliers who
only perhaps in the smoking-room allowed themselves the
occasional courteous departure from language of the highest
tone – certain phrases of genial and good-humoured familiarity,
such as: 'That was a damned good polka you knocked off,
Petya old man'; or: 'Vasya, you old dog, you swished your lady
about with such gay abandon!' For all this, as I've already had
the honour of explaining to my readers, my pen is inadequate,
therefore I remain silent, oh readers! So, let's better return to
Mr Golyadkin, the true and only hero of this my veracious tale.

The fact is, Mr Golyadkin was now in the most peculiar
position, to say the least. He is here too, gentlemen, that is, not
actually at the ball, but *almost* at the ball. He is all right,
gentlemen; although he is going his own way, the road he's
standing on at that moment is not exactly the most direct one.
Now he is standing – strange to relate – at the entrance hall of
the back stairs to Olsufy Ivanovich's apartment. But it is all
right to be standing there, there is nothing wrong with it; he is
quite all right. He, gentlemen, is standing huddled up in a little
corner which, although not really warm is, on the other hand,
comparatively dark, and he is partly hidden by a huge cupboard
and some old screens, amidst all kinds of rubbish, junk and
lumber, hiding until the right time and in the meantime observing the general course of events as a casual observer. He is

simply observing now, gentlemen. He too might also have gone in . . . So, why not go in? He only has to take one step and he will go in – and go in very niftily too. Only now, after standing, incidentally, nearly three hours in the cold, amidst all kinds of rubbish, junk and lumber, between cupboard and screens was he quoting, in self-justification, a phrase of the late-lamented French minister Villèle,[17] namely: 'All things will come in due course to him who has the gumption to be patient.' Mr Golyadkin had read this phrase at some time in a book on some completely irrelevant subject, but now recalled it extremely aptly. Firstly, the phrase suited his present situation admirably, and secondly, what doesn't enter the head of someone who has spent about three hours in a cold, dark entrance hall, awaiting a happy denouement to his tribulations! After quoting, most appropriately, as I have already said, this phrase of the former French minister Villèle, for some mysterious reason Mr Golyadkin immediately recalled the late Turkish Vizier Martsimiris, as well as the beautiful Margravine Louisa,[18] whose stories he had also read at some time or other in some book. Then he recollected that the Jesuits had even made it their rule that all means were justified as long as the end was achieved. Having somewhat reassured himself by a historical point such as this, Mr Golyadkin asked himself who the Jesuits were: they were the most dreadful idiots, to the last man, and he would put them all in the shade! – if only the refreshment room would empty just for a minute (the room whose door led directly to the back stairs and the entrance hall where Mr Golyadkin now found himself), so that despite all those Jesuits, he would pass straight through himself, first from refreshment room to tea room, then into the room where they were playing cards, then into the hall where they were now dancing the polka. He would go straight through, regardless of everything he would go through, just slip through – no one would notice and that would be that; once there he himself would know what to do. So this is the situation, gentlemen, in which we now find the hero of our perfectly veracious story, although it is difficult to explain what exactly was happening to him during that time. In fact, he had managed to reach the entrance hall and back stairs for

the simple reason, as he said, that everyone had got there, so
why shouldn't he? But he did not dare go further – he clearly
did not dare ... not because there was something he did not
dare do, but because he did not want to, because he very much
preferred to do things nice and quietly. And why should he not
wait? Villèle himself had waited. 'But how does Villèle come
into it?' thought Mr Golyadkin. 'Why bring Villèle in? Well,
what if I take the plunge and go through? ... Oh, you're such
a second-rater, you!' Mr Golyadkin exclaimed, pinching his
frozen cheek with frozen fingers. 'You silly fool – you old
Golyadka![19] What a name you've got!' However, these self-
endearments really meant nothing and were made just in passing, serving no real purpose. Now he was about to charge
in and had already moved forward. The time had come: the
refreshment room had emptied and not a soul was there – Mr
Golyadkin could see that through the tiny window. In two
strides he was at the door and had already started opening it.
'Shall I or shan't I? Shall I go in or shan't I? Yes, I will – why
shouldn't I? All ways are open to the bold!' After thus reassuring
himself, our hero suddenly and quite unexpectedly withdrew
behind the screen. 'No,' he thought, 'what if someone came in?
Yes, you see – someone *has* come in! So why did I stand there
dithering when no one was around? Yes, I should have taken
the plunge and barged straight in! But what's the use of barging
in with a character like mine! What a vile disposition I have! I
simply chickened out! That's all I'm good at, chickening out –
that's right! Always making a mess of things, that's the long
and the short of it. Here I am, standing around like a dummy
– that's what! I wish I were at home drinking a cup of tea. Yes,
a cup of tea would be so nice now! If I'm any later Petrushka
will probably start grumbling. Then shouldn't I go home? Oh,
to hell with it all! ... I'm going in and that's that!' Having
resolved his situation this way, Mr Golyadkin whizzed forward
as if someone had touched off a spring inside him. Two strides
and he found himself in the refreshment room; he threw off his
coat, took off his hat, hurriedly thrust everything into a corner,
tidied himself and smoothed himself down, after which he
proceeded to the tea-room, from the tea-room he darted into

yet another room, slipping almost unnoticed between the card players lost in the excitement of their game. And then . . . and then . . . here Mr Golyadkin forgot all that was going on around him and, like a bolt from the blue, stepped straight into the ballroom.

As if it were fated, they were not dancing at that particular moment. The ladies were strolling around the room in picturesque groups. Gathered in small circles, the men were flitting about, engaging partners. Mr Golyadkin was blind to all this. He saw only Klara Olsufyevna, with Andrey Filippovich beside her, Vladimir Semyonovich, two or three officers and two or three other very interesting looking young men who, as could be seen at first glance, either showed great promise or had already fulfilled it. And he saw some other people too. Or perhaps not; he saw no one at all, nor did he look at anyone, but propelled by that same spring that had sent him whizzing uninvited into someone else's ball, he pressed on further and still further. On his way he stumbled into some counsellor, treading on his foot, at the same time he stepped on the dress of a respectable old lady and tore it slightly, bumped into a man with a tray, elbowed someone else and, without noticing any of this – rather, in fact, noticing it but at the same time not looking at anyone – he forged ahead, until suddenly he found himself right in front of Klara Olsufyevna herself. At that moment, without a shadow of doubt, without batting an eyelid, he could have sunk through the floor with the utmost pleasure. But what's done is done – in no way can it be undone . . . So what was he to do? 'If things are bad – I stand firm; if they go well I hold my ground.' Mr Golyadkin was of course not an intriguer, not adept at polishing the parquet with his boots. And this was just how it happened now . . . Besides, here the Jesuits had somehow got involved . . . however, Mr Golyadkin had no time for *them*! Then suddenly, all that walked, talked, made a noise, moved and laughed, suddenly fell quiet, as if at the wave of a magic wand, and gradually began to crowd around Mr Golyadkin. But Mr Golyadkin seemed to see nothing and hear nothing and he could not look – oh no, not for anything could he bring himself to look! He lowered his eyes and simply stood there, having incidentally vowed to blow his brains out that same night somehow or other. After making this vow, Mr Golyadkin thought to himself: 'Here goes!' – and to his own utter amazement he most unexpectedly started to speak.

Mr Golyadkin began with congratulations and appropriate good wishes. The congratulations went well, but our hero stumbled over the good wishes. He felt that once he stumbled everything would immediately go to the devil. And so it did . . . he stumbled, got stuck . . . he got stuck and he blushed; he blushed and grew flustered; he grew flustered and raised his eyes; he raised his eyes and looked around; he looked around and . . . and he froze . . . Everyone had stopped, everyone had gone silent, everyone was waiting. A little way off there was whispering; a little nearer someone burst into laughter. Mr Golyadkin cast a humble and forlorn look at Andrey Filip-povich. Andrey Filippovich responded with a look that would undoubtedly have crushed our hero a second time – if that were possible – were he not crushed already. The silence continued.

'This has more to do with my domestic circumstances and my own personal life, Andrey Filippovich,' articulated the half-dead Mr Golyadkin in a barely audible voice. 'It's not an official occasion, Andrey Filippovich.'

'Shame on you, sir, shame on you!' Andrey Filippovich pro-nounced in a half-whisper, with a look of indescribable indig-nation; this said he took Klara Olsufyevna by the arm and turned his back on Mr Golyadkin.

'I've nothing to be ashamed of, Andrey Filippovich,' replied Mr Golyadkin, also in a half-whisper, utterly lost, looking around with mournful eyes, trying to find his proper milieu and social position among that bewildered crowd.

'Well, it's all right, it's all right, gentlemen! What's wrong? It could happen to anyone,' Mr Golyadkin whispered, shifting slightly and trying to extricate himself from the surrounding throng. They let him through. Our hero somehow made his way between two rows of inquisitive and nonplussed spectators. Fate was carrying him along – he himself felt that fate was carrying him along. Of course, he would have paid dearly now to be at his former stopping-place, near the back stairs, without any breach of etiquette. Since that was definitely out of the question he tried to slip away into some corner where he could simply stand, modestly, decently, on his own, without troubling anyone, without attracting particular attention to himself, but at the same time winning the good graces of both host and guests. However, Mr Golyadkin felt as if something were undermining him, as if he were tottering and about to fall. Finally he managed to reach a corner and stood there, rather like an outsider, a fairly indifferent observer, leaning his hands on the backs of two chairs, thus having claimed full possession of them and trying his utmost to look cheerfully at those guests of Olsufy Ivanovich who had grouped themselves around him. Nearest to him stood a certain officer, a tall, handsome youth before whom Mr Golyadkin felt a mere insect.

'These two chairs are taken, Lieutenant: one for Klara Olsufyevna and the other for Princess Chevchekhanova who is dancing. I'm keeping them for them now, Lieutenant,' Mr Golyadkin said breathlessly, looking imploringly at the lieutenant. The lieutenant gave him a murderous smile and turned away without a word. Having misfired in this direction, our hero decided to try his luck elsewhere and straight away addressed a certain pompous-looking counsellor with an important decoration around his neck. But the counsellor measured him with such an icy stare that Mr Golyadkin felt he had been doused with a bucketful of cold water. Mr Golyadkin fell silent. He decided it would be best to keep quiet, not to start a conversation, to show that he was all right, that he too was like everyone else and that his position was, as far as he could see at least, really quite proper. To this end he riveted his eyes on the cuffs of his jacket, then he raised his eyes and stared intently at a gentleman of the most respectable appearance. 'That gentleman's wearing a wig,' thought Mr Golyadkin, 'and if it were removed there'd be a bald head – as bald as the palm of my hand.' Having made such an important discovery, Mr Golyadkin remembered those Arabian emirs who, if the green turbans they wear as a mark of kinship with the prophet Muhammed were to be removed, are also left with hairless heads. Then, probably because of some peculiar collision of ideas in his mind regarding the Turks, Mr Golyadkin arrived at Turkish slippers, and now he most aptly remembered that the boots Andrey Filippovich was wearing were more like slippers than boots. Mr Golyadkin was, to a certain extent, clearly in command of the situation. 'If that chandelier,' he thought, 'were to come loose now and fall down on the people below, I'd rush immediately to save Klara Olsufyevna. As I was saving her I'd tell her: "Don't be alarmed, miss, it's nothing. I am he who is your saviour."' And then Mr Golyadkin looked to one side, searching for Klara Olsufyevna, and he spotted Gerasimych, Olsufy Ivanovich's old butler, heading straight for him with the most solicitous, solemnly official expression. An unaccountable and at the same time highly disagreeable sensation made Mr Golyadkin shudder and frown. Mechanically, he looked around; the idea almost occurred to him to sneak off somehow, to get out of harm's way and quietly slip and fade into the background – that is, to act as if nothing were wrong, as if the matter didn't concern him at all. However, before our hero had time to come to a decision, Gerasimych was already standing in front of him. Turning to Gerasimych, our hero said, faintly smiling: 'Do you see that candle up there in the chandelier, Gerasimych? It's going to fall any moment. Now, you must go and give orders at once for someone to straighten it. It's definitely going to fall any minute, Gerasimych.'

'The candle, sir? No, sir, it's absolutely straight . . . But someone's been asking for you, sir.'

'Who could there be asking for me, Gerasimych?'

'Can't say for sure who is it, sir. A certain gentleman from somewhere or other. "Is Yakov Petrovich here?" he said. "Well, call him out, he's wanted on some very urgent and vital matter." That's what he said, sir.'

'No, you're mistaken, Gerasimych, you're quite mistaken.'

'That's doubtful, sir.'

'No, Gerasimych, that's not doubtful at all. No one's asking for me, there's no need for anyone to ask for me . . . I'm at home here – I mean this is where I belong, Gerasimych.'

Mr Golyadkin drew breath and looked around. It was just

as he thought! Every single person in the ballroom was straining eyes and ears at him in solemn expectation. The men had crowded closer and were listening hard. A little further off the ladies were anxiously whispering to each other. The host himself appeared not very far away at all from Mr Golyadkin and although it was impossible to tell from his look whether he in turn was taking an immediate and direct interest in Mr Golyadkin's position, as the whole thing was done on a most tactful footing, all this nonetheless gave our hero clearly to understand that the decisive moment had arrived. Mr Golyadkin clearly saw that the time had come for a bold move, the time to bring disgrace on his enemies. Mr Golyadkin was very agitated. Suddenly Mr Golyadkin felt somehow inspired and in a tremulous, solemn voice he turned to the waiting Gerasimych and began afresh:

'No, my friend, no one's asking for me . . . you're mistaken. I'll go further and say you were mistaken this morning when you assured me, when you dared to assure me (here Mr Golyadkin raised his voice) that Olsufy Ivanovich, my benefactor from time immemorial, who has, in a certain sense, taken the place of a father to me, would close his doors to me at a time of the most solemn domestic rejoicing for his paternal heart. (Smugly, but deeply moved, Mr Golyadkin looked around. Tears glittered on his eyelashes.) 'I repeat, my friend,' concluded our hero, 'you were mistaken, you were cruelly and unforgivably mistaken . . .'

It was a moment of triumph. Mr Golyadkin felt that he had achieved exactly the right effect. He stood there with eyes modestly lowered, awaiting Olsufy Ivanovich's embrace. Among the guests there were distinct signs of agitation and bewilderment. Even the unshakeable and imperturbable Gerasimych stumbled over his words: 'It's doubtful, sir!' And then suddenly, for no apparent reason, the merciless orchestra struck up a polka. All was lost, all was scattered in the wind. Mr Golyadkin shuddered. Gerasimych staggered back and all who were in the ballroom surged like the sea – and there was Vladimir Semyonovich, already whisking Klara Olsufyevna along in the leading pair, followed by the handsome lieutenant and

Princess Chevchekhanova. The spectators, curious and enraptured, crowded to watch those who were dancing the polka – an interesting, novel and fashionable dance that had turned everyone's head. For a time Mr Golyadkin was forgotten. But suddenly all was commotion, confusion and bustle. The music stopped . . . something strange had happened. Wearied by the dance, almost breathless from her exertions, cheeks burning and bosom deeply heaving, Klara Olsufyevna finally sank into an armchair, utterly exhausted. All hearts went out to that fascinating enchantress, everyone was vying with one another to compliment her and thank her for the pleasure she had given them – when suddenly right before her stood Mr Golyadkin. Mr Golyadkin was pale and extremely distraught; he too seemed to be in a state of exhaustion and he could barely move. He was smiling for some reason and offering his hand imploringly. In her astonishment Klara Olsufyevna had no time to withdraw her hand and rose mechanically to Mr Golyadkin's invitation. Mr Golyadkin lurched forward once, and then again, then he somehow raised one foot, then he clicked his heels, stamped his foot and then he stumbled . . . he too wanted to dance with Klara Olsufyevna. Klara Olsufyevna screamed. Everyone rushed to free her hand from Mr Golyadkin's and at once our hero was pushed almost ten paces away by the crowd. A small circle formed around him, too. The shrieks and cries of the two old ladies whom Mr Golyadkin almost knocked over in his retreat rang out. The commotion was terrible: everyone was shouting, arguing, questioning. The orchestra fell silent. Our hero was spinning around within his small circle and was mechanically, faintly smiling, muttering something to himself under his breath, to the effect that: Why not? The polka was a novel and most interesting dance, devised to divert the ladies . . . But if this was how things stood now he was by all means ready to acquiesce. But no one was asking for Mr Golyadkin's acquiescence, at least so it seemed to him. Our hero suddenly felt someone's hand fall on his arm, then another pressed down slightly against his back and he felt he was being steered with particular solicitude in a certain direction. Finally he noticed that he was heading straight for the doors. Mr Golyadkin wanted to do something, to say something . . . But no, he no longer wanted anything. He simply laughed it off mechanically. Finally, he became aware that they were putting him into his overcoat and pulling his hat down over his eyes; at length he felt he was out in the passage, in the cold and dark, and then on the stairs. He stumbled and felt he was falling into an abyss; he wanted to cry out – and then suddenly he found himself out in the courtyard. The fresh air wafted over him and he stood still for a moment. At that very instant the sound of the orchestra striking up again reached his ears. Mr Golyadkin suddenly remembered everything: he seemed to have recovered all his lost strength. From where he had just been standing as if rooted to the spot, he tore off and rushed headlong – anywhere, to freedom, to fresh air, to wherever his legs would carry him . . .

CHAPTER V

Every clock tower in St Petersburg that showed and told the hour was striking exactly midnight when Mr Golyadkin, beside himself, ran on to the Fontanka Embankment,[20] near that same Izmaylovsky Bridge, seeking refuge from his enemies, from persecution, from the insults that had rained down on him, from the shrieks of frightened old ladies, from the sobbing and sighing of women – and from Andrey Filippovich's murderous glances. Mr Golyadkin was crushed, absolutely crushed, in the full sense of the word, and if he still had the ability to run at that moment it was solely by some miracle, a miracle in which he himself refused to believe. It was a dreadful November night – dank, misty, raining, snowing, a night fraught with colds, fevers, agues, quinsies and inflammations of every conceivable variety and description – in brief, fraught with all the blessings of a St Petersburg November. The wind howled down the deserted streets, raising the black waters of the Fontanka above the mooring-rings and rattling with a vengeance the feeble lanterns along the embankment which echoed its howling with those shrill, ear-splitting squeaks that make up the endless concert of jarring sounds so very familiar to every inhabitant of St Petersburg. It was raining and snowing at the same time. Sheets of rain, broken up by the wind, sprayed about almost horizontally, as if from a fire hose, stabbing and stinging the face of the hapless Mr Golyadkin like a thousand pins and needles. Amidst the stillness of the night, interrupted only by the distant rumble of carriages, the howling of the wind and the squeaking lanterns, could be heard the mournful sound of water, gushing and gurgling from every roof, porch, gutter and cornice on to the granite pavement. There was not a soul to be seen, either far or near – it seemed there could not possibly be at such an hour and in such weather. And so, only Mr Golyadkin, alone in his despair, was trotting along the Fontanka at this time of night, taking his usual rapid, short steps, hurrying to reach his fourth-floor flat in Shestilavochnaya Street as soon as he possibly could.

Although the rain, the snow and everything that does not even have a name, when a blizzard rages and thick fog comes down on a St Petersburg November night, were suddenly, of one accord, attacking Mr Golyadkin, who was crushed enough by misfortune, allowing him not the least protection or respite, chilling him to the marrow, gluing up his eyes, gusting from all sides, driving him off his path and out of his mind – and although all this descended on Mr Golyadkin at once, as if deliberately conspiring with his enemies to give him a day, evening and night he would never forget – despite all this Mr Golyadkin remained almost unaffected by this final proof of a fate that was pursuing him, so thoroughly shaken and stunned was he by all that had happened to him a few minutes earlier at State Counsellor Berendeyev's! If any disinterested, outside observer had now casually glanced from the side at Mr Golyadkin in his wretched flight he would have at once fathomed the whole awful horror of his tribulations and would doubtless have said that Mr Golyadkin now looked like a man wanting to hide, wanting to run away from himself. Yes! – that really was the case. Let us say more: now Mr Golyadkin not only wanted to escape from himself, but even hide from himself, to be utterly annihilated, to exist no more and turn to dust. At that

moment he was oblivious of everything around, understood
nothing that was happening around him and he looked as if all
the nastiness of that foul night, the long walk, the rain and
wind and snow, did not in fact exist for him. One galosh,
having parted company with Mr Golyadkin's right foot, was
left behind in the slush and snow on the Fontanka pavement, but Mr Golyadkin didn't even consider going back for
it and didn't even notice he had lost it. He was so perplexed
that several times, despite all that was surrounding him, he
would suddenly stop short and stand stock-still in the middle
of the pavement, completely obsessed by the thought of his
recent appalling fall from grace. At those moments he would
die, he would vanish. Then he would suddenly tear off again
like one demented and run and run, without looking back, as
if escaping pursuit or some even more dreadful calamity. His
predicament was truly shocking. At length, his strength exhausted, Mr Golyadkin stopped, leant over the embankment railing
like a man with a sudden nosebleed and stared intently at the
dark, murky waters of the Fontanka. There is no knowing
exactly how long he spent in this occupation. All that is known
is that at that moment Mr Golyadkin plumbed such depths of
despair, was so tormented, harassed, exhausted, so bereft of
any spark of fortitude, so disheartened, that he had forgotten
everything: Izmaylovsky Bridge, Shestilavochnaya Street and
his present plight . . . But what did it matter? Really he couldn't
have cared less. Everything was all over – signed, settled and
sealed. Why should he fret over it? Suddenly . . . suddenly he
shuddered all over and instinctively leapt a couple of steps
sideways. With an indescribable feeling of uneasiness he started
looking around. But no one was there, nothing out of the
ordinary had happened and . . . meanwhile . . . meanwhile he
felt that someone had been standing right beside him just then,
his elbows similarly propped on the railings and – amazing to
relate – had even said something to him, abruptly and hurriedly,
not altogether intelligibly but about something very familiar to
him and which concerned him. 'Well now, have I imagined all
this?' Mr Golyadkin asked himself, looking round again. 'But
where am I standing? . . . Ah, ah!' he concluded, shaking his

head and meanwhile peering with an anxious, dejected feeling, even fearfully, into the wet, murky distance, straining his short-sighted eyes as hard as he could and doing his utmost to penetrate the sodden gloom that stretched before him. However, there was nothing new, nothing in particular caught Mr Golyadkin's eye. Everything appeared to be in order and as it should have been – that is, the snow was falling even harder and thicker, in larger flakes, nothing was visible at twenty paces. The lanterns squeaked even more shrilly than before and the wind seemed to be singing its melancholy song even more mournfully and plaintively than ever, like some importunate beggar pleading for a few copecks for food. 'Eh, eh! What on earth's the matter with me?' Mr Golyadkin repeated, setting off again and constantly looking round slightly. Meanwhile some new sensation took complete possession of his whole being – not really anguish, not really fear . . . a feverish tremor ran through his every sinew. It was an unbearably nasty moment! 'Well, it's nothing,' he muttered to encourage himself, 'it's nothing. Perhaps it's absolutely nothing at all and no stain on anyone's honour. Perhaps it was all meant to be,' he continued, without understanding himself what he was saying. 'Perhaps in its own good time everything will turn out for the best. There'll be nothing to complain about and everyone will be vindicated.' Talking in this way and calming himself with these words Mr Golyadkin gave himself a little shake, shook off the snowflakes that had been forming a thick crust on his hat, collar, overcoat, scarf, boots – on everything, in fact. But he still couldn't brush aside or rid himself of that strange, vague feeling of anguish. Somewhere far off the sound of a cannon rang out. 'What weather!' thought our hero. 'Just listen to that! Could it be a flood warning? Clearly the water's dangerously high.' No sooner had Mr Golyadkin said or thought this than he saw a passer-by walking towards him, most likely someone delayed for some reason himself. It was all of little consequence, it would seem, a chance encounter. But for some mysterious reason Mr Golyadkin became alarmed, afraid even, and he felt somewhat at a loss. It wasn't that he feared that it might be some nasty character . . . well, perhaps . . . 'Who knows who this belated

person could be?' flashed through his mind. 'Perhaps he's part
of the same thing, perhaps he's the most important person in
this business and he's not here for nothing but has a purpose
in coming, in crossing my path and bumping into me.' But
perhaps Mr Golyadkin did not think precisely that and had only
a fleeting impression of something resembling it and extremely
unpleasant. Yet there was no time for thinking or even feeling;
the passer-by was already within a couple of strides. As was his
invariable habit, Mr Golyadkin wasted no time in assuming a
very special look, a look that clearly expressed that he, Mr
Golyadkin, was minding his own business, that he was all right,
that the street was wide enough for everyone and that indeed
he, Mr Golyadkin, was bothering no one. Suddenly he stood
rooted to the spot, as if struck by lightning and then swiftly
turned around after the stranger who had just passed him
– turned around as if someone had tugged him from behind
and turned him as the wind swings a weathercock. The
passer-by was fast disappearing in the snowstorm. He too was
in a hurry like Mr Golyadkin and he too was wrapped up from
head to foot, he too was pattering along the Fontanka pavement
with the same rapid short steps and at a slight trot. 'What,
what's this?' whispered Mr Golyadkin with an incredulous
smile and yet trembling in every limb. Cold shivers ran down
his spine. Meanwhile the passer-by had disappeared completely
and his footsteps could no longer be heard, but Mr Golyadkin
still stood there, gazing after him. Gradually, though, he finally
came to his senses. 'What on earth's going on?' he thought
irritably. 'Have I gone mad, really gone mad?' He turned and
went on his way, quickening his stride the whole time and
trying his level best to avoid thinking of anything at all. To this
end he even closed his eyes. Suddenly, through the howling of
the wind and noise of the storm, he again heard the sound of
someone's footsteps very close by. He started and opened his
eyes. Ahead of him, about twenty paces away, the small dark
figure of a man was rapidly approaching. This little man was
in a hurry, rushing along with short rapid steps; the distance
between them was rapidly diminishing. Now Mr Golyadkin
could clearly make out his new, belated companion – made him

out completely and he shrieked with horror and bewilderment; his legs gave way. It was that very same passer-by, already familiar to him, for whom he had made way and passed ten minutes earlier, who had now appeared before him, again quite unexpectedly. But it was not only this marvel that startled Mr Golyadkin – and Mr Golyadkin was so startled that he stopped, cried out, tried to say something – and then he raced off in pursuit of the stranger, even shouting out to him to stop as quickly as possible. The stranger did indeed stop – about ten paces from Mr Golyadkin, so that the light of a nearby street lamp fell fully on his whole figure – he stopped and turned to Mr Golyadkin and with an anxious and impertinent look waited to hear what Mr Golyadkin had to say. 'Forgive me, I seem to have been mistaken,' our hero said in a quavering voice. Without a word, the stranger turned away in a huff and swiftly went on his way, as if hurrying to make up the few seconds wasted over Mr Golyadkin. As for Mr Golyadkin, he was trembling in every fibre; his knees weakened and buckled beneath him and he squatted on a bollard, groaning. And in fact he had very good reason to feel so distressed. The fact was, this stranger now seemed somehow familiar. That in itself wouldn't have mattered. But he recognized him – he almost completely recognized that man now. He'd often seen that man at some time, quite recently even. Where could it have been? Could it have been yesterday? However, the important thing wasn't that Mr Golyadkin had often seen him; and there was hardly anything special about that man – certainly no one would have given him a second look. So, he was like anyone else, like all respectable people of course and probably even possessed some quite special qualities – in short he was an individual in his own right. Mr Golyadkin didn't feel either hatred or even open hostility, not the slightest enmity towards him: quite the opposite it would seem. And yet (and this circumstance was the essential thing), and yet, not for all the tea in China would he have wanted to meet him and particularly not to meet him as just now, for example. We shall say more: Mr Golyadkin knew that man extremely well; he even knew what he was called, his surname. But at the same time, not for all the tea in China

would he have wanted to name him or agree to admit that, in
a manner of speaking, that's what he was called – Christian
name, patronymic and surname. Whether Mr Golyadkin's confusion was long-lasting or brief, or whether he squatted for
long on that bollard I cannot say, only that, finally recovering
slightly, he suddenly hared off as fast as he could without
looking back, with all the strength he could muster. His lungs
were bursting; twice he stumbled and nearly fell and as a result
of this event Mr Golyadkin's other boot was orphaned, also
abandoned by its galosh. Finally Mr Golyadkin slackened his
pace a little to catch his breath, took a hurried look round and
saw that he'd already run, without noticing it, the whole way
along the Fontanka, had crossed Anichkov Bridge,[21] had gone
down part of Nevsky Prospekt and was now standing at the
junction with Liteynaya Street. Mr Golyadkin turned into Liteynaya Street. His situation at that moment was like that of a
man on the brink of a terrifying precipice, when the ground is
giving way beneath him; it is moving and rocking, it quakes, it
sways for the last time and falls, drawing him towards the
abyss, which the poor wretch has neither the strength nor
the fortitude to leap back from, or to avert his eyes from the
yawning chasm. The abyss is drawing him on and finally he
himself leaps into it, thus hastening his own demise. Mr Golyadkin knew and felt, and was perfectly convinced, that some
new evil would overtake him on his way, that more unpleasantness was bound to erupt over his head, that, for instance, he
might again encounter that stranger. But – strange to relate –
he positively longed for that meeting, considering it inevitable,
and all he asked was that the whole thing should be over and
done with, that his position should be decided quickly, one way
or the other, so long as it was soon. Meanwhile on and on he
ran, as if propelled by some external force, for he felt a growing
weakness and a numbness in his whole being. He couldn't think
of anything, although his mind clutched at everything, like
blackthorn. A wretched stray dog, wet and shivering, attached
itself to Mr Golyadkin and hurried along beside him, its tail
between its legs and its ears laid back, looking up at him
every now and then, timidly and intelligently. Some remote,

long-forgotten idea, the memory of something that had happened long ago, now entered his head, tapping away like a
small hammer in his brain, vexing him and not leaving him in
peace. 'Ugh, that nasty little cur!' Mr Golyadkin whispered,
not understanding what he was saying himself. At length he
caught sight of his stranger at the corner of Italyanskaya Street.
Only this time the stranger wasn't coming towards him but was
also running in the same direction, a few steps ahead. At last
they turned into Shestilavochnaya Street: it took Mr Golyadkin's breath away – the stranger had stopped right in front
of the block where Mr Golyadkin lodged. The sound of a bell
rang out and almost at the same time an iron bolt creaked. The
gate opened, the stranger stooped, flitted past and vanished.
Almost at the same moment Mr Golyadkin arrived too and
flew through the gates like an arrow. Ignoring the grumbling
porter he ran breathlessly into the courtyard and immediately
caught sight of his interesting companion whom he'd lost for
one moment. Then he glimpsed the stranger at the entrance of
the staircase that led to Mr Golyadkin's flat. Mr Golyadkin
hurtled after him. The staircase was dark, damp and filthy.
Every landing was heaped with all kinds of tenants' rubbish, so
that a stranger, unfamiliar with the place and have to face that
staircase after dark, was forced to spend about half an hour
climbing it, risking breaking his legs and cursing his friends
(together with the staircase) for residing in such an inconvenient
locality. But Mr Golyadkin's companion seemed to be perfectly
at home and familiar with his surroundings and he ran up
easily, without any trouble and with a complete knowledge of
the topography. Mr Golyadkin almost caught up with him;
once or twice the tail of the stranger's coat even struck his nose.
And then his heart missed a beat: the mysterious person stopped
right outside the doors to Mr Golyadkin's flat, and knocked
(at any other time this would have startled Mr Golyadkin).
Petrushka opened the door at once, as if he had been waiting
up for him and hadn't gone to bed and followed the man who
entered, candle in hand. Quite beside himself the hero of our
tale ran into his abode; without taking off hat or coat, he went
down the short passage and stopped on the threshold of his

room as if thunderstruck. All Mr Golyadkin's worst misgivings were confirmed. All that he had dreaded and guessed at had now taken place in reality. He gasped for breath, his head went round. There was the stranger, sitting before him on his own bed, also wearing a hat and coat, faintly smiling, screwing up his eyes a little, and giving him a friendly nod. Mr Golyadkin wanted to cry out, but he was unable to; he wanted to protest in some way, but his strength failed him. His hair stood on end and he squatted where he was, insensible with horror. And besides, he had good reason. Mr Golyadkin had fully recognized his nocturnal friend: his nocturnal friend was none other than himself, Mr Golyadkin in person – another Mr Golyadkin, but identical to him in every way – in brief, in all respects what is called his double . . .

CHAPTER VI

Next morning, at exactly eight o'clock, Mr Golyadkin came to in his bed. Immediately all the extraordinary events of the previous day, all that unbelievable night with its well-nigh impossible events, suddenly, all at once, presented themselves to his imagination and memory in their horrifying fullness. Such fierce, hellish malice on the part of his enemies – and particularly this last proof of malice – made Mr Golyadkin's blood run cold. But at the same time it was all so strange, so incomprehensible, so weird, so impossible even, that it was extremely difficult to credit any of the whole business. Even Mr Golyadkin himself was ready to admit that it was all some fantastic raving, some momentary derangement of the imagination or darkening of the mind, had he not known – fortunately for him, from bitter experience of life – to what length malice can drive a man sometimes, to what extremes an embittered enemy can sometimes go to avenge his honour and pride. Besides, Mr Golyadkin's exhausted limbs, his befuddled head, his aching back and his pernicious head cold were powerful enough testimony to confirm the whole plausibility of the

previous night's walk – and in part all the other things that had
happened during the course of that walk. Finally, Mr Golyadkin
had in fact known for ages that they were cooking something
up and that someone else was mixed up in it with them. But
what then? After carefully thinking it over, Mr Golyadkin
decided to keep quiet, to submit and not make his protest before
the time was right. 'Well, perhaps they just thought they'd give
me a fright and when they see that I don't care, that I'm not
protesting, but fully resigned to it and that I'm prepared to grin
and bear it they'll just withdraw, withdraw of their own accord
– yes, they'll be the first to withdraw.'

These were the kinds of thoughts that ran through Mr Golyadkin's mind while he stretched out on his bed, relaxing his
aching limbs and waiting on this occasion for Petrushka's customary appearance in his room. He had already been waiting
nearly a quarter of an hour and could hear that lazy Petrushka
fussing with the samovar behind the partition, but at the same
time he just couldn't bring himself to summon him. We could
go further and say that Mr Golyadkin was even slightly apprehensive of a confrontation with Petrushka. 'God only knows
what that scoundrel will think about all this now,' he wondered.
'He usually keeps his mouth shut, but he's a cunning devil!'
Finally the door creaked and Petrushka appeared with a tray
in his hands. Mr Golyadkin looked at him sheepishly, with a
sidelong glance, waiting impatiently to discover what would
happen next, waiting to hear whether he would have anything
to say regarding a certain circumstance. But Petrushka didn't
say a word – on the contrary, he was even more taciturn and
truculent and angrier than usual, scowling at everything; evidently he was extremely displeased about something. Not once
did he even glance at his master and this, we can say, in passing,
rather piqued Mr Golyadkin. After putting everything he had
brought on the table he turned and vanished in silence behind
his partition. 'He knows, he knows everything, the lazy devil!'
grumbled Mr Golyadkin as he started on his tea. However, our
hero didn't question his manservant about anything, although
Petrushka subsequently entered several times, on different
errands. Mr Golyadkin was in the most agitated state of mind.

What was more, he dreaded going to the office. He had a strong presentiment that it was precisely *there* that something wasn't quite right. 'So, I'll go along,' he thought, 'and what if I run slap bang into something? Wouldn't it be best to try and be patient now? Wouldn't it be best to wait for a bit now? They can do what they like there. Really, I'd better wait here today, get my strength back, get back on my feet, have a good think about all this, then seize the right moment, turn up out of the blue and act as if nothing were wrong.' With these considerations Mr Golyadkin smoked pipe after pipe. The time flew – it was already almost half past nine. 'Ah well, it's already half past nine,' thought Mr Golyadkin, 'so it's too late now to turn up. Besides, I'm ill, of course I'm ill, no question I'm ill. Who'd deny it? What do I care? And if they send someone to check up on me, an administrative clerk, what does it matter, in effect? My back aches, I've a bad cough and a cold in the head. Finally, I couldn't, I couldn't possibly go in this weather. I might be taken seriously ill and then even die; the death rate's particularly high just now . . .' By virtue of these arguments Mr Golyadkin finally eased his conscience completely and justified himself in advance against the dressing-down he could expect from Andrey Filippovich for neglecting his work. Generally speaking, in all such cases our hero was inordinately fond of vindicating himself in his own eyes with various kinds of irrefutable arguments and thus completely salving his conscience. So, his conscience completely salved, he took up his pipe, filled it, and the moment it was drawing nicely he sprang up from the sofa, abandoned the pipe, briskly washed, shaved, smoothed his hair, put on his uniform jacket and all the rest, grabbed some papers and flew off to the office.

Mr Golyadkin entered his department timidly, trembling in expectation of something very bad – expectation which, although unconscious and vague, was nonetheless unpleasant. Sheepishly he seated himself at his customary place next to Anton Antonovich Setochkin, the chief clerk. Without looking at anything or allowing himself to be distracted he investigated the contents of the documents that were lying before him. He had resolved and had promised himself to avoid as far as

possible anything that might provoke him, anything that could
seriously compromise him, namely, indelicate questions, any
kind of jokes and unseemly allusions regarding all the previous
evening's events; he even decided to forgo the usual polite
exchanges with his colleagues, such as inquiring about their
health and so on. But it was also obviously clearly impossible
to maintain this stance. Uneasiness and ignorance about something that intimately concerned him always tormented him
more than the thing itself. So that was why, despite the promise
he had made to himself not to allow himself to become involved
in anything, at all costs, happen what may, to keep aloof from
everything, no matter what, Mr Golyadkin, furtively and
stealthily, occasionally kept raising his head very slightly, slyly
looking to left and right, peering into his colleagues' faces to
try and read from their expressions if anything new or special
concerning him was being concealed for some improper
reasons. He assumed that there was a definite link between all
yesterday's events and everything around him now. Finally, in
his acute distress, he began to wish that everything would be
resolved quickly – God knows how – even if it had to be through
some disaster, no matter what! And here fate took him at his
word: no sooner had Mr Golyadkin time to wish this than his
doubts were suddenly resolved, but in the strangest and most
unexpected fashion.

The door from the next room suddenly opened with a timid,
quiet creak, as if thus announcing the entrance of a very insignificant person, and someone's figure, incidentally very familiar
to Mr Golyadkin, came in and shyly stood before the very desk
at which our hero was seated. Our hero didn't raise his head –
oh no! He only gave this figure the slightest, fleeting glance, but
he already knew everything, he understood everything, down
to the smallest detail . . . He was burning with shame and buried
his wretched head in some documents for the same reason that
an ostrich pursued by the hunter hides its head in the scorching
sands. The newcomer bowed to Mr Golyadkin and after that
he could hear an officially kind voice, the sort in which all heads
of department usually address newly arrived subordinates. 'Sit
here,' Andrey Filippovich said, motioning the new recruit to

Anton Antonovich's desk. 'Sit here, opposite Mr Golyadkin, and we'll give you some work right away,' Andrey Filippovich concluded by making a rapid, suitably commanding gesture to the newcomer and then he immediately absorbed himself in the contents of the various documents lying in a great pile before him.

Mr Golyadkin at last raised his eyes and if he did not faint it was only because he had a foreboding of the whole thing from the start, had been forewarned about everything from the start, and had already divined in his heart the newcomer's identity. Mr Golyadkin's first move was to take a rapid look around to see if there was any whispering, whether any office witticisms on the subject were pouring forth, whether anyone's face was contorted with surprise or, finally, whether anyone had fallen under his desk from fright. But to Mr Golyadkin's extreme amazement he could detect nothing of the kind in anyone. Mr Golyadkin was astounded by the behaviour of his colleages and comrades. It seemed beyond the bounds of common sense. Mr Golyadkin was even scared by such an unusual silence. The reality spoke for itself: it was a strange, ugly, absurd affair. There was good reason to feel disturbed. All this, of course, merely flashed through Mr Golyadkin's mind. He himself felt he was being roasted over a low flame. And he had good reason. The person now sitting opposite Mr Golyadkin was Mr Golyadkin's horror, Mr Golyadkin's shame, Mr Golyadkin's nightmare of the day before: in brief it was Mr Golyadkin himself – not the Mr Golyadkin now sitting on his chair with his mouth agape and his pen frozen in his grasp; not the one who worked as assistant to the head clerk; not the one who liked to be self-effacing and bury himself in the crowd; finally, not the one whose walk clearly announced: 'Don't touch me and I shan't touch you.' No – this was another Mr Golyadkin, a completely different one, but at the same time one who was completely identical to the first – the same height, the same build, the same clothes, the same bald patch – in brief, nothing had been omitted for a perfect likeness, so that if one were to stand them side by side, nobody, absolutely nobody would have ventured to determine who was the real Mr Golyadkin and who the fake, who the old and who the new, who the original and who the copy.

Our hero, if the comparison may be allowed, was now in the situation of someone with whom some prankster was having fun, slyly turning his burning-glass on him for a joke. 'What is this – is it a dream or not?' he wondered. 'Is it real or simply the continuation of yesterday's events? But how can this be? By what right is all this happening? Who engaged such a clerk, who authorized such a thing? Am I sleeping, am I day-dreaming?' Mr Golyadkin tried pinching himself – he even conceived the idea of pinching someone else . . . No, it was no dream and that was that. Mr Golyadkin felt the sweat pouring off him, felt that something unprecedented and hitherto unseen was happening to him and, for that very reason, to crown his misfortune, was improper, for Mr Golyadkin realized and sensed the disadvantage of being the first example of such a scandalous business. In the end he even began to doubt his own existence and although he had been prepared for everything to start with and had longed for all his doubts to be somehow resolved, the very essence of the situation was of course its unexpectedness. His anguish crushed and tormented him. At times he completely lost all capacity for reasoning and remembering. Recovering after such a moment, he noticed that he was automatically and unconsciously moving pen over paper. As he did not trust himself, he began checking all he had written but could not make head or tail of it. At length the other Mr Golyadkin, who up to then had been sitting decorously and demurely at his desk, got up and disappeared through the doorway into another section on some business. Mr Golyadkin looked around – everything was all right, all was still. Only the scratching of pens could be heard, the rustle of turning pages and snatches of conversation in the corners furthest removed from Andrey Filippovich's seat. Mr Golyadkin glanced at Anton Antonovich and since, in all probability, our hero's face fully reflected his present plight and harmonized with all that the present business implied so that consequently it was very remarkable in a certain respect, the kindly Anton Antonovich put down his pen and inquired after Mr Golyadkin's state of health with unusual solicitude.

'I – I'm all right, perfectly well, thank God, Anton Antono-
vich,' stammered Mr Golyadkin. 'I'm all right now, Anton
Antonovich,' he added irresolutely, still not fully trusting Anton
Antonovich, whom he had mentioned so often.

'Ah! I thought you were ill. But that wouldn't surprise me –
who knows what can happen! At the moment there's all sorts
of epidemics going around. Do you know . . .'

'Yes, Anton Antonovich, I know there's epidemics going
around . . . But that's not why I, Anton Antonovich . . .' continued Mr Golyadkin, staring hard at Anton Antonovich. 'You
see, I don't even know how to put it . . . that is, I mean to
say . . . from what angle should I tackle this matter, Anton
Antonovich?'

'What did you say? Well, you know . . . I must confess . . . I
don't really get your drift. You know, you must explain in more
detail in what respect you are having difficulty,' said Anton
Antonovich, who was beginning to have a little difficulty himself when he saw that tears had started to Mr Golyadkin's eyes.

'I . . . really . . . here, Anton Antonovich . . . there's a clerk
here, Anton Antonovich.'

'Well now! I still don't understand.'

'I mean to say, Anton Antonovich, there's a new clerk here.'

'Yes there is, sir, with the same surname as yours.'

'What?!' cried Mr Golyadkin.

'I'm telling you, he's got the same name. He's a Golyadkin
too. Is he your brother?'

'No, Anton Antonovich . . . I . . .'

'Hm! Then please tell me . . . I had the impression that he
must be a close relative of yours. There's a family likeness of
sorts, you know.'

Mr Golyadkin was absolutely dumbfounded and for a while
he lost the power of speech. How could he treat something so
monstrous and unprecedented so lightly, something rare
enough of its kind, something that would have astonished even
the most impartial observer, and talk of a family likeness when
it was as clear as if in a mirror!

'Do you know what I advise, Yakov Petrovich?' Anton
Antonovich continued. 'You should go to the doctor's and ask

his advice. You know, you don't look at all well. Your eyes in particular . . . you know . . . they've such a peculiar expression.'

'No, Anton Antonovich . . . of course I feel . . . I mean, I still want to ask – what do you think about this clerk?'

'Well, what exactly?'

'I mean, haven't you noticed something special about him, something very significant?'

'And what's that?'

'I mean to say, a striking resemblance to someone – to me, for example. Just now, Anton Antonovich, you remarked on a family likeness in passing . . . Do you know that twins are sometimes alike as two peas in a pod, so you can't tell the difference? That's what I meant.'

'Yes,' said Anton Antonovich, after pausing for thought and realized this was the first time he had been struck by such a circumstance. 'Yes sir, you are right! The resemblance is truly amazing and indeed you're not wrong when you say that one could be taken for the other,' he continued, opening his eyes ever wider. 'And do you know, Yakov Petrovich, it's really a miraculous resemblance, a fantastic likeness as they sometimes say . . . that is, he's you to a tee! Haven't you noticed, Yakov Petrovich? I was even intending to ask if you could explain it and I must confess I didn't pay due attention at first. It's a marvel, a sheer marvel! And you're not from these parts, are you, Yakov Petrovich?'

'No, sir.'

'He's not from here either. Perhaps he hails from the same place as you. Now, if I dare ask, where did your mother live most of her life?'

'Did you say . . . did you say, Anton Antonovich, that he's not from round here?'

'No, not from here. But really, it's an absolute miracle,' continued the loquacious Anton Antonovich, for whom it was a real pleasure to have something to gossip about, 'it could really arouse one's curiosity. And how often might you pass him, bump into him or brush against him and not notice. But don't go upsetting yourself. It happens. Do you know – I must tell you this – exactly the same thing happened to an aunt on my mother's side. Before she died she too saw herself doubly . . .'

'No . . . I . . . please forgive me for interrupting, Anton Antonovich, but I'd like to know how this clerk . . . that is, on what basis is he here?'

'Well, he's filled the position left by the late Semyon Ivanovich. The position fell vacant, so they took him on. Oh yes, that poor, good-hearted Semyon Ivanovich. He left three little children, all tiny tots, I've heard say. His widow fell at His Excellency's feet. But they do say she's hiding something: she's got a little money, but she's hidden it away.'

'No, I'm still talking about that other circumstance, Anton Antonovich.'

'What's that? Oh yes! But why are you so interested in it? I'm telling you, don't go upsetting yourself. It's only temporary. And what does it matter? It's got nothing to do with you. It's all the Lord God's work, He arranged it, it's His will and to complain about it is sinful. His wisdom is plain to see. But you, Yakov Petrovich, as far as I understand, are not to blame in any way. The world is so abundant in wonders! Mother Nature is bounteous. No one's asking you to account for this, you won't be held responsible for it. And while we're on the subject, let me give you an example. I hope you've heard of – what on earth do you call them? – oh yes, those Siamese twins,[22] born with their backs joined and they have to live, eat and sleep like that, always together. I've heard people say they're making a lot of money.'

'If you don't mind, Anton Antonovich . . .'

'I understand you, I do understand! Oh yes! Well, what of it? It's nothing! I'm telling you that as I see it there's nothing to feel upset about. So what? He's a clerk like any other and he strikes me as the efficient sort. Says his name is Golyadkin, that he's not from round here and he's a titular counsellor. He gave a good account of himself in person to His Excellency.'

'Well, what happened?'

'Oh, it went well. They say he gave a very good account of himself – provided good arguments. "Well, it's like this, Your Excellency," he said, "I've no money and I'm keen to work here and I should be especially flattered to serve under your distinguished command." – Well, he said all the right things, expressed himself well. He must be a clever chap. Of course, he came with a reference – can't get far without one of those, you know!'

'Well ... from whom? I mean, who exactly had a hand in this shameful business?'

'Oh yes, a good reference, they say. His Excellency, so I'm told, had a good laugh over it with Andrey Filippovich.'

'Had a laugh with Andrey Filippovich?'

'Yes, he simply smiled and said it was all right, that he had no objections, as long as he served loyally.'

'Go on, you're cheering me up a bit, Anton Antonovich! Please go on, I beg you.'

'Forgive me again, there's something else I don't quite ... Ah well, it doesn't matter, it's perfectly simple. Now don't you go upsetting yourself, I say, there's nothing at all dubious about it.'

'No ... I ... that is, I'd like to ask you, Anton Antonovich, if His Excellency added something else – about me, for example?'

'What do you mean? Oh yes! But no, there was nothing, so you can put your mind at rest. Of course, it goes without saying that it's something quite striking and at first ... well, take me, for example, I almost didn't notice it at first. I really don't know why I didn't notice it, until you mentioned it. But you can relax, His Excellency said nothing special, absolutely nothing at all,' added the kindly Anton Antonovich, rising from his seat.

'So I, Anton Antonovich ...'

'Ah, if you'll excuse me ... Here I've been waffling away about trifles and I've important business to see to. It's urgent, I must deal with it right away.'

'Anton Antonovich!' Andrey Filippovich's politely summoning voice rang out. 'His Excellency's asking for you.'

'Right away, Andrey Filippovich, right away.' And Anton Antonovich, picking up a pile of papers, flew off first to Andrey Filippovich, then to His Excellency's study.

'So, how is this?' Mr Golyadkin thought to himself. 'So that's their little game. That's the way the wind's blowing here now ... But it's not so bad. Things must have taken a most pleasant turn,' our hero said to himself, rubbing his hands for joy. 'So, it's quite run-of-the-mill, this business of ours. It's all ending in trivialities, just fizzling out. In fact no one's doing anything – not a squeak out of them, the scoundrels! – they're just sitting there and getting on with their work. Splendid, splendid! I like a good man, always have done, and I always have respect for him But come to think of it, it's not so good ... I'm scared of trusting him with anything, that Anton Antonovich. He's gone terribly grey and he's on his last legs. Still, the most wonderful, stupendous thing is that His Excellency didn't say anything and simply turned a blind eye. That's good, I approve of that. Only, why does Anton Antonovich have to poke his nose into it with that chuckling of his? What's it to do with him? Cunning old fox! Always in my way, always rubbing people up the wrong way, always crossing and spiting a man, always spiting and crossing ...'

Mr Golyadkin took another look around and again his hopes revived. For all that, a remote, nasty thought was troubling him. He even considered for the moment somehow currying favour with the clerks, somehow stealing a march on them even (as they were all leaving work, approaching them ostensibly about office matters) dropping hints during the course of a conversation to the effect: it's like this, gentlemen, there's this striking resemblance, a strange circumstance, a pure farce – so that by treating it all as a joke he could take soundings of the depth of the danger. 'Still waters run deep,' concluded our hero. But this was no more than a thought – and then he changed his mind in time. He realized that this would be going too far. 'That's you all over!' he said to himself, giving his forehead a gentle smack. 'You'll be jumping for joy in a moment, you're so pleased, you honest soul! No, we'd better be patient, you and I, Yakov Petrovich, we'll wait and be patient.' Nevertheless, as we have already mentioned, Mr Golyadkin's hopes were completely revived and he felt as if he'd risen from the dead. 'It's fine,' he thought.' It's like a ton's fallen from my chest! I mean to say – what a circumstance! "And the casket opened easily after all."[23] That Krylov's right, yes, Krylov's right – he's really cunning, he's a master that Krylov – and a great fable-writer!

And as for that fellow, let him work here to his heart's content, as long as he doesn't pester anyone or get in their way. Let him work here – he has my full consent and approval!'

Meanwhile the hours were flying past and before anyone realized it four o'clock struck. The office closed. Andrey Filippovich took his hat and as usual everyone followed suit. Mr Golyadkin hung around a little, just as long as was necessary, and deliberately left later than anyone, ensuring he was last, when all had gone their various ways. Out in the street he felt as if he were in paradise, so much so that he even had the urge to go down Nevsky Prospekt, even if it meant a detour. 'Surely it's fate,' our hero said, 'the whole thing's taken an unexpected turn. And the weather's cleared up, there's a nice frost and the sledges are out. Frosts suit Russians, Russians and frosts get on splendidly. I do like Russians! And there's snow – the first powdering, as a hunter would say. How lovely it would be to go out after a hare over the newly fallen snow! Ah well, everything's fine!'

This was how Mr Golyadkin expressed his delight, yet something was still nagging away in his head, not really what you would call anguish, and at times there was such a gnawing at his heart that he didn't know how to console himself. 'Still, let's wait another day and then we can rejoice. After all, what is the problem? Let's reason it out, have a good look at it. Yes, let's reason the whole thing out, my young friend, let's reason it all out. Well, in the first place there's a man exactly like you, exactly the same. Well, what of it? If that's what he is, do I need to shed tears over it? What is it to me? I'm an outsider; I just whistle my tune and that's that! If that's what it's come to. Let him work here! They say it's a marvel, a real oddity, those Siamese twins ... But why bring those Siamese twins into it? All right, let's suppose they're twins – but even great men sometimes looked very odd. We even know from history that the famous Suvorov[24] used to crow like a cock. But then he did it for political reasons. And the same goes for the great commanders ... but why bring in commanders? I'm my own master, that's what, I don't want to know anyone and in my innocence I despise my enemy. I'm no schemer and of that

I'm proud. Pure, straightforward, neat and tidy, agreeable, inoffensive . . .'

Suddenly Mr Golyadkin fell silent, stopped short and started trembling like a leaf; he even closed his eyes for a moment. Hoping however that the object of his fear was merely an illusion, he finally opened them and timidly stole a glance to the right. No – it was no illusion! There beside him, tripping along, was his acquaintance of that morning, smiling and looking into his face and apparently waiting for the chance to start a conversation. But no conversation got underway, however. Both of them continued walking for about fifty paces like that. Mr Golyadkin's sole concern was wrapping himself up as tightly as possible, burying himself in his overcoat, and pulling down his hat over his eyes as far as it would reach. To add insult to injury, even his acquaintance's overcoat and hat were exactly the same, as if Mr Golyadkin himself had just taken them off.

'My dear sir,' our hero finally declared, trying to speak almost in a whisper and without looking at his friend, 'it seems we're going our different ways. In fact, I'm even convinced of it,' he added after a brief pause. 'Finally, I'm sure that you've completely understood me,' he added quite gruffly, in conclusion.

'I should like,' Mr Golyadkin's companion said at last, 'I should like . . . You'll probably be magnanimous enough to excuse me . . . I don't know who to turn to here . . . my circumstances . . . I hope you'll excuse my impertinence, but I thought you were so moved with compassion that you took a personal interest in me this morning. For my part I felt drawn to you at first sight . . . I . . .' Here Mr Golyadkin wished that the earth would swallow up his new colleague. 'If I dared hope that you would be indulgent enough to hear me out, Yakov Petrovich . . .'

'We – we're here . . . we'd . . . better go to my place,' replied Mr Golyadkin. 'Let's cross Nevsky now – it will be more convenient for both of us that way and then we can go down a side street . . . yes . . . it's best to take a side street.'

'Very well, sir. All right, let's take a side street,' Mr Golyadkin's meek companion timidly observed, as if hinting by the tone of his reply that in his position he had no right to pick and choose and that he was prepared to be satisfied even with a side street. As for Mr Golyadkin, he had no idea what was happening to him. He did not trust himself. He still had not got over his amazement.

CHAPTER VII

Mr Golyadkin recovered a little on the stairs, at the entrance to his flat. 'Ah! what a mutton-head I am!' he mentally cursed himself. 'So, where am I taking him? I'm putting my own head in a noose. What will Petrushka think when he sees us together? What will that rogue dare to think now? He's suspicious . . .' But it was too late for regrets. Mr Golyadkin knocked, the door opened and Petrushka started helping master and guest off with their coats. Mr Golyadkin took a brief look, just a fleeting glance at Petrushka, trying to read his expression and guess what he was thinking. But to his extreme astonishment he saw that his servant was far from being surprised and on the contrary seemed to be expecting something of the kind. Of course, he too was scowling now, squinting sideways and apparently ready to bite someone's head off. 'Has someone cast a spell over everyone today?' wondered our hero. 'Has some demon been doing the rounds? Something certainly very out of the ordinary has got into everyone today. Hell, it's real torment!' Thus reflecting and weighing everything up, Mr Golyadkin led his guest into the room and humbly invited him to sit down. The guest was evidently deeply embarrassed and terribly shy. Meekly he followed his host's every movement, caught his every glance as he apparently tried to deduce his thoughts from them, so it seemed. There was something downtrodden, cowed and abject about every gesture he made, so that at that moment he was – if I may make the comparison – rather like someone who, for lack of any clothes of his own, has put on someone else's: the sleeves ride up, the waist is around his neck and he constantly keeps tugging at his wretchedly short waistcoat, or he stands sideways, tries to hide somewhere, then peers into everyone's eyes and listens hard to discover whether people are discussing his circumstances, whether they're laughing at him or whether they are ashamed of him – and this man blushes, becomes flustered and his pride suffers ... Mr Golyadkin put his hat on the window sill; a clumsy movement sent it flying on to the floor. His guest immediately rushed to pick it up, brushed all the dust off and carefully restored it to the same spot, putting his own on the floor beside a chair, on the edge of which he meekly perched. This trivial incident opened Mr Golyadkin's eyes a little and he realized his guest was in dire straits, so that therefore he didn't bother any more as to how to start with his guest, leaving all that, as was proper, to him. But for his part his guest didn't make a start either – whether from shyness or embarrassment or simply because he was politely waiting for his host to begin was hard to determine. Just then Petrushka entered, stopped in the doorway and stared in the completely opposite direction to that where his master and guest were sitting.

'Shall I bring dinner for two?' he asked in a casual, rather husky voice.

'I, I don't know ... you – yes, bring dinner for two, old chap.' Petrushka went out. Mr Golyadkin glanced at his guest who blushed to the roots of his hair. Mr Golyadkin was a kind person and therefore out of goodness of heart he immediately formulated a theory: 'He's a poor man,' he thought, 'and he's been at his new job only one day. He's probably suffered in his time. Perhaps all he possesses is a decent suit, but has nothing left to feed himself on. Ugh, how downtrodden he looks! Well, never mind. In some ways it's better like that ...'

'Forgive me for asking,' began Mr Golyadkin, 'but please may I inquire – by what name should I call you?'

'I'm ... I'm Yakov Petrovich,' replied his guest, almost in a whisper, ashamed and embarrassed, as if he were begging forgiveness for the fact that he too was called Yakov Petrovich.

'Yakov Petrovich!' our hero repeated, unable to conceal his confusion.

'Yes, sir, exactly, sir ... Your namesake, sir,' replied Mr Golyadkin's humble guest, venturing a smile and allowing himself to say something a little more jocular. But then he immediately sank back and assumed a serious but at the same time rather embarrassed look upon seeing his host was in no mood for jokes just then.

'You, if I may inquire . . . to what circumstance do I owe the honour . . . ?'

'Knowing your goodness of heart and virtues . . .' his guest rapidly interrupted, but in a rather timid voice, half-rising from his chair, 'I made so bold as to appeal to you and ask for your . . . friendship and protection . . .' his guest concluded, evidently having difficulty expressing himself and choosing words that were neither too flattering nor obsequious so as not to compromise his pride, yet not so daring as to suggest an improper equality. In general one could say that Mr Golyadkin's guest was behaving like a noble beggar who, wearing a patched tail-coat and with a nobleman's passport in his pocket, is not yet practised in the art of duly holding out his palm.

'You're confusing me,' replied Mr Golyadkin, surveying himself, the walls of his flat and his guest, 'how can I be . . . I, that is, I'd like to say, in exactly what respect can I be of service to you?'

'I felt drawn to you at first sight, Yakov Petrovich, and – please be gracious enough to forgive me – I built my hopes on you, I dared place my hopes in you, Yakov Petrovich. I . . . I'm like someone forsaken here, I'm poor, I've suffered a great deal, Yakov Petrovich, and I'm still new here. When I found out that you, with the customary innate qualities of your beautiful soul, had the same surname as me . . .'

Mr Golyadkin frowned.

'. . . with the same surname and from the same place as me I decided to come and familiarize you with my painful position.'

'Very good, very good. But really, I don't know what to say to you,' Mr Golyadkin replied in an embarrassed voice. 'Well, let's talk after dinner.'

The guest bowed, dinner was brought. Petrushka laid the table and guest and host proceeded to satisfy their appetites. The dinner did not last long as they were both in a hurry – the host because he wasn't quite himself and felt ashamed that the dinner was poor – ashamed partly because he wanted to feed his guest well and partly because he wanted to show that he did not live like a pauper. For his part the guest was extremely embarrassed and confused. Once, having helped himself to a slice of bread and eaten it, he was afraid to stretch his hand out for another slice, was ashamed to take the best portions and constantly claimed that he wasn't at all hungry, that the dinner was excellent, that he for his part was perfectly happy and would be grateful to him to his dying day. When dinner was over Mr Golyadkin lit his pipe and offered his guest another that he kept for friends; both sat facing each other and the guest began the story of his adventures.

Mr Golyadkin Junior's tale lasted some three or four hours. The story of his adventures consisted, incidentally, of the most trifling, most inconsequential and, one might say, meagre incidents. It told of service in some provincial law-courts, of prosecutors, lawyers and court presidents, of office intrigues, of a sudden change of superiors; it told of how Mr Golyadkin Junior had suffered through no fault of his own; of his aged aunt, Pelageya Semyonovna; of how, in consequence of various intrigues initiated by his enemies, he had lost his position and had walked to St Petersburg; of his life of drudgery and misery here in St Petersburg; of his lengthy and fruitless search for a job; of how he had run through all his money, spending his last copeck to live from hand to mouth; of how he had virtually lived out on the street, eaten stale bread washed down with his tears, and had slept on bare floorboards; and finally, how some kind person had gone to a lot of trouble on his behalf, given him a letter of introduction and magnanimously fixed him up with a new job. Mr Golyadkin's guest wept as he told his tale and wiped away the tears with a blue check handkerchief that strongly resembled oilcloth. He concluded by completely unburdening himself to Mr Golyadkin and confessed that for the time being not only did he not have the wherewithal to live and settle himself in decent lodgings somewhere, but couldn't even afford to equip himself with a uniform. He added that he couldn't even scrape enough money together for a pair of rotten old boots and that his uniform coat had been borrowed from someone for a short time.

Mr Golyadkin became quite emotional and was genuinely

touched. Moreover, despite the utter triviality of his guest's story, every word of it fell on his heart like manna from heaven. The fact was, Mr Golyadkin had shed his last doubts, allowing his heart to feel joyous and free and – finally – he mentally branded himself a fool. It was all so natural! And was there any reason to distress himself so, to press panic buttons? Yes, to be sure, there was in fact that one very ticklish matter, but it wasn't too calamitous: it couldn't tarnish a man's reputation, damage his pride or ruin his career when you were innocent and where nature herself had taken a hand in matters. Besides, his guest was asking for protection, had wept and accused fate, had appeared so artless, so lacking in malice or cunning, so pitiful and insignificant, and apparently he too was perhaps ashamed now – although possibly in another respect – by the strange resemblance of his face to his host's. His conduct was proper in the highest degree, his only concern to please his host and he looked like a man tormented by pangs of conscience and conscious of his guilt before another person. If, for instance, the discussion turned on some doubtful point, the guest immediately concurred with Mr Golyadkin's opinion. If, for instance, he mistakenly advanced an opinion contrary to Mr Golyadkin's and noticed his slip, he would waste no time correcting what he'd said, would explain himself and immediately give him to understand that he held the same views as his host, that he thought like him and looked upon everything in exactly the same way. In brief, the guest made every conceivable effort to win Mr Golyadkin over, so that the latter finally decided that he must be a most amiable person in all respects. Meanwhile tea was served; it was after eight. Mr Golyadkin was in excellent spirits. He cheered up, relaxed, let himself go a little and then he finally embarked on the liveliest and most entertaining conversation with his guest. At times, when in a cheerful mood, Mr Golyadkin was fond of relating interesting items of news. And so it was now: he told his guest a great deal about the Capital, its amusements and beauties, its theatres and clubs; about Bryullov's latest painting;[25] of the two Englishmen who travelled to St Petersburg expressly to take a look at the wrought-iron railings of the Summer Gardens[26] and then went straight home again; about his work, about Olsufy Ivanovich and Andrey Filippovich; about how Russia was approaching perfection hourly, how belles-lettres were flourishing. He related an anecdote he had recently read about in the *Northern Bee*[27] concerning an extraordinarily powerful constricting snake in India; and lastly about Baron Brambeus,[28] and so on and so on. In brief, Mr Golyadkin was perfectly satisfied, firstly because his mind was completely at ease; secondly because far from fearing his enemies he was even now prepared to challenge all of them to a decisive showdown; thirdly because he himself was giving someone protection in his own right and doing a good deed. In his heart, however, he admitted that he was not entirely happy just then, that there was still a tiny worm lurking inside him which, although minute, was gnawing away at him even now. He was much tormented by the memory of the previous evening at Olsufy Ivanovich's. What would he have given for certain of yesterday's events never to have happened! 'Still, never mind!' our hero finally concluded and he firmly resolved to behave well in future and never make such awful blunders again. As Mr Golyadkin was completely relaxed and suddenly felt almost completely happy, he even had the urge to enjoy life a little. Petrushka brought rum and they made some punch. Guest and host drained a glass each, then another. The guest became even more amiable than before and for his part gave more than one proof of his forthright and easy-going, happy-go-lucky nature, sharing in Mr Golyadkin's joy to the full and apparently rejoicing in his joy alone, considering him his sole and true benefactor. Taking up pen and a small sheet of paper, he requested Mr Golyadkin not to look at what he was going to write and when he had finished showed his host all he had written. It turned out to be a rather sentimental quatrain, written in exquisite style and handwriting and evidently his amiable guest's own composition. The lines read as follows:

> If e'r you should me forget,
> I'll never forget thee;
> Whatever in life may happen yet
> Never forget me![29]

With tears in his eyes Mr Golyadkin embraced his guest and finally, overcome with deep emotion, initiated his guest into some of his most intimate secrets and confidences, laying great emphasis on Andrey Filippovich and Klara Olsufyevna. 'Well, it seems that you and I will get on famously, Yakov Petrovich,' our hero told his guest. 'You and I, Yakov Petrovich, will get on like a house on fire, live like brothers. We'll fox them, old chap, we'll be sly – we'll be sly together! We'll be the ones to do the intriguing, to spite them – yes, we'll start intrigues to spite them ... we'll start intrigues to spite them. And don't trust any of them. I know you very well, Yakov Petrovich and I understand your character. You'd go and tell them everything, you honest soul! But you must steer clear of all of them, my friend.' In complete agreement the guest thanked Mr Golyadkin and finally he too shed tears.

'Do you know, Yasha,'[30] continued Mr Golyadkin in a weak voice, trembling with emotion, 'come and live with me for a while – or for good. We'll get along so well. What do you think, old chap, eh? Now, don't you be embarrassed or complain about this strange situation between us. It's sinful to complain, old chap – it's Nature! Mother Nature is bounteous, that's what, Yasha! I'm telling you this because I love you, love you like a brother. We'll be cunning, too, Yasha, we'll lay a few traps of our own and score off them.' Finally the punch reached a third and fourth brotherly glass and Mr Golyadkin began to experience a twofold sensation: one that he was extraordinarily happy and the other that he could no longer stand on his feet. Of course, the guest was invited to stay the night. A bed was somehow made up from two rows of chairs. Mr Golyadkin Junior announced that under a friendly roof even bare boards make a soft bed, that he could in fact sleep anywhere he had to, with humility and gratitude, that now he was in paradise and that, finally, he had been through much grief and misfortune, had seen everything, suffered everything and – who knew what the future held – would perhaps have to endure much more. Mr Golyadkin Senior objected to this and argued that one must put one's whole trust in God. The guest agreed entirely, adding that there was of course no one like God. Here

Mr Golyadkin Senior observed that in a certain respect the
Turks were right in invoking the name of God even in their
sleep. And then, without concurring with the aspersions of
certain scholars directed at the Turkish prophet Muhammed
and recognizing him as a great politician in his own way, Mr
Golyadkin embarked on a very interesting description of an
Algerian barber's shop that he had read about in some miscel-
lany. Guest and host laughed a great deal at the ingenuousness
of the Turks, but they could not help being duly amazed at
their opium-induced fanaticism ... At length the guest started
undressing and Mr Golyadkin, partly because in the goodness
of his heart he thought that his guest probably didn't have a
decent shirt, vanished behind the partition to avoid embarrassing someone who had already suffered enough and partly to
reassure himself as far as possible about Petrushka, to sound
him out, to cheer him up – if he could – and be nice to the man,
so that everyone would be happy and that there should be no
ill feeling. Petrushka, it must be said, still somewhat embarrassed Mr Golyadkin.

'You go to bed now, Petrushka,' Mr Golyadkin said gently
as he went into his servant's quarters. 'You go to bed now and
wake me up tomorrow at eight. Do you understand, Petrushka?'

Mr Golyadkin spoke unusually gently and kindly, but
Petrushka remained silent. Just then he happened to be fussing
around his bed and didn't even turn to face his master, which
he ought to have done, if only out of respect.

'Did you hear, Petrushka?' continued Mr Golyadkin. 'Go to
bed now and wake me up tomorrow at eight. Got it?'

'Well, of course I'll remember – what's the problem?'
Petrushka grumbled to himself.

'All right then, Petrushka, I only mentioned it to make you
feel happy and relaxed, too. We're all happy now, so I want you
to be happy and relaxed as well. And now I wish you goodnight, Petrushka. Sleep, Petrushka, get some sleep. We all have
work to do ... And don't start thinking things, old chap ...'

Mr Golyadkin was about to go on, but stopped. 'Isn't that a
bit too much?' he wondered. 'Haven't I gone too far? It's always
the same with me – always overdoing things.' Highly dissatisfied

with himself our hero left Petrushka. What was more, he was
rather hurt by Petrushka's rudeness and stubbornness. 'You try
to be nice to that good-for-nothing, you go out of your way
to show that good-for-nothing some regard, but he doesn't
appreciate it,' thought Mr Golyadkin. 'But his sort all have that
same vile way with them.' A trifle unsteady on his feet he
returned to his room and when he saw that his guest had gone
to bed he sat down for a moment on the bed. 'Come on,
own up, Yasha,' he started whispering, wagging his head. 'You
scoundrel, Yasha, you're the one who's at fault, after all, you're
my namesake, you know . . .' he continued, taunting his guest
in rather familiar fashion. Finally, after wishing him a friendly
goodnight, Mr Golyadkin retired to bed. Meanwhile the guest
started snoring. In his turn Mr Golyadkin climbed into bed,
chuckling and whispering to himself: 'You're drunk tonight,
Yakov Petrovich my dear, you old rogue, you Golyadka – what
a name you've got!! Well, what are you so pleased about?
Tomorrow you'll be crying your eyes out, you great sniveller!
What am I to do with you?' Just then a rather strange sensation,
something like doubt or remorse, seemed to flood Mr Golyadkin's whole being. 'I really let myself go,' he thought, 'and
now there's ringing in my head and I'm drunk. Just couldn't
control yourself, you damned fool! And he spun me a whole
yarn and was preparing to play tricks on me, the rotter! Of
course, to forgive and forget insults is the first of virtues, but
it's still very bad, that's what it is!' Here Mr Golyadkin got up,
took a candle, and went once more on tiptoe to have another
look at his sleeping guest. For a long time he stood over him,
deep in thought. 'Not a very pretty picture. A caricature – a
pure caricature – that's all you can say about it!'

At last Mr Golyadkin really did retire for the night. His head
was splitting and filled with ringing and buzzing. Gradually
he began to doze off . . . doze off . . . he tried to think about
something, to recall something very interesting, to resolve
some very important, ticklish matter, but he could not. Sleep
descended on his miserable head and he slept the way people
usually sleep who are unused to the sudden consumption of
five glasses of punch at some friendly gathering.

CHAPTER VIII

Next day Mr Golyadkin awoke at eight o'clock as usual; once awake he immediately recalled all the events of the previous evening – he remembered them and he frowned ... 'Made a complete fool of myself yesterday,' he thought, sitting up slightly in bed and glancing at his guest's bed. But how great his astonishment on finding that not only his guest but even the bed on which he had slept had gone from the room! 'What's going on?' Mr Golyadkin almost shrieked. 'What's happened? What on earth's the meaning of this new state of affairs?' While Mr Golyadkin was gaping in open-mouthed bewilderment at the empty space, the door creaked and in came Petrushka with the tea tray. 'But where is he, where on earth is he?' our hero muttered barely audibly, pointing to the place allotted to his guest the night before. At first Petrushka did not answer or even look at his master, but peered into the right-hand corner, so that Mr Golyadkin felt obliged to look into the corner on the right. But then after a silence Petrushka replied in his gruff and husky voice: 'The Master's not home.'

'You fool, *I'm* your master, Petrushka!' exclaimed Mr Golyadkin in a faltering voice, staring wide-eyed at his servant.

Petrushka made no reply, but gave Mr Golyadkin such a look that Mr Golyadkin blushed to the roots of his hair, a look of such insulting reproachfulness that it was tantamount to nothing less than sheer abuse. Mr Golyadkin lost heart, as they say. At length Petrushka announced that the *other one* had left about an hour and a half ago, as he wouldn't wait. Of course, this reply was both probable and plausible. Petrushka was obviously not lying and his insolent look and the words the *other one* were merely the consequence of the whole beastly episode. All the same, he understood, albeit only vaguely, that something was amiss and that fate held in store for him some other present – and not in the least agreeable at that. 'Good, we'll see,' he thought, 'we'll see, we'll get to the bottom of all this, all in good time. Oh Lord!' he moaned in conclusion, already in quite a different tone of voice. 'Why did I have to invite him? What

point was there in doing that? I'm well and truly putting myself
into their thieves' noose and tightening it around my own neck.
Oh, what a head, what a head! Just can't help blurting things
out like some urchin, like some clerk, some low-ranking riff-
raff, some spineless creature, some lousy dishcloth – you gossip,
you old woman! . . . Saints preserve us! And the verses he wrote,
the rogue, declaring his love for me! how could I . . . I mean to
say . . . ? How can I show that scoundrel the door as politely as
possible, should he return? It goes without saying that there's
lots of different turns of phrase, there's many ways. I could say:
"Well, it's like this, what with my meagre salary . . ." or I could
scare him by saying: "Taking this and that into account . . . I'm
obliged to express myself this way . . . you must pay half for
food and lodging and give me the money in advance." Hm!
No, blast it, that won't do! It would sully my reputation. It's
not in the least tactful. Perhaps I could somehow do it like this:
I could get Petrushka to spite him, to neglect him, to be rude to
him somehow and so get rid of him – that way I could play one
off against the other . . . No, damn it, no! It's dangerous And
again, if you look at it from that viewpoint, it's really not good
at all. Not good at all! So what if he doesn't come? Would that
be a bad thing? I gave the game away to him yesterday. Oh, it's
bad, it's really a very bad business. Oh, what a head I've got,
what a damned head I've got! I can't seem to knock what I
need to into my noddle, can't knock any sense into it. Well,
what if he does come and he refuses? But God grant he will
come! I'd be so terribly glad if he did come!' Such were Mr
Golyadkin's reflections as he swallowed his tea, constantly
glancing at the clock on the wall. 'A quarter to nine – it's really
time I was off. But something's going to happen – what will it
be? I'd like to know what's so particularly special that's being
concealed here – I mean the aim and the objective, the various
catches there? It would be good to know exactly what these
people are aiming at and what their first step will be . . .' Mr
Golyadkin could bear it no longer, threw down his pipe half-
smoked, dressed and set off for the office, eager to nip the
danger in the bud and to reassure himself by actually being
there personally. And there *was* danger: that he knew himself,

that there was danger. 'So, now we'll get to the bottom of this,' said Mr Golyadkin, removing his overcoat and galoshes in the vestibule. 'Now we'll fathom it all out.' Having decided on this course of action our hero tidied his clothes, assumed a formal, official air and was about to pass through into the next room when suddenly, right in the doorway, he collided with his friend and acquaintance of yesterday. Mr Golyadkin Junior appeared not to notice Mr Golyadkin Senior, although their noses nearly met. Mr Golyadkin Junior seemed terribly busy and was breathlessly dashing off somewhere. He had such an official, business-like air that anyone could see that he had been 'sent on a special mission'.

'Ah, it's you, Yakov Petrovich,' said our hero, grabbing last night's guest by the arm.

'Later, later . . . please excuse me and tell me later,' cried Mr Golyadkin Junior, pushing forward.

'If you don't mind, but it seems you wanted, Yakov Petrovich, to . . .'

'What's that? Do hurry up and explain . . .' Here Mr Golyadkin's guest of yesterday halted as if he were being forced against his will and he put one ear right up to Mr Golyadkin's nose.

'I must say, I'm most surprised at this reception, Yakov Petrovich, a reception I never could have expected.'

'For everything there is an official procedure. Report to His Excellency's secretary and then make proper application to the gentleman in charge of the office. Do you have a request?'[31]

'Well, I don't know, Yakov Petrovich! You do amaze me, Yakov Petrovich! Either you don't recognize me or you're having your little joke in keeping with your innate cheerfulness.'

'Oh, it's you!' said Mr Golyadkin Junior, as if he'd only now recognized Mr Golyadkin Senior. 'So, it's you. Well, now, did you have a good night?' Here Mr Golyadkin Junior gave a faint smile, a formal, official smile, not at all the kind he should have given (because, after all, he owed Mr Golyadkin a debt of gratitude) and after that formal, official smile he added that for his part he was absolutely delighted Mr Golyadkin had slept well. Then he bent forward slightly, shuffled his

feet, looked right, then left, glanced down at the floor, headed
for a side door and rapidly whispered that he was 'on a
special mission', darting into the next room and disappearing
in a flash.

'Well, there's a nice thing!' whispered our hero, momentarily
stunned. 'There's a pretty kettle of fish! So that's how things
are!' At this point, Mr Golyadkin felt shivers running up and
down his spine. 'However,' he said to himself as he made his
way to his department, 'I've been talking about such circumstances for ages. I had the feeling long ago that he was on a
special mission – yes, only yesterday I said that man was being
sent on a special mission . . .'

'Have you finished that document you were working on
yesterday, Yakov Petrovich?' Anton Antonovich Setochkin
asked Mr Golyadkin, as he took his seat next to him. 'Do you
have it here?'

'It's here,' whispered Mr Golyadkin, looking at his head clerk
with a rather lost expression.

'Right, sir. I'm saying this as Andrey Filippovich has asked
for it twice already. His Excellency will be wanting it before
you know it.'

'It's all right, it's finished, sir.'

'Oh, that's good, sir!'

'I, Anton Antonovich, think I have always performed my
duties conscientiously and I've always taken great care over the
tasks entrusted me by my superiors. I've always dealt with them
most zealously.'

'Yes . . . but what are you driving at?'

'Nothing, Anton Antonovich . . . I only want to explain that
I . . . that is . . . I wanted to declare that sometimes disloyalty
and envy spare no one in their quest for their disgusting daily
sustenance.'

'Forgive me, but I don't quite follow. I mean, to whom are
you referring?'

'All I meant, Anton Antonovich, was that I keep to the
straight and narrow, that I despise deviousness, that I'm not
one for intrigues – if you'll permit me to express myself this
way – and I can very justly be proud of this.'

'Yes, that's so, and as far as I understand it I admit the full justice of your argument ... But allow me to point out, Yakov Petrovich, that in good society personal remarks about other people are not altogether permissible. For example, I'm prepared to tolerate them behind my back, since who isn't reviled behind his back! But, say what you like, I shall not allow anyone to be insolent to my face, my dear sir. I, dear sir, have turned grey in government service and I shall not allow anyone to be insolent to me in my twilight years ...'

'No, Anton Antonovich, don't you see, Anton Antonovich, it appears, Anton Antonovich, you haven't quite understood. I, if you don't mind, Anton Antonovich, can only consider it an honour on my part ...'

'Well then, I beg you to forgive me, too. I was trained in the old school. It's too late for me to learn these newfangled ways of yours. Up to now I think my grasp of things has been good enough to serve my country. As you well know, sir, I have a medal for twenty years' irreproachable service ...'

'Yes, I appreciate that, Anton Antonovich, for my part I really do appreciate all that ... But that wasn't what I meant ... I was talking about a mask, Anton Antonovich ...'

'A mask, sir?'

'I mean ... again you ... I'm afraid you'll misinterpret my meaning, that is, the meaning of what I've just been saying, as you yourself put it, Anton Antonovich. I'm only developing the theory, putting forward the idea, Anton Antonovich, that people who wear masks aren't at all rare now and that nowadays it's hard to recognize the man beneath the mask.'

'Well, you know, it's not so hard. Sometimes it's even fairly easy, sometimes you don't have to look very hard ...'

'No ... I'm talking of myself, Anton Antonovich, I'm talking of myself, for example: when I say that I wear a mask, it's only when I need to; that is, only for carnivals or festive gatherings, speaking literally. But I don't wear one every day in front of people, speaking in a different and more cryptic sense. That's what I wanted to say, Anton Antonovich.'

'Very well, but let's leave all that for the moment. Besides, I just don't have the time right now,' said Anton Antonovich, rising from his seat and collecting some papers from a report for His Excellency. 'I fancy this little business of yours will be cleared up in a very short time. You yourself will see whom you should blame, whom you should accuse, but in the meantime I humbly beg you to spare me any further private discussions and gossip that might be detrimental to work . . .'

'But no, Anton Antonovich,' Mr Golyadkin began telling the retreating Antonovich, paling slightly. 'I, Anton Antonovich, never thought that. "What *is* this? What winds are blowing here and what's the meaning of this new obstacle?" our hero, now left alone, kept thinking to himself. At that very moment when our forlorn and half-crushed hero was preparing to solve this new question, there came a noise, a surge of activity from the next room. The door opened and there appeared in the doorway a breathless Andrey Filippovich, who only a few moments before had gone to His Excellency's room on some business; he called to Mr Golyadkin. Realizing what it was all about and reluctant to keep Andrey Filippovich waiting, Mr Golyadkin leapt from his seat and as was fitting started frantic- ally busying himself putting the required portfolio in order and prepared to follow both portfolio and Andrey Filippovich into His Excellency's study. Suddenly, virtually from under the arm of Andrey Filippovich, who was standing at that moment right in the doorway, in flew Mr Golyadkin Junior, bustling, breath- less and exhausted from his exertions, and with an important, determined air as he rolled right up to Mr Golyadkin Senior: this attack was the last thing he was expecting.

'The papers, Yakov Petrovich, the papers . . . His Excellency is pleased to inquire if you have them ready,' twittered Mr Golyadkin Senior's friend under his breath. 'Andrey Filippovich is waiting for you . . .'

'I know he's waiting, without you telling me,' retorted Mr Golyadkin Senior in a rapid whisper.

'No, Yakov Petrovich, I . . . didn't mean that. That's not what I meant at all, Yakov Petrovich. I sympathize and I'm moved by genuine concern . . .'

'From which I most humbly implore you to spare me . . . Now, if you don't mind . . .'

'Of course, you'll put them in a folder, Yakov Petrovich, and insert a marker on the third page, if you don't mind, Yakov Petrovich . . .'

'If you don't mind, please let me . . .'

'But there's a blot here, Yakov Petrovich. Didn't you notice that blot?'

Just then Andrey Filippovich summoned Mr Golyadkin a second time.

'I'm coming right away, Andrey Filippovich . . . I'm right here . . . just a little . . . Do you understand plain Russian, my dear sir?'

'It's best to get it off with a penknife, Yakov Petrovich, you'd better leave it to me: don't touch it yourself, Yakov Petrovich, rely on me . . . I can get most of it off with a penknife . . .'

Andrey Filippovich summoned Mr Golyadkin for the third time.

'Yes, for heaven's sake – but where is there a blot? There doesn't appear to be any blot at all.'

'And it's a really huge one . . . there it is! There, that's where I saw it . . . allow me . . . just allow me, Yakov Petrovich, I'll do it out of concern for you, Yakov Petrovich, with a penknife, from a pure heart. There, it's done!'

And then, quite unexpectedly, without rhyme or reason, Mr Golyadkin Junior, having got the better of Mr Golyadkin Senior in the momentary conflict that had arisen between them – and at any rate quite contrary to the latter's wishes – Mr Golyadkin Junior seized possession of the document requested by his superiors and instead of scraping it with a penknife from a 'pure heart' as he had treacherously assured Mr Golyadkin Senior, quickly rolled it up, stuffed it under his arm and in two bounds was at the side of Andrey Filippovich, who hadn't noticed a single one of his pranks, and shot off with him into the director's office. Mr Golyadkin Senior remained as if rooted to the spot, holding the penknife and apparently preparing to scrape something off with it . . .

Our hero had not yet fully grasped his new situation. He had not come to his senses. He had felt the blow, but thought it was of no importance. In terrible, indescribable anguish he tore

himself from where he was standing and charged straight into
the Director's office, beseeching heaven on the way that everything might somehow turn out for the best and would be all
right ... In the last room before the Director's he bumped
straight into Andrey Filippovich and his namesake. They were
both already coming back; Mr Golyadkin moved to one side.
Andrey Filippovich was talking cheerfully and smiling; Mr
Golyadkin Senior's namesake was also smiling, fussing about,
tripping along at a respectful distance from Andrey Filippovich,
whispering something in his ear with a rapturous look, to which
Andrey Filippovich nodded in the most favourable fashion. Our
hero grasped the whole situation in a flash. The fact was, his
work (as he learnt later) had almost exceeded His Excellency's
expectations and had been handed in by the deadline, in good
time. His Excellency was extremely satisfied. It was even
rumoured that His Excellency had said thank you to Mr Golyadkin Junior – a very warm thank you – had said that he would
remember it when the occasion arose, and that he would not
fail to forget it ... Of course, Mr Golyadkin's first reaction was
to protest, to protest with all his might, as much as was humanly
possible. Almost beside himself and pale as death, he rushed to
Andrey Filippovich. But when Andrey Filippovich heard that
Mr Golyadkin's business was private, he refused to listen, flatly
pointing out in no uncertain terms that he didn't have a moment
to spare even for his own needs.

The brusqueness of his refusal and chilly tone stunned Mr
Golyadkin. 'Perhaps I'd better try a different approach ... I'd
better go to Anton Antonovich,' he thought. But unfortunately
for Mr Golyadkin, Anton Antonovich was not available either:
he too was busy somewhere. 'So, it wasn't without something
in mind that he asked to be spared explanations and gossip!'
our hero thought. 'So that's what the cunning old fox was
driving at! In that case I'll simply be bold and appeal to His
Excellency.'

Still pale and feeling that his head was in complete turmoil,
thoroughly perplexed as to what exactly he should decide upon,
Mr Golyadkin sat down on a chair. 'It would be much better if
all this were simply a trifling matter,' he constantly thought. 'In

fact, such a fishy business was even highly improbable. Firstly
it was all nonsense and secondly it couldn't possibly happen.
Most likely it was a trick of the imagination, or something
different had happened from what really was the case; or perhaps I must have been walking along . . . and somehow completely mistook myself for someone else . . . in short the whole
thing's absolutely impossible.'

No sooner had Mr Golyadkin decided that the whole thing
was absolutely impossible than Mr Golyadkin Junior suddenly
came flying into the room, with papers in both hands and under
his arm. Having addressed some necessary words to Andrey
Filippovich, exchanging a few more with someone else, politely
greeting another, treating another with easy familiarity, Mr
Golyadkin Junior, having on the face of it no time at all to
waste, already seemed about to leave the room, but fortunately
for Mr Golyadkin Senior he stopped right at the door to talk
to two or three young clerks who happened to be standing
there. Mr Golyadkin Senior rushed straight towards him. The
moment Mr Golyadkin Junior spotted Mr Golyadkin Senior's
manoeuvre, he immediately started looking around in panic to
see where he could slip away the fastest. But our hero had
already grabbed his previous evening's guest by the sleeve. The
clerks surrounding the two titular counsellors fell back and
awaited events with considerable curiosity. The old titular
counsellor Mr Golyadkin Senior understood that favourable
opinion was not on his side and he understood very well that
they were all intriguing against him, which made it all the more
imperative for him to make a stand. It was the moment of truth.

'Well, sir?' asked Mr Golyadkin Junior, looking rather
brazenly at Mr Golyadkin Senior.

Mr Golyadkin Senior was barely breathing.

'I don't know, my dear sir,' he began, 'how to make you
understand how strangely you're behaving towards me.'

'Well sir, do go on.' Here Mr Golyadkin Junior looked
around and winked at the surrounding clerks, as if giving them
to understand that the comedy was just about to begin.

'The insolence and shamelessness of your conduct, my dear
sir, in the present circumstances, denounce you more than any

words of mine could do. Don't bank on the success of the game you're playing – it's a rotten one.'

'Well, please do tell me how you slept, Yakov Petrovich,' asked Mr Golyadkin Junior, looking Mr Golyadkin Senior straight in the eye.

'You, my dear sir, are forgetting yourself,' said our titular counsellor, utterly baffled and barely feeling the floor beneath him. 'I hope you will change your tone . . .'

'My little sweetie-pie!' Mr Golyadkin Junior said, pulling a somewhat unseemly face at Mr Golyadkin Senior. And suddenly, right out of the blue, under the guise of a caress, he pinched his rather chubby right cheek between two of his fingers. Our hero reddened like fire. The moment Mr Golyadkin Senior's friend noticed that his adversary, shaking in every limb, red as a lobster and exasperated beyond all measure, might even decide on a real attack he in turn immediately forestalled him in a most shameless manner. After pinching his cheek twice more, tickling him a couple of times and toying with him in this way for a few more seconds as he stood there motionless and mad with rage, to the not inconsiderable amusement of the young clerks standing around, Mr Golyadkin Junior rounded things off with the most startling effrontery by giving Mr Golyadkin Senior's rather rotund belly a prod and saying with the most venomous leer that hinted at much: 'You're a tricky customer, Yakov Petrovich old chap, you're a tricky customer. We'll be cunning, you and I, we'll be cunning!' And then, before our hero had time to make even the slightest recovery from this latest assault, Mr Golyadkin Junior (after directing only a preliminary grin at the surrounding spectators) suddenly assumed the most business-like, formal and official air, looked down at the floor, huddled up and shrank into himself and after rapidly saying he was 'on a special mission' jerked his stumpy legs into action and darted into the next room. Our hero couldn't believe his eyes and he was still in no condition to come to his senses . . .

But at last he did come to his senses. Realizing in a flash that he was finished, that he had perished, been destroyed in a sense, that he had disgraced himself, sullied his reputation, that he

had been humiliated and made a laughing-stock in the presence
of disinterested parties, that he had been treacherously abused
by the person whom only yesterday he had considered his
greatest and most trustworthy friend, that he had finally fallen
flat on his face – and how! – Mr Golyadkin charged off in
pursuit of his enemy. At that moment he no longer wanted to
think of those who had witnessed the outrage perpetrated on
him. 'They're all hand in glove,' he told himself, 'they all stand
up for one another and each sets the other against me.' However, after about a dozen steps our hero clearly saw that any
pursuit was vain and futile and so he turned back. 'You won't
get away with it!' he thought. 'I'll trump you, all in good time,
you'll get your just deserts!' With fierce sangfroid and the most
energetic determination Mr Golyadkin returned to his chair
and sat down. 'You won't get away with it!' he repeated. No
longer was it a question of some kind of passive self-defence:
there was something decisive and aggressive in the air and
anyone who saw Mr Golyadkin just then, flushed, barely able
to contain his agitation, stabbing his pen into the inkwell, and
the fury with which he set about scribbling on the paper, might
have concluded in advance that the matter would not rest there,
nor could it fizzle out in some old-womanish way. In the depths
of his soul he had made one resolution and deep in his heart he
vowed to carry it out. If truth be told, he didn't quite know
what steps to take – rather, he had no idea at all. But it didn't
matter, it was all right! 'You will achieve nothing by imposture
and insolence in this day and age, my dear sir! Imposture and
insolence lead to no good – only to the gallows. Only Grishka
Otrepyev,[32] my dear sir, succeeded by imposture, deceiving the
blind populace, but even then not for long.' In spite of this last
circumstance Mr Golyadkin decided to wait until masks fell
from certain faces and something would come to light. To
achieve this it was first necessary for office hours to finish as
soon as possible and until that time our hero proposed to
undertake nothing. And then, when the working day was over,
he would take a certain step. Then he would know how to act
and, after taking that step, how to organize his whole campaign
in order to shatter the horn of pride and crush the serpent that

gnawed the dust in impotent scorn. To be used like a rag for people to wipe their dirty boots on – that he could not allow. To that he could not agree, particularly in the present circumstances. But for that last outrage our hero might have taken courage, perhaps he might have decided to remain silent and not protest too strongly. He might have argued a little, complained, demonstrated that he was in the right and then yielded a little and then, perhaps, a little more – and then he would have given his complete agreement, especially when the opposing party had solemnly admitted that he was within his rights; and then perhaps he would even have made peace, would even been rather touched and – who could tell? – perhaps a new friendship would have sprung up – a firm, warm friendship, on an even broader basis than yesterday evening's, a friendship that might in the end have so eclipsed all the unpleasantness of that rather unseemly likeness between two people that both titular counsellors would have been absolutely delighted and would have lived to a ripe old age, and so on. To sum up: Mr Golyadkin was even beginning slightly to regret that he had stood up for himself and his rights, and in consequence had only run into unpleasantness. 'If only he'd given in,' wondered Mr Golyadkin, 'and said it was all a joke, I'd have forgiven him, I'd even have forgiven him all the more if only he'd admitted it out loud. But no, I won't let myself be used as a rag. I've never let such people use me as a boot-cloth and even less will I allow this depraved wretch to attempt it. I'm not a rag, my dear sir, oh no, I'm not a rag!' In short our hero had made up his mind. 'You yourself are to blame, my good sir,' he thought. So, he had decided to protest – and protest to the very last, with all his strength. That's the kind of man he was! He could not possibly agree to let himself be insulted – even less to be used as a rag – and least of all by some completely depraved person. But let us not argue about it, let us not argue. Perhaps if someone had so wanted, if someone had had an irresistible urge, for example, to turn Mr Golyadkin into a rag, then he might have done so without meeting any opposition and with impunity (Mr Golyadkin himself had been aware of this on occasions) and then the result would have been a rag and not a Golyadkin – yes, a rag, a disgusting filthy rag – but not an ordinary rag, though: this rag would have had its pride, this rag would have been endowed with animation and feelings, and even though those feelings would have been mute and hidden deep within the filthy folds of that rag, they would nonetheless have been feelings . . .

The hours seemed to drag past; finally it struck four. Shortly afterwards everyone got up, followed the head of the department and headed homewards. Mr Golyadkin mingled with the crowd. He was on the alert and did not let his quarry out of his sight. Finally our hero saw his friend run up to the office porters who were handing out the coats and in his usual blackguardly way was fidgeting around everyone while waiting for his. It was a moment for decision. Mr Golyadkin somehow managed to squeeze his way through the crowd and he too started fussing about for his overcoat, not wishing to fall behind. But Mr Golyadkin's friend and acquaintance was first to get his coat, for even here he had managed in his own fashion to wheedle, to suck up to everyone, to curry favour, whisper in people's ears and behave like a cad.

After throwing on his overcoat Mr Golyadkin Junior gave Mr Golyadkin Senior an ironic look, thus spiting him openly and brazenly and then, with his characteristic insolence, minced around the other clerks – most probably to leave a favourable impression – making a witty remark to one, whispering something to another, toadying politely to a third, directing a smile at a fourth, giving his hand to a fifth – and then flitting gaily down the stairs. Mr Golyadkin went after him and to his indescribable satisfaction overtook him on the last step and grabbed his coat collar. Mr Golyadkin Junior seemed somewhat dumbfounded and looked around with a lost air.

'What do you mean by this?' he finally whispered weakly to Mr Golyadkin.

'My dear sir, if you are in any way a decent gentleman I trust you will recall our friendly relations of yesterday,' said our hero.

'Ah yes. Well, what now? Did you sleep well?'

For a moment fury deprived Mr Golyadkin Senior of the power of speech.

'Yes, I did, but please allow me to tell you . . . my dear sir, that you're playing a highly complicated game.'

'Who says so? It's my enemies who say that . . . !' the self-styled Mr Golyadkin brusquely replied and suddenly freed himself from the real Mr Golyadkin's feeble grasp. Once free he dashed down the stairs, looked around and, seeing a cab driver, climbed into the droshky and in a flash disappeared from Mr Golyadkin Senior's view. Despairing and deserted by all, the titular counsellor looked around, but there were no other cabs. He tried to run, but his legs gave way beneath him. With an utterly downcast face, his mouth gaping, crushed, shrunken and helpless, he leaned against a lamp-post and there he stayed for several minutes, in the middle of the pavement. All was lost for Mr Golyadkin, it seemed . . .

CHAPTER IX

It seemed that everything, even Nature herself, was up in arms against Mr Golyadkin; but he was still on his feet and unvanquished: yes, he felt that he was unvanquished. He was ready to do battle. He rubbed his hands together when he recovered from the initial shock with such feeling and energy that one might conclude from Mr Golyadkin's look alone that he would not surrender. However, danger was just around the corner, that was obvious; Mr Golyadkin sensed it too. But how was it to be tackled, that danger? That was the question. For one fleeting instant the thought flashed through Mr Golyadkin's mind: 'Why not leave things as they are and simply give up, withdraw from the scene? Why not? Well, it's nothing at all. I'll stand aside, as if it isn't me, I'll let it all pass. It's not me and that's the end of it. He'll keep to himself too and perhaps he'll give up too. Yes, he'll make up to me, the scoundrel, and then the swine will turn away and withdraw. That's it! But I'll win through by my humility. And where's the danger, in fact? Well, what danger? I'd like someone to show me the danger in all this. Such a piffling matter! Such an ordinary business . . . !'

Here Mr Golyadkin stopped short. The words died on his lips. He even berated himself for thinking like that; he even convicted himself of meanness and cowardice on account of that thought. However, his cause had not got under way at all. He felt that it was at that moment an absolute necessity to decide on some course of action. He even felt that he would have paid anyone handsomely who could have told him what exactly he should decide upon. So, how could he guess? But there was no time for guessing. Just in case and in order not to waste time, he took a cab and flew home.

'Well, how do you feel now?' he wondered, addressing himself. 'How are you allowing yourself to feel now, Yakov Petrovich? What will you do? What will you do now, wretch that you are, scoundrel that you are? You've driven yourself into the ground and now you're crying, now you're snivelling!'

Thus Mr Golyadkin taunted himself as he was jolted up and down in the rickety vehicle. Rubbing salt in his wounds and taunting himself at that moment gave Mr Golyadkin a kind of profound pleasure almost amounting to voluptuousness. 'Well, if some magician were to come along, or if something official were to happen, so that they said: "Give up a finger of your right hand, Golyadkin, and we'll be quits, there won't be another Golyadkin and you can be happy – only minus a finger" – then I'd surrender it, surrender it without fail, without making a face! Oh, to hell with all this,' the despairing titular counsellor finally cried out. 'Why all this? Why precisely this, why this, as if nothing else were possible? Well, why did it have to happen? Everything was fine at first, everyone was happy and contented. But no, this had to happen! Well, talking won't get me anywhere – one has to act!'

And so, having almost come to a decision, Mr Golyadkin entered his flat, grabbed his pipe without a moment's delay and sucking on it for all he was worth and scattering puffs of smoke to right and left began running up and down the room in extreme agitation. Meanwhile Petrushka started laying the table. And then, having finally come to a decision, Mr Golyadkin suddenly abandoned his pipe, threw on his overcoat, announced he would not be dining at home and charged out of the flat. On the stairs a breathless Petrushka caught him up, holding his forgotten hat. Mr Golyadkin took it and felt he should say a word or two to justify himself a little in Petrushka's eyes, so that Petrushka should not think anything in particular of it, to the effect that he'd gone and forgotten his hat and so on. But as Petrushka did not even want to look and immediately went away, Mr Golyadkin put on his hat without any further explanations and scurried downstairs, muttering to himself that everything was for the best, perhaps, and that this business would be settled somehow, although he was conscious, nonetheless, of a shivery sensation even in his heels; then he went out into the street, took a cab and hurried off to Andrey Filippovich's. 'But wouldn't tomorrow be better . . . ?' wondered Mr Golyadkin, reaching for the bell-pull at the door of Andrey Filippovich's flat, 'and do I have anything special to say? Well, there's nothing special about it. It's such a wretched business, oh yes! All said and done, it's wretched, trifling – well, almost trifling . . . yes, that's what it is, that's what the whole thing is.' Suddenly Mr Golyadkin pulled the bell. It rang and some footsteps were heard from within. At this point Mr Golyadkin even cursed himself, partly for his hastiness and his audacity. The recent unpleasant incidents which Mr Golyadkin had almost forgotten while at work, and his falling-out with Andrey Filippovich, now came to mind. But it was already too late to escape: the door opened. Fortunately for Mr Golyadkin he was informed that Andrey Filippovich had not returned from the office and he wasn't dining at home. 'I know where he dines – near Izmaylovsky Bridge, that's where,' our hero thought, and he was absolutely delighted. To the footman who inquired as to what message he should give he replied: 'It's all right, my friend, I, my friend, will come back later.' And he ran downstairs, even to a certain degree in high spirits. As he went out into the street he decided to let the cab go and settled up with the driver. When the latter asked for something extra, claiming: 'I've been waiting a long time, sir, and I didn't spare the horse for Your Worship,' he even willingly gave him an extra five copecks and proceeded on foot.

'Well now,' thought Mr Golyadkin, 'it's really the sort of business that can't be left just like that. However, if you think hard about it, think sensibly, then what is there to fuss about? Well, no, I'll keep repeating it – what is there to fuss about? Why should I suffer, struggle, toil and moil, work my fingers to the bone? Firstly, the thing's done and can't be undone ... no, it can't be undone! Let's reason like this: a man comes along – along comes a man, with fairly good references, so to speak, said to be a capable civil servant, of good conduct, only he's poor and has had some nasty experiences in one way or the other – such scrapes! Well, I mean to say, poverty's no crime. Well, that's no fault of mine. And in fact what kind of nonsense is all this? He was suitable, happened to fit the job, nature created him the spitting image of another man, so that they're as like as two peas in a pod. So, why should they refuse to take him on because of that? If it's fate, if it's fate alone, if it's blind fortune that is to blame – well, should he then be treated like a dishcloth, shouldn't he be allowed to work? What justice would there be in that? He's poor, lost, frightened – it makes your heart ache – here compassion demands that he should be taken care of. Oh yes, fine superiors they would be if they argued the same way as I do – you old reprobate! I mean to say, that noddle of mine! At times there's enough stupidity there for ten put together ... ! No, no! They did the right thing and deserve thanks for being charitable to that poor victim of misfortune ... So ... let's suppose, for example, that we were born twins, born so that we're twin brothers – that's all – that's it! Well, what of it? Why, it's all right! All the clerks can be trained to accept it and no outsider coming into the department would find anything unseemly or shocking about such a state of affairs. In fact, there's something even touching here. Yes – here's a thought: Divine Providence, so to speak, created two identical beings and the benevolent authorities, recognizing the hand of Providence, took the twins under their wing. 'Of course,' continued Mr Golyadkin, catching his breath and lowering his voice a little, 'of course ... of course it would have been better – oh yes, it would – if this touching state of affairs had never happened, if there'd have been no twins either. Oh

to hell with it all! Was it necessary? Was there any pressing
need for it that brooked no delay? My goodness! These devils
have really stirred up trouble now. And that character of his,
though, he's got such a nasty, skittish way with him – he's so
frivolous, such a lickspittle, crawler – in fact, a real Golyadkin!
On top of this I dare say he'll behave badly and blacken my
name, the swine! So now I'm supposed to keep an eye on
him and look after him, if you please! I mean to say, what
punishment! Ah well, what of it? It doesn't matter at all. So,
he's a scoundrel, so this Golyadkin's a scoundrel – let him be a
scoundrel – the other one is honest. So, he'll be the scoundrel
and I'll be the honest one and they'll say that that Golyadkin's
a scoundrel, don't take any notice of him, don't mix him up
with the other – but this one's honest, virtuous, meek and mild,
always so reliable at work and worthy of promotion. That's
how it is! Well now, that's fine . . . but what if they . . . you
know . . . go and mix us up? Anything could happen with him
around! Oh, Lord preserve us! He'd supplant someone, that
scoundrel would supplant him, as if he were a piece of rag, and
he'd never stop even to consider that a man isn't a rag. Oh
heavens above! What misfortune.'

Reasoning and lamenting in this way Mr Golyadkin ran
along blindly, almost oblivious of where he was going. He came
to his senses on Nevsky Prospekt – and then only after bumping
so violently into some passer-by that he saw stars. Without
looking up Mr Golyadkin mumbled some apology and only
when the passer-by, having growled something not very compli-
mentary, was some distance away did he raise his head to see
where he was and how things were. After looking around and
finding that he happened to be right next to the same restaurant
where he had taken a rest while getting ready for Olsufy Ivanovich's dinner party, our hero was suddenly conscious of a
tweaking and pinching in his stomach and he remembered that
he had not dined and that there was no prospect of a dinner
party anywhere and therefore without wasting precious time
he dashed up the restaurant stairs to snatch a quick snack
without hanging about any longer. And although everything in
the restaurant was on the expensive side, this minor circum-

stance did not deter Mr Golyadkin on this occasion: he had no
time to linger over such trifles now. In the brightly lit room a
fairly large crowd of customers were standing at a counter piled
high with an assortment of the various comestibles respectable
people consume by way of a light snack. The waiter was hard
pressed, hardly having time to pour drinks, serve, take money
and give change. Mr Golyadkin waited his turn and as soon as
it came modestly reached for a fish pasty. After going away to
one corner, turning his back on the crowd and eating with great
appetite, he returned to the waiter, put his plate on the table
and, as he knew the price, took out a ten-copeck silver piece
and left it on the counter, catching the waiter's eye as if to say:
here's the money for one pasty.

'That'll be one rouble ten copecks,' the waiter said through
his teeth.

Mr Golyadkin was really staggered.

'Are you talking to me . . . ? I . . . I . . . had one pasty only,
I think.'

'You had eleven,' the waiter retorted with great assurance.

'You, as far as I can see, are mistaken. I believe I had only
one.'

'I counted them. You had eleven. If you had them you must
pay for them. We don't give anything away for nothing here.'

Mr Golyadkin was dumbstruck. 'What's going on – is someone casting a magic spell over me?' he thought. Meanwhile
the waiter was awaiting Mr Golyadkin's decision. A crowd
surrounded Mr Golyadkin; Mr Golyadkin had already felt in
his pocket to take out the silver rouble, intending to settle up
at once and withdraw from the scene to avoid further trouble.
'Well, if it's eleven then eleven it is,' he thought, turning as red
as a lobster. 'Well, what of it, if eleven pasties were consumed?
If a man's hungry he'll eat eleven; let him eat to his heart's
content, it's nothing to wonder at or laugh at . . .' Suddenly
something seemed to prick Mr Golyadkin. He looked up and
at once understood the whole mystery, all the witchcraft: all
his difficulties were at once resolved . . . In the doorway to the
next room, almost directly behind the waiter's back and facing
Mr Golyadkin, there in the doorway which until then our hero

had taken for a mirror, stood a man: there he stood, there stood Mr Golyadkin in person, not the old Mr Golyadkin, not the hero of our story, but another Mr Golyadkin, the new Mr Golyadkin. Clearly this other Mr Golyadkin was in excellent spirits. He was smiling, nodding and winking at the first Mr Golyadkin, mincing a little and looking as if at the slightest provocation he would efface himself, slip into the next room and sneak out by a back door, get clean away and all pursuit would be to no avail. In his hands was a piece of a tenth pasty which, right before Mr Golyadkin's eyes, he consigned to his mouth, smacking his lips with pleasure. 'He's passed himself off as me, the blackguard!' thought Mr Golyadkin, flushing fiery red with shame, 'he's not ashamed of doing it in public. Can they see him? I don't think anyone's noticed.' Mr Golyadkin threw down his silver rouble as if he had burnt all his fingers on it and ignoring the waiter's significantly insolent smile, a smile of triumph and unruffled authority, extricated himself from the crowd and dashed off without a backward glance. 'Thank God he didn't compromise me completely!' Mr Golyadkin Senior reflected. 'I must thank that villain – and fate as well – that everything was settled without any trouble. Only, that waiter was rude. Still, the man was within his rights. One rouble ten copecks were owing, so he was within his rights. "We don't give anything away here for nothing," he said. But he could have been a little more polite, the layabout!'

All this was said by Mr Golyadkin as he went downstairs to the porch. But on the last step he stopped as if rooted to the spot and he blushed so furiously from a paroxysm of injured pride that his eyes even filled with tears. After standing stock-still for half a minute he suddenly stamped one foot with determination, leapt in one bound from the porch, ran into the street without a backward glance and rushed off home to his flat in Shestilavochnaya Street, gasping for breath, feeling no fatigue. Once there, without even taking off his outer clothing – quite contrary to his usual habit of making himself comfortable when at home and without even the preliminary picking-up of his pipe – he at once settled himself on the sofa, drew the inkstand closer towards him, took a pen and sheet of notepaper and started scribbling the following epistle, his hand shaking with inner agitation.

My dear sir, Yakov Petrovich!
Never would I have put pen to paper had not my circumstances and you yourself, my dear sir, compelled me to do so. Believe me that necessity alone obliged me to enter upon this kind of explanation with you and therefore I request you, above all, to consider this measure of mine not as a deliberate attempt to insult you, but as the inevitable consequence of those circumstances that now link us together.

'That sounds good, doesn't it, polite and proper and at the same time not without firmness and strength. I don't think he could possibly take offence at that. Besides, I'm within my rights,' mused Mr Golyadkin, reading over what he had written.

Your strange and unforeseen appearance, my dear sir, on a stormy night, after that boorish and unseemly behaviour towards me on the part of my enemies, whose names I pass over in silence out of the contempt I feel for them, sowed the seeds of all those misunderstandings that at present exist between us. Your pig-headed determination, my dear sir, to have your own way and forcibly to insinuate yourself into the circle of my existence and all my relationships in everyday life, transgresses even the limits prescribed by common courtesy alone and the norms of commu-nal life. I consider there is no need to mention your appropriation of my documents and of my own good name, my dear sir, with the intention of currying favour with your superiors – favour you have not merited. I need hardly refer here to your calculated and offensive evasiveness in proferring the explanations that this matter has necessitated. Finally, so that nothing is left unsaid, I make no reference here to your recent peculiar – one might even say incomprehensible – behaviour towards me in the coffee-house. Far be it from me to complain about the futile loss of one rouble, but I cannot help but give full vent to my indignation when I recall your blatant intrusion, prejudicial to my honour and what is more in the presence of several personages who although not actually known to me are nonetheless people of the greatest refinement . . .

'Am I going too far?' wondered Mr Golyadkin. 'Isn't it a bit on the strong side? Isn't it being rather too touchy – that allusion to great refinement, for example? Well, it doesn't matter! I must show him firmness of character! However, in mitigation, I could flatter him and butter him up a little at the end. So, let's see . . .'

But I would not have thought of wearying you, my dear sir, with my letter, were I not firmly convinced that the nobility of your sentiments and your frank and straightforward character would indicate to you yourself the means of rectifying all omissions and restoring the status quo.

In full hope I dare to remain assured that you will not consider this letter in any sense offensive to you and at the same time will not refuse to let me have an explanation on this occasion in writing through the mediation of my manservant.

In anticipation I have the honour to remain
your obedient servant
Ya. Golyadkin

'Well now, that's all very good! The thing's done! So, it's even come to writing letters! But who is to blame? He himself is to blame; he himself drives a man to demand a written reply . . . I'm within my rights . . .'

Having read the letter through a last time, Mr Golyadkin folded and sealed it and summoned Petrushka. Petrushka appeared looking sleepy-eyed as usual and extremely annoyed about something.

'I want you to take this letter, old chap . . . do you understand?'

Petrushka said nothing.

'I want you to take it to the office. There you'll find Provincial Secretary[33] Vakhrameyev – he's duty officer today. Do you understand?'

'I understand.'

' "I understand"! Can't you say "I understand, *sir*?" Ask for

Secretary Vakhrameyev and tell him: "It's like this, so to speak, my master sends his regards and humbly requests you to have a look in our office address book – and find out where this Titular Counsellor Golyadkin lives."'

Petrushka remained silent and Mr Golyadkin fancied he could detect a smile.

'So, Petrushka, you'll ask for the address first and find out where this new clerk Golyadkin is living.'

'Yes, sir!'

'You'll ask for the address and then you'll take this letter to that address. Do you understand?

'I understand.'

'If there . . . well, where you're taking the letter, that gentlemen to whom you're giving the letter . . . this Golyadkin . . . What are you laughing at, you idiot?'

'Why should I be laughing? I wasn't doing anything! What have the likes of me to laugh at?'

'All right . . . Now, if this gentleman should ask how your master is, if he's all right, what he's doing, you know, if he starts questioning you, just keep your mouth shut and tell him: "My master's all right, but he requests a personal, written reply from you." Got it?'

'Got it.'

'So, tell him: "My master's all right and is just about to go and visit someone. But he's asking for a written reply from you." Understand?'

'I understand.'

'Well, off with you.'

'The bother I have with that idiot, too! All he can do is laugh to himself. What's he laughing at? I'm in real trouble now – just see what trouble I've landed myself in! But perhaps all will turn out for the best . . . I bet that rogue will be hanging around for a couple of hours now and then disappear somewhere. Just can't send him anywhere. Oh, what a dreadful mess I'm in! Oh, what trouble I'm in . . .'

Thus fully realizing the trouble he was in, Mr Golyadkin decided to play a passive role for about two hours while waiting for Petrushka. One hour he spent pacing the room and smoking, then he abandoned his pipe and sat down with a book, then he lay down for a while on the sofa and then he took his pipe again, after which he started chasing around the room again. Then he would have liked to reason it all out, but he could reason absolutely nothing out. Finally, as the agony of his passive role had reached its climax, Mr Golyadkin decided to take a certain step. 'Petrushka won't be back for an hour,' he pondered, 'so I can give the key to the porter and in the meantime I myself and . . . well . . . I can go and investigate the matter. I can go and investigate on my own behalf.' Without wasting time, hurrying to investigate the matter, Mr Golyadkin took his hat, left the room, locked the door, went to the porter to give him the key and a ten-copeck tip – for some reason Mr Golyadkin had become unusually generous of late – and set off to where he needed to go. First he went on foot to Izmaylovsky Bridge; the walk took him about half an hour. On reaching his destination he went straight into the courtyard of the house that was so familiar and looked up at the windows of State Counsellor Berendeyev's apartment. Except for three windows with their red curtains drawn, the others were in darkness. 'Olsufy Ivanovich probably doesn't have any visitors today,' mused Mr Golyadkin, 'everyone must be sitting at home on their own now.' Trying to come to some sort of decision, Mr Golyadkin stood for a time in the courtyard. But the decision was not fated to be reached, for Mr Golyadkin evidently had a change of mind, gave it all up as a bad job and returned to the street. 'No, I shouldn't have come here. And what can I do here anyway? I'd better . . . er . . . go now . . . and investigate the matter in person.' Having reached this decision, Mr Golyadkin headed for the office. The walk was not short and, besides, it was terribly muddy and huge flakes of wet snow were falling heavily. But no difficulties seemed to exist for our hero at that moment. True, he was soaked to the skin and he was not a little bespattered with mud – 'that's how it is, but at the same time the objective has been attained,' he thought. And in fact Mr Golyadkin was already approaching his objective. The great mass of the huge government building loomed dark before him in the distance. 'Stop!' he suddenly thought. 'Where am I going now and what shall I do here? Supposing I do find out where he lives – in the meantime Petrushka will most likely have returned with the reply. I'm only wasting precious time – I've already wasted precious time. Well, not to worry, all this can still be sorted out. But really, shouldn't I drop in on Vakhrameyev? But no! I can do that later. Damn, there was no need to come out at all. But that's me all over – it's a knack of mine, always jumping the gun, whether I need to or not ... Hm ... what time is it? Must be nine by now. Petrushka might get back and not find me at home. That was an extremely stupid thing to do, going out. Oh dear, it's all such a bother!'

Frankly admitting to himself that he had acted extremely stupidly, our hero ran back home to Shestilavochnaya Street; he arrived tired and weary. He learned from the porter that Petrushka had not yet condescended to put in an appearance. 'Ah well, just as I expected!' our hero reflected, 'but meanwhile it's nine already. Ugh! What a lazy devil he is! Always getting drunk somewhere. Good Lord! What a wretched day has fallen to my unhappy lot!' Thus reflecting and lamenting, Mr Golyadkin unlocked his room, got some light, undressed completely, lit a pipe and feeling weak, worn-out, dejected and hungry, he lay down on his sofa to await Petrushka. The candle burned down dimly, its light flickering on the walls ... Mr Golyadkin gazed and gazed and thought and thought – and then he fell asleep, dead to the world.

It was already late when he awoke. The candle had burnt right down, was smoking and about to go out altogether. Mr Golyadkin jumped up with a start, roused himself and remembered everything, absolutely everything. From behind the partition resounded Petrushka's heavy snores. Mr Golyadkin rushed to the window – not a light anywhere. He opened the window vent – all was quiet. It was as if the city had become deserted, was sleeping. So, it must have been two or three in the morning – and indeed it was: the clock behind the partition exerted itself and struck two. Mr Golyadkin rushed behind the partition.

Somehow, and not without a lengthy struggle, he managed to rouse Petrushka and made him sit up in bed. At that moment

the candle went out completely. It was about ten minutes before
Mr Golyadkin managed to find and light another. During this
time Petrushka had succeeded in dropping off again. 'You
scoundrel, you damned good-for-nothing!' exclaimed Mr Golyadkin, shaking him again. 'Are you getting up now, are you
awake?' After half an hour's sustained effort Mr Golyadkin
succeeded however in rousing his servant completely and dragging him out from behind the partition. Only then could our
hero see that Petrushka was, as they say, drunk as a lord and
could barely stand up.

'Damned layabout!' shouted Mr Golyadkin. 'You ruffian!
You'll be the death of me! Oh God, what on earth has he done
with the letter? My God . . . where is it? And why did I write
it? Was there any need to? Got carried away, you idiot – you
and your pride! Went in for pride, you did – now see where
pride's landed you! There's pride for you – you scoundrel!
Now, you! . . . what have you done with that letter, you
criminal! Who did you give it to?'

'I didn't give any letter to anyone. I never had any letter – so
there!'

Mr Golyadkin wrung his hands in despair.

'Now you listen, Pyotr, you listen to me!'

'I'm listening.'

'Where did you go? Answer me!'

'Where did I go? I went to see some nice people. Where else?'

'Oh God help me! Where did you go first? Did you go to the
office . . . ? Now, you listen to me, Petrushka – you're drunk,
aren't you?'

'Me drunk?! May I be struck down this minute . . . n-n-not
a drop . . . that's . . .'

'No, no, it's all right if you're drunk . . . I was only asking.
It's quite all right if you're drunk! I don't mind, Petrushka, I
don't mind at all. Perhaps it's just slipped your mind for the
moment and you'll remember everything. Come on, try and
remember. Did you go and see that clerk Vakhrameyev or didn't
you?'

'No, I didn't. There was no clerk with that name. Strike me
down . . .'

'No, no, Pyotr! No, Petrushka, you know I don't mind! You
can see for yourself that I don't ... what of it? Well, it's cold
and wet outside and you had a little drink – there's no harm in
that. I'm not angry, old chap. I had a drop myself today ...
Now ... please tell me, try and remember: did you see that
clerk Vakhrameyev?'

'Well, to be honest, it was like this. I did go – strike me ...'

'Good, Petrushka, it's good that you went. You can see I'm
not angry,' continued our hero, encouraging his servant even
more, patting his shoulder and smiling at him. 'Well, well, so
you did have a little drop, you old devil! Put away about ten
copecks' worth, didn't you? You cunning rogue! Well, that's
all right by me, you can see that I'm not angry, old chap ...
You can see I'm not angry, old chap, I'm not angry ...'

'No, say what you like, sir, but I'm not a rogue. I just went
to see some nice people, but I'm not a rogue ... never have
been ...'

'Oh no, Petrushka, of course not! Now listen, Petrushka. I've
nothing against it, I'm not getting at you by calling you a rogue
– I only meant it nicely. I'm using the word in a noble sense.
All it means is that some men consider it flattering if you call
them a rogue or a crafty devil – it means they're nobody's fool
and won't allow themselves to be duped by anyone. Some men
like that ... Ah well, never mind! Now, tell me, Petrushka,
frankly and openly, like a friend – did you see that clerk Vakhrameyev and did he give you the address?'

'Yes, he gave me the address, too. Good at his work, that
clerk! "Your master," he says, "is a good man, very good."
"Go and tell your master," he says, "that I send my regards,
thank him and tell him I respect your master. Your master's a
good man," he said, "and you, Petrushka, are a good man
too ...", so there you are ...'

'God help me! But the address, the address, you Judas!' Mr
Golyadkin's last words were spoken almost in a whisper.

'Oh, yes, the address – he gave me the address.'

'He did? Well, where does he live, this Golyadkin, this clerk
Golyadkin, this titular counsellor?'

'"You'll find Golyadkin," he says, "in Shestilavochnaya

Street. When you go down Shestilavochnaya Street," he says, "there's a flight of stairs on the right and it's on the third floor. That's where you'll find Golyadkin," he says.'

'You rogue!' cried our hero, finally losing all patience. 'You rotten crook! That's *me*! That's *me* you're talking about! But there's *another* Golyadkin, I'm talking about the other one, you scoundrel!'

'Well, as you please. What is it to me? Do what you like – so there!'

'But the letter, the letter . . .'

'What letter? There wasn't any letter. I never saw any letter.'

'What did you do with it, you scoundrel?'

'I handed it over, I did. I gave it to him. "My compliments and thanks," he says. "He's a good man, your master. Give your master my respects," he says.'

'But who said that? Did Golyadkin say it?'

Petrushka remained silent for a moment and then, grinning all over his face, he looked his master right in the eye.

'Listen to me, you criminal you!' Mr Golyadkin began, choking with rage and almost beside himself. 'What have you done to me? Tell me what you've done to me! You've finished me off, you ruffian. You've taken my head off my shoulders, you Judas!'

'Well, you can do what you like now, what do I care?' Petrushka replied in a decisive tone, retreating behind the partition.

'Come here, come here, you scoundrel!'

'No I won't come now, I just won't! I'm off to see good folk . . . Good folk live honestly. Good people live without deception and never come in twos . . .'

Mr Golyadkin's arms and legs turned to ice and he gasped for breath.

'Yes,' continued Petrushka, 'they never come in twos and they're not an insult to God and they're honest men . . .'

'You're drunk, you lazy devil! Now go and sleep it off, you ruffian. Tomorrow you'll catch it!' muttered Mr Golyadkin, barely audibly.

As for Petrushka, he muttered something else; then he could be heard lying down on his bed so that it creaked, yawned lengthily, stretched himself out and finally started to snore, sleeping the sleep of the just, as they say. Mr Golyadkin was neither dead nor alive. Petrushka's behaviour, his very strange hints, which, although vague and at which there was consequently nothing to take offence, particularly as it was a drunken man speaking, and finally the whole nasty turn of events – all this shook Mr Golyadkin to the core. 'Whatever possessed me to give him a blowing-up in the middle of the night?' our hero wondered, trembling all over from some morbid sensation. 'What the hell made me get involved with a drunk? What sense could I expect from someone drunk? Every word of his is a lie. All the same, what was he hinting at, the ruffian? Oh, my God! Why on earth did I have to go and write all those letters, like a murderer! I'm a suicide, that's what. Just can't keep my mouth shut, had to blab. And for what? I'm ruined, I'm like a rag – but no, that wasn't enough, I had to bring my pride into it. My pride's suffering, you say, so you must salvage it! I'm a suicide, that's what I am!'

Thus spoke Mr Golyadkin as he sat on his sofa, too frightened to move. Suddenly his eyes fixed on an object that aroused his attention in the highest degree. Terrified – was that which had aroused his attention an illusion or figment of his imagination? – he stretched his arm out, hopefully, timidly and with indescribable curiosity. No, it was no trick, no illusion! It was a letter, yes, a letter, no doubt about it and it was addressed to him. Mr Golyadkin picked the letter up from the table. His heart was pounding violently. 'That scoundrel must have brought it back, put it down here and forgotten all about it. Most likely that's what happened . . .' The letter was from the clerk Vakhrameyev, a young colleague and former friend of Mr Golyadkin's. 'But I anticipated all this,' thought our hero, 'I anticipated all the contents of this letter . . .' The letter read as follows:

Dear Sir, Yakov Petrovich!
Your man is drunk and it is impossible to get any sense out of him. For this reason I prefer to reply in writing. I hasten to inform you that I agree to carry out carefully and conscientiously the

task you have entrusted to me, that is, the personal transmission
through my manservant of a letter to a person you know very
well. That person who is familiar to you and who has now taken
the place of my friend and whose name I pass over in silence on
this occasion (for the reason that I do not wish to blacken unfairly
the reputation of a completely innocent man) lodges with us at
Karolina Ivanovna's flat, in the same room which during your
residence with us was occupied by a visiting infantry officer from
Tambov.[34] However, this person is everywhere to be found in
the company of people who are at least honest and sincere, which
cannot be said for some. I intend henceforth to sever all relations
with you, as it is impossible for us to maintain the same spirit
of mutual concord and harmonious comradeship as before, so
therefore I request you, my dear sir, immediately on receipt of
this, my frank epistle, to forward the two roubles owing to me
for razors of foreign manufacture that I sold you on credit, if you
will be so good as to recall, seven months ago at the time of your
residence with us at Karolina Ivanovna's, for whom I have the
most heartfelt respect. I am acting in this fashion since, according
to reports received from judicious people, you have lost your
self-respect and your reputation and become a threat to the
morality of the innocent and uncontaminated, for there are certain individuals who do not live according to the truth, most of
all, their words are false and their show of good intent is suspect.
As for Karolina Ivanovna, who has always been a lady of exemp-
lary conduct and, to boot, a spinster, although no longer young,
but of good foreign family – people capable of defending the
wronged Karolina Ivanovna can be found everywhere, which fact
several persons have asked me to mention in my letter in passing
and to do so speaking for myself.

In any event, you will discover everything in good time if you
have not done so already, despite your giving yourself a bad
name in every corner of the capital, according to the reports of
judicious people and consequently you may already have
received, my dear sir, such information appertaining to yourself,
in many places. In conclusion, my dear sir, I must inform you
that the person known to you, whose name I refrain from mentioning here for certain honourable reasons, is highly respected

by right-thinking people; what is more, is of a cheerful and agreeable disposition, successful both at work and in the company of judicious people, is true to his word and his friends and does not revile behind their backs those with whom he enjoys amicable relations in person.

At all events I remain your humble servant

N. Vakhrameyev

P.S. Get rid of your man: he's a drunkard and in all probability causes you a great deal of trouble. Take on Yevstafy, who used to work here and who now finds himself unemployed. Your present servant is not only a drunkard but a thief into the bargain, since only last week he sold Karolina Ivanovna a pound of lump sugar at a reduced price which in my opinion he could not have done without craftily robbing you of it bit by bit at different times. I am writing this as I wish you well, despite the fact that some people only know how to insult and deceive everyone, particularly those who are honest and of good character. What's more, they revile them behind their backs and misrepresent them, solely out of envy and because they cannot call themselves the same.

N.V.

Having read Vakhrameyev's letter our hero remained for a long time sitting motionless on his sofa. A new kind of light was breaking through that vague and mysterious fog that had been enveloping him for the past two days. Our hero was beginning partly to understand. He attempted to get up from his sofa and take a couple of turns around the room to refresh himself, to collect his scattered thoughts somehow and focus them on a single object and then, having pulled himself together, to give the situation his mature consideration. But the moment he tried to stand up he immediately felt so weak and feeble that he fell back again in his former place. 'Of course, I had a premonition of all this. But how he writes! And what's the direct meaning of all these words? Supposing I do know their meaning – where will it all lead? If he'd told me you must do this and that and said it's like this and that, so to speak, I would have done it. Events have taken a very nasty turn! Ah, how I wish tomorrow would arrive quickly so that I can get down to business! Well, now I know what do to. I'll say: "It's like this, I agree to your arguments but I won't sell my honour." However, how does this person I know of . . . how does this disreputable character come to be mixed up in it? And why did he get mixed up precisely here? Oh, if only I could get to tomorrow quickly! Until then they'll keep dragging my name in the mud, they're scheming, they're working to spite me! The main thing is not to waste time and now I must write a letter, for example, simply to say there's this and that, that I agree to such and such. And first thing tomorrow I'll send it and then I'll move in on them from another direction and forestall them, the darlings! They'll drag my name in the mud, that's what!'

Mr Golyadkin drew some paper towards him, picked up his pen and wrote the following epistle in reply to Provincial Secretary Vakhrameyev's:

Dear Nestor Ignatyevich,
It was with heartfelt sorrow and amazement that I read your letter, so insulting to me, as I can clearly see that you are alluding to me when referring to certain unprincipled persons and others of suspect loyalty. With genuine sorrow I see how rapidly, how successfully and to what depths slander has sunk its roots, to the detriment of my welfare, my honour and my good name. And it is all the more deplorable and insulting that even honest, truly high-minded people, and, most importantly, people endowed with straightforward and open characters, should abandon the interests of noble people and should cling with the best qualities of their hearts to that pernicious putrefaction that in our troublous and immoral times has unfortunately been so widely and so insidiously propagated. In conclusion, I will say that I shall consider it my sacred duty to repay in its entirety the debt of two roubles to which you referred.

As to your references, my dear sir, to a certain person of the female sex, regarding the intentions, calculations and various projects of this same person, I must confess that I vaguely and dimly comprehend them. Allow me, dear sir, to preserve unsullied

my lofty mode of thought and my good name. At all events, I am
personally prepared to condescend to entering into explanations
with you, preferring the trustworthiness of personal contact to
the written word and, what's more, I am preparing to enter into
various peacable and mutual agreements. To this end I beg you,
dear sir, to convey to this person my readiness to reach a personal
settlement and furthermore to ask that person to suggest a time
and place to meet. Your insinuation that I insulted you, betrayed
our original friendship and spoke ill of you, made bitter reading.
I ascribe all of this to misunderstandings, to base calumny and
to the envy and ill will of those whom I can justifiably term my
deadliest enemies. But they are probably unaware that innocence
is strong by virtue of its own innocence, that the shamelessness,
insolence and scandalous familiarity of various people will sooner
or later earn them the stigma of universal contempt and that such
persons will perish from nothing but their own indecency and
depravity. In conclusion, I beg you, my dear sir, to convey to these
people that their strange pretensions and ignoble and fantastic
desire to oust others from the positions occupied by those other
people by reason of their very existence in this world and to supplant them, are deserving only of amazement, contempt and pity
and – in addition – of the madhouse. Above all, such relations are
strictly prohibited by the law and this, in my opinion, is perfectly
just, since everyone should be content with his own place. There
are limits to everything and if this is a joke then it is a most
improper one – I will say more, my dear sir, that my ideas outlined
above regarding *knowing one's place* are purely moral.

At all events I have the honour to remain

Your humble servant

Ya. Golyadkin

CHAPTER X

All in all one could say that the events of the previous day had
shaken Mr Golyadkin to the very core. Our hero passed an
extremely bad night and was unable to get any proper sleep,

even five minutes. It was as if some practical joker had scattered bristles in his bed. He spent the whole night in a half-sleeping, half-waking state, tossing and turning from side to side, sighing and groaning, nodding off one moment and waking a minute later. All this was accompanied by peculiar anguish, vague memories, horrid visions – in brief, by every conceivable nastiness. First, in the strange, mysterious half-light, he would glimpse Andrey Filippovich, a dry, wrathful figure with a dry, harsh gaze, uttering cruelly courteous rebukes. And the moment Mr Golyadkin began to approach Andrey Filippovich, somehow to justify himself this way or that and claim that he wasn't as black as his enemies had painted him, but was like this and that and even possessed many virtues over and above his ordinary inborn qualities, in one way or the other, then there would appear a certain person notorious for his beastly tendencies and by the most scandalous means would destroy every initiative of Mr Golyadkin's and practically before Mr Golyadkin's very eyes thoroughly blacken his name, trample his pride in the mire and then, without a moment's delay, usurp his place both at work and in society. At other times Mr Golyadkin felt his head smarting from some insult recently dispensed and humiliatingly accepted, either in the company of his fellows or while carrying out his duties and against which insult any form of protest would have been difficult ... And while Mr Golyadkin began to rack his brains as to why exactly it was so very difficult to protest even against any kind of insult, in the meantime the idea of the insult was imperceptibly being recast into another form – into the form of some small or fairly significant act of nastiness that he witnessed, heard of, or recently carried out himself – carried out frequently even, not on any sordid basis, not even from some vile motive, but sometimes by chance, for example, out of delicacy, at other times because of his utter defencelessness and finally ... in brief, Mr Golyadkin knew very well *why*! Just then he blushed in his sleep and as he tried to suppress his blushes he too would mutter to himself that here, for example, he might have shown firmness of character, could have shown considerable firmness of character in this case ... and then he concluded by asking

why firmness of character and why bring that up now! ...
But what incensed and exasperated Mr Golyadkin more than
anything else was, whether summoned or not, at that precise
moment a certain person notorious for his disgusting and scandalous behaviour would invariably turn up and although the
facts were sufficiently well known would mutter with a nasty
little grin: 'What's firmness of character got to do with it? What
firmness of character do you and I have, Yakov Petrovich?'
Then Mr Golyadkin would dream that he was in the company
of distinguished people, renowned for the wit and refinement
of every single member; that Mr Golyadkin in turn was distinguished for charm and wit and that everyone came to like him
– even some of his enemies who were present came to like him,
which Mr Golyadkin found extremely pleasant; all that gave
him precedence; and finally that Mr Golyadkin had the pleasure
of overhearing the host singing Mr Golyadkin's praises while
taking one of the guests aside ... Then suddenly, for no earthly
reason, there again appeared the person notorious for his perfidious ways and bestial impulses, in the shape of Mr Golyadkin
Junior and in a flash, in one fell swoop, Golyadkin Junior
destroyed Mr Golyadkin Senior's entire triumph and glory,
eclipsed Mr Golyadkin Senior, trampled Mr Golyadkin Senior
in the mire and finally demonstrated that Mr Golyadkin Senior,
who was also the real one, was not the real one at all, but a
fake and that *he* was the genuine one and that Golyadkin Senior
was not at all what he seemed but simply this and that, and
consequently ought not and in fact had no right to belong to
the company of honourable people of good taste. And all this
happened so very quickly that Mr Golyadkin Senior did not
manage to open his mouth before everyone, in body and soul,
defected to the dastardly and counterfeit Mr Golyadkin Junior,
rejected him, the authentic and innocent Mr Golyadkin, with
the profoundest contempt. Not a single person was left whose
attitude had not been altered in one flash by the repellent Mr
Golyadkin to suit his own ends. Not one person remained –
even the most insignificant out of the entire gathering – to
whom the spurious and worthless Mr Golyadkin wouldn't have
sucked up in the most unctuous manner, to whom he didn't

toady, before whom he didn't smoke something extremely pleasant and sweet as a sign of his extreme pleasure so that the person enveloped in smoke could only sniff and sneeze until the tears came. And, most important, it all happened like lightning: the speed of movement of the suspect and worthless Mr Golyadkin was amazing! For example, no sooner had he finished sucking up to someone to win his good graces, than in the blink of an eyelid he'd be with someone else. Ever so slyly he'd butter up another, extract a benevolent little smile from him, jerk his thick, round, rather dumpy legs into action and then be off and away, making up to a third, toadying to him in friendly fashion. And before you could open your mouth to show your surprise – there he'd be with a fourth, up to the same tricks with him! It was horrible, sheer sorcery and nothing less! And everyone was delighted with him, everyone liked him, everyone praised him to the skies and everyone proclaimed in unison that for amiability and satirical cast of mind he was superior to the innocent, authentic Mr Golyadkin, thus putting the real and authentic Mr Golyadkin to shame; and they rejected and drove out the genuine, truth-loving Mr Golyadkin, showering insults on Mr Golyadkin, so well known for his love for his neighbour.

Filled with anguish, terror and rage, the suffering Mr Golyadkin ran out into the street and tried to hire a cab to speed him straight to His Excellency's, or if not there then at least to Andrey Filippovich's. But – oh, the horror! The cabbies refused point-blank to take Mr Golyadkin, saying: 'We can't take two gents exactly the same, sir. A good man tries to live honestly, sir, not just anyhow and he never comes in twos.' In a paroxysm of shame the perfectly honourable Mr Golyadkin kept looking around and in fact saw for himself, with his own eyes, that the cab drivers and Petrushka, who was in league with them, were all in the right: for the depraved Mr Golyadkin was actually close by, not at all far away, and in his customary dastardly way was even here at that critical moment undoubtedly preparing to do something very improper, showing no sign of that nobility of character that is normally acquired by education, that nobility upon which the revolting Mr Golyadkin II was so pluming himself at every opportunity. Beside himself with shame and despair, the ruined and completely authentic Mr Golyadkin rushed off blindly, at the mercy of fate, wherever. But with every stride, with every thud of his foot on the granite pavement, there would spring up, as if from under the ground, a completely identical Mr Golyadkin, utterly similar in depravity. And the moment they appeared, all these perfect replicas would start running one after the other and, stretching out in a long chain like a gaggle of geese, would hobble behind Mr Golyadkin so that there was no escaping these replicas, so that the eminently pitiable Mr Golyadkin couldn't catch his breath for horror, so that in the end such a terrifying multitude of exact replicas was spawned that the whole city was finally jammed with these perfect replicas and a police officer, observing such a breach of the peace, was obliged to grab all these perfect replicas by the scruff of the neck and fling them into a lock-up that happened to be close at hand ... Our hero would wake up, rigid and frozen with horror and – rigid and frozen with horror – he felt that even his waking hours were hardly spent more cheerfully ... it was cruel, sheer agony ... The anguish was such that it seemed his heart was being gnawed out of his breast.

In the end Mr Golyadkin could endure it no longer. 'This shall not happen!' he shouted, resolutely sitting up in bed, and after this exclamation he completely came to.

It was evidently very late in the day. In the room it was somehow unusually light. The sun's rays were filtering through the frosty windowpanes and scattering themselves over the whole room, to the not inconsiderable surprise of Mr Golyadkin, for normally only at noon did the sun peer into his room as it followed its daily course. As far as Mr Golyadkin could recall no deviation from the heavenly luminary's usual course had ever occurred. Our hero barely had time to wonder at this than the wall clock behind the partition whirred preparatory to striking. 'Oh yes!' thought Mr Golyadkin as he prepared to listen with dull expectancy. But to Mr Golyadkin's complete and utter consternation the clock exerted itself and struck only once. 'What sort of nonsense is this?' our hero shouted, leaping right out of bed. Unable to believe his ears he dashed, just as he was, behind the partition. The clock really did show one. Mr Golyadkin glanced at Petrushka's bed, but there wasn't even a whiff of Petrushka in the room. His bed had evidently been made and vacated long before; his boots were nowhere to be seen either – a sure indication that Petrushka really had gone out. Mr Golyadkin rushed to the door: the door was shut. 'But where on earth's Petrushka?' he continued in a whisper, terribly agitated and feeling a quite significant trembling in every limb. Suddenly a thought flashed through his mind . . . Mr Golyadkin rushed to the table, inspected it and rummaged around – yes: that letter written yesterday to Vakhrameyev was not there; nor was there any sign of Petrushka behind the partition. The clock showed one, and several new points that had been introduced into Vahkrameyev's letter of yesterday that at first reading had struck him as utterly vague were now perfectly clear to him. Finally – Petrushka, too – obviously a bribed Petrushka! Yes, yes, that was it!

'So that's where the main knot was being tied!' Mr Golyadkin cried, striking his forehead and opening his eyes ever wider, 'so it's in that niggardly German woman's nest where all the devilry is lurking! So, it must have been only a strategic diversion when she directed me to Izmaylovsky Bridge – she was distracting me, confusing me (the old hag!) and that's how she's been undermining my position!! Yes, that's it! You only have to consider it from that angle to see exactly how the whole thing is. And it also fully accounts for that scoundrel's appearance. Yes, it all adds up now, it all makes sense. They've been keeping him in reserve for a long time, preparing him and saving him for a rainy day. And now it's all come out in the wash; that's how it's all turned out. Ah well, never mind! No time has been lost!' Here Mr Golyadkin remembered with horror that it was already after one in the afternoon. 'What if they've already managed to . . . ?' A groan broke from his chest. 'But no, they're lying, they couldn't have had time – let's see.' He somehow dressed himself, grabbed pen and paper and scribbled the following epistle:

Dear Yakov Petrovich,
It's either you or me, but there's no room for both of us! I'm
telling you quite frankly that your strange, absurd and at the
same time impossible desire to appear as my twin and pass
yourself off as such will serve no other purpose than to bring
about your complete disgrace and defeat. So therefore I must
request you, for your own sake, to step to one side and make
way for those who are truly noble and with honourable intentions. Failing this I am prepared to resort even to the most
extreme measure. I lay down my pen and await . . . However,
I remain at your service – and with pistols.

                                               Ya. Golyadkin

When he had finished this note our hero vigorously rubbed
his hands together. Then, pulling on his overcoat and putting
on his hat, he opened the door with a second, spare key and set
off for the office. But when he arrived he could not make up
his mind whether to go in. It was too late: Mr Golyadkin's
watch showed half past two. Suddenly an apparently extremely
trifling circumstance resolved some of Mr Golyadkin's doubts:
from around the corner of the office building there suddenly
appeared a small, breathless, flushed figure which stealthily,
darting like a rat, scuttled up the steps and then into the lobby.
It was the copy clerk Ostafyev, a man well known to Mr
Golyadkin, in somewhat straitened circumstances and ready to
do anything for ten copecks. Knowing Ostafyev's weak side
and aware that after an absence on some very urgent, private
business he was probably all the more susceptible to ten-copeck
pieces, our hero decided to be generous with them and immediately tore up the steps and then into the hall after Ostafyev,
called to him and with a mysterious air invited him into a
secluded corner behind a huge iron stove. Having led him there
our hero began cross-examining him.
    'Well, my friend, how's it going, um . . . er . . . if you get my
meaning?'
    'I do, Your Honour and I wish Your Honour good health.'
    'Good my friend, good. I'll make it worth your while, dear
friend. Well, tell me now – how are they?'

'What are you inquiring about, sir?' Here Ostafyev for a moment gave a little support with one hand to his unexpectedly gaping mouth.

'I'm . . . well you see, my friend, I'm . . . er . . . now don't you go thinking things. Well now, is Andrey Filippovich here?'

'He's here, sir.'

'And are the clerks here?'

'Yes, sir, they're all here, as they should be, sir.'

'And His Excellency as well?'

'His Excellency too, sir.'

Here for a second time the clerk gave a little support to his mouth that had fallen open again and gave Mr Golyadkin a somewhat quizzical, peculiar look. At least so it appeared to our hero.

'And nothing special to report, old chap?'

'No, sir, nothing at all.'

'I mean, about me – is there anything going on there to do with me, my friend, anything at all . . . eh? I was just asking, you understand.'

'No, sir, haven't heard a thing up to now.' Here the clerk again supported his mouth and gave Mr Golyadkin another peculiar look. The fact was, our hero was now trying to penetrate Ostafyev's expression and read something there, to see whether he was keeping something back. And he really did seem to be keeping something or other back. Actually, Ostafyev was now becoming ruder and more off-hand and didn't show the same concern over Mr Golyadkin's interests as at the beginning of the conversation. 'He's partly within his rights,' thought Mr Golyadkin. 'After all, what am I to him? Perhaps he's already been buttered up by the other side, so that's why he was absent on urgent private business. Ah well, I'd better give . . .' Mr Golyadkin understood that the time for ten-copeck pieces had arrived.

'Here you are, dear chap.'

'I'm deeply obliged to Your Honour.'

'And there'll be more for you.'

'Yes, Your Honour.'

'I'll give you even more and when our business is finished as much again. Understand?'

The clerk said nothing, stood to attention and fixed his eyes on Mr Golyadkin, without blinking.

'Now tell me, has anything been said about me?'

'I don't think so sir ... er ... nothing for the time being,' Ostafyev replied in a slow drawl, also like Mr Golyadkin maintaining a mysterious air, twitching his eyebrows a little, staring at the floor and trying to strike the appropriate tone – briefly, doing his utmost to earn what had been promised, as what had been given he already considered his own and fully earned.

'So, there's nothing at all?'

'Not for the moment, sir.'

'But listen ... um ... er ... perhaps there *will* be something?'

'Later, of course, sir, something might come up.'

'That's bad,' thought our hero.

'Listen, here's some more for you old chap.'

'Much obliged to Your Honour.'

'Was Vakhrameyev here yesterday?'

'That he was, sir.'

'And was there anyone else? ... Try and remember, old fellow.'

The clerk rummaged in his memory for a moment but could find nothing to fit the bill.

'No, sir, there was nothing else.'

'Hm!' Silence followed.

'Listen, old chap, here's another ten copecks for you. Just tell me all you know, all the ins and outs.'

'Yes, sir.'

Ostafyev stood there as meek as a lamb: this was exactly what Mr Golyadkin needed.

'Tell me, old chap, what sort of footing is he on?'

'Not bad, sir – very good, sir,' the clerk replied, staring hard at Mr Golyadkin

'So, how good?'

'He's all right, sir.' Here Ostafyev twitched his eyebrows significantly. But now he was decidedly all at sea and did not know what to say. 'That's bad!' thought Mr Golyadkin.

'Is there really nothing further to report, with him and Vakhrameyev?'

'Everything's as it was before.'

'Think hard.'

'Well, they do say that . . .'

'What do they say?'

Ostafyev propped his mouth again for a moment.

'Isn't there a letter for me from there?'

'Well, Mikheyev the caretaker went to Vakhrameyev's flat today, to that German woman of theirs, so I'll go and ask if you like.'

'Please do me the favour, old chap, for God's sake! I'm only saying . . . Now don't you go thinking things, I'm only just saying. But ask a few questions, find out if they are cooking anything up that concerns me. Find out how he's acting. That's what I need to know. Now you go and find that out, dear chap, and I'll reward you for it later . . .'

'Yes, Your Honour, but Ivan Semyonych was sitting in your place today, sir.'

'Ivan Semyonych? Oh, was he now?! Really?'

'Andrey Filippovich showed him where to sit, sir.'

'Oh, really? How did that come about? Now you go and find that out, for God's sake, go and find that out. If you find everything out I'll reward you for it, dear chap. That's what I want . . . But don't go thinking things, old chap.'

'Yes, sir, I'll go up right away, sir. But aren't you coming in today, Your Honour?'

'No, my friend, um . . . er . . . I've only come to have a look. But I'll show you my gratitude later, my dear chap.'

'Very good, sir,' the clerk swiftly and zealously ran upstairs and Mr Golyadkin was left alone.

'This is bad,' he thought. 'Oh, it's bad, very bad! Oh dear! That little business of ours – how bad it seems now! What could all this mean? What exactly did some of that drunkard's hints mean, for example, and whose trickery is it? Ah! Now I know whose trickery it is! This is the kind of trickery it is: they probably got to know, then they sat him there . . . But hold on a moment . . . Did *they* put him there? It was Andrey Filippovich who put him there, that Ivan Semyonovich, but why did he make him sit there, for what precise purpose did he put him there? They probably found out ... It's all Vakhrameyev's work. No, not Vakhrameyev's, he's as thick as two planks, that Vakhrameyev. But all of them are working for him and that's precisely why they put that scoundrel up to it! And that one-eyed German slut went and complained! I always suspected that there was more to this simple intrigue, that there was something behind all those old wives' tales. I said as much to Krestyan Ivanovich: "They've vowed to murder someone," I said, "in the moral sense – and they've got Karolina Ivanovna in their clutches." No, there are clearly experts at work here, that's for sure! Yes, my dear sir, an expert's hand is at work here, not Vakhrameyev's! I've said all along that Vakhrameyev's stupid and this is ... but now I know who's working for all of them here – it's that blackguard who's working for them – that impostor! He's clinging to that one thing – and it partly helps to explain his success in the highest society. But really, I'd like to know what footing he's on now ... what's he doing there with them? But why on earth did they take on Ivan Semyono-vich? What the hell did they need him for? As if they couldn't get anyone else. Still, it would have come to the same thing whoever they put there, but what I do know is that I've had my suspicions about Ivan Semyonovich for a long time. I noticed it ages ago: what a nasty old man he is – so vile – they say he lends money and charges exorbitant interest just like a Jew. And all this is masterminded by the Bear. The Bear's mixed up in the whole proceedings. That's how it all began. It was at Izmaylovsky Bridge, that's how it all began ...' Here Mr Goly-adkin screwed up his face as if he had bitten into a lemon, most likely having remembered something very unpleasant. 'Well now, it doesn't matter,' he thought. 'All this time I've been worry-ing about my own troubles. But why doesn't that Ostafyev come? Probably sitting down somewhere or been held up for some reason. It's partly a good thing in fact that I'm doing some intriguing and undermining of my own. I only had to give Ostafyev ten copecks and he's ... well ... on my side. But that's the thing – *is* he really on my side? Perhaps for their part they've done the same from *their* side too ... and for their part they're intriguing together, they're in collusion with him. Yes

. . . he looks like a bandit, the ruffian, a real bandit. He's holding something back, that crook! "No, there's nothing," he says, "and I'm deeply obliged to Your Honour." Ugh, you rotten crook!' There was a noise. Mr Golyadkin shrank back and jumped behind the stove. Someone came down the stairs and went out into the street. 'Who could that be leaving at this time?' our hero wondered. A minute later someone's footsteps rang out again. Here Mr Golyadkin couldn't resist poking out the tip of his nose ever so slightly from behind the parapet – and he immediately withdrew it, as if someone had pricked it with a pin. This time someone he knew was passing by, that is, that scoundrel, that intriguer, that debauchee, tripping along as usual with those nasty little steps, pattering and jerking his legs as if he were about to kick someone. 'The scoundrel!' our hero muttered to himself. However, Mr Golyadkin could not fail to notice that under the villain's arm was a huge green portfolio belonging to His Excellency. 'He's on another special mission!' thought Mr Golyadkin, flushing and shrinking into himself still more in annoyance. No sooner had Mr Golyadkin Junior flashed past Mr Golyadkin without even noticing him than footsteps were heard for a third time and on this occasion Mr Golyadkin guessed they were the clerk's. And in fact the little figure of some greasy-haired clerk did peer from behind the stove at him. However, the figure was not that of Ostafyev but of another clerk nicknamed Scribbly. Mr Golyadkin was amazed. 'Why has he been letting others into the secret?' our hero wondered. 'What barbarians! That lot hold nothing sacred!'

'Well, what then, old chap?' he asked, turning to Scribbly. 'Who sent you, my friend?'

'Well, it's about that little business of yours. No, there's no news so far from anyone for the time being, sir. But if there is anything we'll tell you.'

'And what about Ostafyev?'

'He just couldn't get away, sir. His Excellency's already walked through the department twice and I've no time now . . .'

'Thanks, my dear chap, thank you. Only, tell me . . .'

'Honest to God, I've no time now. Every minute he keeps asking for us. But if you would care to stand here a little

longer, sir, we'll let you know if there's any news regarding
your business.'

'No, my friend, you tell me . . .'

'Please excuse me, but I don't have the time,' Scribbly replied,
breaking away from Mr Golyadkin, who had grabbed him by
the lapel. 'I really don't . . . If you'll please stand here a bit
longer we'll keep you informed.'

'Just a moment, just a moment, my dear friend! Just a
moment! Now, here's a letter, my friend. And there'll be something for you, dear friend.'

'Yes, sir.'

'Try and give it to Mr Golyadkin, dear chap.'

'Mr Golyadkin?'

'Yes, my friend, Mr Golyadkin.'

'Very well, sir, as soon as I've cleared up here I'll take it. And
in the meantime you stand here. No one will see you.'

'No, my friend, don't go thinking that . . . I'm not simply
standing here so that no one can see me. But I won't be here,
my friend . . . I'll be over there, in the side street. There's a
coffee-house there. I'll be waiting there and if anything crops
up you must come and tell me all about it – understand?'

'Very good, sir. Only, please let me go now . . . I understand.'

'And I'll reward you, dear chap,' Mr Golyadkin shouted after
Scribbly, who had at last managed to free himself. 'He's a
blackguard, seems he got a bit ruder later on . . .' thought our
hero, stealing out from behind the stove. 'There's another catch
here, that's clear enough . . . First it was yes sir, no sir . . . But
perhaps he really was in a tearing hurry. Perhaps His Excellency
did walk through the department twice. And what was that in
connection with? Oh well, it doesn't really matter, perhaps it's
absolutely nothing . . . but now we'll see . . .'

Here Mr Golyadkin was about to open the door and already
intending to go out into the street when suddenly, at that very
moment, His Excellency's carriage clattered up to the entrance.
Mr Golyadkin had managed to collect himself, then the carriage
door opened from the inside and its occupant jumped out on
to the porch. The new arrival was none other than that same Mr
Golyadkin Junior, who had gone off himself only ten minutes

before. Mr Golyadkin Senior remembered that the Director's
apartment was just around the corner. 'He's on some special
mission,' our hero thought. Meanwhile, after grabbing the fat
green portfolio inside the carriage, with some other papers, and
after giving orders to the coachman, Mr Golyadkin Junior flung
open the door, almost hitting Mr Golyadkin Senior with it,
deliberately ignoring him and therefore trying to spite him, and
shot up the stairs to the department. 'This is bad!' thought Mr
Golyadkin. 'See what's happening to our little business now!
Good God, just look at him!' For about half a minute longer
our hero stood motionless; finally he came to a decision. Without much further pause for thought and feeling moreover a
violent palpitation in his heart and a trembling in every limb,
he chased up the staircase after his friend. 'Well, here goes:
what do I care? I'm to one side of all this,' he reflected, removing
his hat, overcoat and galoshes in the ante-room.

It was already dusk when Mr Golyadkin entered his department. Neither Andrey Filippovich nor Anton Antonovich was
in the room. Both were in the Director's office with their
reports. The Director, as rumour had it, was in turn hurrying
to report to His Supreme Excellency. As a result of these circumstances and also because dusk was infiltrating here, too, and
office hours were drawing to a close, several clerks, mainly the
juniors, were whiling away the time in a kind of busy inactivity
just as our hero entered, having gathered in small groups, chatting, arguing and laughing, while some of the very youngest,
that is, those of the very lowest rank were amidst all the noise
enjoying a quiet game of pitch-and-toss in a corner over by the
window. Aware of decorum and feeling just at that moment a
special need to find favour and 'get in' with everyone, Mr
Golyadkin immediately approached whoever he was on good
terms with to wish them good day, etc. But his colleagues
responded somewhat strangely to Mr Golyadkin's greetings.
He was unpleasantly struck by the general chilliness, dryness
and one might even say a certain steeliness in the reception he
got. No one held out his hand. Some simply said 'hello' and
walked away; others merely nodded, one just turned his back,
pretending not to have noticed him. Finally several of them –

and this riled Mr Golyadkin most of all – several of the youngest
clerks, the lowest of the low, mere whippersnappers who, as
Mr Golyadkin so rightly commented, were fit only for playing
pitch-and-toss given the chance and loafing around somewhere,
gathered in small groups, gradually surrounding Mr Golyadkin
and thus almost barring his exit. They all stared at him with a
kind of insolent curiosity.

The omens were bad. Mr Golyadkin realized that and sensibly prepared, for his part, to take no notice. Suddenly a
completely unexpected event finished him off, as they say,
utterly annihilated Mr Golyadkin.

Among the small crowd of the young surrounding colleagues,
as if deliberately, at the most distressing moment for Mr Golyadkin, there suddenly appeared Mr Golyadkin Junior, cheerful
as ever, smiling and frivolous as ever: in short, mischievous,
capering, toadying, guffawing, nimble of tongue and foot as
ever, just as before, just as yesterday, for example. He grinned,
gambolled, pranced and twisted around with a smile that
seemed to say 'Good evening' to everyone. He wormed his way
into the small crowd of clerks, shaking hands with one, patting
another on the shoulder, hugging another, explaining to a
fourth exactly the kind of mission His Excellency had employed
him for, where he had gone, what he had done, what he had
brought back with him. To a fifth – probably his best friend –
he gave a smacking kiss, right on the lips – in brief, everything
was happening exactly as in Mr Golyadkin Senior's dream.
After having had his fill of dancing about, after finishing with
everyone in his own unique way, manipulating them all to his
own ends, whether he needed to or not, having slobbered over
all and sundry to his heart's content, Mr Golyadkin Junior
suddenly and most probably in error (up to that moment he
had not had time to notice his oldest friend) even offered his
hand to Mr Golyadkin Senior as well. Probably also in error,
although he had in fact ample time to notice the dishonourable
Mr Golyadkin Junior, our hero immediately eagerly grasped the
so unexpectedly extended hand and shook it in the friendliest,
firmest manner, shook it as if prompted by some strange, quite
unexpected inner impulse, with a lachrymose feeling. Whether

our hero had been deceived by his worthless enemy's first movement or was simply at a loss, or sensed and acknowledged in
his heart of hearts the full extent of his own defencelessness, is
difficult to say. The fact is, Mr Golyadkin Senior, in full possession of his faculties, of his own free will and before witnesses,
solemnly shook hands with the person he had termed his mortal
foe. But what was the amazement, the frenzy and rage, the
horror and shame of Mr Golyadkin Senior when his foe and
his deadly enemy the ignoble Mr Golyadkin Junior, observing
the error of the persecuted and innocent man he had so perfidiously deceived, without shame, without feeling or compassion,
suddenly, with insufferable effrontery and rudeness, snatched
his hand away from Mr Golyadkin Senior's. Not only that: he
shook his hand as if he had just dirtied it on something really
nasty, spat to one side, accompanying all this with the most
obscene gesture; what is more, he took out his handkerchief
and there and then, in the most unseemly manner, used it to
wipe every one of his fingers that had momentarily been resting
in Mr Golyadkin Senior's hand. Acting in this manner, Mr
Golyadkin Junior, in his usual dastardly fashion, looked around
deliberately, made sure that everyone was witnessing his
behaviour, looked everyone in the eye, clearly trying to inspire
them with all that was most unfavourable with regard to Mr
Golyadkin Senior. The loathsome Mr Golyadkin Junior's conduct seemed to arouse the universal indignation of the surrounding clerks. Even the empty-headed, most junior clerks
showed their displeasure. All around there was murmuring
and discussion. The general stir could not fail to escape Mr
Golyadkin Senior's ears. But suddenly a well-timed little witticism that had meanwhile been simmering on Mr Golyadkin
Junior's lips shattered and destroyed our hero's last hopes,
tipping the balance once again in favour of his deadly and
worthless enemy.

'This is our Russian Faublas,[35] gentlemen. Allow me to introduce the young Faublas!' squeaked Mr Golyadkin Junior, with
his own unique insolence, mincing and winding his way through
the clerks, pointing out to them the petrified and at the same
time frenzied, genuine Mr Golyadkin. 'Give us a kiss, sweetie-

pie!' he continued with intolerable familiarity, moving towards the man he had so treacherously insulted. The worthless Mr Golyadkin's witticism seemed to have found a ready response in the right quarters, all the more so as it contained a cunning allusion to a certain incident that was clearly already public knowledge. Our hero felt the heavy hand of his enemies on his shoulders. However, his mind was already made up. With eyes blazing, a fixed smile on his pallid face, he managed to extricate himself from the crowd and with uneven, hurried steps headed straight for His Excellency's office. In the penultimate room he was met by Andrey Filippovich, who had only just left His Excellency, and although there were quite a number of other people of all kinds in the room, at that moment complete strangers to Mr Golyadkin, nonetheless our hero did not choose to pay any attention to such a circumstance. Boldly, directly, decisively, almost surprised at himself and inwardly praising himself for his daring, without further ado he directly accosted Andrey Filippovich, who was considerably startled at such an unexpected assault.

'Ah, what do you ... what do you want?!' asked the departmental chief, not listening to Mr Golyadkin, who had stumbled over some words.

'Andrey Filippovich ... I ... may I, Andrey Filippovich, have a talk right away, face to face with His Excellency?' our hero articulated volubly and distinctly, giving Andrey Filippovich the most determined look.

'What, sir? Of course you can't,' Andrey Filippovich replied, looking Mr Golyadkin up and down, from head to foot.

'I'm saying this, Andrey Filippovich, because I'm amazed no one here is prepared to unmask an impostor and scoundrel.'

'Wha-at, sir!?'

'A blackguard, Andrey Filippovich!'

'And to whom are you pleased to refer in such a manner?'

'A certain person, Andrey Filippovich. I, Andrey Filippovich, am referring to a certain person. I'm within my rights ... I think, Andrey Filippovich, that the authorities should encourage such actions,' added Mr Golyadkin, clearly forgetting himself, 'you can probably see for yourself, Andrey Filippovich, that this honourable action demonstrates my undivided loyalty and good intentions – to accept the authorities as a father, Andrey Filippovich, to accept the benevolent authorities as a father, and I blindly entrust my destiny to them. That's to say, so to speak, that's how it is . . .' Here Mr Golyadkin's voice trembled, his face grew flushed and two tears trickled down his eyelashes.

As he listened to Mr Golyadkin, Andrey Filippovich was so amazed that he involuntarily staggered back a couple of steps. Then he looked around uneasily . . . It is difficult to say how all this would have ended . . . But suddenly the door to His Excellency's room opened and he emerged in person, accompanied by several officials. Every single person in the room followed in his wake. His Excellency summoned Andrey Filippovich and walked beside him, embarking on a conversation about some business matters. When they had all moved on and left the room, Mr Golyadkin came to his senses. A little more relaxed now, he took shelter under the wing of Anton Antonovich Setochkin, who in turn came stumping along last of all and as it seemed to Mr Golyadkin with a terribly stern and apprehensive look. 'I've really let my tongue run away with me and made a mess of things here as well,' he thought. 'Ah well, not to worry.'

'I hope, Anton Antonovich, that you will at least agree to hear me out and investigate my circumstances,' he said quietly, his voice still trembling somewhat with emotion. 'Rejected by all, I appeal to you. I am still at a loss as to the meaning of Andrey Filippovich's words, Anton Antonovich. Please explain if you can.'

'All will be explained in its own good time,' Anton Antonovich replied sternly and deliberately and with a look that gave Mr Golyadkin clearly to understand that he had no desire whatsoever to continue the conversation. 'You'll know everything very soon. You'll be officially notified about everything today.'

'What do you mean *officially*, Anton Antonovich? Why exactly officially, sir?' our hero inquired sheepishly.

'It's not for us to question the decisions of the authorities, Yakov Petrovich.'

'But why the authorities, Anton Antonovich?' asked Mr

Golyadkin, even more daunted, 'why the authorities? I can see no reason why they need to be troubled on this score, Anton Antonovich ... Perhaps you want to say something about what happened yesterday, Anton Antonovich?'

'No, it has nothing to do with yesterday. There's something else that's not up to scratch as far as you're concerned.'

'What's not up to scratch, Anton Antonovich? I don't think there's anything about me that's not up to scratch, Anton Antonovich ...'

'Well now, with whom were you intending to get up to crafty tricks?' Anton Antonovich sharply interrupted the completely flabbergasted Mr Golyadkin, who winced and turned as white as a sheet.

'Of course, Anton Antonovich,' he said in a barely audible voice, 'if you heed the voice of slander and listen to your enemies without letting the other side justify itself, then of course ... of course one has to suffer, Anton Antonovich – suffer innocently, for nothing.'

'Exactly. But what about your unseemly conduct prejudicial to the reputation of that noble young lady who belongs to that virtuous, highly respected and well-known family that has been so good to you?'

'What conduct do you mean, Anton Antonovich?'

'What I say. Regarding your "laudable" behaviour towards that young lady, who, although poor, is of honourable foreign extraction – are you not aware of that either?'

'Excuse me, Anton Antonovich ... please be good enough to hear me out!'

'And your perfidious conduct, your slandering another person, accusing another person of something you yourself are guilty of – eh? What would you call that?'

'I, Anton Antonovich, didn't turn him out,' said our hero, beginning to tremble. 'And I never told Petrushka – my man-servant, that is – to do anything of the sort. He ate my bread, Anton Antonovich, he enjoyed my hospitality,' our hero added with such deep feeling and expressiveness that his chin twitched slightly and the tears were ready to well up again.

'You're only just saying that he ate your bread, Yakov

Petrovich,' pAnton Antonovich replied with a grin and with such cunning in his voice that Mr Golyadkin felt a nagging anxiety in his heart.

'If I may humbly be permitted to ask once more, Anton Antonovich: is His Excellency aware of the whole affair?'

'Well, what do you think, sir? But now you must let me get on. I've no time for you now . . . Today you'll find out all you need to know.'

'For God's sake – please – just one more minute, Anton Antonovich!'

'You can tell me later, sir.'

'No, Anton Antonovich. I, sir, you see, sir, please just listen a moment, Anton Antonovich. I'm not in the least a free-thinker, Anton Antonovich, I avoid free-thinking like the plague . . . For my part I'm quite ready . . . and I've even advanced the idea that . . .'

'Very well, very well . . . I've heard it all before.'

'No, you haven't heard this, Anton Antonovich. It's something different, Anton Antonovich, it's good, really good, and makes for pleasant listening . . . I've advanced the idea, Anton Antonovich, as I explained before, that Divine Providence has created two people exactly alike and our benevolent superiors, seeing Divine Providence at work, have provided sanctuary for the two twins, sir. That's good, Anton Antonovich. You can see that's very good and that I'm far from being a free-thinker. I accept our benevolent authorities as a father. It's like this, so to speak, you know, and um . . . well, a young man needs to work. Please lend me your support, Anton Antonovich, please intercede for me. I don't mean anything, Anton Antonovich . . . For God's sake, Anton Antonovich, just one more tiny word . . . Anton Antonovich . . .'

But Anton Antonovich was already some distance from Mr Golyadkin. So shaken and confused by all that he had heard and what was happening to him, our hero had no idea where he was standing, what he had heard, what he had done, what had been done to him and what else was going to be done to him.

With an imploring look he tried to find Anton Antonovich

in the crowd of clerks with the intention of justifying himself even further in his eyes and to tell him something extremely loyal, inspiring and pleasant regarding himself . . . However, a new light was gradually beginning to break through Mr Golyadkin's confusion, a new and ghastly light that suddenly, all at once, illuminated a whole vista of circumstances until then completely unknown and even totally unsuspected. Just then someone nudged our utterly devastated hero in the side. He looked around. Before him stood Scribbly.

'A letter, Your Honour.'

'Ah! So you're back already, old chap.'

'No, it was brought here this morning, as early as ten o'clock. Sergey Mikheyev the porter brought it from Provincial Secretary Vakhrameyev's flat.'

'That's good, my friend, that's good. I'll show you my gratitude for that, old chap.'

This said, Mr Golyadkin hid the letter in a side pocket of his uniform which he had buttoned all the way up. Then he looked around and to his astonishment saw that he was already in the office vestibule, among a little group of clerks who, now that office hours were over, were crowding towards the exit. Not only had Mr Golyadkin failed to notice this last circumstance up to then but he did not notice or remember how he suddenly came to be wearing his overcoat and galoshes and be hat in hand. All the clerks were standing motionless, respectfully waiting. The fact was, His Excellency had stopped at the bottom of the steps to await his carriage, which had been delayed for some reason and he was having a very interesting conversation with two counsellors and Andrey Filippovich. A little removed from these two counsellors and Andrey Filippovich stood Anton Antonovich Setochkin and some of the other clerks, all of whom broke into broad smiles when they saw that His Excellency was pleased to laugh and joke. The clerks who had congregated at the top of the stairs were smiling too and waiting for His Excellency to start laughing again. Only Fedoseich, the pot-bellied commissionaire, who stood to attention grasping the door handle, impatiently awaiting his daily ration of pleasure, which was throwing one half of the doors open with one sweep

of the arm and then bending almost double and respectfully
standing to one side to allow His Excellency to pass, wasn't
smiling. But it was clearly Mr Golyadkin's unworthy and
ignoble enemy who was experiencing the greatest pleasure and
joy. At that moment he had even forgotten all the other clerks,
had even stopped weaving, mincing, twisting and turning
among them in his usual obnoxious way – he even missed the
opportunity of sucking up to someone at that moment. He had
become all eyes and ears, was strangely withdrawn, probably
trying to hear better and was looking away from His Excellency.
Only occasionally did his arms, legs and head twitch in barely
perceptible spasms to reveal all the secret, innermost impulses
of his soul. 'Just look, he's so full of himself!' our hero thought,
'everyone's favourite, it seems – the crook! I'd like to know
exactly why he's so successful in high-class society. No brains,
no personality, no education, no feelings. That rotter has all
the luck! Heavens above! Really, if you think about it, how
quickly a man can come along and "get in" with everybody!
That man will go far – I swear he will, that swine . . . he'll
prosper, he will – the lucky devil! I'd like to know exactly what
it is he keeps whispering to everyone. What confidences does
he share with these people and what secrets are they discussing?
Heavens above! If only I could . . . er . . . get in with them a
little as well . . . I could say: "It's this and that . . ." Or perhaps
I could say: "That's how it is, I won't do it in future . . . It's
my fault and a young man needs to work these days, Your
Excellency. I'm not in the least embarrassed by my dubious
situation." Yes – that's it! So, is that how I should act . . . ? But
you can't get through to that scoundrel, you can't get through
to him with words. It's impossible to hammer any sense into
that desperado's head. Still, I'll have a try. If I happen to hit on
a good time I'll have a shot at it . . .'

   In his anxiety, agitation and confusion, feeling that he could
not possibly leave things as they were, that the critical moment
was now at hand, that he needed to have things out with
someone, our hero was gradually moving a little nearer to
where his unworthy and mysterious friend was standing, but
at that moment the long-awaited carriage clattered up to the

entrance. Fedoseich pulled open the door, bent double, and let His Excellency pass. All the clerks who had been waiting surged forward in one mass towards the exit and for a moment shoved Mr Golyadkin Senior away from Mr Golyadkin Junior. 'You won't get away!' our hero thought, forcing his way through the crowd without taking his eyes off his quarry. Finally, the crowd gave way. Our hero felt free now and rushed off in pursuit of his enemy.

CHAPTER XI

Mr Golyadkin gasped for breath as he flew as if on wings after his fast-retreating enemy. He felt a terrible inner energy. But for all that, Mr Golyadkin had every reason to think that at that moment even an ordinary mosquito, had it been able to exist in St Petersburg at that time of year, could very easily have broken him with one touch of its wing. What was more, he felt that he had gone downhill, grown utterly weak, and that he was being borne along by some completely strange, alien force, that he himself wasn't walking at all – on the contrary: his legs were giving way and refused to obey him. However, it all might turn out for the best. 'Whether for the best or not for the best,' thought Mr Golyadkin, barely able to catch his breath from running so fast, 'it's a lost cause – of that there's not the slightest doubt. That I'm done for, as we now know, is signed, settled and sealed.' In spite of this it was as if our hero had risen from the dead, that he'd survived a battle and snatched victory when he managed to grab his enemy's overcoat just as the latter was putting one foot on the step of the droshky he had just hired.

'My dear sir! My dear sir!' he shouted at length to the infamous Mr Golyadkin Junior whom he had finally caught up with. 'My dear sir, I trust you will . . .'

'No, please don't have any hopes on that score,' Mr Golyadkin's callous enemy replied evasively, standing with one foot on the step of the droshky, doing his utmost to get over to the other side of the carriage, vainly waving the other foot in the air as he tried to keep his balance and at the same time wrench his overcoat from Mr Golyadkin Senior, who, for his part, was holding on to it with all the strength nature had conferred on him.

'Yakov Petrovich . . . just ten minutes . . .'

'Forgive me, I haven't the time.'

'You yourself must agree, Yakov Petrovich, . . . please, Yakov Petrovich, for God's sake, Yakov Petrovich! Let's have it out, let's face up to it . . . Just one second, Yakov Petrovich!'

'My dear fellow, I haven't time,' Mr Golyadkin's falsely honourable enemy replied with ill-mannered familiarity but in the guise of goodheartedness. 'Some other time. I, believe me, with all my heart and soul . . . But now – well, really, I honestly can't.'

'Scoundrel!' thought our hero.

'Yakov Petrovich!' he exclaimed miserably. 'I have never been your enemy. Spiteful people have depicted me unfairly . . . For my part, I'm ready . . . if you like, shall we, you and I, Yakov Petrovich, pop into this coffee-house now . . . There, with pure hearts as you so rightly put it just now and in straight-forward, noble language . . . here, into this coffee-house. Then everything will explain itself – that's it, Yakov Petrovich. Then everything is bound to be explained of its own accord.'

'Into this coffee-house? Very well, sir, I've no objections, let's drop in, my dear chap, only on one condition – on one condition: that everything will explain itself of its own accord. So, it's like this, so to speak, sweetie-pie,' said Mr Golyadkin Junior, getting out of the cab and shamelessly slapping our hero on the shoulder. 'You're such a good pal, you are. For you, Yakov Petrovich, I'm prepared to go down a side street (as you so rightly suggested at that time, Yakov Petrovich). You're a real rogue you are – you do just what you like with a man!' continued Mr Golyadkin's false friend with a faint smile, hover-ing and turning around him.

Far from the main streets, the coffee-house that the two Mr Golyadkins entered happened at that moment to be completely empty. The moment they rang the bell a rather plump German woman appeared at the counter. Mr Golyadkin Senior and his unworthy enemy went through into the second room where a puffy-faced urchin with close-cropped hair was fussing around the stove with a bundle of firewood, trying to resuscitate the fire that was about to go out. At Mr Golyadkin Junior's request chocolate was served.

'She's a scrumptious dish,' said Mr Golyadkin Junior, roguishly winking at Mr Golyadkin Senior.

Our hero blushed and said nothing.

'Oh yes, do forgive me, I quite forgot. I know your taste. You and I, dear sir, are partial to little Fräuleins, aren't we? You and I, Yakov Petrovich, my dear honest soul, fancy nice Fräuleins who are not lacking in certain other attractions, however. We rent rooms from them, lead them morally astray, dedicate our hearts to them for their *Biersuppe* and *Milchsuppe*, and promise them different things in writing – that's what we do – you Faublas, you gay deceiver!'

While he was saying all this Mr Golyadkin Junior, thus making an utterly futile but nonetheless crafty allusion to a certain person of the female sex, hovered around Mr Golyadkin, warmly smiling at him in a false show of cordiality and delight at their meeting there. But when he noticed that Mr Golyadkin Senior was by no means so stupid or by no means so completely lacking in education and refinement as immediately to trust him, the infamous man decided to change tactics and be open about everything. So after those vile remarks the spurious Mr Golyadkin concluded by slapping the respectable Mr Golyadkin on the shoulder with deeply distressing effrontery and familiarity and, not contenting himself with this, started teasing him in a manner quite improper in well-bred society. He suddenly hit upon the idea of repeating his earlier filthy trick, that is, of pinching the exasperated Mr Golyadkin Senior on the cheek, despite the distressed Mr Golyadkin Senior's resistance and faint cries of protest. At the sight of such depravity our hero flew into a rage but held his tongue . . . only for the time being, however.

'That's what my enemies say,' he finally replied in a quavering voice, sensibly restraining himself. At the same time our hero uneasily looked round at the door. Mr Golyadkin Junior was evidently in excellent spirits and ready to embark on all kinds of pranks, impermissible in a public place and generally speaking not tolerated by the rules of etiquette, especially as observed in society of the most refined tone.

'Ah well, just as you please,' gravely responded Mr Golyadkin Junior to Mr Golyadkin Senior's idea, putting his empty cup that he had drained with unseemly greed down on the table. 'Well now, there's no point in my staying long with you, but . . . Well, how are you getting on now, Yakov Petrovich?'

'There's only one thing I have to tell you, Yakov Petrovich,' our hero replied coolly and with dignity. 'I have never been your enemy.'

'Hm . . . and what about Petrushka? That's his name, isn't it? Of course it is! How is he? All right? Same as ever?'

'He's the same as ever, too, Yakov Petrovich,' replied Mr Golyadkin Senior, somewhat startled. 'I don't know, Yakov Petrovich, but for my part . . . from an honourable and frank point of view, Yakov Petrovich, you yourself will agree, Yakov Petrovich . . .'

'Yes, sir. But you yourself know, Yakov Petrovich,' replied Mr Golyadkin Junior in a soft and expressive voice, thus falsely making himself out to be a man dejected, remorseful and worthy of compassion, 'you yourself know that these are hard times . . . I refer to *you*, Yakov Petrovich. You're an intelligent man and you'll make a fair judgement,' added Mr Golyadkin Junior, basely flattering Mr Golyadkin Senior. 'Life isn't a game, you know that yourself,' concluded Mr Golyadkin Junior meaningly, thus trying to pass himself off as a learned and intelligent man capable of conversing on lofty subjects.

'For my part, Yakov Petrovich,' our hero answered with animation, 'as one who despises beating about the bush and who speaks boldly and openly, in straightforward, noble language, thus putting the whole business on a lofty basis, I can tell you, I can affirm candidly and honourably, Yakov Petrovich, that I am completely innocent and that as you yourself know, Yakov Petrovich, there can be mutual misunderstandings – anything can happen – the judgement of society, the opinion of the servile mob. I'm telling you quite frankly,

Yakov Petrovich, anything can happen. And I'll say more, Yakov Petrovich: if you judge things like that, if you consider the business from a noble and lofty point of view, then, I boldly maintain, I shall say this without any false shame, Yakov Petrovich, that it would even be a pleasure for me to discover I was mistaken – and even a pleasure to confess to it. You yourself know that, you're an intelligent man and high-minded into the bargain. Without shame, without false shame – I'm ready to confess it,' our hero concluded with nobility and dignity.

'It's fate, it's destiny, Yakov Petrovich! But let's leave it at that,' sighed Mr Golyadkin Junior. 'Let's rather spend these brief moments together in more profitable and agreeable conversation as is proper between two colleagues. Really, I don't think I've managed to say two words to you all this time. But I'm not the one to blame for it, Yakov Petrovich.'

'Nor am I,' our hero heatedly interrupted. 'Nor am I! My heart tells me I'm not the one to blame for all this. We must blame it all on fate, Yakov Petrovich,' added Mr Golyadkin Senior in a positively conciliatory tone. His voice was gradually beginning to weaken and quaver.

'So, how about your health in general?' the errant one inquired in a sugary voice.

'I've a bit of a cough,' our hero replied in an even more sugary voice.

'You must be careful. With all these infections going around you could easily catch quinsy and I admit I've already started wrapping myself in flannel.'

'Oh yes, Yakov Petrovich, you can easily catch quinsy ... Yakov Petrovich!' our hero said after a brief silence. 'Yakov Petrovich! I can see that I was mistaken! With deep emotion I recall those happy moments we spent together beneath my humble – dare I say – hospitable roof.'

'But that's not what you wrote in your letter,' somewhat scornfully retorted the completely justified Mr Golyadkin Junior (but only in this respect was he completely justified).

'Yakov Petrovich! I was mistaken ... Now I can clearly see that I was wrong to write that unfortunate letter of mine, Yakov Petrovich, I feel ashamed to look at you, you won't believe ...

Now give me that letter so that I can tear it up before your eyes, Yakov Petrovich, or if that's really out of the question I beg you to read it the other way round, completely the other way round, that is, with a deliberately friendly intention, giving all the words their opposite meaning. I was in the wrong. Please forgive me Yakov Petrovich, I completely . . . I was grievously wrong, Yakov Petrovich.'

'You were saying?' Mr Golyadkin Senior's perfidious friend suddenly asked, quite nonchalantly and absent-mindedly.

'I was saying that I was mistaken, Yakov Petrovich, and that for my part it was completely without false shame . . .'

'Oh well – that's good! It's very good that you were mistaken,' rudely replied Mr Golyadkin Junior.

'I even had the idea, Yakov Petrovich,' nobly added our candid hero, completely failing to notice his deceitful friend's appalling perfidy, 'I even had the idea that here two identical twins have been created . . .'

'Ah! So that's your idea!'

Here the notoriously worthless Mr Golyadkin Junior rose and picked up his hat. Still failing to notice the deceit, Mr Golyadkin Senior got up, too, smiling ingenuously and good-naturedly at his spurious friend and attempting in his innocence to be nice and encouraging to him, so striking up a new friendship with him.

'Farewell, Your Excellency!' Mr Golyadkin Junior suddenly shouted. Our hero shuddered, observing something almost Bacchic in his enemy's face, and simply in order to get rid of him thrust two of his fingers into the degenerate's outstretched hand. But here Mr Golyadkin Junior's shamelessness exceeded all bounds. Grabbing two fingers of Mr Golyadkin Senior's hand and first squeezing them, that worthless man decided there and then to repeat before his very eyes the shameless trick he had played on him that morning. It was more than flesh and blood could stand.

He was already stuffing the handkerchief on which he had wiped his fingers into his pocket when Mr Golyadkin Senior recovered and rushed after him into the next room where, true to his usual obnoxious habit, his uncompromising foe slipped away in a hurry. There he was, standing at the counter, as if nothing had happened, eating pies and, just like any virtuous gentleman, calmly exchanging pleasantries with the German proprietress. 'Not in front of a lady,' thought our hero and he, too, went up to the counter, beside himself with agitation.

'Really, not a bad little dish at all! What do you think?' said Mr Golyadkin Junior, embarking on those lewd sallies of his again and no doubt counting on Mr Golyadkin Senior's infinite patience. For her part, the fat German looked at both her customers with blank, pewtery eyes, smiling affably, since she evidently didn't understand a word of Russian. At these words of the utterly shameless Mr Golyadkin Junior, our hero, flushed as red as fire and losing all self-control, finally launched himself at him with the clear intention of tearing him limb from limb and thus finishing him for good. But Mr Golyadkin Junior, with his customary vileness, was far off by now – he had taken to his heels and was already outside the front door and on the top steps. It goes without saying that after the first, momentary fit of stupefaction that had naturally come over Mr Golyadkin Senior, he dashed full tilt after the offender, who was already getting into the cab that had been waiting for him and with whose driver he obviously had an agreement. But at that very moment the fat German, seeing that her two customers were fleeing, shrieked and rang her bell as hard as she could. Almost in mid-air our hero turned round, threw her some money, both for himself and for the shameless man who had not paid, and without asking for change and despite the delay this occasioned still managed – although again almost in mid-air – to catch up with his enemy. Clinging to the splashboard with all the strength bestowed on him by nature, our hero was carried some way along the street as he attempted to clamber on to the carriage, while Mr Golyadkin Junior did his level best to fend him off. Meanwhile the driver, with whip, reins, feet and exhortations, urged on his broken-down nag which, quite unexpectedly, the bit between its teeth, broke into a gallop, kicking out its hind legs – a nasty habit it had – at every third stride. Finally our hero managed to perch himself on the droshky, facing his enemy, leaning with his back to the driver, his knees pressed

against his enemy's and with his right hand gripping for all he
was worth the badly moth-eaten fur collar of his depraved and
fiercest enemy's coat . . .

The two enemies were carried along for some time in silence.
Our hero could barely catch his breath. The road was dreadful
and he kept bobbing up and down at every stride, in great
danger of breaking his neck. What was more, his fierce enemy
still would not concede defeat and was trying to tip his opponent
over into the mud. The crowning nastiness was the frightful
weather; the snow was falling in large flakes, which were doing
their utmost, for their part, to creep somehow under the unbuttoned coat of the genuine Mr Golyadkin. All around it was
murky, difficult to see anything and to tell where they were
going and along which streets. It struck Mr Golyadkin that
there was something familiar about what was happening to
him. For a moment he tried to remember whether he had had
a kind of hunch the day before – in a dream, for example.
Finally his misery turned into the most acute agony. Leaning
with all his weight against his pitiless enemy, he was about to
utter a cry. But his cry died upon his lips. There was a moment
when Mr Golyadkin forgot everything and decided that everything was all right, that it was all simply happening in some
inexplicable way and that in this case it would have been
superfluous to protest, a complete lost cause . . . But suddenly
and almost at the moment when our hero was coming to this
conclusion, a careless jolt changed the whole complexion of the
matter. Mr Golyadkin toppled off the droshky like a sack of
flour and rolled away somewhere, admitting to himself as he
fell – and quite rightly – that in fact he had let himself get
excited most inopportunely. Finally, leaping up, he saw that
they had arrived somewhere: the droshky was standing in the
middle of a courtyard and at first glance our hero recognized it
as belonging to the very same house in which Olsufy Ivanovich
resided. At that very moment he noticed that his enemy was
already going up on to the porch – probably he was going to
visit Olsufy Ivanovich. In indescribable anguish he was about
to dash off and overtake his foe but fortunately for him he
prudently had second thoughts. Not forgetting to pay the

driver, Mr Golyadkin tore down the street for all he was worth, wherever his legs would carry him. As before, the snow was falling heavily and it was wet, murky, dark. Our hero did not run but flew, knocking over everyone in his path – men, women, children – and he in turn rebounded from men, women and children. All around and from behind could be heard cries of distress, shrieks and screams ... But Mr Golyadkin seemed oblivious of it all and did not deign to pay attention to any of it. But at Semyonovsky Bridge he came to his senses – and only then as a result of somehow managing to collide awkwardly with two peasant women, knocking them over together with their wares and then toppling over himself. 'It's all right,' thought Mr Golyadkin, 'all this can very easily be settled for the best.' And immediately he felt in his pocket for a silver rouble to pay for the spilt gingerbread, apples, peas and sundry items. Suddenly a new light dawned on Mr Golyadkin: in his pocket he felt the letter given him by the clerk that morning. Happening to remember that not far away was a tavern he knew, he ran into it and without wasting a moment in settling himself at a small table lit by a tallow candle and without paying attention to anything, without listening to the waiter who had come to take his order, he broke the seal and read the following, which completely stunned him:

Noble one who is suffering on my behalf and who is eternally dear to my heart!

I am suffering, I am perishing – save me! A slanderer, an intriguer, notorious for his worthless ways, has ensnared me and I am undone! I am fallen! To me he is abhorrent, while you ... ! They have kept us apart, my letters to you have been intercepted and it is all the work of an immoral one taking advantage of his only good quality – his resemblance to you. In any event one can be ugly but still charm with intellect, powerful feelings and pleasant manners ... I am perishing. I am to be married against my will and the one who is intriguing most is my father, my benefactor, State Counsellor Olsufy Ivanovich, doubtless wishing to usurp my place and relations in good society ... But my mind is made up and I protest with all the powers that nature has given me. Wait for me in your carriage outside Olsufy Ivanovich's windows at exactly nine tonight. We are giving another ball and that handsome lieutenant is coming again. I shall come out – and we shall fly away. Besides, there are other places where one can still be of service to one's country. At any rate, my friend, remember that innocence is strong by virtue of its very innocence. Farewell. Wait at the entrance with the carriage. I shall throw myself into the shelter of your embrace at two o'clock in the morning.

Yours to the grave
Klara Olsufyevna

After reading this letter our hero remained for some time as if thunderstruck. In terrible distress, in terrible agitation, white as a sheet, he paced the room several times with the letter in his hand. To crown all his appalling tribulations our hero failed to notice that at that moment he was the object of the exclusive attention of everyone in the room. Probably his disordered clothes and his uncontrollable agitation, his walking – rather, his scurrying – his two-handed gesticulations and perhaps the several enigmatic words spoken down the wind in absent-mindedness – all this must have lowered Mr Golyadkin significantly in the opinion of all present. Even the waiter was beginning to look at him suspiciously. When he came to his senses our hero found he was standing in the middle of the room, staring in an almost improper, discourteous manner at one old gentleman of the most venerable appearance who, having dined and said a prayer before an icon, had returned to his seat and for his part couldn't take his eyes off Mr Golyadkin. Our hero gazed vacantly around and noticed that everyone there, every single person, was looking at him with the most ominous and suspicious expression. Suddenly a retired military man with a red collar loudly demanded the *Police Gazette*.[36] Mr Golyadkin started and blushed. Happening to look down he saw that his clothing was so unseemly that it was not fit to be worn even in his own home, let alone in a public place. His boots, trousers and the whole of his left side were completely caked with mud; his right trouser-strap was torn off and his tail-coat even torn in many places. In inexhaustible distress our

hero went over to the table where he had read the letter and saw
that the waiter was approaching with a strange and insolently
insistent expression on his face. Flustered and quite deflated,
our hero set about inspecting the table at which he was now
standing. On it lay plates yet to be cleared away from someone's
dinner, a soiled napkin and a knife, fork and spoon that had
just been used. 'Who can have been dining here?' our hero
wondered. 'Could it have been me? Anything is possible! I must
have had dinner and didn't even notice. What on earth shall I
do now?' Looking up Mr Golyadkin saw that the waiter was
again beside him and about to say something to him. 'How
much do I owe you, old chap?' our hero asked in a trembling
voice.

Loud laughter broke out all around Mr Golyadkin. Even the
waiter himself grinned. Mr Golyadkin understood that he had
blundered again, committed some awful gaffe. Realizing all this
he was so embarrassed that he felt compelled to grope in his
pocket for his handkerchief, probably for the sake of doing
something instead of simply standing there. But to his own
and everyone else's indescribable amazement, instead of his
handkerchief he pulled out the phial containing some kind of
medicine prescribed four days earlier by Krestyan Ivanovich.
'Get it at the same chemist's as before', ran through Mr Golyadkin's mind. Suddenly he gave a start and almost shrieked
with horror. A new light was dawning ... The dark, revolting
reddish liquid shone into Mr Golyadkin's eyes with a sinister
gleam. The bottle dropped from his grasp and immediately
shattered on the floor. Our hero screamed and jumped back
from the spilt liquid ... he was trembling in every limb and
beads of sweat broke out on his temples and forehead. 'So, my
life is in danger!' he said. Meanwhile there was uproar and
general commotion in the room. Everyone surrounded Mr
Golyadkin, everyone spoke to Mr Golyadkin, some even
grabbed hold of Mr Golyadkin. But our hero was speechless
and motionless, seeing nothing, hearing nothing, feeling
nothing ... Finally, as if tearing off, he rushed out of the
tavern, pushing aside each and every one of those who were
endeavouring to detain him, slumped almost unconscious into

the first droshky that happened to come along and sped off to
his flat.

In the entrance hall he met Mikheyev, the office porter, bearing an official envelope in his hand. 'I know, my friend, I know
everything. It's official,' our exhausted hero replied in a weak,
suffering voice. And in fact the envelope contained an order to
Mr Golyadkin, signed by Andrey Filippovich, for him to hand
over all the files in his possession to Ivan Semyonovich. After
taking the envelope and giving the porter ten copecks, Mr
Golyadkin entered his flat and found Petrushka getting all his
things together, all his rubbish and bits and pieces and wordly
possessions, with the clear intention of abandoning Mr Golyadkin and going over to Karolina Ivanovna, who had enticed
him there as a replacement for Yevstafy.

CHAPTER XII

Petrushka entered the room with a rocking motion, in a peculiarly off-hand manner and with a look that combined servility
and triumph. Evidently he had devised some plan, felt quite
within his rights and looked like a complete stranger – that is,
like someone else's servant, only nothing like Mr Golyadkin's
former servant.

'Well, you see, my dear man,' our hero began breathlessly,
'what's the time?'

Without a word Petrushka withdrew behind the partition
and returned to announce, in a rather independent tone, that it
would soon be half past seven.

'Good, dear man, that's very good. So you see, old chap . . .
let me tell you that everything appears to be over between us.'

Petrushka did not reply.

'Well, now that everything is over between us, you can tell
me frankly, as a friend, where you've been, old chap.'

'Where I've been? To see good people, sir.'

'I know, my friend, I know. I've always been satisfied with

you, dear chap – I'll give you a good reference . . . Well, what were you doing there?'

'Why, you know very well, sir! It's a fact that a good man won't teach you bad ways, sir.'

'I know, my dear man, I know. Good people are rare nowadays, my friend. You must value them. Well, how are they?'

'What do you mean, sir? You know how they are! Only, I can't stay in service here any more, sir. You know that for yourself.'

'Yes, I do, dear man, I do. I know how zealous and diligent you are . . . I've seen all that, taken note of it, my friend. I respect you. I respect a good and honest man, even if he's only a flunkey.'

'Why of course, sir! The likes of me, sir, as you know very well, must go where they're best off. That's how it is. What's it to me? You know very well that it's impossible without a good man.'

'Oh, all right, old chap, all right! I appreciate that . . . Well, here's your wages and your reference. Now let's kiss and let's say farewell, old chap . . . But there's one last service I ask of you,' said Mr Golyadkin solemnly. 'You see, my dear chap, all sorts of things can happen. Sorrow, my friend, lurks even in gilded palaces and you can't escape from it anywhere. I reckon, my friend, I've always been good to you.'

Petrushka said nothing.

'I think I've always been good to you, dear fellow. Well, how much linen do we have, dear chap?'

'All present and correct, sir. Linen shirts – six, sir; socks – three pairs; shirt-fronts – four, sir; one flannel vest and two sets of underwear. You know that's all, sir. I've got nothing of yours, sir . . . I, sir, look after my master's possessions. You know that very well, sir . . . and as for me doing anything I shouldn't have – never, sir!'

'I believe you, my friend, I believe you. But that's not what I meant, my friend, not that. You see, it's this, my friend . . .'

'Of course, sir. We know that very well, sir. Take when I was still working for General Stolbnyakov – they let me go, as

they were moving to Saratov[37] – that's where the family estate
was . . .'

'No, my friend, it's not about that . . . It's nothing . . . now
don't start thinking things, my friend.'

'Of course, sir. You know it's easy to speak ill of the likes of
us, you know that very well . . . But everywhere they've been
satisfied with me. Ministers, generals, senators, counts – I've
worked for them all: Prince Svinchatkin, Colonel Pereborkin,
General Nedobarov – he also went off to his family estate, sir.
It's a fact, sir.'

'Yes, my friend, yes. That's very good, that's very good. And
now I'm going away, my friend. We all have different paths to
travel, my friend, and there's no telling what path you may
finally tread. Well, my friend, put my things out so I can get
dressed. Lay out my uniform jacket, too . . . and my other
trousers, sheets, blankets, pillows . . .'

'Shall I bundle them all up?'

'Yes, my friend, please do bundle them up. Who knows what
may happen to us? And now, dear man, you can go and find a
carriage.'

'A carriage, sir?'

'Yes, my friend, a carriage – a nice, spacious one, for a fixed
period. And don't start thinking things, my friend.'

'Do you intend going far, sir?'

'I don't know, my friend, that's something I don't know
either. You'd better pack the feather-bed, too. What do you
think? I'm relying on you, my dear chap.'

'But you don't want to go right away, do you, sir?'

'Oh yes, my friend, I do! A circumstance has arisen . . . that's
how it is, dear chap, that's how it is.'

'Of course, sir. It was the same with a lieutenant in my
regiment, sir. Carried off a landowner's daughter he did . . .'

'Carried off? What do you mean? My dear chap, you . . .'

'Yes, he carried her off and they got married on a different
estate. It was all planned in advance. There was a hue and cry.
But the late prince stuck up for them and it was all patched up
in the end.'

'How did you know all this about it?'

'Well, I just know! News travels fast, sir. We know everything sir ... of course, who hasn't been guilty of sin? Only, if I may be permitted to mention it now, sir, in plain servant's talk, if this is what it's come to then I'll tell you, sir – you have an enemy – you have a rival, sir, a powerful rival, that's what, sir ...'

'I know, my friend, I know. You know it yourself, dear chap ... So, I'm relying on you. Well, how are we going to do it now, my friend? What do you advise me to do?'

'Well, sir, if you're going in for that kind of thing, roughly speaking, what you'll be needing to buy are sheets, pillows, another feather-bed – a double, sir – and a good quilt, from a neighbour, a tradeswoman who lives downstairs, sir. And she's got a very nice fox fur coat. You could go down there right away, sir, have a look and buy it. It's just what you'll be needing now, sir. It's a fine coat, satin – lined, with fox fur.'

'Very good, my friend, that's good. I agree. I'm relying on you entirely, my friend, but we'll have to be quick! I'll go and buy that coat – only for God's sake please be quick! It will soon be eight. Be as quick as you can, my friend, for God's sake hurry! Be quick, my friend!'

Petrushka abandoned the linen, pillows, blankets and various odds and ends he had not finished bundling up and rushed headlong from the room. Meanwhile Mr Golyadkin grabbed the letter again but he could not read it. Clutching his wretched head in both hands he leant against the wall in amazement. He was unable to think about anything, nor could he do anything. He himself didn't even know what was happening to him. Finally, seeing that time was getting on and that neither Petrushka nor the coat had appeared, he decided to go himself. Opening the door into the hall he heard voices – arguing and altercations from down below. A few women neighbours were shouting, quarrelling and passing judgement on something. Mr Golyadkin knew very well about what. He heard Petrushka's voice and then footsteps. 'Good God! They'll bring the whole world in here next!' groaned Mr Golyadkin, wringing his hands in despair and rushing back to his room. Once there he fell almost senseless on to the sofa, burying his face in the cushion.

After lying there for about a minute he leapt up and, without waiting for Petrushka, put on his galoshes, overcoat and hat, seized his wallet and charged headlong downstairs. 'I don't need anything, old chap, I don't need anything, dear chap! I'll see to everything myself. I don't need you for the moment and perhaps the whole thing will even turn out for the best in the meantime,' Mr Golyadkin muttered to Petrushka when he met him on the stairs. Then he ran out into the courtyard and away from the house. His heart stopped beating – he still hadn't decided what he should do, what steps he should take at this present critical juncture.

'Yes, I mean, what should I do, for God's sake? Why on earth did all this have to happen?' he finally cried out in despair, as he trotted blindly and aimlessly along the street. 'Why did all this have to happen? If it hadn't been for this, precisely this, then everything would have been settled once and for all, at one stroke – at one clever, energetic, powerful stroke everything would have been settled! I'd stake my finger that it would have been settled! I even know exactly how it would have been settled. It would be done like this: I'd simply say: "It's like this, my dear sir, it's this and that. If you don't mind my saying so it's neither one thing nor the other as far as I'm concerned. Things aren't done that way, so to speak," I'd have said, "and imposture, my dear sir, will get you nowhere here. An impostor, my dear sir, is . . . er . . . hm . . . someone's who's worthless, no use to his native country. Do you understand that, sir? Do you understand that, my dear sir?" That's how it would have been, you know . . . But no . . . Now why am I talking all this non-sense, you utter idiot! I'm a suicide, that's what. No . . . that's not it at all, you suicide! But this is how it's being done now, you old reprobate . . . ! Well, where shall I go now, what shall I do with myself, for example, just tell me what I'm fit for now? Well, to give an example . . . Poor old Golyadkin – you unworthy fellow! Well, what now? I need to hire a carriage, so she says, I should go and get a carriage or we'll get our feet wet, so to speak, if there isn't any carriage. And who would have thought it? Well done, my fine, well-behaved young lady, our much-praised young miss! You've really excelled yourself,

young lady, no doubt about it, really excelled yourself! And it
all comes from an immoral upbringing. Now that I've looked
into this and got to the bottom of it I can see it all stems from
nothing else but an immoral upbringing. Instead of giving her,
so to speak, the occasional thrashing when she was a child, they
stuff her with all kinds of sweetmeats and bons-bons and the
old man drools over her. "You're my pretty darling," he says.
"You're my this and that and we'll marry you off to a count!"
And now she's turned out like this and shown her hand. "That's
what our game is," she says! Well, instead of keeping her at
home they send her to boarding-school, some French madame,
some émigrée lady, some Madame Falbala[38] or whatever. And
she learns all sorts of good things at that émigrée Madame
Falbala's, so that's why it always turns out like this. "Come
and rejoice!" she says, "be with the carriage under my window
at such and such a time and sing me a sentimental Spanish
serenade. I'll be waiting for you and I know you love me and
we'll run away together and we'll live in a little hut." But in the
end it simply can't be done, if this is what it's come to, young
lady, it can't be done as it's against the law to carry off an
honest and innocent girl from her parents' home without the
parents' consent. And finally, what's the point, what's the need
for it? If only she married someone she ought to marry, the one
preordained by fate, that would be the end of the matter. But
I'm a working man, I could lose my job over this! I might end
up in court, my dear young lady! That's how it is – as if you
didn't know! It's that German woman's work. It all comes from
her, the witch, she's the spark that set the house on fire. Because
a man's been slandered, because they've made up some old
woman's gossip about him, some brazen cock-and-bull story,
on Andrey Filippovich's advice – that's where it all comes from.
Otherwise why on earth should Petrushka be mixed up in it?
What's it to do with him? What need does that scoundrel have
to get involved? No, young lady, I can't, I really can't – not for
anything. On this occasion you must excuse me, it all comes
from you, young lady, it's not the German that everything
comes from, not from the old witch at all, but purely from you,
as the witch is actually a good woman, because the witch is not

to blame for anything, but it's *you*, young lady, you are to blame! That's how it is! You, young lady, are leading me into making wrongful accusations. A man's disappearing here, a man's losing sight of himself and he can't keep a grip on himself – so what kind of wedding can there be here? And how will it all end? How will it be arranged? I'd give a great deal to find that out!'

So reasoned our hero in his despair. Suddenly recovering himself he noticed that he was standing somewhere in Liteynaya Street. The weather was awful: a thaw had set in and it was snowing and raining – well, exactly as it had been on that never-to-be forgotten night, at that dread midnight hour when all Mr Golyadkin's misfortunes began. 'What kind of journey can one make in this!' thought Mr Golyadkin, looking at the weather, 'everything's dead around here . . . Good God! Where can I find a carriage, for example? Yes, I think I can see something black over there at the corner. Let's go and investigate. Oh Lord!' continued our hero, directing his feeble and faltering steps towards what looked like a carriage. 'No, this is what I'll do. I'll go there, I'll go and fall at his feet if I can, I'll humbly implore him and say: "It's like this and that, I put my fate in your hands, into the hands of my superiors . . ." I'll tell him: "Your Excellency, protect and be benevolent to a man; it's like this and that, and such and such, it's an unlawful act. Don't ruin me, I look upon you as a father, don't desert me . . . save my pride, honour, and my name . . . and save me from that scoundrel, that depraved man . . . He's a different person, Your Excellency, and I'm another, too. He's someone apart and I'm also someone in my own right. Really, someone in my own right, Your Excellency, really someone in my own right." That's how it is, I'll say. "I can't be like him," I'll say. "Please be kind, please authorize the change and put an end to that godless, wilful substitution, so that it won't serve as an example for others, Your Excellency. I look upon you as a father. Of course, benevolent and caring superiors must encourage such actions . . . There's even something chivalrous about it. I take you benevolent authorities as a father and I put my fate in your hands and I shan't contradict you. I entrust myself to you and

I myself will stand aside from the whole business . . . That's how it is!"'

'So, you're a cab driver, dear man?'

'Yes.'

'I need a carriage, old chap, for the whole evening.'

'Will you be wanting to go far, sir?'

'I want it for the evening, the evening. And to go wherever I need to, my dear man.'

'You won't be going out of town, will you, sir?'

'Perhaps, my friend, perhaps even out of town. I myself don't know for sure yet and I can't tell you for sure, dear chap. The fact is, it all might turn out for the best! That's so, my friend.'

'Well of course it's so, sir. God grant that happens for everyone.'

'Yes, my friend, yes. Thank you, dear man. Well, how much will you charge, dear chap?'

'Will you be wanting to go right away, sir?'

'Yes . . . that is . . . no. You'll have to wait at a certain spot . . . yes . . . you won't have to wait long, dear chap.'

'Well, if you want to hire me for the whole evening I couldn't possibly charge less than six silver roubles . . . not in this weather, sir.'

'All right, my friend, all right. And I'll show my gratitude, dear chap. So, you can take me there right away, dear chap!'

'Get in, sir . . . no, excuse me . . . I'll just tidy it up a bit inside first . . . Now please get in, sir. Where to, sir?'

'To Izmaylovsky Bridge, my friend.'

The driver clambered up on to the box and was about to get his pair of scrawny nags going – which he had difficulty in tearing away from their trough of hay – and drive to Izmaylovsky Bridge. But suddenly Mr Golyadkin pulled the cord, stopped the carriage and implored the driver to turn back and go to some other street and not to Izmaylovsky Bridge. The driver turned into another street and within ten minutes Mr Golyadkin's newly hired carriage drew up before the house where His Excellency lived. Mr Golyadkin alighted, entreated the driver to wait, dashed up to the first floor and with a sinking feeling rang the bell.

'Is His Excellency at home?' Mr Golyadkin asked, addressing the servant who opened the door to him.

'And what do you want, sir?' asked the footman, looking Mr Golyadkin up and down.

'I . . . my friend . . . er . . . um . . . I'm Golyadkin, civil servant, titular counsellor. Say it's like this and I've come to explain things . . .'

'You'll have to wait. It's impossible . . .'

'No, my friend, I can't wait. My business is important and it brooks no delay!'

'Who are you from? Have you brought some documents?'

'No, I'm here on a private matter. Please announce me. Tell him this and that, tell him I've come to explain. I'll show my gratitude, my friend.'

'But I can't. Orders are to receive no one. He has visitors just now. Please come back in the morning at ten o'clock.'

'Now do go and announce me, dear fellow. I can't wait – it's impossible! You'll answer for this, my man!'

'Oh, go on and announce him, what's the matter – saving on boot leather, eh?' said another footman who was lolling on a chest and had not said a word until then.

'To hell with boot leather! Orders are not to receive anyone, that's what. *Their* turn's in the mornings.'

'Oh, go on, announce him. Frightened your tongue'll drop off, or something?'

'Oh, all right, I'll announce him. But my tongue won't drop off. I've orders not to . . . that's what he said. Now, come through.'

Mr Golyadkin entered the first room. A clock stood on the table. He glanced at it – it was half past eight. His heart ached and he was about to turn back but at that very moment a lanky footman stationed at the threshold of the next room thunderously announced Mr Golyadkin. 'What a foghorn!' thought our hero in indescribable anguish. 'Now I should have said: "Um . . . it's like this, so to speak, I've come most humbly and dutifully to explain . . . er . . . please be good enough to receive me . . ." But my business is all ruined, my business has been blown away in the wind. Ah well, never mind!' But there

was no point in reflecting, however. The footman returned and
announced: 'This way please,' and led Mr Golyadkin into the
study.

The moment he entered our hero felt as if he'd suddenly gone
blind, as he could see absolutely nothing. However, he caught
a glimpse of two or three figures and the thought, 'Yes, they
must be visitors' flashed through Mr Golyadkin's mind. At
length our hero could clearly distinguish a star on His Excellency's black frock-coat and then, taking a gradual approach,
he progressed to the frock-coat itself, until finally he regained
the faculty of full vision.

'Well, sir?' asked a familiar voice above Mr Golyadkin's
head.

'Titular Counsellor Golyadkin, Your Excellency.'

'Well?'

'I've come to explain myself.'

'What's that? What did you say?'

'Yes, it's like this, so to speak, I've come to explain myself,
Your Excellency.'

'And . . . who are you?'

'M-m-m-mister Golyadkin, Your Excellency, titular counsellor.'

'Well, what do you want?'

'It's like this, so to speak. I consider him my father . . .
I myself am withdrawing from the whole affair . . . protection
from my enemies – that's what I want!'

'What's that . . . ?'

'It's well known . . .'

'What's well known?'

Mr Golyadkin didn't reply; his chin started to twitch
slightly.

'Well?'

'I thought it's chivalrous, Your Excellency . . . there's a touch
of chivalry about it, I thought, and I look upon my superior as
a father . . . so to speak . . . that's it . . . So please protect me
. . . w-with t-t-tears in my eyes I b-b-beseech you . . . such
actions should be en-en-encouraged . . .'

His Excellency turned away. For several moments our hero's

eyes could distinguish nothing. He felt a tightness in his chest; he was short of breath; he had no idea where he was standing ... he felt somehow ashamed and sad. God knows what happened after that. When he recovered our hero saw that His Excellency was talking to his visitors, apparently engaged in a vigorous and sharp debate with them. Mr Golyadkin at once recognized one of the visitors. It was Andrey Filippovich; but the other he didn't recognize. However, his face was somehow familiar – it was a tall, thick-set elderly figure, endowed with very bushy eyebrows and whiskers and a keen, expressive look. Around this stranger's neck was a decoration and in his mouth a cigar. This stranger was smoking and without taking the cigar from his mouth he nodded significantly as he glanced occasionally at Mr Golyadkin. Mr Golyadkin began to feel somewhat awkward. He averted his eyes and at once caught sight of yet another very strange visitor. In a doorway which until then our hero had taken for a mirror, as sometimes happened with him, *he* appeared – it's obvious who – Mr Golyadkin's very intimate friend and acquaintance! Until then Mr Golyadkin Junior had been in another little room writing something in a great hurry. Now he was apparently needed and he appeared with papers under his arm, went up to His Excellency and, fully expecting everyone's exclusive attention, managed very cleverly to worm his way into the general discussion, stationing himself behind Andrey Filippovich's back and partly screening himself with the cigar-smoking stranger. Evidently Mr Golyadkin Junior was taking a great interest in the conversation, on which he was now eavesdropping in the most dignified manner, shuffling his feet, smiling and constantly glancing at His Excellency as if by his glance he was asking that he too might be allowed to get his word in. 'The scoundrel!' thought Mr Golyadkin and he involuntarily took a step forward. At that moment His Excellency turned around and he himself approached Mr Golyadkin rather hesitantly.

'Well, all right, all right. Off with you now, I'll look into your case and I'll get someone to show you out.' Here the general glanced at the stranger with the bushy side-whiskers. The latter nodded in agreement.

Mr Golyadkin felt and fully realized that he had been mistaken for someone else, not at all as he should have been. 'One way or the other,' he thought, 'I really must explain myself. "It's like this, so to speak, Your Excellency", I'll say.' Just then, in his bewilderment, he looked down at the floor and to his amazement saw a sizeable white stain on His Excellency's shoes. 'Surely they can't have split, can they?' he wondered. Soon Mr Golyadkin discovered that in fact they hadn't split at all but were acting as powerful reflectors, a phenomenon fully explained by the fact that they were of extremely glossy patent leather. 'That's called a *high-light*,' thought our hero. 'The term is used particularly in artists' studios, but in other places these reflections are simply called flashes of light.' Here Mr Golyadkin looked up and saw that it was time to speak, since the whole business might easily take a turn for the worse. Our hero stepped forward.

'It's like this and that, so to speak, Your Excellency,' he said, 'these days imposture will get you nowhere.'

The general made no reply and gave a hard tug on the bell pull. Our hero took another step forward.

'Your Excellency,' said our hero, beside himself, almost dying with fear, but nevertheless boldly and determinedly pointing at his unworthy twin who at that moment was prancing about near His Excellency. 'He's a depraved and vile man. Say what you like, but I'm referring to a certain well-known person.'

Mr Golyadkin's words were followed by a general stir. Andrey Filippovich and the unfamiliar figure nodded. His Excellency impatiently tugged with all his might at the bell pull to summon the servants. Here Mr Golyadkin Junior in turn stepped forward.

'Your Excellency,' he said, 'I humbly beg permission to speak.' In Mr Golyadkin Junior's voice there was an extremely determined note; everything about him showed that he felt he was completely within his rights.

'Allow me to ask you,'[39] he began, again anticipating His Excellency's reply in his zeal and this time addressing Mr Golyadkin, 'allow me to ask in whose presence are you explaining yourself, in whose presence are you standing, in whose study are you?' Mr Golyadkin Senior was in an unusually agitated state, his face was red and burning with indignation and anger. Tears even came to his eyes.

'The Bassavryukovs!' bellowed the footman, who had appeared in the doorway, at the top of his voice.

'A good aristocratic name, of Ukrainian origin,' thought Mr Golyadkin and immediately someone laid a hand on his back in the friendliest fashion and then another hand was laid on his back. Mr Golyadkin's vile twin bustled around in front, showing the way, and our hero could clearly see that he was being steered towards the large study doors – and then he found himself out in the entrance hall. 'Just as at Olsufy Ivanovich's,' Mr Golyadkin thought. As he looked round he saw beside him two of His Excellency's footmen and one twin.

'The overcoat, the overcoat, my friend's overcoat! My best friend's overcoat!' twittered the depraved man, snatching the coat from one of the footmen and tossing it right on to Mr Golyadkin's head as a despicable and mean joke. As he struggled out from under his overcoat Mr Golyadkin Senior could clearly hear the two footmen laughing. However, listening to nothing and oblivious to all around, he left the hall and found himself on a brightly lit staircase. Mr Golyadkin Junior was following him.

'Goodbye, Your Excellency!' he shouted in Mr Golyadkin Senior's wake.

'Scoundrel!' our hero muttered, beside himself.

'So, I'm a scoundrel . . .'

'Depraved wretch!'

'So, I'm a depraved wretch,' the worthy Mr Golyadkin's unworthy foe replied, looking down at him without blinking, straight in the eye, from the top of the staircase with his characteristic vileness, as if inviting him to continue. Our hero spat in indignation and ran out on to the front steps. He was so crushed that he had absolutely no recollection of who helped him into the carriage or how. When he recovered he saw that he was being driven along the Fontanka. 'So, I must be going to Izmaylovsky Bridge,' thought Mr Golyadkin Senior. Now he wanted to think of something else, but he could not. It was all so

horrible that it defied explanation. 'Well, never mind!' concluded our hero as he drove off to Izmaylovsky Bridge.

CHAPTER XIII

It seemed that the weather was trying to change for the better.
In fact, the wet snow that had been falling up to then in great
clouds gradually began to fall more thinly and finally stopped
almost completely. The sky became visible, with a few tiny stars
twinkling here and there. It was just wet, muddy, damp and
steamy – especially for Mr Golyadkin, who already had difficulty catching his breath. His coat, which was soaked and
weighed down by the wet, made him feel a disagreeable warmth
and dampness all over and its weight made his already terribly
weak legs buckle. A feverish trembling spread all over his
body, producing a sharp, tingling sensation. Sheer exhaustion
squeezed a cold, sickly sweat out of him, so that at this suitable
moment Mr Golyadkin forgot to repeat his favourite phrase,
with his characteristic determination and resolve, that somehow it might possibly, surely, undoubtedly, certainly, turn out
for the best. 'Still, none of this matters for the moment,' added
our plucky and undaunted hero, wiping from his face the drops
of cold water streaming in all directions from the brim of his
hat that was too sodden to hold any more water. Adding that
everything was still all right, our hero tried to take a seat on a
large log lying near a stack of firewood in Olsufy Ivanovich's
courtyard. Of course, there was no question now of thinking
of Spanish serenades or silken ladders. But what he did need to
think about was finding a quiet little corner which, if not actually warm, would at least be comfortable and secluded. He
was strongly tempted, let it be mentioned in passing, by that
particular little corner on Olsufy Ivanovich's landing, where
our hero had once before, almost at the beginning of this
veracious story, waited for a whole two hours between the
cupboard and some old screens, among all kinds of domestic
rubbish and unwanted junk. The fact was that even now he had

been standing waiting two solid hours in Olsufy Ivanovich's courtyard. But now there were certain inconveniences that had not existed before concerning his former quiet and cosy little corner. The first was that the place had probably now been noted since that scandal at Olsufy Ivanovich's last ball and precautionary measures taken. Secondly, he must now await the agreed signal from Klara Olsufyevna, since there must be some kind of agreed signal. That was the way these things were always done and 'We're not the first and we shan't be the last', as he put it. Just then, most opportunely, Mr Golyadkin remembered in passing a novel he had read a long time before, where the heroine had given a prearranged signal to Alfred in exactly similar circumstances, by tying a pink ribbon to her window. But now, at night, and with the St Petersburg climate, so notorious for its dampness and unreliability, a pink ribbon was out of the question – in brief, it was quite impossible. 'No, this isn't the time for silken ladders,' thought our hero. 'I'd better stay where I am, on my own – stand here, for example, nice and quietly where no one can see me.' And he selected a spot in the courtyard directly opposite the windows, near the stack of wood. Of course, many postilions, coachmen and visitors were constantly passing through the courtyard, and in addition there were wheels clattering and horses snorting and so on. But for all that it was a convenient spot: whether he was noticed or not, there was now at least the advantage that everything, in a manner of speaking, was to some extent in shadow, so that he could see absolutely everything and no one could see Mr Golyadkin. The windows were brightly lit; some kind of ceremonial gathering was in progress at Olsufy Ivanovich's. As yet no music could be heard. 'So, it can't be a ball, they must have gathered for another reason,' our hero thought, his heart sinking. 'But is it today?' flashed through his mind. 'Was there a mistake about the date? Well, it's possible, anything is possible. Oh yes, anything is possible . . . It's possible it was yesterday that the letter was written but it didn't reach me – it didn't reach me because Petrushka got involved in it – the scoundrel! Or perhaps "tomorrow" was written there, that is . . . I . . . that everything had to be done tomorrow, that is, to be waiting with a carriage . . .' Here our hero went cold all over and fumbled in his pocket for the letter, so that he could check. But to his amazement the letter was not in his pocket. 'How is this?' the half-dead Mr Golyadkin whispered. 'Where could I have left it? Does this mean I've lost it? Well, that's the last straw!' he groaned at length. 'What if it falls into evil hands now? (Perhaps it already has!) Good heavens! What will be the upshot of all this! The upshot will be that . . . Oh, my wretched fate!' Here Mr Golyadkin trembled like a leaf at the thought that his shameless twin, when he had got wind of it from Mr Golyadkin's enemies, had perhaps hurled his coat over his head with the express purpose of stealing that letter! 'What's more, he's intercepting it as evidence . . . but why evidence?' After the initial shock and stupor of horror the blood rushed to Mr Golyadkin's head. Groaning, gnashing his teeth and clutching his burning head, he sank down on his log and started thinking about something . . . But somehow his thoughts wouldn't connect with anything. There were glimpses and memories of faces, at times vividly and vaguely of others and of long-forgotten events; silly song-tunes filled his head. The anguish, the anguish was really unnatural! 'Oh God!' he thought, slightly recovering and suppressing the dull sobs in his breast, 'Oh God! Grant me fortitude in the bottomless depths of my tribulations! But there's no doubt whatsoever that I'm done for, I've disappeared, gone from this world completely and all this is in the natural order of things and just couldn't be otherwise. To start with I've lost my job, I must have lost my job, in no way could I not have lost it. Well, supposing it will all be sorted out there. Supposing the little bit of money I've got will be enough to begin with. I'll need a different little flat, a few bits of furniture . . . But for a start I shan't even have Petrushka with me. I can cope without that scoundrel . . . and I'll have lodgers as well, that's good! And I can come and go as I please and Petrushka won't be there to grumble if I'm late. That's good, that's why it would be a good thing to have lodgers. Well, supposing that's all very good, only why do I always talk about the wrong thing, always the wrong thing completely?' Here the thought of his present predicament again lit up his memory. He looked around. 'Oh God! Oh God! What am I talking about now?' he wondered, clutching his burning head in utter confusion . . .

'Will you be wanting to go soon, sir?' said a voice above Mr Golyadkin. Mr Golyadkin gave a start. But it was only his cab driver, also soaked to the skin, chilled to the marrow, having taken it into his head, in his impatience and from having nothing to do, to come and have a look at Mr Golyadkin behind the woodpile.

'I'm all right, my friend . . . I . . . my friend soon, very soon . . . so please wait.'

The cab driver went away, grumbling to himself. 'What's he grumbling about?' thought Mr Golyadkin through his tears. 'After all, I hired him for the evening so . . . really . . . er . . . I'm within my rights now – that's it! I hired him for the evening and that's the end of it, it makes no difference even if one has to stay here like this. I can please myself. I'm at liberty to go or not to go. And the fact that I'm standing here behind the woodpile . . . well, there's nothing at all wrong with that . . . and don't you dare contradict me! I say, the gentleman chooses to stand behind firewood . . . so he stands behind firewood . . . and he won't blacken anyone's name by so doing – that's right! That's how it is, my dear young lady, if you really want to know. In our day and age just no one, so to speak, lives in a hut. And in this industrial age, young lady, you'll get nowhere without good behaviour, of which you provide such proof. One has to be a magistrate's clerk and live in a hut by the sea.[40] Firstly, young lady, there are no magistrate's clerks on the seashore and secondly you and I couldn't even get a job as one of those magistrate's clerks. Let's suppose, for example, I apply for the job and present myself and say: "It's like this and that . . . and to be a magistrate's clerk and . . . you know . . . and protect me from my enemy" – they'll tell you, young lady, such and such, that there's lots of magistrate's clerks and here you're not at Madame Falbala's where you learned good behaviour, of which you provided such a baneful example. Good behaviour, young lady, means staying at home, respecting your father, and not hankering after nice suitors before the time is ripe, young lady. Suitors, young lady, will come along all in good time –

that's how it is! Of course, there's no doubt that you need to
have acquired various talents, such as playing the piano now
and then, speaking French, knowing history, geography, div-
inity and arithmetic – that's how it is! But you don't need more
than that. And cookery in addition. A knowledge of cookery
should definitely be within the sphere of knowledge of every
well-behaved young lady! Otherwise what is there? Firstly, my
beauty, my dear young lady, they won't let you go but they'll
raise a hue and cry and you'll be trumped – and then it's into a
convent. So what then, young lady? What would you have me
do then? Would you have me go to a nearby hill and dissolve
in tears, after the fashion of certain novels,[41] as I contemplate
the cold walls of your confinement and finally expire after the
example of certain bad German poets and novelists – isn't that
so, young lady? But first allow me to tell you as a friend that
things aren't done that way; and secondly I'd give you and your
parents a good thrashing for letting you read French books, for
French books will teach you no good. There's poison in them,
pernicious poison, my dear young lady! Or do you think, if I
may ask, do you think this and that, so to speak, that we'll run
away unpunished and there's ... um ... so to speak ... a hut
for you by the seashore and we'll start billing and cooing and
talk about different feelings and live happily ever after? And
then along comes a nestling, so we'll ... well, it's like this,
it's this and that, so to speak. We'll tell our father and State
Counsellor Olsufy Ivanovich that a nestling's come along, so
on this auspicious occasion will you withdraw your curse and
bless the couple? No, young lady, once again things aren't done
like that and the first thing is that there won't be any billing
and cooing, so please don't pin your hopes on that. Nowadays
the husband, young lady, is master and a good well-brought-up
wife must try and please him in everything. Displays of affection
aren't in fashion in this industrial age. The days of Jean-Jacques
Rousseau are past, so to speak. For example, these days a
husband comes home hungry from work and asks if he could
have a little snack before dinner, darling, perhaps a glass of
vodka to drink and a bit of herring? Well, young lady, you
must have vodka and herring all ready for him. The husband

will eat heartily and won't so much as give you a look – all he'll say is: "Just pop into the kitchen, my little kitten, and see to dinner." And perhaps, just once a week, if you're lucky, he'll give you a kiss and a pretty casual one at that! That's the way we do it, so to speak – and even then indifferently! That's how it will be if we think about it like that, if that's what things have come to, if that's the way we've started looking at things . . . But what's it all to do with me? And why, young lady, have you mixed me up in your idle fancies? "A benevolent man who is suffering for my sake," you say, "in so many ways dear to my heart, and so on." Well, firstly, young lady, I'm not suited to you – you know that yourself, I'm no expert at paying compliments, I don't like uttering all that sweetly scented nonsense to the ladies, I've no time for womanizers and I must confess my looks have never got me anywhere. You won't find any false bragging or false modesty in me and now I confess it in all sincerity. That's how it is, so to speak. All I possess is a straightforward, open character and good sense. I don't get mixed up in intrigues. I'm not an intriguer, so to speak, and I'm proud of it – so there you are! I don't wear a mask when I'm with decent people and to tell all . . .'

Suddenly Mr Golyadkin gave a start. The drenched ginger beard of his cab driver again appeared around the woodpile.

'Coming right away, my friend,' Mr Golyadkin replied in a trembling, languishing voice. 'I'm coming right away.'

The driver scratched the back of his head, then stroked his beard, then took one step forward . . . he stopped and eyed Mr Golyadkin mistrustfully.

'I'm coming right away, my friend . . . you see, my friend . . . I'll only be here a few seconds . . . you see . . . my friend . . .'

'Aren't you going anywhere at all?' the driver finally said, going up to Mr Golyadkin, resolutely and decisively.

'Oh yes, my friend, I'm coming right now. You see, my friend, I'm waiting . . .'

'Yes, sir.'

'I, you see, my friend . . . what village are you from, my dear man?'

'I'm a serf.'

'Do you have a good master?'

'He's all right.'

'Well, my friend, you just wait here, my friend. You see, my friend – have you been long in St Petersburg?'

'Been driving a cab for a year.'

'Are you doing well, my friend?'

'All right.'

'Yes, my friend, yes. Thank Providence, my friend. You, my friend, should try and find a good man. These days a good man is rare, my friend; he'll bathe you, give you food and drink, my dear chap. But sometimes you see that even money doesn't bring happiness – you see a lamentable example of that, my friend. That's how it is, dear chap.' The cab driver suddenly appeared to feel sorry for Mr Golyadkin.

'All right, as you like, I'll wait, sir. Will you be waiting much longer, sir?'

'No, my friend . . . I . . . er . . . well, you know how it is . . . I shan't wait any longer, dear man. What do you think, dear chap? I'm relying on you. I shan't be waiting here any longer . . .'

'So do you want to be going anywhere?'

'No, my friend, no. But I'll show my gratitude, dear man . . . that's it. Well, how much do I owe you, dear chap?'

'What we agreed on, sir – that's what you should give me. I've been waiting a long time, sir. Please don't be hard on me, sir.'

'Well, here you are, my friend, here you are.' Mr Golyadkin paid the cab driver the full six silver roubles and having decided in earnest not to waste any more time – that is, to leave while the going was good, particularly now that the matter had finally been settled and the driver sent away there was no point in waiting any longer – he walked out of the courtyard, out through the gates, turned left and without a backward glance, panting and rejoicing, broke into a run. 'Perhaps it will all be settled for the best,' he thought, 'and this way I've avoided trouble.' In actual fact Mr Golyadkin had suddenly grown unusually light at heart. 'Ah, if only it could be settled for the best,' our hero wondered, but he did not put very much trust in his own words. 'Now I can . . .' he thought. 'No, I'd better

try a different approach, but on the other hand . . . wouldn't it
be better to do . . . ?' With these doubts and seeking a key and
a solution to all his doubts our hero ran as far as Semyonovsky
Bridge and having run as far as Semyonovsky Bridge he prudently and finally decided to turn back. 'That's best,' he
thought. 'I'd better take a different approach, I mean, like this.
I'll simply be an outside observer and that's the end of the
matter. I'll say I'm an observer, someone not involved – that's
all, and whatever happens there I'm not to blame. That's it!
That's how it will be now!'

Having decided to return our hero did in fact turn back,
particularly in view of the fact that, thanks to his happy idea,
he had now set himself up as a complete outsider. 'That's best:
you're not responsible for anything and you'll just see what
comes of it . . . that's the way!' Therefore his calculations were
absolutely correct and the matter would be closed. Having set
his mind at rest he withdrew into the tranquil haven of his
comforting and protective woodpile and began to concentrate
his attention on the windows. This time he did not have to
watch and wait for long. Suddenly there was a strange kind of
movement at the windows, all at once, figures were glimpsed,
curtains drawn back and Olsufy Ivanovich's windows became
crowded with whole groups of people, all of them searching
for something in the courtyard. Secure behind his woodpile our
hero in turn watched the general commotion with curiosity,
stretching his head to right and left, at least as far as the
short shadow the woodpile that was concealing him allowed.
Suddenly he was struck dumb, shuddered and sat cowering on
the spot in horror. He realized – in brief he had guessed correctly
– that they were not looking for anyone or anything: they were
simply looking for *him*, Mr Golyadkin. Everyone was looking
in his direction, everyone was pointing in his direction. To run
away was impossible . . . they would see him! The dumbstruck
Mr Golyadkin huddled as closely as he could to the woodpile
and only then did he notice that the treacherous shadow had
betrayed him by failing to conceal all of him. With the greatest
pleasure our hero would have agreed to creep into a mousehole
in the woodpile and sit there quietly – if only that were possible!

But it was absolutely impossible. In his agony he finally began to stare directly and boldly at all the windows at once; that was best ... Suddenly he blushed furiously with shame. He had quite clearly been spotted, everyone had seen him at the same time, everyone was beckoning to him, everyone was nodding, everyone was calling out to him; several windows clicked open, several voices started shouting something to him simultaneously. 'I'm amazed those sluts aren't thrashed when they're still little girls,' he muttered to himself, utterly flustered. Suddenly *he* (we know who) came running down the steps, wearing only his uniform, hatless, breathless, prancing and frisking, perfidiously giving expression to his overwhelming joy at seeing Mr Golyadkin at last.

'Yakov Petrovich!' twittered that man, so notorious for his worthlessness. 'Are you here? You'll catch cold, Yakov Petrovich, it's cold here. Please come in.'

'Yakov Petrovich! No, I'm all right, Yakov Petrovich,' our hero muttered submissively.

'But you can't, you can't, Yakov Petrovich. They're begging you most humbly, they're all waiting. "Do make us happy," they say, "and bring Yakov Petrovich here!" That's what they're saying.'

'No, Yakov Petrovich, I'd better ... you see ... I'd better be going home now,' our hero said, so mortified and horrified that he felt as if he were being roasted over a slow fire and at the same time freezing with shame and horror.

'No-no-no-no!' twittered the loathsome man. 'No-no-no. Not for anything! Let's go!' he said with determination, dragging Mr Golyadkin towards the porch. Mr Golyadkin Senior had no desire whatsoever to go; but since everyone was watching it would have been silly to struggle and dig his heels in. So in went our hero – however, it couldn't be said that he went, because he had positively no idea what was happening to him. But then, at the same time, it was all right!

Before our hero had time to somehow recover and come to his senses he found himself in the reception hall. He was pale, harassed and dishevelled; he glanced at the whole crowd with lacklustre eyes – and, horror!: the reception hall, all the rooms

were filled to overflowing. There were masses of people, a whole
hothouse of ladies; all were milling around Mr Golyadkin, all
were surging towards Mr Golyadkin, and he could see very
well that they were pushing him in a certain direction. 'Surely
not to the doors!' flashed through his mind. Indeed, they were
not pushing him towards the doors, but straight towards Olsufy
Ivanovich's comfortable armchair. On one side of the chair
stood Klara Olsufyevna, pale, languid and melancholy, but
sumptuously attired. Mr Golyadkin was particularly struck by
the little white flowers in her black hair that created such a
wonderful effect. On the other side of the chair, in black tail-
coat and with his new decoration in his buttonhole, stood
Vladimir Semyonovich. Mr Golyadkin, as we have already said,
was taken by the arms and escorted straight towards Olsufy
Ivanovich – on one side by Mr Golyadkin Junior, who had
now assumed an extraordinarily decorous and loyal air, which
gladdened our hero no end, and on the other by Andrey
Filippovich, wearing the most solemn expression. 'What could
it be?' wondered Mr Golyadkin. But when he saw that they
were leading him to Olsufy Ivanovich it all dawned on him in
a flash. The thought of that intercepted letter darted through
his brain. In unbounded agony our hero stood before Olsufy
Ivanovich's chair. 'What shall I do now?' he thought. 'Of course
it should all be on a bold footing, that is, with candour not
lacking in nobility. I'll say this and I'll say that, and so on.' But
what our hero had evidently been fearing did not come to pass.
Olsufy Ivanovich seemed to give Mr Golyadkin a very warm
reception and although he did not offer his hand he at least,
when looking at him, shook his hoary head that inspired great
respect – shook it with a sad yet at the same time well-disposed
air. At least, so it seemed to Mr Golyadkin. He even thought
he could detect glistening tears in Olsufy Ivanovich's lacklustre
eyes. He looked up and it seemed to him that there was also
a tiny tear gleaming on an eyelash of Klara Olsufyevna, who
was standing close by, and that something of the kind was
also visible in Vladimir Semyonovich's eyes; and that, finally,
Andrey Filippovich's calm, imperturbable dignity was no less
appropriate amidst all that general lachrymose sympathy and

that even the young man who had once so strongly resembled an important counsellor was sobbing bitterly, taking advantage of the moment. Or perhaps it was all in Mr Golyadkin's imagination, since he himself had burst into tears and was acutely conscious of his hot tears coursing down his cold cheeks . . . In a voice filled with sobs, reconciled with mankind and destiny, at that moment overflowing with affection not only for Olsufy Ivanovich and all the guests taken together but even for his pernicious twin who was evidently not in the least pernicious now and not even Mr Golyadkin's twin but a somehow extraneous and extremely amiable person in himself, our hero attempted to address Olsufy Ivanovich with a touching effusion and soulful outpouring. But in the fullness of all that had been accumulating within him, he could not express anything at all but could only point with an eloquent gesture at his heart . . . At length, Andrey Filippovich, probably wishing to spare the hoary-headed old man's sensibilities, drew Mr Golyadkin a little to one side and left him completely to his own devices. Smiling and muttering to himself, somewhat bewildered, but in any event almost entirely reconciled with mankind and destiny, our hero began to make his way somewhere through the solid crowd of guests. Everyone made way for him, everyone looked at him with a kind of strange curiosity and a mysterious, unaccountable sympathy. Our hero passed into the next room and was accorded the same attention everywhere. He was vaguely aware of the entire crowd following hard on his heels, noting his every step, furtively discussing among themselves something extremely interesting, shaking their heads, talking, arguing, passing judgement and whispering. Mr Golyadkin longed to know what they were passing judgement on, arguing and whispering about. Looking around our hero saw Mr Golyadkin Junior at his side. Feeling the urge to grab his arm and take him aside, Mr Golyadkin earnestly implored the other Yakov Petrovich to cooperate with him in all his future undertakings and not to abandon him at a critical juncture. Mr Golyadkin Junior nodded gravely and firmly squeezed Mr Golyadkin Senior's hand. Our hero's heart started palpitating from an excess of emotion. At the same time he felt he was

suffocating, being hemmed in, terribly hemmed in; that all those
eyes fixed on him were somehow oppressing and crushing him.
Mr Golyadkin happened to catch a glimpse of the bewigged
counsellor who was giving him a severe, searching look, quite
unmoved by the general mood of sympathy . . . Our hero almost
decided to go right up to him in order to smile at him and to
have things out with him there and then but for some reason
this came to nought. For a moment Mr Golyadkin almost
completely lost consciousness, lost his memory and all feeling.
When he recovered he noticed that he was rotating in a wide
circle of guests who had gathered around him. Suddenly someone shouted Mr Golyadkin's name from the next room and this
shout was immediately taken up by the entire crowd. Everything
became agitated, noisy, everyone in the rooms rushed to the
doors of the reception hall. Our hero was almost carried aloft
with them; just then the stony-hearted, bewigged counsellor
turned up right beside Mr Golyadkin. Finally he took the latter
by the arm and sat him on a chair next to him, opposite Olsufy
Ivanovich's chair but at a quite considerable distance from
him. Every single person became hushed and quietened down;
everyone observed a solemn silence, everyone kept looking at
Olsufy Ivanovich, evidently expecting something not quite in
the normal run of things. Mr Golyadkin noticed that the other
Mr Golyadkin, together with Andrey Filippovich, had taken
their places next to Olsufy Ivanovich's chair and also exactly
opposite the counsellor. The silence continued; they really were
expecting something. 'Yes, exactly like in a family when someone's going away on a long journey. All we need to do now is
stand up and say a prayer,' reflected our hero. Suddenly there
was a great stir which cut short all Mr Golyadkin's reflections.
That long-expected something had come to pass. 'He's coming,
he's coming!' ran through the crowd. 'Who's coming?' ran
through Mr Golyadkin's head and some strange sensation made
him shudder. 'It's time!' said the counsellor, looking attentively
at Andrey Filippovich, who in turn glanced at Olsufy Ivanovich.
Olsufy Ivanovich nodded solemnly and gravely. 'Let us all be
upstanding' said the counsellor, helping Mr Golyadkin to his
feet. Everyone stood up. Then the counsellor took Mr Goly-

adkin by the arm, while Andrey Filippovich took Mr Golyadkin Junior's and both solemnly led the two absolutely identical men through to the middle of the crowd that had gathered around and whose eyes were straining in expectation. Our hero looked around in bewilderment, but he was immediately stopped and his attention directed to Mr Golyadkin Junior, who offered his hand. 'They want us to make peace,' our hero thought and, deeply moved, stretched out his hand to Mr Golyadkin Junior; and then he leant his head towards him. The other Mr Golyadkin followed suit. At this point Mr Golyadkin Senior had the impression that his treacherous friend was smiling, that he had given a fleeting, roguish wink at the entire surrounding crowd, that there was something sinister in the improper Mr Golyadkin Junior's expression, that he had even grimaced at the moment of his Judas-kiss ... There were ringing noises in Mr Golyadkin's head, there was darkness before his eyes; it seemed that a great multitude, a whole file of absolutely identical Golyadkins was noisily forcing open every door in the room. But it was too late. A resounding kiss of betrayal had rung out and ...

And then something totally unexpected happened. The doors of the reception hall opened with a crash and on the threshold appeared a man whose look alone made Mr Golyadkin's blood run cold. His legs became rooted to the spot. A cry of terror died away in his tightened chest. However, Mr Golyadkin had known this all along and had long been expecting something like it. The stranger solemnly and gravely approached Mr Golyadkin ... Mr Golyadkin knew that figure very well. He had often seen it, had even seen it that very same day ... The stranger was a tall, thickset man, wearing a black tail-coat and with an important-looking decoration in the form of a cross around his neck and he was endowed with thick, jet-black side-whiskers; only a cigar was needed to complete the likeness. But the stranger's stare, as we have said already, made Mr Golyadkin go cold with horror. With solemn and grave countenance, this terrifying person approached the sorry hero of our tale ... Our hero stretched out his hand to him; the stranger took it and hauled him along after him. With a lost, crushed expression our hero glanced around.

'This is Krestyan Ivanovich Rutenspitz, Doctor of Medicine and Surgery, an old acquaintance of yours, Yakov Petrovich!' someone's loathsome voice twittered right into Mr Golyadkin's ear. He looked around: it was Mr Golyadkin's twin, so repulsive for the vile qualities of his soul. An unseemly, malicious glee shone in his face. He was rubbing his hands in delight, rolling his head in delight, pattering around everyone in delight; he seemed ready to dance for delight right away; finally he leapt forward, grabbed a candle from one of the servants and walked ahead to light the way for Mr Golyadkin and Krestyan Ivanovich. Mr Golyadkin could clearly hear everyone in the hall surge after him, crowding and jostling one another and all of them repeating with one accord: 'It's all right, don't be afraid, Yakov Petrovich, after all it's your old friend and acquaintance Krestyan Ivanovich Rutenspitz.' Finally they came out on to the main, brightly lit staircase; the staircase too was packed with people. The doors on to the porch were flung open with a crash and Mr Golyadkin found himself on the steps together with Krestyan Ivanovich. A carriage harnessed with four impatiently snorting horses was drawn up at the bottom. In three bounds the gloating Mr Golyadkin Junior reached the bottom of the steps and opened the carriage door himself. With an imperious gesture Krestyan Ivanovich invited Mr Golyadkin to take a seat. However, there was no need at all for such a gesture, as there were sufficient people there to help him in. Numb with horror, Mr Golyadkin looked back: the entire brightly lit staircase was swarming with people; inquisitive eyes were looking at him from all sides. On the uppermost landing, in his armchair, presided Olsufy Ivanovich himself, watching attentively and with profound interest all that was taking place below. They were all waiting. A murmur of impatience ran through the crowd when Mr Golyadkin looked back.

'I hope there's nothing here ... reprehensible ... nothing that might provoke disciplinary measures and draw everyone's attention to my official relationships,' our hero said in bewilderment. There was a clamour all around; everyone shook their heads negatively. Tears streamed from Mr Golyadkin's eyes.

'In that case I'm ready ... I fully entrust myself ... I put my fate in Krestyan Ivanovich's hands . . .' The moment Mr Golyadkin spoke of fully entrusting his fate to Krestyan Ivanovich a terrible, deafening, joyous cry rolled in the most sinister echo among the whole expectant throng. Then Krestyan Ivanovich from one side and Andrey Filippovich from the other took Mr Golyadkin by the arm and began putting him in the carriage. As for his double, he was helping him in from behind in his usual dastardly way. The hapless Mr Golyadkin Senior took a last look at everyone and everything, and shivering like a kitten drenched with cold water – if the comparison may be permitted – climbed into the carriage. Krestyan Ivanovich followed him immediately. The carriage doors slammed; the crack of a whip was heard and the horses jerked the carriage into motion . . . everyone rushed after Mr Golyadkin. The piercing, frenzied cries of all his enemies rolled after him like a valediction. For a while a few figures could still be seen running around the carriage that was bearing Mr Golyadkin away; but gradually they fell further and further back until they were finally completely lost to sight. Mr Golyadkin's unseemly twin kept up longer than all the others. With hands in the trouser pockets of his green uniform he ran along with a contented look, leaping up first on one side on the carriage and then the other; at times he grabbed the window frame and hung from it, poking his head in and blowing farewell kisses at Mr Golyadkin; but even he too began to tire, his appearances grew fewer and fewer until he finally vanished altogether. Mr Golyadkin's heart was filled with a dull ache. The hot blood rushed into his head and throbbed; he was suffocating and wanted to unbutton his coat, to bare his chest and sprinkle it with snow and pour cold water over it. Finally he lapsed into unconciousness . . . When he came to he saw that the horses were bearing him along some unfamiliar road. To right and left loomed dark forests; all around it was bleak and deserted. Suddenly his heart stood still: two fiery eyes were peering at him out of the darkness and those two eyes were burning with malevolent, hellish glee. But it was not Krestyan Ivanovich! Who was it? Or *was* it him? It was! It was Krestyan Ivanovich – not the earlier one but a different, fearful Krestyan Ivanovich!

'Krestyan Ivanovich . . . I . . . I think I'm all right,' our hero
tried to begin, timidly and trembling, wishing at least somehow
to mollify the fearful Krestyan Ivanovich with his meekness and
submission.

'You vil haf kvarters, mit vood, licht und serfants of vich you
do not diserf,' Krestyan Ivanovich's reply rang out, stern and
dreadful as a judge's sentence.

Our hero shrieked and clutched his head. Alas! He had long
been expecting this!

Notes

NOTES FROM UNDERGROUND

1. *collegiate assessor*: Eighth grade in Table of Ranks, equivalent to army major (see p. liv).
2. *'sublime and beautiful'*: See Introduction, note 6, p. liv.
3. *l'homme de la nature et de la vérité*: This phrase appears differently in Rousseau's *Confessions* (1782–9), and it seems Dostoyevsky is deliberately and sarcastically misquoting *Première Partie*, Livre Premier: 'Je forme une entreprise qui n'eut jamais d'exemple, et dont l'exécution n'aura point d'imitateur. Je veux montrer à mes semblables un homme dans toute la vérité de la nature, et cet homme, ce sera moi.' ('I am undertaking something which has never had a precedent and whose execution will have no imitator. I wish to portray to my fellows a man in the whole truth of nature – and that man will be me.')

   Dostoyevsky here follows Heine's total scepticism concerning the possibility of true autobiography. Affirming that no one up to then had succeeded in writing a true autobiography, Heine states in Part 10 of volume two of the French edition of *De l'Allemagne*, in his *Confessions* (1853–4): '... ni le Genevois Jean-Jacques Rousseau; surtout ce dernier qui, tout en s'appellant l'homme de la vérité et de la nature, n'était au fond pas moins mensonger et dénaturé que les autres.' ('... neither the Genovese Jean-Jacques Rousseau; above all the latter who, calling himself a man of nature and truth, was basically no less mendacious and perverted than others') .
4. *Once it is proven to you, for example, that you're descended from the apes...*: Interest in the question of man's origin had particularly sharpened at the beginning of 1864 with the appearance in translation, in St Petersburg, of T. H. Huxley's *Evidence as to Man's Place in Nature* (1863).

5.   *... despite all the Wagenheims in the world ...*: According to a
     directory, in the mid-1860s there were no fewer than eight den-
     tists of this name in St Petersburg; signboards advertising their
     services were to be seen all over the city.
6.   *... like a person "divorced from the soil and his native
     roots" ...*: This phrase occurs frequently in articles appearing in
     Dostoyevsky's journals of the early 1860s – *Time* and *Epoch*.
7.   *... the artist Ge*: Dostoyevsky is here attacking an article by
     the novelist and publicist M. E. Saltykov-Shchedrin praising a
     painting by N. N. Ge (1831–94), *The Last Supper*, shown at
     the Academy of Arts autumn exhibition of 1863. This painting
     aroused conflicting criticisms and Dostoyevsky later reproached
     Ge for deliberately mixing the historical with the contemporary,
     which resulted in falsehood (*Diary of a Writer*, 1873, IX). 'For
     your satisfaction' was an article of Saltykov-Shchedrin's, printed
     in *The Contemporary*, 1863.
8.   *... affirming with Buckle ...*: H. T. Buckle (1821–62), in his
     History of Civilisation in England (1863), had expounded the
     idea that the development of civilization leads to the cessation of
     war between nations.
9.   *There's your Napoleon ... the present-day one*: Napoleon I and
     Napoleon III are mentioned in view of the great number of wars
     waged by France during their reigns.
10. *There's your North America ...*: Reference to the American Civil
     War (1861–5).
11. *... there's your grotesque Schleswig-Holstein*: By 'grotesque'
     Dostoyevsky is probably referring to the immensely complicated
     history of Schleswig-Holstein. Briefly, the duchies of Schleswig
     and Holstein became the personal possessions of the King of
     Denmark in 1460, with a largely German population. Holstein
     was included in the German Confederation (1815). In 1848
     Prussia intervened to stop a Danish attempt to annex the duchies
     and, together with Austria, forced Denmark to give them up
     (1864), Austria taking Holstein and Prussia Schleswig.
12. *Attila*: King of the Huns (c. 406–53) who overran much of the
     Byzantine and Western Roman Empires. He came to be called
     the 'Scourge of God'.
13. *Stenka Razin*: Don Cossack (?–1671) who led a peasant revolt
     in 1670, causing widespread devastation and massacring land-
     owners. There is a portrait of him in Turgenev's story 'Phantoms',
     published together with *Notes from Underground* in the same
     issue of *Epoch*.

14. *Cleopatra*: Queen of Egypt (69–30 BC). Her name was mentioned frequently in the Russian press in 1861, in connection with the reading at a literary evening in Perm of her monologue in Pushkin's 'Egyptian Nights' (1835), by Madame Tolmachev, a civil servant's wife. This reading is mentioned with great relish by the libertine Svidrigaylov in *Crime and Punishment*.

15. *Then the Crystal Palace will be erected*: The Crystal Palace is referred to in 'The Fourth Dream of Vera Pavlovna' in N. G. Chernyshevsky's utopian novel *What is to be Done?* (1863), the main target of Dostoyevsky's polemic in *Notes from Underground*. Chernyshevsky describes a cast-iron crystal palace as presented by Charles Fourier in his *Theory of Universal Unity* (1841); in this crystal palace members of a social commune or phalanstery live in complete harmony. Here the model (for the palace) was the Crystal Palace built in 1851 for the Great Exhibition in London.

16. *Colossus of Rhodes*: Bronze statue of Helios 31 metres high, cast in 280 BC and one of the Seven Wonders of the World.

17. *Mr Anayevsky*: A. E. Anayevsky (1788–1866), author of literary articles, the object of constant ridicule in journals of the 1840s–60s. In his brochure 'Enchiridion for the Curious' he writes: 'The Colossus of Rhodes was erected, some writers affirm by Semiramis, others claim it was not erected by human hands, but by Nature.'

18. *aux animaux domestiques*: To domestic animals.

19. *. . . Heine claims . . . lie about himself*: In *De l'Allemagne*, volume two in his *Confessions* (1853–4), Heine wrote: 'To execute one's own self-portrait would not only be an awkward undertaking but simply impossible . . . for all one's desire to be sincere, not one man can tell the truth about himself.' In the same book he affirms that in his *Confessions* Rousseau 'makes false confessions to hide his true actions behind them' (see also note 3).

20. *. . . apropos of the wet snow*: The memoirist P. V. Annenkov in his article 'Notes on Russian Literature' observed that 'fine drizzle and wet snow are indispensable elements of the St Petersburg cityscape with writers of the Natural School and their imitators'.

21. *When from error's murky ways . . .*: From the poem by the civic poet N. A. Nekrasov (1845). This poem was one of the first where Nekrasov treats a fallen woman with great compassion and it had been mentioned ironically in *The Village of Stepanchikovo* (1859).

With the three etceteras that unceremoniously close the quotation, Dostoyevsky is treating with much sarcasm the redeemed prostitute theme originating in French Social Romantic novelists such as Eugène Sue, Victor Hugo and George Sand, and which appears in Chernyshevsky's *What is to be Done?*, which he is polemicizing in *Notes from Underground*. There is a strong resemblance between the episode in *What is to be Done?* where a hero saves a fallen woman who eventually dies of tuberculosis, and that in the second part of *Notes from Underground*.

22. *Kostanzhoglos and Uncle Pyotr Ivanoviches*: Kostanzhoglo, a model landowner portrayed by Gogol in Part Two of *Dead Souls* (1843–6); Pyotr Ivanovich (Aduyev): the uncle in Goncharov's *An Ordinary Story* (1847), the epitome of hard-headed practicality.

23. *... because he thinks he's the 'King of Spain'*: Poprishchin in Gogol's *Diary of a Madman* (1835) is under the illusion he's King of Spain.

24. *... like Gogol's Lieutenant Pirogov*: In *Nevsky Prospekt* (1835) Pirogov, after being flogged by the tinsmith Schiller for flirting with his wife, wishes to put in a written complaint to the authorities.

25. *Fatherland Notes*: (1839–84) Founded by A. Krayevsky and considered the leading journal of the Westernizers. Works by Lermontov, Belinsky, Turgenev, Herzen and Nekrasov were published in it.

26. *Nevsky Prospekt*: St Petersburg's main thoroughfare, about two and a half miles long, the hub of the city's shopping and entertainment district. Gogol's description of it in his story of that name makes an interesting comparison with Dostoyevsky's.

27. *Gostiny Dvor*: Shopping arcade opening off Nevsky Prospekt. It is visited by Golyadkin on his mad shopping spree in *The Double* (pp. 138–9).

28. *Manfredian*: After Manfred, eponymous hero of Byron's dramatic poem (1817), the personification of romantic despondency.

29. *... rout the reactionaries at Austerlitz*: The hero imagines himself as Napoleon, victor over the combined Russian and Austrian forces (1805). There is possibly a reflection here of a novel known to Dostoyevsky, E. Cabet's *Voyage en Icarie* (1840), where the philosopher-reformer of mankind also smashes the coalition of the 'retrograde' emperors at Austerlitz.

30. *... the Pope agrees to leave Rome for Brazil*: Refers to conflict between Napoleon I and Pope Pius VII – as a result of which

Napoleon was excommunicated – from 1809 to 1814, during which time the Pope was a virtual prisoner of Napoleon.

31. *... ball for the whole of Italy at the Villa Borghese*: Refers to celebration in 1806 of the foundation of the French Empire, arranged to coincide with the birthday of Napoleon. The Villa Borghese was established in Rome in the first half of the eighteenth century. At the time it belonged to Camillo Borghese, husband of Napoleon's sister Polina.

32. *Five Corners*: Place in St Petersburg at the junction of Zagorodny Prospekt, Chernyshev Alley, Razezzhaya Street and Troitskaya Street.

33. *Zverkov*: From *zver* (wild animal), a name that reflects its bearer's character. This may be compared with the name of Simonov's other guest, *Trudolyubov* (p. 57), from '*trud*' (toil) and '*lyubov*' (love), which suggests an industrious person.

34. *droit de seigneur*: Medieval feudal custom where the lord had the right to spend the wedding night with the bride of one of his vassals.

35. *Silvio*: From Pushkin's story *The Shot* (*Tales of Belkin*, 1830). After a wealthy count refuses to treat a duel seriously, Silvio retains the right to fire at the count at any time. Bursting in on the happily married count and his wife, however, he takes pity and wastes his shot.

36. *Masquerade*: Drama by Mikhail Lermontov, written in 1835–6, where the demonic villain Arbenin poisons his wife on suspicion of infidelity, only to go insane when he learns that she is innocent.

37. *the Haymarket*: Originally fodder and livestock were sold there in the 1730s. The surrounding area was inhabited by the poor and the whole neighbourhood was filled with brothels, gambling dens and low pubs. The dreadful squalor there is vividly evoked in *Crime and Punishment*.

38. *Volkovo Cemetery*: Volkovo Kladbishche, or Wolves' Graveyard, so called as the area was originally overrun with vicious wolves. Founded for the burial of the poor, the cemetery grew in size and became the last resting place of the famous, including Turgenev, Belinsky, Kropotkin, Witte and Blok.

39. *the Sadovaya, and near the Yusupov Gardens*: Sadovaya Street runs through the Haymarket as far as Nevsky Prospekt. The Yusupov Gardens lie just to the south of the Haymarket, off Sadovaya Street.

40. *And boldly and freely . . .*: From the poem by Nekrasov that appears as epigraph to Part II of *Notes from Underground* (p. 38).

THE DOUBLE

1. *Titular Counsellor*: Grade 9 in the fourteen ranks established by Peter the Great in 1722 (see p. liv).

2. *Shestilavochnaya Street*: Lit. Street of the Six Shops, now Mayakovsky Street, in Liteynaya district of central St Petersburg.

3. *. . . bundle of nice green, grey . . . banknotes*: The value of banknotes according to colour was: green – 3 roubles; grey – 50 roubles; blue – 5 roubles; red – 10 roubles. The notes were known by these colours in everyday speech.

4. *Nevsky Prospekt*: Famous avenue in St Petersburg, about two and a half miles long, running from the Admiralty to the Aleksandr Nevsky Monastery. The main focus of St Petersburg life.

5. *'It's a Russian proverb'*: The basic meaning is a present, a delicacy. In the metaphorical sense it signifies an unexpected 'treat' – or unpleasantness.

6. *'. . . promotion to assessor's rank'*: This is collegiate assessor, grade 8 – one grade higher than titular counsellor in the Table of Ranks (see p. liv).

7. *Gostiny Dvor*: Or Trading Rows, the commercial centre of St Petersburg at the beginning of the eighteenth century and still a centre of business activity. The original wooden stalls were destroyed by fire in 1736 and rebuilt (1761–85) by Vallin de la Mothe. About half a mile long, it is bounded on one side by Nevsky Prospekt. With its columned arcades, it was a fashionable promenade in the nineteenth century.

8. *flimsy national newspaper*: Most probably the *Northern Bee*, arch-reactionary journal published 1825–64 by the 'reptile journalists' F. V. Bulgarin and N. I. Grech.

9. *registrar clerks*: Collegiate registrars, the lowest grade (14) in the Table of Ranks (see p. liv).

10. *'Izmaylovsky Bridge'*: Spans the Fontanka River (see also note 20, below).

11. *'. . . sans façon'*: Simply, without ceremony.

12. *State Counsellor*: Fifth in the Table of Ranks (see p. liv).

13. *Belshazzar's Feast*: After Belshazzar, son of the last Babylonian emperor who saw the 'writing on the wall' at a great feast which foretold his own fate and that of Babylon.

14. *Yeliseyev and Milyutin*: Purveyors of high-quality foods and drinks. Yeliseyev's was founded by Pyotr Yeliseyev, a peasant, in 1813, and is still trading today.

15. *Demosthenic eloquence*: A reference to Demosthenes (384–22 BC), the famous Athenian orator.

16. *collegiate counsellor*: Sixth in the Table of Ranks (see p. liv).

17. *... French minister Villèle*: Jean Baptiste, Joseph, Comte de Villèle (1773–1854), reactionary President of the Council under Louis XVIII. The quoted phrase was Villèle's political slogan.

18. *... Turkish Vizier Martsimiris as well as the beautiful Margravine Louisa ...*: Reference to the highly popular cheap novel by M. Komarov (c. 1730–1812), *The Tale of the Adventures of the English Milord George and the Margravine Fredericka Louisa of Brandenburg, with the Appended History of the Former Turkish Vizier Martsimiris and Queen Terezia of Sardinia* (1782). It went into an eighth edition in 1840.

19. *'... you old Golyadka'*: *golyadka* means 'beggar'.

20. *Fontanka Embankment*: The Fontanka is the widest of St Petersburg's waterways, about four miles long and once the city border.

21. *Anichkov Bridge*: A three-span bridge that carried Nevsky Prospekt across the Fontanka. Built in 1839–41, it is famous for Pyotr Klodt's sculptures of wild horses at each corner.

22. *'Siamese twins ...'*: Conjoined twin brothers Chang and Eng (1811–74) left Siam (Thailand) and earned considerable amounts by giving lectures in Europe and the United States, becoming 'celebrities' of the time. They married two sisters in North Carolina and between them produced twenty-one offspring. All conjoined twins were subsequently called 'Siamese'.

23. *'And the casket opened easily after all'*: Reference to 'The Casket', a fable by I. A. Krylov (1769–1844), in which every possible way of opening the casket is attempted except the obvious.

24. *'the famous Suvorov'*: From *Anecdotes of the Prince of Italy, Count Suvorov-Rymniksky*, published by Ye. Fuchs in St Petersburg, 1827. Count A. V. Suvorov (1730–1800) was one of Russian's greatest military commanders.

25. *about Bryullov's latest painting ...*: Reference to K. P. Bryullov's famous painting, *The Last Days of Pompeii*, finished in Italy and shown in St Petersburg at the Academy of Arts.

26. *... wrought iron railings of the Summer Gardens*: Created in 1771–84, in the reign of Catherine the Great, the fine filigree iron grille, or railings, extend along the Neva Embankment and are the work of Yury Velten and Pyotr Yegorov. The railings referred to in Pushkin's *The Bronze Horseman* (1833).

27. *Northern Bee*: See note 8, above.

28. *Baron Brambeus*: *Nom de plume* of Osip Senkovsky (1800–1858), editor of *Library for Reading*, Russia's most widely read journal, catering for provincials, low-grade civil servants and those with a taste for cheap sensationalism.

29. *'If e'er you should me forget...'*: Album verses very popular among girls at boarding-school, etc.

30. *'...Yasha'*: Affectionate diminutive of Yakov.

31. *'Report to His Excellency's...'*: These lines are strongly reminiscent of those spoken by the Very Important Person to Akaky Akakievich in Gogol's 'The Overcoat': 'It's high time you knew that first of all your application must be handed in at the main office, then taken to the chief clerk, then to the departmental directory, then to my secretary, who *then* submits it to me for consideration...'

32. *'...Grishka Otrepyev'*: Or False Dmitry. Also known as 'First Pretender'. He opposed the rule of Boris Godunov, claiming to be Dmitry, a son of Ivan the Terrible. He was recognized as Tsar after Godunov's death in 1605, but was deposed and put to death in 1606.

33. *'...Provincial Secretary'*: Grade 13 in the Table of Ranks (see p. liv).

34. *Tambov*: Large town about 300 miles south of Moscow.

35. *'...our Russian Faublas'*: Faublas, cunning deceiver and hero of the French libertine novel *Amorous Adventures of Ch. de Faublas*, 1787–90, by J. B. Louvet de Couvry (1760–97). (French title *Les Amours du Chevalier de Faublas par Louvet de Couvry*.) The novel appeared in Russian translation, 1792–96; 1805.

36. *Police Gazette*: Full title *St Petersburg City Police Gazette*, published 1839–1917. It gave details of daily events in the capital.

37. *Saratov*: A city on the Volga, once capital of the Lower Volga region.

38. *Madame Falbala*: Derives from the French for a frill or flounce. In Pushkin's poem *Count Nulin* (1825), a Madame Falbala is the owner of a pension for young ladies:

> ... she was not educated
> According to her father's rule,
> But in a noble boarding-school,
> At émigrée Madame Falbala's.

39. *'Allow me to ask you...'*: These lines recall those spoken by the Very Important Person in Gogol's 'The Overcoat': 'Do you realize

who you're talking to? Do you know who is standing before you?' etc. (See also note 31, above)

40. '. . . *a hut by the sea* . . .': This theme appears in Friedrich Schiller's poem, *The Youth by the Stream* (1803; Russian translation 1838). Dostoyevsky was passionately fond of the German poet, particularly in his younger days.

41. '. . . *after the fashion of certain novels* . . .': Reference to similar situations in Schiller's ballad 'The Knight Toggenburg' (1797), which appeared in a Russian translation by the poet Zhukovsky in 1818; also to the sentimental, highly popular novel *Siegwart* (1776) by I.-M. Miller (1750–1814).

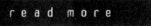

PENGUIN CLASSICS

THE HOUSE OF THE DEAD
FYODOR DOSTOYEVSKY

'Here was the house of the living dead, a life like none other upon earth'

In January 1850 Dostoyevsky was sent to a remote Siberian prison camp for his part in a political conspiracy. The four years he spent there, startlingly re-created in *The House of the Dead*, were the most agonizing of his life. In this fictionalized account he recounts his soul-destroying incarceration through the cool, detached tones of his narrator, Aleksandr Petrovich Goryanchikov: the daily battle for survival, the wooden plank beds, the cabbage soup swimming with cockroaches, his strange 'family' of boastful, ugly, cruel convicts. Yet *The House of the Dead* is far more than a work of documentary realism: it is also a powerful novel of redemption, describing one man's spiritual and moral death and the miracle of his gradual reawakening.

This edition includes an introduction and notes by David McDuff discussing the circumstances of Dostoyevsky's imprisonment, the origins of the novel in his prison writings and the character of Aleksandr Petrovich.

Translated with an introduction and notes by David McDuff

PENGUIN CLASSICS

THE IDIOT
FYODOR DOSTOYEVSKY

> 'He's simple-minded, but he has all his wits about him,
> in the most noble sense of the word, of course'

Returning to St Petersburg from a Swiss sanatorium, the gentle and naive Prince
Myshkin – known as 'the idiot' – pays a visit to his distant relative General
Yepanchin and proceeds to charm the General, his wife and his three daughters.
But his life is thrown into turmoil when he chances on a photograph of the
beautiful Nastasya Filippovna. Utterly infatuated with her, he soon finds himself
caught up in a love triangle and drawn into a web of blackmail, betrayal and,
finally, murder. In Prince Myshkin, Dosteyevsky set out to portray the purity of 'a
truly beautiful soul' and to explore the perils that innocence and goodness face in a
corrupt world.

David McDuff's major new translation brilliantly captures the novel's idiosyncratic
and dream-like language and the nervous, elliptic flow of the narrative. This
edition also includes an introduction by William Mills Todd III, further reading,
a chronology of Dostoyevsky's life and work, a note on the translation and
explanatory notes.

Translated by David McDuff with an introduction by William Mills Todd III

PENGUIN CLASSICS

THE DEATH OF IVAN ILYICH AND OTHER STORIES
LEO TOLSTOY

> 'Every moment he felt that … he was drawing nearer and nearer
> to what terrified him'

Three of Tolstoy's most powerful and moving shorter works are brought together in this volume. *The Death of Ivan Ilyich* is a masterly meditation on life and death, recounting the physical decline and spiritual awakening of a worldly, successful man who is faced with his own mortality. Only in his last agonizing moments does Ivan Ilyich finally confront his true nature, and gain the forgiveness of his wife and son for his cruelty towards them. *Happy Ever After*, inspired by one of Tolstoy's own romantic entanglements, tells the story of a seventeen-year-old girl who marries her guardian twice her age. And *The Cossacks*, the tale of a disenchanted young nobleman who seeks fulfilment amid the wild beauty of the Caucasus, was hailed by Turgenev as the 'finest and most perfect production of Russian literature'.

Rosemary Edmonds's classic translation fully captures the subtle nuances of Tolstoy's writing, and includes an introduction discussing the influences of the stories and contemporary reactions towards them.

Translated with an introduction by Rosemary Edmonds

PENGUIN CLASSICS

THE KREUTZER SONATA AND OTHER STORIES
LEO TOLSTOY

> 'We were like two prisoners in the stocks,
> hating one another yet fettered to one another by the same chain'

'The Kreutzer Sonata' is the self-lacerating confession of a man consumed by sexual jealousy and eaten up by shame and eventually driven to murder his wife. The story caused a sensation when it first appeared and Tolstoy's wife was appalled that he had drawn on their own experiences together to create a scathing indictment of marriage. 'The Devil', centring on a young man torn between his passion for a peasant girl and his respectable life with his loving wife, also illustrates the impossibility of pure love. 'The Forged Coupon' shows how an act of corruption can spiral out of control, and 'After the Ball' examines the abuse of power. Written during a time of spiritual crisis in Tolstoy's life, these late stories reflect a world of moral uncertainties.

This lucid translation is accompanied by an introduction in which David McDuff examines Tolstoy's state of mind as he produced these last great works, and discusses their public reception. This edition also contains notes and appendices.

Translated with an introduction by David McDuff

THE STORY OF PENGUIN CLASSICS

Before 1946 ... 'Classics' are mainly the domain of academics and students; readable editions for everyone else are almost unheard of. This all changes when a little-known classicist, E. V. Rieu, presents Penguin founder Allen Lane with the translation of Homer's *Odyssey* that he has been working on in his spare time.

1946 Penguin Classics debuts with *The Odyssey*, which promptly sells three million copies. Suddenly, classics are no longer for the privileged few.

1950s Rieu, now series editor, turns to professional writers for the best modern, readable translations, including Dorothy L. Sayers's *Inferno* and Robert Graves's unexpurgated *Twelve Caesars*.

1960s The Classics are given the distinctive black covers that have remained a constant throughout the life of the series. Rieu retires in 1964, hailing the Penguin Classics list as 'the greatest educative force of the twentieth century.'

1970s A new generation of translators swells the Penguin Classics ranks, introducing readers of English to classics of world literature from more than twenty languages. The list grows to encompass more history, philosophy, science, religion and politics.

1980s The Penguin American Library launches with titles such as *Uncle Tom's Cabin*, and joins forces with Penguin Classics to provide the most comprehensive library of world literature available from any paperback publisher.

1990s The launch of Penguin Audiobooks brings the classics to a listening audience for the first time, and in 1999 the worldwide launch of the Penguin Classics website extends their reach to the global online community.

The 21st Century Penguin Classics are completely redesigned for the first time in nearly twenty years. This world-famous series now consists of more than 1300 titles, making the widest range of the best books ever written available to millions – and constantly redefining what makes a 'classic'.

The Odyssey continues ...

The best books ever written

PENGUIN CLASSICS

SINCE 1946

Find out more at www.penguinclassics.com